Also by Cameron Judd

BOONE: A Novel Based on the Life
and Times of Daniel Boone

CROCKETT OF TENNESSEE:
A Novel Based on the Life
and Times of David Crockett

PASSAGE TO NATCHEZ

Available from Bantam Books

IT WAS A TIME WHEN THE LINE BETWEEN COURAGE AND CRUELTY, MERCY AND MASSACRE, LOYALTY AND BETRAYAL VANISHED IN THE RUSH OF HISTORY....

AMY DEACON—Torn between loyalty to her father and her passionate belief in the Union cause, she is banished from her home and forced to fend for herself, determined to find a way to make a difference.

GEORGE "DOC" DEACON—A virulent Secessionist, he expects absolute loyalty from all around him, even at the expense of his own family. But in losing his daughter he will be exposed for what he really is: a man whose rage borders on madness.

RUFUS—The Deacon family slave, he has inspired Amy with the spirit of freedom. In return for that gift she vows to support him in his own quest for liberty—a journey that could divide them forever.

BEN SCARLETT—Down on his luck, whiskey his only solace, he is a man whose loyalties are determined solely by who's holding the bottle. Now he has one last chance to save his life, but to do so he'll have to make the most difficult decision of all: to renounce his past.

HANNIBAL DEACON—Apparently neutral in the growing conflict, he is not what he seems. A man of remarkable courage, his true loyalties—and daring exploits—could lead him straight to the gallows.

SAM COLTER—Because circumstances make him unable to stand up and fight for what he believes, there are those who call him a coward. But this is a war that no one can escape.

All too soon Sam will discover that his very survival could depend on learning how to kill.

GREELEY BROWN—An old family friend of the Colters, he was a man who'd known his share of sorrow. As tough as the mountains he roamed, he would find his role in the coming war, hoping lightning wouldn't strike twice in the same place.

JOE COLTER—Unlike his brother Sam, he is no stranger to violence. Driven by a desire to avenge the murder of their uncle, he sets out to take the law into his own hands. For him the war is a mere backdrop to his personal obsession, a chance to answer death with death.

JIM MATOY—One of the few remaining Cherokee who have not been forcibly removed from their people's mountain homeland, he joins the conflict, a reluctant Confederate. But in the crucible of battle he discovers that years of suffering and oppression can be turned to fierce and bloody advantage.

The
Shadow Warriors

BOOK I IN THE MOUNTAIN WAR TRILOGY

A Novel of Unionist Resistance
in Tennessee and North Carolina,
September 1860 ~ January 1863

CAMERON JUDD

BANTAM BOOKS
NEW YORK • TORONTO • LONDON • SYDNEY • AUCKLAND

THE SHADOW WARRIORS

A Bantam Book/March 1997

ISBN 0-553-57698-4

Published simultaneously in the United States and Canada

Bantam Books are published by Bantam Books, a division of
Bantam Doubleday Dell Publishing Group, Inc. Its trademark,
consisting of the words "Bantam Books" and the portrayal of a
rooster, is Registered in U.S. Patent and Trademark Office and in
other countries. Marca Registrada, Bantam Books, 1540
Broadway, New York, New York 10036.

PRINTED IN THE UNITED STATES OF AMERICA

OPM   0   9   8   7   6   5   4   3   2   1

To Bonnie

AN INTRODUCTORY NOTE . . .

During the grim days of the American Civil War, there was in the hills and mountains of western North Carolina and East Tennessee a large population of people, mostly rural and agrarian, who remained staunchly loyal to the Union while living within the bounds of the Confederacy. Some of these loyalists struggled, often vainly, to remain publicly neutral. Many others risked their freedom and even their lives to "stampede" through rebel-occupied territory and reach the Federal lines to volunteer service to the Union military. Others went underground or under cover within the Confederacy itself, acting as citizen insurgents, burning railroad bridges, fighting as irregulars, serving as Union spies, smugglers, bushwhackers, or "pilots" for those fleeing north for Union military service. Some smuggled both escaped slaves and fleeing loyalists along the Underground Railroad. For such "Tories" the war experience was often not so much one of great battles between formal armies on vast battlefields, but gritty, brutal, underground warfare fought at their very doorsteps, often by men and women who never wore uniforms or held military commissions. These loyal hill people and mountaineers, isolated in the midst of a rebel-controlled region, saw the ugliest underbelly of the Civil War. Many were deprived and abused, or conscripted into military service for a cause they opposed. Some were imprisoned for their political beliefs, some were murdered, some were hanged under authority of the Confederacy.

Some endured and ultimately forgave. Others never did, and learned to dole out bitterness for bitterness, brutality for brutality.

Their story is seldom told. It is told here.

On the banks of the battle-stained river
I stood, as the moonlight shone,
And it glared from the face of my brother
As the sad wave swept him on!

Where my home was glad, are ashes;
And horrors and shame had been there—
For I found, on the fallen lintel,
This tress of my wife's torn hair.

—From S. Teackle Wallis
"The Guerrillas" (1864)

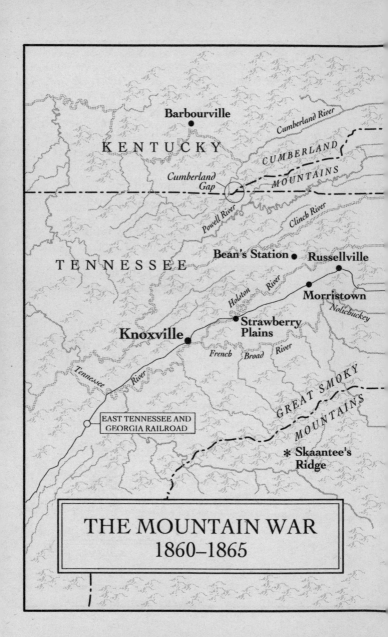

THE MOUNTAIN WAR
1860–1865

VIRGINIA

Clinch River

N. Fork Holston R.

EAST TENNESSEE AND
VIRGINIA RAILROAD

Watauga

River

Elizabethton

Lick Creek

Colter
✱
Jonesborough

Greeneville

River

Shelton Laurel Cr.

Warm Springs

Marshall

NORTH CAROLINA

Asheville

0   20   40
Scale of Miles

✱ fictional sites

Part I

SECESSION HILL

Chapter 1

Ben Scarlett jolted awake as the shed door jerked open beside him. Cool air hammered his raggedly clad body and sunlight burned eyes that moments before had rested in the blissful darkness of a drunkard's undreaming sleep. He sat up, confused, lifting his arm to block the unwelcome glare. The burly form of merchant Daniel Baumgardner filled the doorway and leaned toward him with grasping hands.

"Ben Scarlett! I figured it would be you!" bellowed Baumgardner, a red-faced man with a horrendous underbite and breath perpetually tainted by tobacco and coffee. He grabbed Ben by the collar of his worn woolen coat and began dragging him out the door into the light. "How many times have I told you to stay out of this shed, Ben? You think I run a hotel? Phew, man! Take a smell of yourself! You reek like a whiskey still!"

He hauled the blubbering Ben completely out of the shed and into the fenced little dirt courtyard in which it stood. Overlooking the enclosure was the ugly backside of the three-storied dry goods store Baumgardner had owned and operated for the past fifteen years. The shed in which Ben had been sleeping was built against the back of the store and contained mostly tools, firewood, and a few items of merchandise too old or damaged to sell, but which the packrat Baumgardner was unwilling to throw away.

"On your feet, swill!" Baumgardner barked, pulling up on Ben's collar so hard his ancient coat was almost ripped off him. Ben struggled for footing, but Baumgardner's man-handling had him off balance and he never fully rose. His head reeled from the aftereffects of a drunken binge the prior evening, and now the first throbs of an intense headache bored through his skull like an auger. He groaned.

"You're a nuisance, Ben!" Baumgardner bellowed. "A drunken, stinking, pants-peeing, no-'count nuisance!" He gave up trying to pull Ben to his feet and pushed him down instead. Ben collapsed, a dirty, reeking, grizzled raggedy man with a month's worth of whiskers. He was in his mid-thirties but looked ten years older.

Baumgardner leaned over and shook a thick finger in Ben's face as he took on a lecturing tone, his wide face crimson and a vein in his neck visibly pulsing. "Ben, this is the fifth, sixth time I've found you in my shed. I've told you I don't want you sleeping off your drunks in there, but you won't listen. This time I ain't going to overlook it. I'm going to take you down to the jail and have you locked up for tres-passing, for breaking into my building . . . and if I find one thing has gone missing, one thing—"

"But it wasn't locked," Ben protested as best he could with a dry tongue that at the moment felt too big for his mouth.

"What of it? You know my rule. I've told you often enough."

"I'm sorry, Mr. Baumgardner . . . I forgot." This was true; the night before, Ben had been so drunk he would have scarcely been able to remember his own name. Even now he couldn't remember having entered Baumgardner's shed. "I'll go away, no trouble . . . I won't sleep here no more. . . ."

"I've heard it before, Ben. Your promises mean nothing. No more slack on your rope! It's time you learned a lesson."

Escape, Ben thought wildly. *I must escape.* An alley run-ning alongside Baumgardner's store opened into the court-yard and provided the only exit from it unless one opted to leap the fence itself, which Ben couldn't hope to do on his best day. Ben looked longingly at the alley's mouth, evaluating his chances for a successful bolt for freedom. A vain prospect. He would never outrun Baumgardner. Besides, his head ached miserably; the idea of jolting along on the run was too agonizing to consider. There would be no escape.

Joints snapping and creaking, he came to his feet slowly, lachrymose and sure that Baumgardner was going to cause him real trouble this time. He grew whiningly contrite. "Mr. Baumgardner, I'm ashamed of myself. I was drunk last night, I admit, and I reckon I just forgot you had told me not to sleep here."

"Don't try to gain my pity. Come on. Let's go pay call on the law."

"Please, Mr. Baumgardner . . ."

"Don't beg. It won't sway me. It's high time you were called to account for your ways. Maybe it'll do you some good." Baumgardner puffed up self-righteously. "These are not days for a man to be a drunkard, Ben. These here are sober times, and all the more sober they'll soon become, if war comes."

The mention of war reminded Ben that someone had told him Baumgardner was one of Knoxville's most avid Secessionists. Perhaps, he thought, a few good words for that cause might generate some needed good grace. So he said, "I hear a lot declare that if any war comes, it won't last long. The South would win any war right off. And them Yankee devils know it. They'll never start no war they know they can't win. They'll just fuss and threaten and . . ."

He trailed off, seeing that the look on Baumgardner's face was not that of a man hearing words that pleased him. Ben realized he had surely been misinformed about Baumgardner's politics. Had he been a dog, he would have laid back his ears and cringed.

"Not only a drunk, but a Secesh to boot!" Baumgardner declared. "You're talking to an American Union patriot here, Ben Scarlett, and I'll hear no blabber about disunion from the likes of you! Let's go. I'm tired of talking."

Just then fortune did Ben a curious favor. A fit of coughing wracked his thin frame, making him bend forward and hack so terribly he might have emptied his belly had there been anything in it. The coughing was authentic—he had been developing a terrible rasp over the past week as the weather cooled—but as soon as it began he wildly seized on it as another possible tactic for earning Baumgardner's pity, and with luck, pardon. He added some theatrical heaves and wheezes, followed up with a loud and not completely feigned groan.

Baumgardner studied Ben with narrowing eyes. "You sick or something, Ben?"

"Mighty sick, Mr. Baumgardner. My chest, it hurts like a hot iron has been thrust through it." Another hack and groan. "God help me, God help me. Please, sir, don't have me locked up. I swear I'll die in that cold old jail. I've been in it before." He leaned to one side, grimacing, gripping his chest, wheezing.

Baumgardner frowned, backing off a step and chewing at his moustachioed upper lip with the row of outthrust bottom teeth that made him the most distinctively featured merchant in Knoxville. "You ain't consumptive, are you?"

"I pray it ain't so, Mr. Baumgardner. I pray it ain't so." Ben hacked and spat.

Baumgardner backed away another step and eyed his forlorn companion with an evident mix of disgust, pity, and fear of catching something contagious. More lip-chewing, then he swore to himself, shook his head and said: "Aw, get off with you, then, Ben Scarlett. I won't cast a sick man in a cold jail, and God knows I don't want to keep close company with you all the way to the jail with you harking that way. I believe you're awful ill. You'd best find yourself a doctor before that cough kills you."

"I will, Mr. Baumgardner. God bless you, sir. God bless your soul." He reached out as if to shake Baumgardner's hand, causing the merchant to dance away from him. Ben secretly enjoyed that fully anticipated reaction. There was yet a bit of playfulness in his soul, though he had lost any good cause for lightheartedness years ago.

"Get out of here, Ben, and take whatever affliction you got with you. And don't let me find you about this place again, you hear me?"

"Yes sir. Yes sir. God bless you for your mercy, sir." Ben turned and headed out the alley, walking in a slump, pausing only long enough to force a few more coughs and make as sorrowful looking a departure as he could.

"You need to visit a doctor, Ben!" Baumgardner yelled after him. Ben nodded without looking back.

When he reached the end of the alley he cut left and made off at a much faster clip. He coughed some more, real coughs, and wondered if he truly was bad sick. He was used to being at least a little ill almost all the time, but fancied he felt worse than usual. Of course, he was hungover and had undergone a very rough awakening, and besides that was weak with hunger. Counting back, he calculated that his most recent meal had been on the morning of the day before. No wonder he felt bad. But he had no money for food.

Baumgardner's store stood on Gay Street, so named by Knoxville's original surveyor in honor of a street of the same name in Baltimore. All of Knoxville was familiar to Ben, who had been born in a little house, long since torn down, which had stood southeast of his present location and above the bluff overlooking the Tennessee River. He had grown up in Knoxville, received a rudimentary education in reading and ciphering, become a hardworking sawmill hand and eventually foreman . . . but tragedies had come, whiskey had offered its solaces, and he had accepted. Now he worked very rarely, and never for long. Whenever he received the occasional question as to how he managed to survive, he could only shrug and shake his head in reply. He honestly didn't know.

He lingered on a corner, listening to his stomach grumble, and wished he were still asleep in Daniel Baumgardner's shed. A sleeping man knows no illness, no worry, no hunger, no craving for liquor. But Ben could hardly dare return to that shed, one of the warmest and driest in the city—and he knew, having slept in almost all of them. He had taken advantage of Baumgardner's shed far more often than Baumgardner knew. And would again, when some time had passed and the merchant had cooled down. Maybe around Christmas. Baumgardner was always in better spirits around Christmas.

It was a brilliant, cold, early-autumn day. The sunlight

made Ben's bleary eyes water profusely. Squinting, he looked to the left, down toward the river, and watched a wagon hauling a load of logs bound for the mill. The wagon bisected a small herd of beef cattle being driven along a side avenue and went on its way.

A look to the right, up toward the railroad and depot, revealed a newly hung homemade banner bearing the words SOUTHERN INDEPENDENCE! and beneath it a group of rowdy boys pointing and laughing at a frightened cur dog to whose tail they had affixed a crude hand-lettered banner: Knoxville Dogs for Disyoonyun. Children of local Unionists, obviously, making mockery of the rebellious banner above them, because sons could get away with it while their fathers—who stood to one side, grinning—could not. Another group of men, glowering and puffing disapprovingly on their pipes, stood in the shade of a storefront porch nearby, silently watching the boys. Ben grinned wanly. These were obviously the Secessionists for whose annoyance the boys' contemptuous show was being orchestrated. There were plenty from both the Secession and Unionist camps in Knoxville. Ben was substantially indifferent to both. Politics was of little personal importance to him. Whatever happened, life would be all the same: a daily quest for enough food to stay alive and enough liquor to stay happy.

"I'm neutral," he muttered to himself, watching the dog trying to scoot the sign off its rear end. "Plain old get-along-with-everybody neutral. I'll sing whatever song needs singing to get by." He eyed the Secession flag, flapping in the cold wind, and wondered if there really would be a war. No. It was impossible. Try as he would, he couldn't imagine it actually happening.

He sauntered off, thinking about food and wishing his head would quit hurting. But he knew it wouldn't, not completely at least, until he was drunk again.

An hour later, when Ben was down to seriously considering exploring the back lots of the local cafés in hopes of finding an old thrown-out loaf or fragment of moldy pie, an enticing aroma of cooking meat reached him like an unexpected

wind from heaven. Pausing, nostrils twitching lustily, he
tried to trace the origin of the scent. He heard a singing male
voice from somewhere on the other side of a meat packing
house that stood nearby, and smiled.

The voice was that of Charlie Douglass, a fellow Knoxville
vagrant. "Charlie, I hope you're in the humor to share with
your fellow man this fine day," Ben murmured to himself.

He sniffed the air as he headed toward the packing house
and then around the rear of it. The aroma was that of goat's
head soup. The proprietor of the packing house was a good
and kindly man who often gave goats' heads to the poor
folk of Knoxville. A frequent recipient was Charlie Douglass, who, like Ben Scarlett, was often drunk, and whom
Ben sometimes regarded as nearly a friend and other times
strongly disliked. The problem was Douglass's own incon-
sistency toward him. He was friendly when drinking, hostile
when sober and suffering.

This morning's singing indicated Douglass had some
liquor in him, which meant prospects were good for hospitality and a serving or two of soup. Maybe even a sip of
whatever he was fortunate enough to be drinking so early in
the day. Ben supposed it was some of the homemade liquor
that was one of Douglass's two sources of fame throughout
Knoxville.

The second source of fame was one that Ben didn't like
nearly as much as the first: Douglass's constant political
ranting. Ben knew no other vagrants besides Douglass who
cared at all about politics. Douglass more than cared; to him
it was an obsession to be gushed about constantly. Douglass
was a rabid Unionist and believed that anyone who wasn't
deserved no respect. Many times Ben had watched Douglass loudly harass leading local disunionists right in the
streets, doing all he could to embarrass them publicly.
Douglass was utterly shameless about it and could not care
less whom he offended.

Because of that, other vagrants didn't fraternize with Douglass much. His partisan outspokenness made him imprudent
company for those whose survival partly depended upon the
charitable inclinations of moneyed urban citizens, many of

whom were disunionists. Most Knoxville vagrants, like Ben, played both sides of the political field, depending upon from whose pocket they were trying to obtain a coin. Too much association with Charlie Douglass just wasn't advantageous for those who needed to stand in good favor with potential bene-factors of all political stripes.

So there were good reasons for Ben to stay away from Charlie Douglass. At the moment, though, the scent of goat's head soup made Knoxville's most ragged and out-spoken Unionist seem the most desirable of companions to Ben Scarlett.

He hurried around the rear of the packing house, his belly aching with hunger, and located Douglass's cook fire by the thin white plume of smoke rising from it. The fire burned in a little brushy lot about two hundred feet back from one corner of the packing house. The lot was cleared of undergrowth at its center, where rough huts built by Knoxville's vagrants stood. These had occasionally pro-vided shelter for Ben, though he usually preferred sheds and barns. He put his foot on the narrow, trash-strewn footpath that led through the brush into the clearing.

Douglass was singing at the top of his voice. He gave Ben a smile as he entered the clearing, never breaking from song. Ben was encouraged by the smile. The aroma of the steaming soup was delicious. His mouth watered.

Ben approached the fire and knelt in its warmth, sniffing the marvelous redolence rising from Douglass's kettle. He waited until Douglass finished his melody, then smiled, nodded, and said a simple hello.

"And hello to you, Ben Scarlett," Douglass replied in a hearty, friendly tone. "Where have you been keeping yourself?"

"Here and there. Spent last night in Dan Baumgardner's shed until he run me out this morning."

"I do despise that man," Douglass said. "He's run me out more than once. Treats that shed of his like a sacred shrine that no down-trod soul like me and you should ever sully. No heart beats in that man. And he's a Secesh to boot."

Ben remembered just then who had misinformed him

about Baumgardner's political views. "He ain't a Secesh, Charlie. You had told me he was, and that nearly got me in a fix this morning."

"What kind of fix?"

"Baumgardner was fixing to haul me to jail for trespassing in his shed, so I talked Secesh talk hoping to make him feel agreeable toward me. He like to have took my head off for it. He's a Union man, like you. Strong one."

Douglass arched his brows. "Is that right? I'll be! I reckon I've misjudged good Mr. Baumgardner."

Ben might have sneered. *Good Mr. Baumgardner . . .* and only a moment ago Douglass had been deploring the man. It was just like Charlie Douglass to judge people solely on where they stood on Secession.

"That soup smells mighty prime, Charlie. You got enough to share? I'll pay you when I can."

Both knew it would never happen. Any money that reached Ben's hand almost always went straight into the pocket of some saloon operator. Douglass, however, jovially went along with the pretense. "You are welcome, Ben," he said. "Find yourself something to eat from, and go to it. A man ought not dine alone if he can help it, eh?"

"Thank you, Charlie. You are a good man. And I will pay you, later on."

Ben scrounged about until he found an old empty meat tin. It was so clean it had probably been licked out by dogs, but Ben wasn't the kind to worry about it. He merely swiped the tin out a little more with a corner of his woolen coat, then dug a horn-handled spoon from an inner pocket. He always carried a spoon and fork, never knowing when he might stumble upon a meal and need cutlery.

The soup was delicious despite a deficiency of salt. While Charlie Douglass chattered out Unionism in his unlistening ear, Ben ate a tinful, a second, a third, and was wondering if he dared go for a fourth when he happened to glance toward the street fronting the brushy lot. A gap in the leafless foliage gave him a view of the boardwalk, and there he saw a young woman standing, looking at him and Douglass. The moment Ben's eye caught hers, she quickly turned away and strode off. Ben watched her cross the street and enter what looked like a warehouse.

Ben's face was pallid when he turned back to Douglass. "Lord in heaven! Just like Angel! If I didn't know better, I'd swear it was her!"

Douglass, whom Ben had just interrupted in full rant, asked, "What'd you say?"

"That gal—did you see her just now?"

"No."

"There was a young lady there, on the boardwalk, looking at us. She went into that warehouse yonder ... there, Charlie! I see her again, in the window!"

Douglass rose, moving to where he too could see through the gap in the brush and across to the warehouse, and squinted. "Ah! *Her!* The Deacon gal. Pretty, ain't she!" He grinned and winked. "She makes your fire burn, does she, Ben?"

"No," Ben said. "It ain't like that. It's that she looks like somebody else I once knowed, a long time ago."

" 'Knowed,' you say. Where is she now?"

"I don't know. Long gone. Angel Beamish was her name. I was engaged to marry her once upon a time."

"Well, don't be thinking that's her. Because I know who that is, and it ain't no Angel Beamish."

Ben was insulted. "I know it ain't Angel. All I said was, she looks like Angel looks. Or used to look back when me and her was to be married. I don't know what she'd look like now."

"Why didn't you marry her?"

"Whiskey. I had to choose between her or the whiskey, and the whiskey did the choosing for me. She gave me back my ring and went off. I sold the ring, bought liquor with the money, and stayed drunk for days." He gestured toward the young woman in the window. "That gal there, you called her by the name of Deacon?"

"Yes indeed, and around her lies quite a story," Douglass said. "Now that you've filled your belly, share a swallow or two with me and I'll tell it to you—part of it, leastways."

All offense at Douglass vanished. Ben smiled as Douglass pulled a flask from beneath his coat. *A good man, Charlie Douglass,* Ben thought. *Better than me. If it was me with that flask, I sure wouldn't be sharing it with him.*

He cast one more glance at the warehouse. The young woman was seated just on the other side of the dirty window glass at a high desk, her profile illuminated by the oil lamp just in front of her. She took up a pen and began to write. Ben gazed at her a moment more, then turned his attention to Douglass's proffered flask.

The whiskey burned deliciously against his throat. He handed the flask back to Douglass with reluctance. Douglass wrapped his lips around the short neck, turned it up, drank.

Thoughts of his past had made Ben contemplative. Memories of a good life before liquor claimed his mind and soul swarmed through his head, and with them a troubling question: *What was it that brought you so low, Ben Scarlett, to render you nothing but a drunk sharing a vagrant's flask beside a pork house? How was it you let go of the best and chose the worst?* Such self-chiding thoughts came from time to time when Ben encountered something or someone to make him think of his earlier life, but seldom lasted for more than a few moments. They were too painful to be allowed a longer life span.

"Now, Ben, about the Deacon gal," Douglass said, smacking and wiping his lips. To Ben's disappointment he stoppered the flask and put it back under his coat. "Her name is Amy. Amy Deacon. And her father is none other than old Doc Deacon himself." Douglass paused to let that obviously significant information sink in.

It took a couple of moments for Ben to grasp it. "Doc Deacon . . . Oh! *The* Doc Deacon? The big Secesh newspaperman?"

"That's right. Dr. George 'Doc' Deacon of *The Secession Advocate.*" Douglass voiced the name of that radical publication very mockingly, it being the embodiment of every idea he loved to ridicule. "Doc Deacon is indeed her pap. And yonder warehouse, though it has no sign on it, that's his building. The Doc made himself a print shop in the front part of it. That's where he printed up that doctoring book of his that made him famous to begin with, and now it's where he puts out his trash Secesh newspaper. He and his gal work in there, along with a young fellow name of Birch Lewis. That's the whole kaboodle of the *Advocate*, just them three, with the Doc's darky helping some, too."

"Well, I'll be." Ben knew *The Secession Advocate* quite well, and for more reason than that at the moment a page from an old copy was folded and stuck inside his left shoe to cover a hole in the sole. No one could live in Knoxville in the 1860s without encountering the *Advocate* and its fire-breathing sermons of rebellion. It was the most radical of the Secession journals of Tennessee, and the philosophical opposite of pro-Union papers such as that published by the acid-penned clergyman named William "Parson" Brownlow, a man whose sour and vindictive attitude toward those who disagreed with him was written all over a wedge-shaped and chinless face.

On the slavery issue, the *Advocate* vied chiefly against an irregularly published local abolitionist journal, *Reason's Torch*. Dr. Deacon, an inheritance-moneyed local physician who was publisher of the *Advocate*, was famous now for his radical Secessionism, abrasive personality, powerful polemics, and seething hatred of abolitionism. But his initial rise to prominence had come through the publication of his popular *A Medical Companion for the Home and Family*, a reference book that translated medical matters into understandable terms for the untrained person. The book had become a classic of its kind, and with proceeds from its sales, Dr. Deacon established a newspaper that published classic novels in an inexpensive newspaper format, one chapter per edition. This too had been a popular money-maker. But Deacon's interests had turned increasingly to politics; he had dropped the classics and now devoted all his publishing efforts solely to *The Secession Advocate*, while still maintaining a token medical practice in Knoxville, seeing mostly long-term patients and seeking no new ones. As a publisher, Deacon's current mission in life seemed to be proving that anything other than unvarnished Secessionism was actually, in one of his best-known expressions, "the wolf of diabolical abolitionism clothed in the white wool of the 'patriotic' sheep."

Ben peered closely at the seeming flesh-and-blood

phantom of a past love. "Look's like she's writing something."

"She is . . . and therein lies the heart of the story I mentioned. But I ain't going to tell you that part. Not yet."

"Why not?"

"I ain't telling. Not till the time is just right. When that time comes, everybody is going to know. Everybody."

"What? Is it some big secret?"

"Mighty big secret, mighty big. Big enough to destroy old Doc Deacon if it got out, too. That's why I'm keeping mum. Biding my time. But I don't aim to bide it much longer. That secret will get out, very soon. 'Bout a week or so."

"Now, how do you come to be knowing such big secrets about Doc Deacon?" Ben asked skeptically.

Douglass haughtily examined the dirt under his nails. "I move in the right circles, Ben. I move in the right circles."

Ben restrained a disdainful snort. The only circles Charlie Douglass moved in were those he circumscribed while drunk and staggering. True, the Unionists of Knoxville knew Douglass quite well, but that was only because he made such a public spectacle of himself by taunting prominent Secessionists on the streets. The Unionists naturally enjoyed seeing him embarrass their political enemies, but no one took Charlie Douglass seriously or considered him part of any inner political circle. At best he was a mascot, a clown, a harmless source of entertainment for Unionists, an annoying public gadfly for their opponents.

Ben doubted that Douglass really knew any secrets. Probably he was merely fantasizing, building up a self-deluding image of greatness. Ben wasn't about to air such speculations before Douglass, however, and risk making him mad, not as long as there was still liquor in his flask. Ben licked his lips. "Reckon I could have another swallow of your whiskey, Charlie? Just enough to warm me, you know?"

"Well . . . I reckon. One more, that's all." Douglass pulled out the flask and handed it to Ben, then watched closely as Ben drank, monitoring the amount imbibed. Douglass hurriedly took back the flask, weighed it in his hand, looked displeased, and put it away. Ben knew he would receive no other swallows. When Douglass's whiskey ran low, so did his hospitality.

Without asking permission and thereby risking its denial, Ben ate one more serving of the goat's head soup, now mostly broth. Douglass did not eat, but sipped at his whiskey, thoughtful eyes turned toward the *Advocate* building.

Rising, Ben abandoned his emptied tin, pocketed his spoon, thanked Douglass for the food and liquor, warmed his hands briefly above the fire, then walked out onto the street that ran between the *Advocate* warehouse and the vagrants' lot. He meandered slowly on, going nowhere in particular, until moody thoughts gave way to questions about where he could find more liquor, or more money with which to buy some. It was likely to be cold this evening, and he would need his liquor just to keep him warm.

Chapter 2

Late afternoon, the same day

Amy Deacon hefted the heavy bundle of broadsides into a more comfortable position and continued on down the boardwalk in an off-balance stride, her breath steaming before her in white puffs, her face reddened by the cold evening breeze. It was dusk; already a few lights were beginning to appear in windows here and there on the street.

She had begun her trek at the intersection of Gay and Main, up a block or so from the river. Moving north, she stopped at the next corner and dropped her bundle. Stooping, she pulled the top broadside off the stack, produced a little hammer and couple of tacks from a small leather tool bag, and tacked the broadside to a pole. Stepping back, she eyed it to make sure it was straight, then hefted up the bundle again and continued up the street toward the Lamar House Hotel, originally built almost fifty years before as a residence for the father of Dr. Thomas W. Humes, rector of Knoxville's St. John's Episcopal Church. Humes was one of the many notable Union-leaning local men her father despised. Dr. George Deacon despised so many men it was often hard for her to keep track of them all.

Because a regrading in 1847 had greatly lowered the street level and forced the Lamar House's owners to convert its basement into its first floor, the main entrance was on the second level and was fronted by a balcony that overlooked the street. George Deacon and other public figures had given many a speech from that balcony in past years. Amy paused at the Lamar House long enough to hang another broadside, then continued up the street toward the intersection with Church.

Ben Scarlett stepped from the shadows beneath the Lamar House balcony. He watched Amy Deacon going on up the street, then went over to examine the broadside she had just hung. It began with a large-type banner headline—COME, ADVOCATES OF INDEPENDENCE!—followed by a second and slightly smaller headline reading, AND THOSE OF OPEN MIND AND TRUE SOUTHERN HEART, and went on to announce a large Secession rally, sponsored by *The Secession Advocate*, to be held in an empty lot farther up Gay Street the Thursday evening a week hence. Music from a small brass ensemble would be featured, along with coffee, lemonade, and fried apple pies, free of charge. At the end was a string of random Secessionist slogans—DISUNION FOR LIBERTY! HAIL TO THE FREE SOUTHERN MAN! STATES' RIGHTS! RISE UP, TENNESSEANS! Ben didn't read those portions. His eye was fixed on the promise of food and beverage. Next Thursday would be a good day to favor Secession, at least until the Unionists held their own rally and offered free edibles.

Ben leaned against the pole and watched Amy Deacon, who was nearly a block away by now, as she again dropped her bundle and prepared to hang another broadside. He was again filled with the sense of seeing his long-gone fiancée, an illusion enhanced by the softening effects of distance and twilight. The way she stood, the way she wore her hair, the way she moved . . . Amy Deacon was the image of Angel Beamish as she had been at about the age of twenty. Ben felt a warmth in his eyes, and a tear emerged to slide down his grimy face and vanish into the forest of his beard. He glanced down, wiping at his eye with his forefinger, and noticed a small leather pouch at his feet.

Stooping, he picked it up. It was the pouch containing Amy Deacon's tacks and little hammer. He looked up, saw her retracing her steps back toward him, and knew she had just detected her missing tools. When he looked at her, she paused uncertainly, then came on again, watching him closely. For the first time in weeks Ben Scarlett was unpleasantly conscious of how ragged he looked and how bad he smelled.

She stopped about twenty feet from him and smiled cautiously. "Good evening, sir. I believe that pouch you have is mine." Even her voice was much like Angel's.

"Yes, ma'am, it is. I was bringing it to you. Here you are." He extended it toward her.

She came closer and took the pouch. "Thank you, sir." She turned and walked away.

He was entranced by this living image of his departed love and couldn't bear to let her walk off. "Uh, ma'am?"

She stopped and looked back. "Yes?"

He searched for something to say. "Ma'am, uh, you are Miss Deacon? Doc Deacon's daughter?"

"Yes. But you have the best of me, sir. Do I know you?"

"Oh, no, ma'am. No reason you would know me. I know you just because of your pap being famous. Everybody knows about Doc Deacon!"

She smiled, just a little. A lovely smile, Ben thought. "I suppose most people do know of him," she said.

"Yes, ma'am. Miss Deacon, my name is Scarlett, Ben Scarlett . . ." He fumbled off his hat, having just remembered he was wearing it. ". . . and I just wanted to tell you that . . . well, it sounds foolish, saying it straight out, but . . . you look an awful lot like a very fine lady I knew some years ago before I became a . . . somebody I knew some years ago." He looked toward the ground. "I seen you earlier today, ma'am, and noticed it, and I just wanted to tell you that you put me so much in mind of Angel that today it's been a bit like being near her again. And so I just wanted to thank you." He scuffed his feet self-consciously. "I told you it sounded foolish."

"Hardly, sir. I think it's perhaps the finest compliment I've received, and I thank you for telling me."

Her words pleased him. "It ain't nothing."

Amy Deacon smiled at him, then reached into a hidden pocket somewhere in the billows of her dress and pulled out a dollar coin, which she held toward him with an uncertain expression. "I'd like to offer this to you, sir, if it won't offend you."

Ben dropped his head. He wanted the coin, but was ashamed—quite an odd thing. He had never felt ashamed to take a handout from anyone before. It was like Angel herself was offering the handout . . . not that Angel would have ever done that. She would have scolded him for lack of discipline, told him to throw away the bottle that trapped him and to go to work like an honest man if he wanted to marry and keep her. That's what Angel would have done . . . what, at one time, she really had done.

"Ma'am, I ain't done nothing to earn no dollar."

"Well . . . then do earn it. I have a heavy bundle, hard for me to carry. You could carry it for me, Mr. Scarlett."

He accepted the offer with a grin and nod.

He maintained a discreet distance as he followed her, proud to be helping such an appealing and refined female. They reached the pile of broadsides; he stooped to pick them up. A new outburst of coughing struck him, worse even than the fit he had suffered outside Daniel Baumgardner's store shed. He turned away, still stooped over, and hacked.

"Mr. Scarlett, are you all right?"

By sheer will he got control of his cough and stood up, feeling the ache in his lungs. His throat was raw, his voice froggy. "I'm fine, ma'am. Just choked a bit, that's all." He picked up the broadsides, then waited with bundle in arms while she tacked one of them up.

"Come this way, Mr. Scarlett. Father wants at least two of the broadsides on every block." She paused. "My father is a doctor as well as a publisher, you know. If your lungs are troubling you, he could help you."

"I'm fine, ma'am. I always get a touch of cough this time of year. Besides, I got no money to pay a doctor. I'm ashamed to admit it, Miss Deacon, but I drink some. Too much, really. But you know that. You saw me drinking with Charlie Douglass over by the meat packing house this morning."

"Oh? That was you?" She did not fool him; he could tell she already knew.

"Yes, it was. I ain't proud of what I am, ma'am."

"That was Charlie Douglass with you?"

"Yes, ma'am. I reckon you know who he is, don't you? He's sort of famous in this town."

"Yes." She paused. "My father hates . . . my father doesn't much like Charlie Douglass."

"Charlie has a big mouth on him and he can be right hard on Seceshes. To tell you the truth, Charlie don't much like your father, neither."

"There are a lot of people who don't like my father," she said. "He isn't an easy man to like."

Ben chuckled. "Well, he's got *you* to like him, even if other folks won't. A daughter ain't got much choice but to like her own father, does she!"

She said nothing.

Ben rattled on. "My own father, I thought the world of him. He was a fine man. Never touched whiskey. He's been dead now for nigh upon twenty years. If he was living, I expect he'd be on your father's side of things. He lived many a year in Alabama. Likely he'd be strong Secesh."

"And what about you, Mr. Scarlett? Are you Secessionist or Unionist?"

"Me? I ain't neither one. I'm neutral most of the time." He grinned. "But one thing you can count on: When this here rally happens Thursday night, I'll be as Secesh as I can be as long as the food lasts."

She laughed, gratifying him. To have amused her was an accomplishment. "You are honest, Mr. Scarlett. There's far too little of that to be found these days."

"I reckon you're right fierce in favor of the Secesh side all the time, huh? No being neutral for a Deacon, I don't figure!"

"You would assume so, I suppose, considering who my father is."

"What do you do there at the newspaper? You help with the printing?"

"Have you heard of a 'printer's devil'? I do that sort of thing, mostly. I roll the ink roller over the type and so on. And I deliver newspapers, or extra jobs like what we're doing right now."

"You don't do no writing, do you? You was writing

something today, it looked like, when you was at the window."

She turned her head quickly and glanced at him, lips tightening with a smile of some private amusement that escaped him. What had he said that was funny? "I help my father, any way I can. I, uh, copy down things for him sometimes. I was doing that today."

They continued up the street, stopping every half block or so to put up a new broadside, and crossing and recrossing the street to make sure both sides got approximately the same number of broadsides. Ben studied the posters as they went along. "Did you print these at the *Advocate*?"

"Yes."

"You enjoy working there?"

"I never think about whether I enjoy it. It's something I do for my father."

They stopped again to tack up another flyer. Ben stood looking around and whistling through his teeth. It was growing very dark. Lights were on all up and down the street. Ben felt the weight of the dollar he had been given—no, this time he had *earned* his dollar, and that filled him with pride. He anticipated the coming pleasure of how he would spend that dollar when this job was finished.

"Your father must be a bold man, to be as outspoke as he is," Ben contributed, just to keep the conversation going so he could listen to her talk.

"He is bold, yes."

"You're proud of him, I reckon."

"A daughter ought to be proud of her father, shouldn't she?"

Ben was not overly observant, but he was beginning to detect an evasive quality in the way Amy spoke of Dr. Deacon. It was puzzling, but he sensed he shouldn't pursue it.

Suddenly Ben broke into more coughing and had to lay down his bundle for a moment.

"You really should visit a doctor, Mr. Scarlett."

"Just a cough, Miss Deacon. It'll go away."

They worked another half hour, and then the broadsides were all posted and it was done. Ben Scarlett looked around and realized they had worked their way around to the little knob of a hill upon which stood the three-storied residence of Dr. George Deacon. Local Unionist firebrand Parson Brownlow had derisively dubbed Deacon's home as "Secession Hill" in one of his published rants in *The Knoxville Whig*, a newspaper that enjoyed a level of circulation Dr. Deacon could only envy, but Deacon had turned the joke on Brownlow by proudly accepting the name, even flaunting it by having it painted on a big sign that now stood in the yard.

In a moment, Ben knew, Amy Deacon would be going inside and he would be alone again. He would be free to go spend his dollar in a tavern . . . but it would be nicer if they could just keep on walking and tacking up broadsides. It was such a pleasant, normal, human thing to be doing. Something besides his usual routine of drinking and scrounging and going hungry and feeling cold and alone. He'd gladly walk the whole of Knoxville if he could do it with Amy Deacon.

"Mr. Scarlett, thank you for your help."

"It was a pleasure, ma'am."

Up on Secession Hill a door opened. Ben saw a tall, broad, very straight-backed figure fill the doorway, visible only in silhouette because of the light behind him. Doc Deacon himself! He stared down at his daughter and the ragged man with her like Zeus gazing down from Olympus.

"My father," Amy said. Her voice was suddenly different. Stiff, lower, spoken almost in a whisper. "I must go. Thank you again, sir . . . and please have that cough tended to."

"Thank you. I'm fine. Good evening, ma'am. Obliged for the dollar." He tipped his hat, glanced up and nodded a humble, sheepish greeting at the big man limned in the doorway—a greeting that went unreturned—then headed off down the walk and into the dark.

Amy climbed the stone stairs that led up to the house.

"Well? Did you get the broadsides hung?" Dr. George Deacon asked.

"Yes. Two every block, just as you said."

"Who was that man?"

"Just a vagrant. I paid him to carry the broadsides for me."

"A vagrant? Not one like babbling old Charlie Douglass, I hope?"

"No, Father. No one like Charlie Douglass would have helped me hang broadsides for a Secession rally. That man's name is Ben Scarlett. He knows Charlie Douglass—I saw him drinking with Charlie Douglass in that clearing beside the meat packing plant this morning, in fact—but don't worry, he says he isn't a Unionist, and said he's coming to the rally besides. And he had some complimentary things to say about you, for what it's worth. That you were famous, and bold, and so on."

"I see." Dr. Deacon cleared his throat and stood a little straighter, absorbing the indirect praise with obvious pleasure, and Amy had to marvel at an ego so perpetually hungry it savored even the plaudits of a town drunk. She had never known so vain a man as her own father. "Well, he sounds like a sensible fellow. But you should be careful about his kind. He might have robbed or hurt you."

"I don't think this one was that type, Father. He told me I reminded him of a woman he was once was engaged to. He carried the broadsides for me. I gave him a bit of money to pay him. He was a gentleman." She looked out into the night. "I felt sorry for him. He seemed lonely, and he's sick. A bad cough. I told him to come see you, but he probably won't. He wouldn't admit to being ill."

"His kind, that's how they are. Spend every dollar on drink, never eating, sleeping outdoors. Taking ill. Dying young. But if he came to me, I would treat him, even if he couldn't pay, considering that he stands on the correct political ground."

Amy laughed inwardly, remembering Ben's open admission that he stood on no political ground at all except that which was prudent at the given moment. All she had told her father was that Ben was no Unionist; he had misconstructed Ben into a Secessionist on his own. But if that misperception would help Ben obtain the doctor's good graces and free medical care, fine. She had liked the amiable vagrant; his identification of her with a lost love, if not a contrivance, had been touching. She decided to keep an eye on the vacant lot near the *Advocate* office over the next few days, in hopes of seeing Ben Scarlett there again. She would tell him that her father was willing to treat his lung problem at no cost.

They ate a silent supper together, father and daughter, in the dining parlor just off the kitchen, served by Dr. Deacon's slave of many years, Rufus. He hovered silently in the background, a dark, tall, lean, looming vulture of a man whose thoughts remained his own and whose words were mostly confined to "Yes, sir, Mr. George," and "No, sir, Mr. George," and "Yes indeed, Miss Amy." For all of Amy's life Rufus had been there, and such his reserve had always been in the presence of his master. But in private, how the man could talk! Amy knew far better than her father the music of Rufus's sonorous voice and the depths of conversation he was capable of. She had learned much from Rufus, things that had shaped her mind in ways of which her father had no inkling.

Amy read silently in her favorite stuffed chair until nine o'clock, then declared herself ready to retire. Her father, puffing his big pipe, nodded a good-night. She glanced at the portrait of her late mother that hung above the fireplace and said her own secret good-night to her as well, then climbed the stairs to her room.

She closed and quietly locked the door, then went to her desk and opened a drawer. She removed a small box, which when opened revealed a ring that had been her mother's. She removed the ring and the slitted padding that held it, then a small key the padding had hidden.

With the key, she opened a trunk at the base of her bed. Removing quilts and folded cloaks and dresses, she reached into the trunk and pressed on the bottom, making it tilt. It was in fact a false bottom, hiding stacks of papers covered with her neat scrawl. She shuffled through the stack until she found the papers she was looking for. Removing them, she went to her desk, sat down, and began to read and occasionally edit the words. When she reached the end, she began writing some more. The pen scratched steadily, words flowing out in a fluid script across the paper with hardly a break. She paused occasionally, listening to the sounds of the house beyond her bedroom door, until she knew that her father was in bed. His vibrant snores echoed in a quiet rumble up the stairs from his room below. At last she completed her work, blowing the newest inkings dry. She read through the entire essay one more time and was satisfied.

When she opened her bedroom door, she found Rufus already waiting in the hallway. "I do hear him snoring, don't I, Rufus?"

"Yes. He'll sleep sound tonight. He drank three glasses of wine before he went to bed."

"Good. Are you willing to make the run?"

"You know I am."

"Be careful. Don't let anyone see you."

"Nobody going to see me, Miss Amy. I always make sure of that."

"Tell Horatio to look this over carefully and change it any way he sees fit, if he wants. Tell him it would be good if we could publish by Thursday, because of Father's rally."

"Yes. I'll tell him."

"Rufus, do be careful. If we should be caught . . ."

"I know. You don't need to tell me. I know more than you what the cost of getting caught might be, Miss Amy. I'll be careful."

"Rufus, lately Birch Lewis has said things to me, dropped hints that maybe he knows. Maybe he's seen you, some time or another. Maybe he's overheard me talking to you at the newspaper office. Maybe he's seen you meeting with Eaton." The latter was the more likely option, in Amy's opinion. Though she had said nothing about it to anyone, twice now she had seen Birch Lewis lingering around Secession Hill late at night, watching the house . . . watching for *her*, probably. She knew Lewis had feelings for her; whether romantic, lustful, or both, she did not know. Certainly they were unreciprocated; her skin crawled every time the *Advocate*'s editor turned his lizardlike eyes on her. But the crucial thing was: If Lewis did sometimes watch the house by night, he might have seen Rufus make one of his nocturnal sneaks to meet Eaton at a certain designated spot on a quiet lane.

Rufus looked worried. "I hope he don't know, Miss Amy. And if he does know, pray to God above that he keeps his mouth shut. Your pap, he can't never find out about this. Never."

She nodded. Rufus tucked the papers under his coat, descended the stairs without making even one creak—a trick that Amy had never mastered despite the fact she weighed at least fifty pounds less than Rufus—and slid out the front door into the night. Amy returned to her room and waited by the window for an hour, until she heard Rufus return. He came up the stairs, rapped gently on her door. "Good night, Miss Amy."

She smiled, deeply relieved. That *good night* was the standard signal that all had gone as planned one more time. "Good night, Rufus."

She changed into her nightgown and crawled into bed, where she fell asleep almost instantly. It had been a most exhausting day.

Chapter 3

The following Thursday, early evening

The weather had grown clear and cool. In a banner-draped Gay Street lot, a huge bonfire spilled light and heat that reflected off the brick walls of tall buildings on either side, generating a pleasant warmth as people filed in. The western sky bore the last trace of daylight and the promise of a brilliant starry display before the rally was through. Carpenters had finished constructing the rough but sturdy speaker's platform ahead of schedule in the afternoon, and the number of people already gathering indicated that the crowd would be large.

George Deacon stood to the side of the stage, counting and recounting the growing crowd, sipping on a glass of lemonade and occasionally nodding in a satisfied manner to himself. A man who had advocated the disunionist cause since the 1850s, he had reason to feel proud. At the first, too few had taken his line of thought seriously, but at last momentum was growing. In the crowd he saw the faces of people who had long hung fire on the issue; perhaps tonight he would be able to persuade several of them to his way of thinking. The mere fact the undecideds were here indicated they were at least open to hearing his arguments.

His arguments . . . for the tenth time that evening he

patted his coat for reassurance that his speech was safely tucked into his pocket. Though he had the gift of making any talk he gave sound extemporaneous, in truth he was very dependent upon prewritten speeches. Usually he memorized them, practicing them in private, complete with just enough pauses and lapses to make them sound improvised and authentically his own. He hadn't had time to fully memorize this one, though, and would have to hold the paper in his hand while he spoke. He was a bit concerned about this, but not seriously. This was a planned, prescheduled rally. No one would necessarily be expecting an extemporaneous speech.

He looked toward the long, draped table where Amy was handing out fried pies and glasses of lemonade for any who requested them. His thick brows moved a quarter inch closer together. Could Amy smile no more brightly, no more authentically, than that? He knew Amy lacked enthusiasm for his politics, suspected she disagreed with some of his beliefs— mere and typical feminine fractiousness, in his assessment, and therefore unimportant—but confound her, could she not at least try a little harder to *look* like she had some enthusiasm? Surely she owed him that as a daughter and an employee. He would have words about this with her later.

Dr. Deacon glanced at his pocket watch, straightened his spine, drew in a deep breath, and nodded at Birch Lewis, the young man who served him officially as editor of the *Advocate*, but in fact was more a pressman, mechanic, and newspaper deliverer than wordsmith. As an editor he was mostly a figurehead. He gathered and wrote a bit of minor local news, scoured major newspapers from other cities for reprintable material. But the real core components of the *Advocate*, the Secession dogmatics that gave it its soul and identity, these Birch Lewis had little to do with.

Lewis mounted the stage and crossed to the center of it. He waved his hands and shouted, "Attention! Attention!" Dr. Deacon frowned. Lewis's words sounded a touch slurred. Lately he had begun to suspect that his editor was drinking fairly heavily. Not good. There were certain delicate private matters to which Lewis was privy because of his job, and what secrets reigned at the *Advocate* needed to remain secrets and not be spilled unwittingly in some tavern by an employee with a liquor-loosened tongue. Furthermore, he fancied he had caught Lewis looking at Amy lately in a manner he didn't like.

"Attention!" Lewis yelled again. The milling, eating, lemonade-and-coffee-guzzling crowd quieted into some semblance of order. Lewis thanked them for attending, encouraged them to partake freely of the edibles as long as they lasted, and launched at once into an introduction of Dr. James Gettys McGready Ramsey, a fellow physician to Dr. Deacon, president of the Knoxville branch of the Bank of Tennessee, resident of a fine house called Mecklenburg, a leading historical authority who had personally interviewed many of Tennessee's founding figures, an influential advocate for railroad development, and all in all one of the most respected and persuasive states' rights spokesmen in Knoxville. Deacon was thrilled that Dr. Ramsey had agreed to give an initial brief speech this evening. His mere participation lent an air of dignity and credibility to the occasion. It was no small thing that Ramsey had agreed to come, in that his personal dislike of George Deacon was well known.

Dr. Deacon didn't let Ramsey's dislike, or that of anyone else, bother him. He knew both his own abilities and limitations. His chief ability was the moving and motivation of masses of people; his chief limitation was a chronic inability to forge and maintain individual relationships. Very few people had ever called him friend. Even his late wife had managed to simultaneously love him and dislike him; he sensed that it was much the same now with Amy. He accepted it. George Deacon could live without the affection of individuals as long as he had the devotion of a significant bloc of the public. He demanded nothing but to be taken seriously, to be recognized as a man of influence and power, and to be faithfully obeyed by those under his authority. His attitude was: Hate me if you wish, but do not betray me, and never hold me up for ridicule.

Ramsey's lean figure worked through the crowd to the stage. He mounted it to a healthy round of applause, but Deacon heard a few catcalls mixed in. He studied the crowd to ferret out the source, and saw a line of known Unionist

men back along the edge of the block near the street. He
sighed. Too bad one had to put up with such disrespectful
dissenters. He hoped they wouldn't grow too obnoxious.
With that in mind he looked specifically for Charlie Douglass and was relieved not to see him. With any luck the sorry
drunk was off draining cups in some tavern.

Ramsey gave his talk without further harassment from
the Unionists, and Deacon was digging out his own speech
when he glanced again toward the street and felt a surge of
dismay. Douglass! The well-known vagrant, grinning like a
hungry man headed for a banquet, came weaving up off the
street and pushed into the crowd until he was almost
squarely in the center of it, near the diminishing bonfire.
Deacon shook his head and asked his Creator why, why,
why was Charlie Douglass a necessary ingredient of the
world? And why did he have to pick just *this* moment to
show up? From the corner of his eye Deacon studied Douglass's ruddy, grinning face, and felt the heat of a long-
standing hatred. An honorable foe Dr. Deacon could abide;
a drunken, jeering fool he could not. Charlie Douglass
served up a dish Deacon could not stomach: disrespect.

Lewis was back up on the stage again, introducing the
little brass band hired to play just before Deacon's speech.
As the band hefted up shining instruments and began
blasting out a vigorous march, Deacon made his way to the
side of the stage and gestured for Lewis. The editor looked
worried. *No doubt afraid I'll smell liquor on his breath,*
Deacon thought.

Lewis knelt near the side of the stage and leaned over
just a little toward Deacon, and it did appear he was trying
to hold his breath as much as possible. "Yes, Doc?"

Deacon raised his voice just enough for Lewis to hear
him over the brass band. "I saw Charlie Douglass come into
the crowd. He's drunk and looks like he's set to give us
trouble. I want you to go stand near him, and if he starts
causing problems, tell him to come with you and you'll buy
him a bottle . . . no, two bottles of good whiskey if he'll just
go away and leave us in peace tonight. He won't be able to

resist that." He dug money from a pocket. "Here. You can pay for it with this."

Lewis nodded and looked back across the crowd. "Oh, yes . . . I see him. I'll go stand near him so . . . oh, no."

"What?"

"Out across the street—it's old Free the Slaves Eaton, setting up a stand. Big pile of papers."

Deacon swore, craning his neck to look. Sure enough, the sparely built, brilliantly red-haired abolitionist was emplacing himself and a stack of his journals on the other side of Gay Street. If there was a man in Knoxville Deacon hated almost as much as Charlie Douglass, it was Eaton. The man had the gall to publish his heresies with the same vigor with which Deacon published his own material, and it often seemed that Eaton took pains to specifically target the ideas pushed by the *Advocate*. Sometimes it even seemed that Eaton had some uncanny precognizance of what the newest *Advocate* was going to contain. "Blast! I hope he doesn't start bellowing at us from across the street. Maybe he'll just give out his little abolition rag and keep quiet."

"I've never known him to bellow," Lewis contributed. "That seems to be more Charlie Douglass's style."

"Eaton bellows on paper, and that's nearly as bad. Worse, because it lasts longer. Ah, well. Nothing to do but hope for the best, maybe call in the law if Eaton makes a disturbance. I'd herald the chance to have that abolition rat hauled off and locked up. In fact, I'd like to schedule a public exhibition in which Horatio Eaton and Charlie Douglass cudgel each other to death with axes. And I wouldn't even charge admission. That would be a display any and all should see, free of charge."

Lewis provided the obligatory laugh. Deacon did little bantering, but when he did, he expected some worthy mirth in response. "Don't worry, Doc. Nobody much takes him serious. You'll find very few Unionists, even, who want to see the darkies free. Why, even most of the abolition societies won't take darkies for members!"

Deacon gazed at Lewis coldly, thinking this was surely the most stupid man he could have ever graced with the title of editor. The man obviously did not even realize he had just contradicted one of Deacon's fundamental tenets: Always, *always* portray Unionism in any form as ultimately equivalent to abolitionism! Ah, well, he wouldn't attempt to educate a fool at such a moment as this.

Abruptly, Deacon stuck his face closer to Lewis's and took a deep sniff. "Birch, your breath smells of rum and you have a slur in your voice. Just how much have you been drinking?"

The band finished its music with a grand flourish, signaling that it was time for Lewis to introduce his employer. Grateful to have been saved from answering Deacon's question, Lewis bounded and headed for center stage, joining in the applause of the crowd and smilingly nodding at the musicians as they left the stage.

"They'll be back with more music in just a few minutes, after our next speaker concludes," Lewis said, making an obvious effort not to speak with a slur. "And it is with great pride I now have the honor of making that speaker's introduction. You all know him well—a man Georgian by birth but Tennessean by choice, a man who wears the hat of publisher, of physician—"

"And anybody else's hat he can sneak off with when they ain't watching!"

The interrupter was, predictably, Charlie Douglass. His loud yell caused those around him to frown at him, but a titter of laughter passed through the crowd as a whole. And from the Unionists on the perimeter, loud guffaws.

Lewis looked rattled, but tried to pick up and go on. "As I was saying . . . the hat of physician, the hat of—"

"Physician? Hey, I need a physician!" Douglass said loudly, putting a mock painful quiver in his voice. "I got the windy bowels mighty bad, Doc, mighty bad! Help me, Doc! Oh, how I'm a-cramping! Mercy!"

The more proper people among the crowd looked offended; a few called for Douglass to shut up. But a large share laughed. The Unionists at the rear were in ecstasy. "Charlie Douglass for president!" one yelled.

Lewis, red-faced and flustered, tried to go on. "Uh, I was saying that Dr. Deacon, our next speaker, is a man of, uh—"

Douglass put the heel of his hand against his mouth and

blew, making a loud, rude, razzing noise. "Never mind 'bout that windy bowel, Doc!" he yelled. "I just took care of the problem my own self!"

"There's a Secession wind a-blowing, Doc!" a Unionist mocked, evoking riotous laughter.

A circle had opened around Douglass; Dr. Deacon's followers in the crowd had no desire to stand near the hated heckler. But one big man among them balled up his fists and advanced upon Douglass. "Charlie, you'd best shut up or I'll shut you up myself."

"Why, don't do that, Bob! Then I wouldn't be able to tell your wife 'bout that little yaller gal you been visiting over on the Kingston road."

The man drew back his fist and would have struck the drunk, but somebody grabbed his arm. "No!" the intervener said. "Bob, don't let him get to you. He's naught but an old sot, not worth an assault charge."

"I ain't been seeing no yaller gal!"

"We know, Bob, we know," said his soother gently.

Dr. Deacon mounted the stage and waved his bewildered and defeated editor away, whispering: "Get that maggot out of here. Promise him three bottles if you have to!" With most eyes fixed on Charlie Douglass, few had noticed the doctor's ascent to the stage.

The Falstaffian Deacon took advantage of the moment to unfold his papers, glance at them, and momentarily tuck them aside. Personal pride demanded that he throw a barb or two at Douglass before beginning his talk. "My friends!" he bellowed in a stentorian voice. Everyone turned back toward the stage. Charlie Douglass grinned foxily. His prior heckles had been mere warm-ups. With his favorite target on stage, he was ready to let go with his most lethal charges.

Meanwhile, Birch Lewis was trying to work his way back toward Douglass.

"My friends!" Deacon bellowed again.

"As I hear it, you got no friends!" Douglass shot back. The Unionists in the back roared as if that were the funniest line ever spoken. Meanwhile, a few of the burlier Unionists worked their way up through the crowd to surround Douglass, silently defying anyone to try anything physical to silence the man. Birch Lewis saw it and frowned. Deacon saw it too, and wondered if this meant he was doomed to put up with Douglass's presence all evening.

Deacon said, "Friends, right now many of you are angry at the rudeness of one who stands among us in body but not in spirit. *Our* kind of spirit, at least—we all know that Mr. Charles Douglass stands among spirits of a different variety far too much for his own good."

The Secessionists clapped and cheered. Douglass doffed his hat and bowed, as if he had just been highly complimented, and up on the stage Dr. Deacon wondered how to shame a man who did not seem to know what shame was.

"My fellow citizens, pay no heed to our loudmouthed monkey. He's not worthy of your attention. Why, this is a man I once treated for a broken finger—it seems somebody had struck him in the nose."

The crowd, after a moment's pause to interpret the jest, roared appreciatively. Douglass tried to look untouched, but Deacon saw that he had gigged him with that one.

"Actually, ladies and gentlemen, we have hired Mr. Douglass here as part of our evening's educational effort, to show you an edifying specimen of the level of intellect that advocates keeping our growing, thriving South in bondage to a tyrannical Union. Of course, I've dealt with far more stupid souls than this pitiful fellow." He paused, grinning slyly. "I've dealt with actual northern politicians!"

That line brought nods and applause. Charlie Douglass seemed momentarily cowed. Deacon went on: "We'll dispense with Mr. Lewis's fine and much-appreciated efforts at introduction, and I'll get right on with what I came to discuss with you."

Douglass opened his mouth to heckle, but one of the Unionists beside him nudged him and subtly shook his head. Deacon was relieved; maybe the more sober Unionists, even if they did enjoy Douglass's jibes, would prevail in keeping him under reasonable control. He hoped so; Birch Lewis was having no luck in breaking through the circle of Unionists to reach Douglass with the offer of whiskey.

Deacon opened his papers again and glanced at the first

lines of the speech that had been written for him. Exceptionally written, in fact. The audience this night would hear some particularly well-turned phrases, especially logical arguments, and unusually clever analogies. They would take them as his original work, and he would do nothing to correct that misperception.

He knew the true author of his speech would voice no complaint about this. She would stand where she was, dipping cups of lemonade, hearing a viewpoint with which, he suspected, she did not fully agree, spoken back at her in her own words. She would not reveal that the ringing words Dr. Deacon spoke into the night, like the burning words that filled his radical journal, were not his at all, but the product of his quiet daughter. Secession Hill's famed resident, known as a great communicator, was in fact a very poor one in the area of politics. Without the unknown labors of his daughter on his behalf, he was a speaker without a voice, a writer without a pen. Outside of the simply worded medical reference volume that had initially made his name known, he had required extensive help for virtually everything he had written.

As Deacon began to speak, Amy looked across the street at Horatio Eaton. He gave a subtle tip of his head in acknowledgment. She quickly looked back toward her father.

She was reminded by Eaton's presence that there were other and greater secrets to be kept than her father's. Just as Dr. Deacon did not want it known that his daughter supplied his words, so also she did not want it known that there was a journal besides the *Advocate* that benefited from her writing skill. Where she gave the *Advocate* her labor out of daughterly duty, the other journal received it out of heartfelt personal persuasion. In the *Advocate*, Amy crafted propaganda she did not even believe herself; in the other journal she poured out her soul.

Amy watched her father on the stage and thought of what Rufus had often told her: *Don't never let him catch you at what you're doing, Miss Amy. Your father, he's a harder and badder man than you know. Especially to them who do him a hurt.*

Several times she had asked Rufus what he meant by

such statements. *Best you don't know, Miss Amy,* he had consistently replied. *Best you don't know.*

The bonfire logs shifted, snapped, sent sparks flying skyward. Amy dipped herself a glass of lemonade and took a small swallow, listening to her father's voice booming out its ghostwritten words, but her mind was on the silent abolitionist across the street and the secret they shared.

Chapter 4

Dr. Deacon at his best was an effective speaker in the classical dramatic orator's tradition. The material Amy provided made it easy for him to be at his best. She comprehended the natural rhythms and baritone effusions of his speaking style and wrote his speeches accordingly.

"My fellow Tennesseans, there is no mystery in why I stand before you," Deacon intoned. "I come to advocate the freeing of a noble people from an oppressor who cares nothing for the rights properly vested in the states under the original scheme upon which our nation was founded, but from which a northern-dominated government has sadly departed. The South, my friends, has been married for years to a spouse that has proven unfaithful. It is my sober view, and the view of many other wiser men than George Deacon, that a divorce is inevitable."

He glanced again at his papers, then continued through a few more paragraphs of basically introductory commentary. Douglass stared at him contemptuously but kept quiet. Deacon peered up briefly and saw Lewis had given up trying to work his way over to Douglass. Lewis eyed his employer abashedly, shrugged, and stayed where he was.

Out on the street, Ben Scarlett came sauntering along, half drunk. He had found a partially full whiskey bottle that afternoon, gripped in the hand of another vagrant drunk, one who had passed out before finishing it off. Ben made sure the remaining whiskey hadn't gone to waste. Now he had his mind on the free food promised in the broadsides he'd helped hang earlier in the week. It looked like this was going to be a rewarding day all around.

Deacon was saying: "Let me ask you to look with me at the life of the blessed land upon which we stand tonight. It is a land that is growing and changing, maturing into its primo. A land that has passed through its childhood, its youth, and now stands on the verge of independent adulthood—if it is allowed the freedom to achieve it.

"Friends, I well recall that day back in May of 1858 when I and many others of you here stood between the towns of Blue Springs and Bull's Gap and watched the laying of the final rail of the East Tennessee and Virginia Railroad. I recall my feelings, my happiness at knowing that with the laying of that rail, a vital line of economic life was completed for our region. In the singing rails and rumbling trains we possess a link tying the market cities of the South with the seaboard towns. The railroad has joined us here in East Tennessee to the major cities of the American South. The mountains in whose shadows we live, the mountains we cherish and love, but which have often cut us off from the world around us—these are no longer a barrier to our divinely destined progress.

"Many of you here are businessmen, mechanics, merchants. You have traveled the railroads, visited others like yourselves in the deeper South, and have learned that they are our brothers in a way the indifferent North can never be. Our life, our economy, has become increasingly linked with the life and economy of the South as a whole. No longer are we in East Tennessee forced to drive great herds of swine along muddy, poor roadways in order to sell them. No! Thanks to the railroad, no longer is it difficult for us to convey the produce and livestock we raise here to those in the deeper South who in turn provide for us the manufactured goods we require."

He was working his way into the spirit of his talk now, forgetting about Charlie Douglass and Horatio Eaton across the street. He also forgot, as often when he was orating at full tilt, that these words had not come from his own mind. The concepts were his, certainly, but the words were Amy's. Her skill was a treasure Dr. Deacon sometimes appreciated, but more often took for granted.

Ben Scarlett had snaked deep into the crowd, eyeing the food tables and watching Amy Deacon, who did not notice him. He felt a warm affection for her. He had unconsciously bestowed on her some of the fondness he once held for the beloved Angel Beamish.

On the stage, Deacon was eloquently describing the development of the East Tennessee region, how its original settlers had been among the first Americans to create their own government in the Watauga Association. He lauded the bravery of the settlers and praised those "Overmountain Men" who had traveled over the mountains to defeat Ferguson at King's Mountain. He described the growth of agriculture through the years, its gradual shift from subsistence farming to trade farming. He talked of the growth of cities along the rivers, the development of roads leading from the East Tennessee farming centers to towns such as Chattanooga, Lynchburg, Richmond. He recalled the days, not long past, when 175,000 hogs a year would be driven along the French Broad River road into Carolina, with countless more moving along other routes to market. He told how East Tennessee farmers had become stronger, more independent, how more than half of them now owned their own land and farmed a hundred, two hundred acres each.

Then he talked of wheat, an old crop that had been given new life through the market access provided by the railroads.

And with his own slave Rufus standing almost invisibly in the background of it all, he talked of slavery. "They tell us that our dispute is not truly about slavery," he said. "They tell us they are not abolitionists. But hear me: If war comes, it will not take long before all will see that it is indeed a war of abolition. It will move toward that cursed error with the relentlessness and inevitability of water

coursing from high ground to low. Most hide their abolitionism, but even now there are those who mindlessly seek
to abolish the venerable old institution of slavery, which
has helped build this land." He looked pointedly across the
crowd toward the fiery-haired Eaton. "They declare it a
moral abomination. They say that no man should own another. I say to you that no man can nor should own another
man—does not God and God alone own us all?—but one
can indeed exercise authority over the labor of another
man, and may through that authority even extend a better
life to that man than he could know on his own, especially
if that man be of a race that has not progressed in morality
and intellect to the level of self-sufficiency. There is not a
nation, not a culture, that has not recognized and indeed
practiced, at some phase of its life, some form of the institution of slavery. This unanimous voice cannot be ignored.
It tells us that if slavery is an evil, the experiences of our
forebears have proven it a lesser evil than its alternatives.
It is an ancient and revered institution. It brings lower
races under the helpful tutelage of the higher. It is right in
the eyes of God: Religious scholars whom I have no right
to question tell us they find no scriptural objections to
slavery, and indeed, many sanctions. And though we here
in our portion of the state own few slaves—there are fewer
than 2,500 of them in our own county of Knox—do not
think that because of that the question of our *right* to own
slaves is of little relevance. To the contrary, it is of utmost
relevance and will only become more crucial as time
passes. We have few plantations in East Tennessee, but we
have growing farms and more land under cultivation every
year. A source of labor to work those farms is vital. We
dare not see it cut off from us. The right to own slaves
must be preserved!"

"Hear! Hear!" someone in the crowd shouted.

"As for those who say slavery is evil, well, to you I say
that there is nothing at all that requires you to practice it. If
slavery offends you, then let it alone. But do not seek to
impose your private morality upon others! Those of you
who preach abolition from the pulpit—recall that in our
nation we enjoy freedom of conscience, and the privilege of

not having the religious views of others forced upon us! To all, I say: The right to utilize the practice of slavery must remain for those who desire it—nay, who *require* it for the sake of their livelihood and the public welfare!"

"Preach it out, Doc!" This from a supporter.

"Preach it out, Doc!" This in mocking imitation, from Charlie Douglass, followed up by another loud mouth-against-hand razz. Douglass was no abolitionist, but was unwilling to let a good opportunity to heckle Deacon pass, even if Deacon was at the moment saying things Douglass agreed with.

Ben Scarlett had not realized Douglass was present. He craned his neck and saw him. Sounded like Charlie was going to do another typical performance. Then he remembered Douglass's talk about revealing Deacon's big "secret," and wondered if this was the time and place he had been talking about. Ben still doubted there was any secret there to be revealed, outside Douglass's self-enhancing imaginations.

Deacon, meanwhile, was jolted by Douglass's interruption. He shuffled his papers and tried to find his place—and then an ill-timed burst of wind snatched half the papers from his hand and sent them flying. Deacon froze. The portion of the speech he had lost was the part he had not yet given.

Most of the sheets were recovered by people in the crowd and handed back up to the speaker, but three crucial pages whirlwinded right into the bonfire and were destroyed. Charlie Douglass cackled loudly, and said something that caused Deacon to freeze on the stage and Amy to snap her head around to stare at Douglass in shock:

"Well! Now you'll just have to get by without your daughter's fine words to help you, Doc Deacon!"

Your daughter's fine words . . . Deacon glanced at Amy and saw she had gone pale. He felt himself do the same. *God help me,* Deacon thought, *he knows that Amy wrote the speech!* His legs felt weak beneath him. *But how could he know?* Then Deacon's eyes fell on the aghast expression of Birch Lewis, and he knew who had betrayed him.

Scoundrel! he thought. *Unfaithful, whiskey-guzzling, Judas of a betrayer! You've been talking in the taverns!*

"Why ain't you talking, Doc?" Douglass yelled in the midst of Deacon's extended silence. "Where's them pretty words you're always taking credit for? Can't you come up with none without your little papers in hand? Maybe you ought to put your girly up there and let her spout a few for you! Hell, it's her who writes all your bilge anyhow!"

Lewis, looking downright sickly, shoved his way through the Unionist barrier and reached Douglass. "Charlie," he whispered desperately, "let's me and you go buy some whiskey. All you want—I'll pay. Please, Charlie, just come on. Don't say any more."

"What? You want to drink with me again, like you've done over many a past evening, Mr. Editor of the *Advocate*?" Douglass said loudly as one of the Unionists pushed Lewis roughly away. "You want to tell me some more of Doc Deacon's secrets—like them you told me already?"

"Shut up!" Lewis yelled, suddenly ready to fight. It was his turn now to know what it was to be betrayed. "Shut up, Douglass! You're lying! He's lying, Doc! I didn't tell him anything!"

"Then who did tell me, if you didn't, Mr. Editor?" Douglass chortled. "The fact is, Doc, he told me plenty. Sung like a pretty springtime bird! Doc, you got a big-mouthed editor, and when he's drunk, my, my, how he talks!"

"I'll kill you! God help me, I'll kill you!" Lewis lunged toward Douglass, but there was no hope of reaching him through his protective circle.

Douglass mocked him. "You told all sorts of interesting news to me, didn't you, Mr. Editor! Like how it ain't really the Doc who writes all that newspaper rubbish and these big pretty Secesh speeches!" Douglass was growing ever more bold and loud. "No sir, folks! It ain't Doc Deacon's words you read in the *Advocate*! Never has been! It ain't his words you've heard him spewing on that stage tonight! It's his *daughter* who writes it all! Birch Lewis told me that with his own lips! He says to me, he says, 'Mr. Douglass, did you know that the old Doc can't string two words together unless his little girl does it for him? Did you know there ain't hardly a word that's been published under his name that he wrote on his own? If Doc didn't have his little girl writing for him, he'd be silent as a rock.' That's the very thing he told me!"

"It's a lie, a damned lie!" Birch Lewis yelled. But the crowd was already rumbling in response to Douglass's claims, so few heard Lewis and fewer still believed him. Charlie Douglass spoke with the firm ring of truth.

Ben Scarlett stood unnoticed in the midst of the crowd, as stunned as anyone there by what he was hearing. Now that he knew the great secret Douglass had hinted at there by the meat packing house, he grudgingly admired Douglass's cruel cleverness in keeping the secret until he could reveal it with maximum damaging effect. It astonished Ben to consider that so common a cur as Douglass had been able to get a death grip on the throat of so prominent and influential a show dog as Dr. Deacon.

On the stage, a suddenly listless Deacon let the papers that remained in his hand drop. They fluttered off in the breeze. He turned and walked stiffly toward the side of the stage.

"Don't you go slinking off, Doc Deacon! There's more yet for you to hear!" Douglass shouted.

Over by the table, Amy thought: *Oh, no.* Rufus slipped up behind her and whispered, "Miss Amy, I hope to God he ain't going to say what I think he is."

But Douglass did say it, very loudly. "Did you know, Doc Deacon, that the same pretty little daughter what writes your *Advocate* rot writes for another journal in this here town, too? Didn't know that, did you? Can you guess which one it is, Doc? Horatio Eaton's free-the-slaves abolition rag, that's what! Birch Lewis told me all about that, too! Told me how he's watched your darky man Rufus carrying her stories by night and slipping them to Eaton! Told me how he's heard them talking about it all when they thought there was nobody to hear. It's true, Doc. Your own little girly, the same one what puts your words in your mouth, is an abolitionist! You hear that, folks? Doc Deacon's girl is an *abolitionist*, and he's never even knowed it! His own daughter, she's played him for the fool he is!"

Looking out over the astonished crowd, Deacon felt like his legs had turned to immobile stone. To the side, Amy slumped forward, feeling faint, putting palms down on the table to keep from falling. The lemonade pitcher spilled and broke at her feet. Rufus reached out and grasped her shoulders to steady her. He was trembling. "We're ruint, Miss Amy. Ruint. Now he knows. Now *everybody* knows."

Out on the street Horatio Eaton felt the impulse to turn and run, but he couldn't, not and leave Amy Deacon to face this calamitous situation alone. It was he who had recruited her as an anonymous writer and encouraged her to perpetuate a potentially dangerous betrayal of her father. But he did not know what to do. Should he come forward, should he deny what was being said? He was utterly unprepared to deal with this.

"Lewis, is all this true?" someone asked.

Please, Birch, say it's not, Amy silently pleaded. *Deny it! Deny it!*

Birch Lewis stammered and babbled, then broke into tears. He turned to the stage. "I'm sorry, Doc," he said. "I didn't think he'd tell nobody. I didn't."

Amy closed her eyes. Birch Lewis, intimidated by no more than a loud drunk, had just confirmed it all when a denial might have saved the situation.

Up on the stage, Dr. Deacon, though shaken by what he had just heard, forced himself back into control and made his own desperate salvage effort. "Lies and slanders!" he shouted. "This is a conspiracy to discredit me! My daughter does not write my words, and to call her an abolitionist, to accuse her of writing for Eaton, of all people—it's a malicious falsehood! A drunk's babble!"

"Ask *her* if it's true!" someone called out.

Scores of eyes turned toward Amy. "Well, girl, tell us!" the same voice shouted. "Do you write Doc's words for him?"

"No! Of course I don't!" She said it as loudly and firmly

as she could. But she sensed that few believed her. She began to shake.

"Well, then, are you an abolitionist? Do you write for Eaton?"

"No! How could anyone believe that!"

"There's Eaton himself back yonder, in the street!" one of the Unionists shouted. "Bring him up here! Let's see what he has to say about this!"

The people of the crowd, Unionist and Secessionist alike, were of one curiosity-filled mind now. A dozen or more men broke out of the lot and mobbed over to surround Eaton and all but dragged him into the rally.

"All right, nigger lover! Tell us the truth: Does Amy Deacon write for your rag in secret?"

Eaton looked like a trapped, terrified animal. Amy despaired. He was a good man, a right-thinking man in her view, but she knew of the weakness he had confessed to her: Horatio Eaton could hold his own with any antagonist on a battlefield of paper and ink, but face-to-face confrontation left him overwhelmed. He was in that way very unsuited for the controversial calling he had chosen.

At the moment, Eaton looked like he feared a lynching. "No, no . . . it's not true," he protested far too feebly. "Amy doesn't write for me . . . I mean, Miss Deacon doesn't write—I don't even know her."

"Hah! He's lying!" declared a burly man who held Eaton by the shoulders. "Listen at him! You can tell he's lying!"

"No, no . . . it's the truth . . . really." Eaton sounded small and pitiful. He slumped weakly in the hands of his captors; had they let him go, he certainly would have hit the ground.

Just then, with everyone's attention distracted by Eaton, Birch Lewis managed to get to Charlie Douglass and strike him in the jaw. Someone intervened and struck Lewis in turn, who fell back hard against the heavyset wife of one of the Unionists. She hit the ground hard, letting out a grunting scream. Her husband swore and swung his fist into Lewis's chin.

Suddenly there was general tumult—yelling, cursing, fighting. Banners crashed down; the crowd scattered, people either running, trying to hide, or throwing themselves into the fight. Ben, caught up in the surge, turned for the street. After much bumping and shoving, he made it, ran hard, and looked back over his shoulder to see the rally breaking into a major brawl behind him, while the distinguished Dr. Ramsey extricated himself and began striding away, no doubt vowing to himself never to lend his support to any of George Deacon's public affairs again.

Amy watched it all in numb disbelief. In a matter of minutes a great deception at the heart of her life for two years had been revealed. It didn't matter that public opinion would probably be divided, some believing the charges, others her denials. What mattered was that her father had heard her secret, and in the end would recognize it for the truth it was. Denials would not work with him. He would not take her word for it. He would scour old copies of his own journal and of Eaton's, and compare the style, the content. He would finally understand why the themes and arguments of particular editions of Eaton's journal so uncannily correlated with the concurrent editions of his own, though from the opposite viewpoint, as if written in direct answer to it—because they were.

Amy looked across the surging, brawling mob to her father, who stood stiffly on the platform, a stunned and wounded man. His head swung slowly around and his eyes met hers, and she knew that from that moment on nothing between them would be as before. Though Amy loved her father as much as he would allow her to, there had never been much affection between them at best. Their relationship had evolved into a substantially formal, functional one. It would not survive the blow it had received tonight. She had betrayed a man for whom betrayal was an unpardonable sin, had put up for ridicule a man who could not abide being laughed at. In the midst of bedlam, father and daughter stared at one another, and then the brawl waved up onto the platform and Dr. Deacon was swept into the middle of it.

Out on the street, Ben Scarlett was still running. He was no fighter, nor did he want to be around when the law arrived to break up the fight. As he neared the next intersection and leaned into his run to turn the corner, his ailing lungs spasmed and he began violently coughing. He was still coughing as he ran, staggering and distracted, around the corner, and thus did not notice the approaching wagon until it was right upon him. Ben felt himself dragged down and under. A crushing weight descended upon his left arm. He screamed, the world began to grow dark and blank, and he was sure he was dying.

Chapter 5

Ben did not die, but suffered greatly that night.

He passed out when the wagon struck him, though only for a moment. When he came around again, the wagon was rumbling on down the street, the driver frenetically whipping his team, trying to get away before anyone saw what he had done. Ben was on his back, his left arm initially hurting, then quickly going numb. He sat up; the arm dragged limply on the ground at his side. Gripping it, he stood, then staggered off toward an alley.

Ben was not a rational being at this moment. His mind was stunned by shock and told him he must run and hide. He was an injured animal seeking its burrow. Collapsing behind a rain barrel at the end of the alley, he held his numb arm and whimpered to himself.

He remained there an hour. Gradually shock faded and common sense returned. His arm was beginning to hurt again and swell. Though it was too dark for him to see much, he was sure it was terribly bruised. Judging by feel, the skin was badly abraded but not broken open. He gingerly probed about on the arm, isolating the place where the pain was worst. Broken at that point? If not, at least very bruised and strained.

He needed medical attention. But Ben didn't care for doctors. They cost money. They invariably preached at him because of his drinking, warning him of grim consequences he didn't like being reminded of. But his arm throbbed. Maybe a doctor could give him some medicine to numb away the suffering, and if the arm was broken, splint it up to heal the right way.

Doctors were hard to find by night, however, unless one went to their homes and roused them. Ben didn't know where any doctors lived, except Dr. Deacon on Secession Hill, and Deacon wasn't likely to be practicing medicine tonight. Not after what Charlie Douglass had done to him.

Ben shifted his arm into a position that hurt less, and thought back over the evening to take his mind off his injury. So Amy Deacon was not only her father's secret voice, she was an insincere voice at that, her own beliefs being radically different from Dr. Deacon's! If Douglass's claims were true—and Ben's instinct was that they were—it all was very remarkable, and very bad for Dr. Deacon. He had taken public credit for a long time for work that wasn't his. He had foisted himself off as a wise man, a great writer, a moving, quick-witted speaker—but it had been a sham.

A sham that could not go on, thanks to Charlie Douglass. Ben couldn't imagine anyone taking Deacon or his journal very seriously now that everyone knew it presented ideas framed by a mere young woman who didn't even believe in what she wrote. Ben hoped Deacon wouldn't make matters too hard for Amy in retaliation.

He remained in the alley all night, sleeping sometimes, other times trying merely to find a comfortable way to sit and hold his hurt arm. The morning was welcome. He rose, found a rag and made a sling for his arm, then set out to find a doctor. There was time to kill, of course; doctors weren't likely to be up and about just after dawn.

He walked out onto the street, back to the corner where he had been run over, and onto Gay Street. He paused at the lot where the rally had been held. The banners were shredded and trampled. The stage was strewn with trash, and the table where Amy had served lemonade stood cockeyed, a leg broken. Must have been quite a fight, Ben thought, glad he had gotten away from it. He might have come out of such a brawl with worse than a hurt arm.

Ben meandered along the walks and through the alleys until he found himself near the medical office of Dr. George Deacon, a place whose doors he didn't expect would be open today. But when he came nearer he was surprised to see a light burning and hear someone moving about inside.

He went to a window and peered in, squinting, trying to see if the doctor was at work. Suddenly the door before him opened and Dr. Deacon thrust out his head.

"What do you want?" he asked gruffly. He looked terrible, his face bruised and swollen, his hair poorly combed, one eye blackened.

Ben, startled, said, "Uh, well, I've got a hurt arm. I was needing a doctor to—"

"I'm not open. Not going to be open today. Probably won't be open for a week or more. Go somewhere else."

Ben nodded, turned and began walking off. A few paces on he heard Deacon give out a loud sigh.

"Ah, blast it all! Wait a minute, man. Come back here. I'll look at your arm."

"You ain't got to, Dr. Deacon. I can go somewhere else. I didn't come by expecting to find you here, not after . . ."

"After what? After my evening of humiliation? You were there, were you?" Deacon said sternly. "Is that where you hurt your arm?"

"I was hurt running off from the fight. A wagon went over the top of me."

"Do tell! Well, you're lucky to be alive, man. Might have been your neck as easily as your arm." Deacon came closer and looked at him intently. "Do I know you?" As he asked that, Ben caught a whiff of his breath. Whiskey. The doctor had been drinking, and it was just after dawn. Ben wondered if Deacon had been in that office, drinking and sulking, since the collapse of the rally last night.

"No, but you might have seen me some," Ben said. "I helped your daughter hang broadsides for the rally a few days ago. You came out onto the porch there at Secession Hill while I was still there."

Deacon stiffened visibly at the mention of his daughter. Ben realized he had brought up a painful subject and figured he would be run off again because of it. But Deacon merely said, "Yes, I remember. It seems a long time ago, now. Let's see, your name is . . ."

"Scarlett. Ben Scarlett."

"Come inside, Mr. Scarlett. Let's take a look at that arm."

The arm wasn't broken, but Deacon did splint it up and bind it. He provided Ben with a better sling than his improvised one, and told him to keep the arm immobile for two weeks, then return to him to have it checked again. Ben listened and nodded, but his mind was more on the doctor's situation than his own. He was fascinated by the black eye, and Deacon noticed.

"Well, now that we're done with you, I'll go ahead and satisfy your none-too-subtle curiosity, Mr. Scarlett. Yes, I did receive this black eye in that brawl. I received it, as a matter of fact, from a friend of yours. Mr. Charlie Douglass."

Charlie had done that? Ben wondered if the doctor had gone after Douglass in the brawl, or vice versa. "Now, I admit to knowing Charlie Douglass, yes sir, but I don't know that he's that much of a friend."

"Really? I recall being told once that you've done some drinking with Mr. Douglass."

Amy must have told him about seeing me over by the pork house. "Yes, sir, I have. But the honest truth is, Doctor, I'll drink with anybody who offers me whiskey." He paused, thinking of that alcoholic odor on the doctor's breath. His passion for liquor overcame any polite reticence. "In fact, sir, I'd drink with you, right now, if you was to offer it. Maybe it'd even make my arm quit hurting me so."

Deacon arched a brow. "A bit early in the morning for drinking, isn't it, Mr. Scarlett?"

"Maybe so. But I notice that—" Ben realized he was about to cross a line he shouldn't, and stopped.

"You notice that I've been doing some drinking myself already—is that what you were going to say? Indeed I have,

Mr. Scarlett. It isn't my normal custom—but last night was not a normal night." He looked wistful. "Perhaps the hardest night of my life."

"I regret it for you, sir. I reckon it must have been right difficult."

"Humiliating is the word, Mr. Scarlett. Humiliating. I'm a man with a reputation, you know. A man perceived as wise, as a communicator, an orator, a writer . . . but the fact is, beyond that first book of popular medicine, I've never been able to write well on my own. I can communicate mere facts ably enough, as in my medical volume, but *ideas* . . . that's something else again. It wasn't until Amy . . . until my daughter began to help me that my ideas began to receive notice and make an impression on the public mind. She has a way, you see, a skill, that I wish I had myself. It's been because of her that me and my newspaper . . . and more importantly, the *ideas* that it champions, have been able to make a difference."

"I reckon she must be an intelligent young woman, your daughter."

Deacon combed fingers through thinning gray hair. "Intelligent. Yes. But the fact is she is nothing *but* an intelligent young woman. And a young woman like that is something like a trained monkey, or a horse that counts with its hoof, don't you see. Interesting to observe, impossible to take seriously. A man in my position couldn't have it known that I was so dependent on a mere *girl*. So we kept our arrangement secret. I gave her the concepts, the gist of what I wanted said, and she crafted it into words for me. No one knew except me, her, my editor—my *former* editor, I should say—and Rufus, my slave. You understand why we had to do it that way, don't you, Mr. Scarlett?"

Ben was flattered that Deacon even cared what he thought. He wasn't used to being given credence by anyone. "I understand it, Dr. Deacon. It wouldn't look right, a girl being give all the credit. Folks wouldn't have listened to you."

"Correct. You're quite perceptive," Deacon said. He paused and looked sad. "Of course, it doesn't matter now. It's over. My daughter has betrayed me. . . . God! How she's betrayed me!" Sadness became anger that burst from him so quickly, Ben was startled. "How could she have done that? How could she have gone so far astray? Writing for that—that damned *abolitionist* dung-sheet, that heretical rag of free-the-darkies nonsense! Damn and blast! She might as well have dragged the Deacon name through a cesspool! And to think she actually *believes* in such bilge-water! I had sensed long ago that she wasn't fully persuaded of my own views, as good as she was at expressing them for me. But *this*! An *abolitionist*! God help us all!" His face was blotchy red. He shook his head, calmed a bit, then said again, much more softly, "God help us all."

"I'm mighty sorry, Doctor," Ben said quietly, groping for the right response to such an outburst. "I can see you're taking it hard. And I reckon it must hurt pretty fierce, having your own child turn 'way from you and deceive you and all."

Deacon looked at him, one eye black and puffy, the other red-rimmed, bloodshot. "Yes. Yes." He seemed sad again, no more fury. Suddenly he smiled. "Mr. Scarlett, I rather like you. What would you say if I offered you a swallow or two of whiskey despite the hour? Might that be something you could keep under your hat—or are you a betrayer at heart, too?" The smile declined a little as he said that.

"I ain't no betrayer, no sir. And I'd be proud to drink with you. It'd be a honor. Why, you're the most famous man I ever talked to, face-to-face."

"Some might tell you that *infamous* is the most accurate word at this point, Mr. Scarlett. Inglorious. Ignoble. Discredited—all because of a common drunk and a wild-eyed abolitionist newspaperman." The doctor sighed, rose, and went to a cabinet, from which he withdrew a bottle and glass. His own glass, damp from his earlier drinking, was already on the table. "Well, here you are, Mr. Ben Scarlett, drinking with Doc Deacon, only days after drinking with Charlie Douglass," the doctor said as he sat the bottle on the desktop. "You're working the full span, aren't you!"

"Reckon so, sir. But like I said, Charlie Douglass ain't no true friend of mine." Ben's friendships, like his politics, shifted depending upon who held the bottle.

Deacon swallowed a mouthful of liquor, smacking his lips. "I despise Charlie Douglass, you know. Loathe him. Hate him. Have for quite some time. And after last night, doubly so. I abominate him. Detest him. It's because of him all this has come out into the sun for everyone to see. He's made a mockery of me, Mr. Scarlett. He and Eaton both."

Ben had his eye on the whiskey. "Charlie's a wicked man, Doctor. A wicked man. And Eaton, he's a fool and troublemaker."

"You see things my way, then! About Charlie Douglass, abolition, Unionism, politics . . ."

"Oh, yes sir. I'm Secesh to the bone. Always have been." Ben reached out, eagerly received the shot glass proffered to him, and pulled it straight to his lips. Dr. Deacon watched him drink, a deepening, thoughtful expression on his vein-dappled face.

"I do like you, Mr. Scarlett. Indeed I do."

"I appreciate that, Dr. Deacon. You're kind to say that. I like you, too."

"More whiskey?"

"Yes indeedy."

Again the doctor watched Ben empty his glass. There were thoughts churning behind his eyes, veiled from Ben. "I'm glad you wandered by, Ben—you don't mind me calling you Ben, do you? Good. Call me Doc. It's been a dismal night for me. Having someone to talk to this morning, someone who listens and comprehends as well as you—that has brightened my spirits considerably."

"You been here since last evening, Dr. Deacon . . . Doc?"

"Since three this morning. Before that I was on Secession Hill, having a very painful talk with my daughter." He grunted. "My *former* daughter, as far as I'm concerned. I'll not consider her my daughter again, not until she repents before me for what she's done. She cried aplenty—but no tears of repentance."

Ben concealed his shock. Deacon was casting off his own daughter? That was a far more extreme reaction than he would have expected from any father. He said, "Maybe

Charlie Douglass was lying about some of that truck he said about her."

"Lying? No, Ben. He was telling the truth. I confronted Amy about it last night. She denied it a minute or two, then admitted it all. Her disagreements with my views, her secret work with Eaton, the involvement of Rufus. All of it. Said she didn't intend me to be hurt, this and that, but that she believed she had done what was right. Bilge. Pure bilge. How could she not have expected me to be hurt? She's a betrayer, Ben. That's one thing I won't abide . . . betrayal. Those who put themselves on my side, under my eye, I expect them to stay where they are and do what they have agreed to. You're that kind of man, I'll bet. Right?"

"Well, I hope I am. I wouldn't want never to betray nobody."

"Of course you wouldn't. I see mettle in you, sir. More whiskey?"

"Thank you. Yes."

The doctor, smiling slightly now, watched Ben drain off his third glass. "Yes, Ben, I'll bet you are a faithful man. A straight shooter. Reliable."

"I reckon I'm good enough." The whiskey was fine, making him feel a familiar, happy warmth. His slinged arm didn't hurt much now.

"Another glassful, Ben?"

I've found heaven, Ben thought. He grinned and stuck out his glass. Deacon filled it and watched Ben drink it down.

"My life is going to be very different from now on, Ben. I'm not sure what will come of all this. But I'll be living alone for the time being. I'm sending Amy and Rufus— another Judas, that two-faced African!—off to live with my brother in Greeneville. I'll not have them in my house any longer."

"Your brother, he won't mind having them put off on him?"

"He'd best not, for their sake. Because they certainly will *not* stay with me."

"What if he won't take them?"

"Then they can go dig a hole in the ground and live in

that. They'll find no forgiveness or welcome in my home or my heart."

Ben thought the man surely was exaggerating. "But she is your own daughter, Doc."

"You think me a hard man?"

"Well . . . it does seem right hard, putting your own girl out." Ben would have never spoken so freely had not his tongue grown loose from the whiskey.

"She's grown. She's intelligent. I'll make some monetary arrangements for her. She'll survive. Believe me, I'll be more faithful to her than she has been to me."

Ben still had a troubled look. The doctor saw it and seemed annoyed. "You needn't worry. My brother *will* take her in. It's in his nature. I'll be sending him a wire, and then an extended and detailed letter, explaining the whole muddle. My brother's a softhearted fellow, and fond of Amy. He'll take her in. So you see I'm not as hard a man as you thought . . . though I am far from soft, especially when I've been wronged. I always have been that way. I have never been able to master the art of forgiving." He paused. "Ben, I tell you, it's as much for her own good as mine that I'm sending Amy off. I could never treat her in any kind way if she stayed. I don't have the ability to overlook wrongs that have been done to me."

Ben had never run across anyone who could talk with such objective disconcern about his own offspring. But the doctor's business was his own. "Well, I reckon you know the best way to handle your own family, Doc." Ben was looking at Deacon's injured eye again as he spoke. "Doc, you said Charlie Douglass busted that eye of yours? What happened to him after?"

"He was hauled off and thrown into the jail for provoking a disturbance," Deacon said. "He'll not be in long. He'll be out again before you know it, stirring up trouble." He paused, smiled coldly. "Or maybe finding some trouble for himself."

"You're going after him, are you?"

"Suffice it to say that I'll not forget what he has done to me. Nor Eaton. I'll find a way to even the score with both of them when the time is right." He smiled coldly. "Perhaps more than even it. Like I said: I don't forgive."

Ben wondered how a man with such a mean spirit had managed to raise so kindly a young woman as Amy Deacon. He still looked back on that brief time of walking with her, helping her hang her broadsides, as a golden-hued memory, a happy, fleeting interlude during which he had been glad to be Ben Scarlett.

Ben sensed it was time to go, and that brought up a touchy matter. "Doc, I . . . I ain't got no money to pay you for patching me up."

Deacon waved him off. "I don't expect payment. Not in money, at least. Perhaps there will be some way on down the road you can pay me. With work. Service of some kind." He smiled.

"Thank you, sir. Thank you very much. And thank you for the whiskey." He stood. "Come back in a couple of weeks, you say?"

"I'll tell you what, Ben—come back sooner than that. Come back tomorrow, about suppertime. We'll have another of these good talks. Eat a meal. Drink some more whiskey."

Ben smiled. "Yes sir. I'll be here."

Deacon said, "I seem to have made you my human confessional booth, eh? I find you an easy man to talk with, Ben. And I do sense a kind of strength and faithfulness in you. There are indeed some things you might be able to do for me on down the road."

"What kind of things is that, Doc?"

"We'll talk about that some other time. I'll be seeing you tomorrow evening?"

"Yes sir. I'll be here."

"Take care of that arm, Ben. Oh . . . and here." He dug a handful of money from his pocket. "Buy yourself a good meal. *Food*. Not whiskey. You want whiskey, I'll give it to you when you come back tomorrow."

"I'll be here," Ben said. "I 'preciate you being so hospitable. This money . . . I'll spend it on food. I promise."

"Good. Ben, I believe you and I may be able to do some

worthwhile business together. Until tomorrow, then." He shook Ben's hand.

As Ben left he wondered what kind of business a doctor could possibly consider having with a town drunk. Whatever it was, he was willing to go along—as long as Deacon kept that whiskey bottle available.

He bought himself some breakfast with part of the money Deacon had given him. At midday he purchased a loaf of bread and ate it for his lunch. The rest of the money he put in his pocket, pledging to himself to save it until the next day so he could buy more food, but by that evening he was in one of the local saloons, and the money was long gone by the time he drunkenly crawled into an unlocked storage building at the railroad depot and found himself a place to sleep for one more night. Before he lay down, he glanced out the single dirty window and saw Deacon's big white house on Secession Hill. Lights burned in only a couple of windows. He wondered what was going on inside, what words had been spoken, and if tears had been shed. He knew that Amy Deacon must surely be very sad at this moment.

She would be going to Greeneville, Dr. Deacon had said. An exile, cut off from her own father. Ben tried to remember if he had ever visited Greeneville. . . . Yes, he had, one time while he was still a boy. He could remember hardly a thing about it.

Whatever kind of town it was, he hoped that Amy Deacon would be happy there. He couldn't forget how kind she had been to him. He would probably never lay eyes on her again, once she left Knoxville, a thought that made him despondent. He stood by the window, watching Secession Hill until the lights in the windows finally winked out.

Part II

THE EXILE

Chapter 6

Aboard a Greeneville-bound train

Her uncle's first name was Hannibal. In Amy Deacon's early childhood he had inspired her with fear—instinctive fear, unspecific, the intuitive fear of a child who enters a certain house, or meets a certain stranger, and simply *knows* there is something ominous in it all that adults cannot detect. As Amy had grown up she came to understand that what had scared her about Hannibal Deacon had really been innocuous things: his extraordinary physical height and breadth, which she associated with the monsters of childish nightmares; his booming voice, which sounded to her like a continual shout; his shag of blondish-brown hair that stuck up, out, and every which way, making her think of madmen. And there was the fact that Hannibal had been a soldier in the Mexican campaign; her father often talked proudly of Hannibal's war-making, which made the child Amy think of him as a hardened killer.

But with maturity came perspective. Hannibal Deacon lost his fearsomeness and she learned to laugh at her childish perceptions of him. She came to know him as a kindly, jovial man, the opposite of all she had discerned as a little girl.

Now she feared him again. As the East Tennessee and

Virginia Railroad passenger train chugged along through the little town of Blue Springs, with Greeneville and Uncle Hannibal Deacon waiting only a few miles ahead, Amy was full of dread and loneliness, even though her beloved Rufus was on the train with her, guarding the baggage. She was wounded, and it hurt. Her own father—her very *father*! . . . she could still hardly comprehend it—had rejected her and now hated her, all because she was unable to share his political views.

No, whispered a voice in her head that she did not want to hear. *Hated for more than that . . . hated because you betrayed him, and George Deacon will not stand for betrayal.*

She bit her lip, looking out the window and fighting tears. This struggle was hard because it was unfamiliar: Amy Deacon seldom cried. She was a strong and controlled young woman, always had been . . . her father's accolade for as long as she could remember had been that she was "three-quarters grit, one-quarter pride." She had never let him know how gratified she felt when he described her that way; wasn't part of being one-quarter pride knowing how to hide it? Sensing he liked seeing her as controlled and unemotional, she worked hard to make herself more that way. When emotions rose, she reached out and snatched them, bringing them under her command before they could bring her under theirs. All these things she had done for her father, and it came to her now that maybe she had loved him more deeply and longed for his affection more than she'd known.

The train rolled on, carrying Amy deeper into rural exile. Through the trees lining the tracks Amy saw the rolling fields, the occasional wooded hills, and the rich, level Lick Creek bottomland that defined the farm country between Blue Springs and Greeneville. Smoke from the big engine stack billowed back across the train, murking the view. Not long now until the dreaded meeting. She could comfort herself only with the idea that meeting her uncle Hannibal couldn't possibly be as miserable as it had been to leave her father at Secession Hill.

The parting had occurred in a cold chill of rejection. He had not even accompanied her to the train station. He had not kissed her good-bye. She had kissed him, but his check was cool and unyielding at the touch of her lips, his eyes staring straight ahead, refusing to acknowledge her. That was the moment she had come to believe he hated her, and the experience was a little like dying young. She had thought of what Rufus told her many times before: how she didn't know the man her father was even as well as he did, and how she should be glad not to know. Maybe now she did know, a little better.

Here on the other side of her departure from Secession Hill, nothing in her life was as clear as it had been before. Despite her refusal to repudiate her actions before her father, the things she had done no longer laid themselves out in her mind in the familiar neat, moral order. Could it be that her father was at least partly right? Had she been wrong to follow a duplicitous course in pursuit of what she saw as the good? She struggled for an answer.

The answer remained unfound as the train at last rolled into the hilly town of Greeneville. Amy put thoughts of recent trials behind her to concentrate on new ones at hand. She swallowed hard, strengthened her will. She would not show her uncle a face of fear or sadness. She would not let him intimidate her. Amy anticipated a cold reception from Hannibal Deacon; she was, after all, being more or less forced upon him by a brother with whom his relationship was distant at best. George Deacon had never really been close to anyone, not to his late wife, to his brother, to his daughter.

Amy had heard her father complain many times that Hannibal was not willing to publicly air Secessionist political convictions—something the doctor simply couldn't understand, because he assumed that any brother of his would naturally be a stalwart Secessionist. "It's because he has to live and make commerce among those cursed Greene County Unionists, that's what it is," Dr. Deacon had theorized until he finally accepted the theory as settled fact. "They force Hannibal to claim neutrality instead of taking a strong stand for what he knows is right. Expedience. That's all that keeps him quiet. Expedience and practical discretion. But he won't be able to hold out that way forever. When the fence falls, that will be the end of straddling." George Deacon had frequently been vocal with such criticisms of Hannibal's political inactivity, and yet—a point painfully clear to Amy at the moment— Deacon had not rejected his brother as a brother just because he refused to publicly blow the Secession trumpet. It seemed terribly unfair to Amy that a brotherly bond could survive political differences, while a father-daughter bond could not. But then, her offense had been far greater. Hannibal simply annoyed and bewildered his brother by being expediently neutral on questions that stirred Dr. Deacon's fire. She, on the other hand, had worked actively in opposition, all the while putting on such a cunning pretense of support for Secession that she had thoroughly fooled even her own father. She had betrayed him, and in so doing, exposed him to public ridicule. In his eyes she could have fallen no farther had she put on a whore's frock and sold herself on the streets.

Amy rose, gathering her bag and parasol. Smoke from the stack billowed back and downward in a gusty wind, making the air acrid and reddening her eyes, which annoyed her because she feared her uncle would perceive the redness as the aftermath of crying. Sending up a pleading prayer, she rose and joined the general human shuffle leading toward the door of the train and the platform outside.

She saw Hannibal Deacon as soon as she detrained. Tall, broad, his hair now liberally salted with gray and his beard almost white, his face was much more lined and sagging than the last time she saw him, some three years earlier. Yet he was still the Hannibal Deacon she had known and feared as a child. He was wearing spectacles—a new feature—and looked at her with a coldness that only worsened her dread. But she would not let him see.

She straightened her spine, put a tight smile onto her face, and strode directly up to him. "Hello, Uncle Hannibal."

"How are you, Amy?" He did not smile, even with his eyes; now that she was near, she noticed uncomfortably that, as he aged, Hannibal was beginning to look much more like her father.

"I am well enough," Amy replied.

"Good. How fine it is that you should be well."

The sarcasm hurt, but she did not flinch at all.

He studied her unsmilingly. It seemed incongruous that a man who looked as imposing and authoritative as a judge was actually a mere grocer and local agent for a commission merchant company out of Virginia. He lived better than most grocers, however, in that he and Amy's father had shared an inheritance from their own father, who had made himself modestly rich building steamboats during the first half of the century, then sold out at an opportune moment. It had done him no good; in his sixtieth year, after the sudden death of his wife, a personal bout with illness, and an investment crisis that briefly threatened to wipe him out, he had suffered a mental breakdown that made him leave home and vanish for seven years. When his sons managed to track him down, he was a sick old man, perceived as penniless, breathing out his last in the Blackwell's Island Lunatic Asylum in New York. They brought him home again just in time for him to die.

Amy looked around. "Where is Aunt Lena?"

"I came alone. She had things to do . . . we can hardly alter every part of our schedule just to meet you at the train station, you must understand."

"Of course." *It's worse than I feared. He obviously resents me being forced upon him and is punishing me already.*

He brushed away a long strand of his wild hair, which the wind had blown down into his eyes. "George has written me with the full details of why he sent you away. My! Haven't you been quite the daughter . . . helping your father and his cause in public, playing the Judas child behind his back. He is a deeply shamed man, Amy. Deeply shamed. You've stricken him the hardest blow of his life. I worry for his mental stability. He's the same age as your grandfather was when he went mad, you know."

Amy looked him in the eye, unanswering. *I will not grovel. I will not.*

Silence lingered between the two for a few moments. All about them were the happy noises of the train station: passengers greeting, hugging, kissing those awaiting them, porters shuffling baggage, railroad crewmen shouting to one another, hustling about at the endless, always hurried tasks of their profession. Amy heard and saw none of it. She kept her eyes locked on her uncle's face. If he could stare at her, by heaven, she could stare at him.

After a moment he grunted and moved. Amy gave a silent inner cheer. She had won the stare-down! At a time full of shame and defeat, that tiny victory counted for much.

"I understood that George's slave was to be with you," Hannibal said.

"Yes." Amy turned and looked among the crowd until she picked Rufus out of the human mix behind them. He had already retrieved her trunk and was lugging it along. "There he is, coming toward us. His name is Rufus."

"He has been one of your tools, I hear? Conveying abolition propaganda to that publisher fellow there in Knoxville. What's his name? Horatio Eaton?"

"Rufus was not a tool. He was only being a faithful servant, doing what I asked him to do."

"And betraying his master in the process. You consider that faithfulness? That boy is fortunate that George hasn't imposed some punishment on him far worse than being sent to me. He deserves a lashing. You know, there are still places to be found with whipping agents. Hand your nigger a note to be redeemed in forty lashes, send him down to the whipping agent to have it redeemed, and there's a stripe-backed darky who won't turn on you again! Quite an effective system, don't you think?"

Amy was quickly growing dismayed. Fearful as she had been of Hannibal, she had hoped that perhaps he would turn out to be sympathetic and gentle, soothing in a time when she was already emotionally wounded. She had even dared to hope that instead of being a silent Secessionist, as her father assumed him to be, he was a silent Unionist. Clearly it was not to be. Hannibal's disdain for Negroes was obvious, and seemingly aired blatantly in order to offend her. And clearly he saw himself as surrogate punisher for his brother—sort of a symbolic "whipping agent" himself, laying the lashes on his betraying niece on behalf of his sibling. Apparently the bond of loyalty between the Deacon brothers was stronger than Amy had thought, and their attitudes far more similar.

Hannibal turned to Rufus as he came up. "Rufus, I'm Hannibal Deacon. You'll answer to me now that you are here. I expect you'll be a good and obedient boy."

"Boy," he says, thought Amy. *Rufus is almost as old as he is.*

Hannibal continued, "Your master has turned you over to me and expects you to obey me as you would him—and no betrayals. Do you understand that, Rufus?"

"Yes, sir."

"See that wagon yonder? Load that trunk into it, and sit on the back."

Minutes later the wagon rolled away from the train station, which sat on a wide, high rise overlooking the town, and out onto a down-sloping street lined with a mix of residences and commercial enterprises. They passed one of the town's finest homes, a mansion built early in the century by the town's first postmaster for his daughter. Amy felt many eyes upon her and wondered just how much, if anything, the people of this town knew about her and what had happened. Would Hannibal Deacon seek to keep her situation quiet to spare family embarrassment, or would public humiliation be part of her punishment?

She shivered in the cold breeze as the wagon reached Main Street, where it rumbled past more houses, stores, and churches, past the simply named Big Spring that had led to the formation of the town at this spot back in frontier days, and on up another slight rise and across it until Hannibal Deacon's big house loomed on the left. Amy hadn't been to the seventy-seven-year-old town of Greeneville in years, but it was all very familiar, having scarcely changed since her girlhood visits here with her father long before the rising winds of political battle had turned him from a simple physician to an activist, and her from a mere schoolgirl to a conniver and secret abolitionist. Perhaps it would have been best if they both had just left such things alone, she thought. But she couldn't imagine what life would have been like in a non-political household. Living, motherless, with a father who did not know how to give or receive affection, her moral and political views had given her life meaning and even excitement.

"Here we are," Hannibal said, stating the obvious as they pulled into the driveway. "Amy, you will go inside. Your room is upstairs—the same room you've always used when visiting."

"You want me to go there now?"

"Yes. Go there and stay there until I come home this evening."

"So I'm to be a prisoner in my room?"

"Heavens, girl, you'll have the run of the house as you need it. But unless there is cause for you to roam about, I do expect you'll spend most of your first days in your room. This is not a happy visit, Amy. You have injured your father deeply, and we have much serious talking to do, you and I. There is a shelf of books in the room, so you'll have something to occupy you for now. Very soon I'll be having you do other reading."

He intends to "educate" me, to reform me, Amy thought. *He's going to begin working on my mind, trying to shame me for what I did, even though there was no wrong in any of it.* She failed to notice that the moral self-doubt she had suffered all the way from Knoxville to Greeneville was suddenly gone. Now that she had parted from her father and gotten past the initial dreadful meeting with Hannibal, she was beginning to realign her mind along older, well-thought-out patterns, and Hannibal himself was spurring the process along, however unwittingly. Hannibal's clear intent was to subject her rebellious mind to heat in hopes of melting and remolding it. Amy resolved to show him that heat doesn't always melt, but sometimes tempers.

She asked, "Will Rufus stay here?"

"When I'm not working him at my store, yes. But that won't be often. He'll work hard for me, far harder than he has for George, I might add. I'll give him time to concentrate on matters other than helping rebellious young hotheads betray the fathers who raised them. He'll soon be wishing he was a house servant again, believe you me."

Amy had nothing to say to that, though it angered her. She climbed down from the wagon before Hannibal had time to descend and come around to help her. She had no desire for *his* help. Obviously she and her uncle were going to have a hard time of it. She wondered if he was already preparing an arsenal of propaganda designed to reverse her errant opinions. The thought roused scorn, Was there any Secessionist argument with which she was not already intimately acquainted? Had she not presented every one of them in her father's ghostwritten newspaper harangues, and answered each in turn in Horatio Eaton's *Reason's Torch*? If he wished to change her persuasions, let him try!

She entered the house in silence and walked up the stairs to the room awaiting her. Like the rest of the house, it had hardly changed over the years. There was even a musty, familiar old rag doll sitting in the familiar little brown toy chair— a reminder that this room had once belonged to Amy's cousin, a girl named Marie who had been the only child of Hannibal and Lena Deacon, and who had died at the age of seven. Amy barely remembered her.

Rufus carried her trunk into the room and sat it on the floor, with Hannibal supervising. "Very good, Rufus. Now let's you and I go and leave Amy to herself. No doubt you could use a rest after your train ride, Amy."

Rufus glanced at her; their eyes caught and a silent communication passed: *We will make it through this.* Her heart warmed for Rufus; she thanked God that he was here. He was a familiar and dear old friend, and knowing that he too was enduring trials for his part in the great "betrayal" would make her stronger in bearing her own.

When they were gone, Amy settled into the big fourposter bed and closed her eyes. The silence in the house was so intense she could hear it. The longer she lay there, the sadder she felt, and now she remembered that this room had always made her feel this way. The spirit of death had seemed to linger inside these walls since the passing of her little cousin so many years ago. It was oppressive and gloomy. Depression settled over Amy and she wanted to cry. But she refused. No tears. Amy Deacon was three-quarters grit and one-quarter pride. She put forth a wrenching effort and generated a smile that was hard and tense as granite. She stared at herself in the mirror over the bureau. She would *not* cry!

She rolled over on her side and pulled a quilt over herself. *I will not cry!* The granite smile shivered, renewed, shivered, then shattered and crumbled away to a grimace of sorrow. She buried her face in the muffling quilt and sobbed without control, without any percentage of grit or pride.

Amy sat at Hannibal Deacon's supper table, listening to her uncle loudly chewing and swallowing, while his wife, the gentle, soft-eyed Lena, cast her repeated glances and small smiles, but few words. Amy wished Lena would talk to her. Lena had always been a comfortable person, and anything would be more pleasant than enduring this silence.

Rufus, meanwhile, was in the kitchen, eating his supper alone. Amy had never seen him looking so worn-out as when he came home with Hannibal just after six o'clock. Hannibal must have worked Rufus very hard down at his store. Punishment by labor—and Rufus was accustomed to the relatively easier work of a house servant. It seemed intensely unjust. Amy ate her supper in a cloud of bitter anger at her uncle, her father, and an entire way of life that could abide seeing a poor slave abused merely for playing one small role in a scenario with which he had little to do.

Amy's interactions with and observations of Rufus through the years had been one of the initial forces driving her to abolitionism. His quiet influence, the stories he shared with her when Dr. Deacon didn't know, had shaped her life and perceptions. From being around Rufus she had first begun to understand what it was to be a slave, and to suspect, then forcefully believe, that the slavery institution could not be morally justified.

What little conversation there was at supper was dominated by Hannibal. All dull talk of what had happened at the store, of something old Thomas Arnold had said about the upcoming national presidential election, of how Dr. Crawford had been compelled to remove a little boy's infected finger the day before because the parents had let it go untreated too long, and how somebody all the way from Newark, New Jersey, was in the store, saying that if the presidential election went in favor of Lincoln, lots of workmen in industries dependent upon heavy commerce with the South were expected to lose their jobs forthwith. Bad omen in that, Hannibal said. It showed how seriously the prospect of rebellion and war was being taken in the North, and how dire a matter it would be for Lincoln to come into office.

Aunt Lena said benign and unoriginal things in response, and Amy developed the feeling that there was something orchestrated and false in all this. Part of Hannibal's plan to reeducate her in the "right" way of thinking? Or perhaps the tension in the atmosphere was generated by the mere fact she was out of place here and both she and they knew it.

When the unenjoyed meal was done, Rufus was put to restocking the piles of wood beside the seven fireplaces of the house, and told to go to bed when he was finished because the morning would come early and there would be much to be done. Rufus's room was a little shed attached to the rear of the house, inaccessible from the house interior. Amy hoped its thin walls and small iron stove would be sufficient to keep Rufus warm over the cold nights.

"Amy, you and I must talk now," Hannibal said as he wiped his mouth on a plain white napkin. "You are not here merely as a visitor, you know. Your father wants me to help you come to an understanding about the things you have done."

Don't patronize me, Uncle. "I am not a criminal, Uncle Hannibal."

"You've held your father up for public shame. That's crime enough. But we'll not discuss this here. Come into the parlor. We'll talk there."

Why not just beat me and shear off my hair and brand me

and be done with it! she thought defiantly. *I'd just as soon endure that as to have to talk to you!*

She said nothing of the sort, of course. Instead she obediently rose and walked into the parlor, determined to endure with a martyr's bravery whatever mental humiliations he had planned for her.

Chapter 7

At least there was a fireplace in the parlor. The dining room had been terribly drafty and cold. But to Amy's surprise, the parlor was colder yet, its fire having been allowed to burn low.

Hannibal seated himself directly in front of the feeble fire, with Amy directly across from him. His substantial body absorbed what scant heat the fire provided. For a full, intimidating half minute he sat staring at his niece from beneath his bushy, sandy brows, his glasses making his eyes look smaller than they were. Amy Deacon stared straight back, refusing to be cowed. If she shivered, it was only because the room was so cool, or so she told herself.

"Tell me, Amy, precisely what you did and why," he finally said. "Start at the beginning. Tell me the events that turned your mind toward rebelling against your own father."

In a calm voice Amy went back to her early years and told him how her views on slavery had developed, though she minimized Rufus's role out of fear he would be held more culpable in her offense. She somewhat overemphasized the influence of two secretly abolitionist teachers she had known in the small private academy for females where she had been educated. She described how, at the academy, she had first learned of abolitionism and realized it suited her innate moral sensibilities far better than did her father's views. She related how, as her viewpoint began to drift far away from George Deacon's, she protected herself from him by learning to mask her opinions under pretended agreement with his.

As the years passed and the issues that now burned so hotly in the public fires had taken their shape, Amy's views and her father's grew even farther apart, even as they as individuals had done the same, their relationship becoming false and functionary. Devouring abolitionist literature, she had slowly been drawn into the movement. It was all private at first, then bit by bit she began to reveal her views to certain like-thinking individuals. After she met Horatio Eaton through one of her fellow antislavers, he persuaded her to become an active but anonymous participant in the abolition movement. The chance to actually *act* on her views, not merely dwell on them in secret, filled her with a sense of life and purpose she had never known before. She secretly wrote pamphlets, broadsides, letters to newspapers that she signed with false names. Eventually, in order to bury the secret of her forbidden viewpoint even deeper, she became a writer for her father, actually honing and shaping for him the very arguments with which she most violently disagreed. Meanwhile, she answered those same arguments in Horatio Eaton's abolitionist paper—anonymously, of course.

"But was it not wrong, dear, to do what you knew your father would have forbidden?" Hannibal asked.

Don't call me "dear." "He did not forbid it. He never told me, 'Amy, don't write for abolitionist publications.' "

Hannibal rolled his eyes. "Hah! You are playing with words, Amy, and you know it. You worked against the cause that drives your father's life. You have no regrets?"

"I regret the pain this has brought. I regret the division that it's generated between me and Father—not that we were particularly affectionate toward one another before. And I regret you've been forced to take me in when you obviously don't want me. But I don't regret it morally. I did what I knew was right."

"You're truly devoted to your views? Nothing will shake you?"

"Nothing."

"We'll see." And then it began all over again. The same questions, the same forced recounting of her experience, and then strong attempts to shame her into recanting. Still she held fast. Then, abruptly, he told her to go to bed and read before she went to sleep. "I want you to read your own writings in the *Advocate*. Read them as if they were written by another, and see if you don't agree with the arguments. Tomorrow evening we'll talk again, and discuss your thoughts."

It seemed a waste of time to Amy to read her own words, but she did it so she would not have to lie the next night when he asked her if she had. She rolled over and slept, dreaming of her dead cousin.

After breakfast the next morning, Hannibal handed her two books. "This book presents a case for Secession. This one discusses the moral validity of slavery. I want you to read both today. Every page. We'll include them in our discussion tonight."

"It appears Father was right about you, Uncle Hannibal," she said, taking the books. "You are obviously a Secessionist, hiding behind the pretense of neutrality out of expedience."

He smiled. "Not all things can be shown publicly as what they are, dear. Prudence sometimes causes the wise man to keep his political views private—particularly the wise man of business in a town of divided opinion. Now go. Be a good girl and read the book."

"I thought I might write Father a letter tonight." She had thought no such thing, but wasn't about to acquiesce before his every command without defiance.

"No letters. I forbid you to contact him."

"You forbid . . . what do you mean, you . . . how dare you! Father will be furious when he finds out!"

"It's at his instruction, dear. He is a wounded man. He doesn't want to hear from you. He made it very clear to me. So don't write him—and by the way, for the time being, don't leave this property without Lena or I being with you."

It was growing worse by the moment. "So I really am a prisoner?"

"Don't think of it that way, my dear. Use that nimble mind of yours and think a moment. You are a somewhat famous figure since the little episode there at George's rally. Parson Brownlow and others of his Union ilk have made sure that the story of the shaming of your father has gotten out far and wide. It's merely sensible and proper that you withdraw from the public for now so as not to be a continual reminder to everyone of the unfortunate thing that has happened to your father."

"The 'unfortunate' thing,' you say. The only thing that has happened to my father is that the world has chanced to learn the truth about the origins of his great words, and that he has chanced to learn the truth about his daughter's viewpoints. Why should truth be unfortunate for anyone?"

"Save your debating skills for later, when we have another of our little parlor talks. You'll need them."

You arrogant, patronizing miscreant! she thought. *How dare you assume that you'll outdebate me! I've shattered better arguments than any you'll come up with on your best day, my dear uncle! I'll show you who'll need debating skills!*

She clenched the books tightly in her hand, rising, hating Hannibal Deacon, this house, Aunt Lena, this town. But she did read the books. She would not give Hannibal grounds to criticize her for uncooperativeness.

The first book was a poorly written volume, a hodge-podge of various writings from prominent Secessionists. Several of the chapters had been published in the *Advocate* and were already familiar, so she had only to scan them. She thought: *If this is representative of your own level of thinking, I'll have no problem besting you, Uncle.* The book attempting to justify slavery, on the other hand, was more tightly reasoned, but presented no arguments Amy hadn't thoroughly demolished in her own mind years before. By the end of the day and the return of Hannibal, she had both books' arguments lodged firmly in mind, her own answers to them stabled beside them, pawing to break out.

Rufus was even more weary tonight than previously. It

saddened Amy to think he was being worked overly hard by her uncle as punishment. It was partly her fault. If not for her secret abolitionist life, Rufus would have never gotten involved in the things that had brought them this exile. He would still be at Secession Hill, living out the dull but protected life of a house servant.

After supper Amy and Hannibal went into the parlor again. The fire was even smaller than on prior evenings. Once again the questions, the recounting of the road she had followed to abolitionism and "betrayal," and then an intense quizzing about the arguments she had read in the *Advocate* and in the books. Amy, coming into the debate confident of her ability to brush off Hannibal Deacon with minimal effort, was unhappily surprised to find he did a much better job of framing Secession arguments than had the book he had forced on her, and she had to fight harder than expected to hold her own. Grudgingly she admitted to herself that Hannibal's knowledge of the issues was impressive. But as she assessed their battle of words, she perceived herself as winner. A battle-scarred one, maybe, but still a winner.

If Hannibal perceived her as victorious, though, it didn't show at all in his manner. At nine o'clock he cheerfully declared the "discussion" at an end for the night and told her to go to bed. "We'll talk again tomorrow night. And please, Amy, try not to be intimidated by me."

She tossed in bed for two hours, seething with fury at that final snide comment, until she realized that he had surely said it just to disconcert and anger her, thereby giving him a prior advantage. *He's a sly old devil! If I let him make me angry, I'll hand him the victory.* So she forced herself to calm down and fell asleep.

That night she dreamed she was wrestling a bear, and though she somehow managed to pin each paw before it could maul her, the bear had the most annoying grin on its face, and no matter what happened, the grin remained.

The next day there was another book to read, more arguments against which to develop arguments. Then again, another tense supper, another visit to the parlor, another too-small fire

and too-cold room. By now Amy was sure there was strata-
gem in all Hannibal Deacon did: Just as his patronization was
designed to insult and anger her, thus making her weak, so
the cold room was intended to chill and discomfort her, thus
making her distracted.

Let him play his little chilly parlor game. It wouldn't
work. He could freeze her into a block of ice and she would
not surrender her abolitionism.

Sunday gave her a reprieve from argument. After attending
services with Hannibal and Lena at the big, high-steepled
Presbyterian Church on Greeneville's Main Street—during
which she received many glances from a handsome, well-
dressed young man with thick brown hair and penetrating
eyes, and also from a nondescript, skinny, sandy-haired fellow
she heard Hannibal speak to as Sam—Amy returned to the
Deacon house to spend the first truly pleasant afternoon of her
stay. Hannibal napped and Lena read, and even Rufus was
given freedom from his labors, and rested on his narrow bed in
the little room out back.

In mid-afternoon Amy put a question to Lena in as nonchalant a manner as possible: "Who was that young man seated
across the aisle from us in church this morning? I noticed he
just couldn't keep still in his seat."

"Sam, you mean?"

"No . . . I think I know which one was Sam, and this was
another fellow. Tall. Thick dark hair . . ."

Lena smiled. "Quite a pretty fellow, that one. Mundy's
his name. Pleadis Mundy. He's a student at Tusculum College, and works part of the time as a furniture maker in a
shop over near the railroad. He's quite a good furniture
mechanic, they say, but supposedly he has his eye on being
a doctor. If not a soldier first. He's very caught up in the
Secession movement, like so many of the young college
men."

"Oh. I see. I do wish he'd learn to sit still in church. He
was very distracting." She tried to sound idle and unconcerned, but in truth she was disappointed. A Secessionist . . .
He didn't seem quite so appealing anymore.

"For what it's worth, Sam's a Union boy," Lena threw in, licking her thumb to turn a page.

"Good for him," Amy replied, and went up to her room.

Monday morning came too soon, and Hannibal handed her yet another book as he prepared to leave for his store. She was deeply surprised when she read the title: *The Impending Crisis of the South and How to Meet It*. The author was one Hinton Helper.

"You want me to read *this* book?" she asked.

"Are you familiar with it already?"

"Yes. I've read Horatio Eaton's copy twice. This is considered wicked, wicked literature among those of your viewpoint, Uncle Hannibal. One of the most hated books that exists. Not at all flattering to the way of life my father is so eager to preserve."

"I'm aware of the book's content, and its reputation. Believe me, it's hard to come by a copy of it; the darn thing is banned, you know. But I want you to read it and present to me the strongest arguments you can"—his eyes took on a keen glitter—"*against* what it advocates."

Now she saw his scheme. "So you're trying to force me to think against my own natural inclinations, are you?"

"I'm presenting you an educational challenge, that's all. Develop your arguments, dear. We'll talk about them tonight. I'll play devil's advocate, and we'll see if you do any better this time than before."

I've done quite well, thank you. It's you who's taken the beating night after night. "Good day, Uncle Hannibal." She smiled so thinly the sourness underneath showed right through, just as intended.

Amy spent the day with the Hinton Helper book and was glad of it. After having been exposed exclusively to disunion literature in this house, it was a pleasure—and a mystery—to read a scathing indictment of the southern system. And what an infamous and controversial indictment this volume was! Helper's book had stirred tremendous anger all over the South and was pointed to often as indicative of how intolerant and wicked the northern view of the South really was.

Amy's mind began to wander in the afternoon, and she laid the book aside for a while and sat by the window, staring out with chin in hand, elbow on windowsill.

She was growing confused. For some odd reason, she was beginning to actually like her uncle, even though she fought a nightly intellectual war with him and he treated her with disdain—although the latter often seemed more strategic than sincere. The fact was, Hannibal was proving himself a worthy opponent, and the nightly debates were honing her viewpoints and making her feel all the more secure in them. And surely he had noticed that! Surely by now he had seen that his strategy was making more of a Unionist out of her, more of an abolitionist, not less. But still he kept it up.

Something was afoot. Hannibal was too smart not to see what was happening, and that could only mean he was content to let it be so. But why? What sense did it make?

She decided to be ever more cautious. His goal, after all, was not to strengthen her but to break her. Perhaps this sudden twist, this shifting of postures in asking her to defend *his* view against that advocated in the *Impending Crisis* volume was the first stage of some ploy intended to break her down and start her on the road to "correction."

It won't work. I'll never let you break me. Never!

She rubbed straining eyes and picked up the book again. Forcing away the world around, she threw herself into it, preparing for the night's battle of ideas with the intensity of a student studying for a graduation examination.

She paused a moment, though, noticing something she wondered why she hadn't noticed before. This volume was extremely dog-eared and worn. Many lines were underscored by hand. Someone had read it very thoroughly, many more times than once. It must have been done by others before it ever came into Hannibal's possession. A Secessionist such as he would never read such a contrary book *that* closely, even for the sake of developing a response. No, whoever had worn out this volume had been enthralled with it, intrigued with it, in agreement with it. And that couldn't have been Hannibal Deacon.

Prince Street, Knoxville, Tennessee

Ben Scarlett knocked again at the office door of Dr. George Deacon but heard no responding sounds inside. He went to the window, palmed away some of the dust that covered it, and peered in. No sign of life. No lights. Plenty of disorder, however. It was puzzling. A bit disturbing, too. He had been drinking here with the doctor every day since his initial visit. This was the first time Deacon hadn't been here awaiting him.

"Out birthing a baby or some such, most likely," Ben muttered to himself. But if so, it was the first time since the ill-fated rally that Deacon had practiced any medicine beyond treating his arm. Deacon had withdrawn from public life, medical practice, everything, and spent all the time that Ben was around him in drinking, talking about his humiliation, and expressing growing hatred for Charlie Douglass and Horatio Eaton.

A boy trailed by a mangy cur pup came striding around the corner and examined Ben. "If you're looking for Doc Deacon, I seen him going into his newspaper office," the boy said. "Down there scrubbing on the wall, I'll betcha." He grinned slyly.

Ben wondered what the wall-scrubbing reference was about. "I'll go look there, then," he said to the boy.

On his way to the newspaper office, Ben pulled his injured arm out of its sling and swung it freely. It didn't hurt him now and he saw no reason to keep it bound up. But when he got near the office he put it back in the sling, not wanting a scolding.

At the door of the warehouse Ben paused, confronted by big letters painted onto the wall right beside the door:

> OLD DOC DEACON HAD A DAUGHTER,
> HELPED HIM SAY THE THINGS HE OUGHTER,
> WROTE HIS PAPERS, WROTE HIS SPEECHES,
> IN HIS HOUSE SHE WORE THE BRITCHES.
> THEN HE FOUND THAT SHE WAS SNEAKING,
> SCRIBING FOR THE MADMAN EATON,
> SO THE DOC HE ROARED AND WAILED
> AND SENT HER RIDING UP THE RAIL

BECAUSE SHE BROKE HIS SACRED RULE:
"DON'T SHOW YOUR PAPA FOR A FOOL."
BUT FOOL HE IS, AND FOOL HE'LL BE,
NO ONE WILL TAKE HIM SERIOUSLY,
AND POOR OLD DOC HAS NAUGHT BUT TROUBLE,
SINCE CHARLIE DOUGLASS POPPED HIS BUBBLE.

Ben read the doggerel, then reread it, shaking his head. Folks were mighty cruel.

Mere days ago he would have laughed at the rhyme. But days ago he hadn't learned what a fine man Dr. Deacon was, how generous he was with liquor and money, how he treated a common vagrant like a worthy fellow, not just a drunk. Unconsciously Ben had made a conversion in favor of Dr. Deacon, his point of view, his wisdom, everything. The whole world might laugh at George Deacon, mock at him, but in Ben Scarlett he had found a devotee who would not fail him or betray him. Deacon seemed to appreciate it, too; over their weekend of drinking, he had made some encouraging noises about Ben taking up lodging on Secession Hill itself. Ben liked that idea very much and hoped it would come up again.

The warehouse door opened and a glowering Deacon stormed out, bucket of paint in hand. Ben jumped back, out of the way, as Deacon threw the paint explosively against the wall, instantly obliterating the doggerel. Red paint ran like blood from a fresh wound down the wall and onto the walk. Deacon, grunting with satisfaction, flung the paint bucket out into the street behind him. Red drops and splatters flew; a couple struck Ben across the chest and he had to duck to miss being hit by the bucket itself.

"Hey there, Doc! Watch where you're flinging there!" he exclaimed.

Deacon turned, surprised and glowering, but smiled to see who was there. "Ben! Sorry, man. Didn't see you." The glower returned; he gestured at the wall. "Did you see that?"

"Yes sir. Wicked thing. Folks got no business messing up the property of others like that, and making fun of good citizens."

"Ruffians. Disrespectful Unionist ruffians and vandals,"

Deacon said. "I hope the day speeds on when we'll have no more such to deal with. Well, Ben, come inside. I'm sorry I wasn't at my office. Somebody told me about that bilge on the wall, and I came down to take care of it."

Ben followed Deacon inside. This was his first visit to the facilities of the *Advocate*. They waded through the print shop area toward Deacon's office. The floor was covered with wadded paper, spilled type, and leaked oil. A big puddle of ink stood like a black pond on a low portion of the uneven floor. Ben wondered if it was always this messy.

"Ignore the mess," Deacon said as he entered a little cubicle office built in one corner of the printing room. "I'm not a neat man, and I expect that now I'll be worse than ever. No help, you know. Have to do it all myself."

"You been working on a new edition, have you? I didn't know that."

"Been thinking about one. Toying with ideas. Nothing yet." Deacon sighed. "The fact is, I need Amy's help as much as ever, and now I don't have it. Wouldn't take it if it was offered. And don't you say a word of that to anyone, hear?"

"I won't. I ain't a betrayer, Doc. You know that. I'm on your side, start to finish."

"Good. Good man." He reached into a cabinet and pulled out a whiskey bottle and two glasses. He filled them, gave Ben his, and set the bottle roughly aside on the desk. It wobbled on its base and settled to stillness.

"Ben, I don't know if I can put out a new edition or not," Deacon said. "I tell you, man, it's not easy to write. Let no one tell you it is. It's a task and a challenge. The ideas come easily, but putting them down—well!" He took a swallow. "Quite a struggle. Quite a struggle. I may have to call an end to the *Advocate*. Ben, you're a literate man—much to my surprise, I must say. Have you ever tried to write anything?"

For a moment Ben wondered if he were actually about to be offered the chance to try his hand at journalism . . . but no. It was too absurd. "No, Doc. I can read, sure, but writing . . . I never do it."

"Not letters? Not anything?"

"I've got nobody to write letters to."

"You have no family left, Mr. Scarlett?"

"My parents are dead. I had two brothers. One's dead. He got killed in the big fire at the state penitentiary a few years back. You remember that? He was locked up for stealing livestock. The other brother, I don't know where he is. He's like me. Took to drinking, you know. Last I heard he was in Baltimore. I got no living aunts or uncles. A few cousins, but I don't know a one of them."

Deacon grunted and took another swallow. "Tragic thing, having no kin."

"Yes sir."

"The sad thing is, if something happened to you . . . injury, illness, getting hauled off to jail, maybe, or worse, God forbid—there'd be no one to grieve or care about it. If you, say, disappeared, you might not even be missed."

Ben thought that a rather cruelly forthright way to talk. "Well, I reckon not."

"Tragic. Tragic. And you've never been married, I gather?"

"No. Almost was, once. But she changed her mind."

"The liquor?"

"Yes sir."

"Well, that's a blow. Where is she now?"

"Lord, I don't know. That was long ago. A fine and beautiful lady. Too good for me. It was my drinking that made her leave me, and I suppose she was wise to do that."

"Tragedy is hard. But liquor eases the pain, right, my friend?" Another swallow. Ben watched the doctor and recognized the beginnings of a very familiar downward slide, one he himself had made years before.

The doctor wiped the back of his hand over his mouth. "Well, sir, I had a wife, too. Died on me, she did. Left me with only my Amy. We did well enough, Amy and me. A good, happy home. Now, of course, she's betrayed me and that happy home is gone, and I'm left here to get by as best I can." He emptied his glass and poured more. Suddenly he was angry—he had a way of bounding from one emotion to another, Ben had noticed. "Did you see what was on my wall outside? Did you see that?"

"Yes sir. Don't you remember? I was there when you threw that paint on it."

"Oh . . . yes. Of course. Damned Unionists. Hateful, wicked folk they are, to do such a thing to a man who has already been humiliated."

"Reckon Parson Brownlow was behind it?" Ben put forth. He had thought of the acidic Brownlow, Knoxville's most vociferous Unionist, as soon as he saw the verses.

"Brownlow? No. He pays no heed to me. He's always been afraid to take me on, knowing I would best him."

Ben knew that wasn't true. Parson Brownlow wasn't afraid of anyone. Furthermore, a recent edition of Brownlow's *Whig* had featured a full, gleeful description of how Dr. Deacon had been humiliated and exposed by a drunkard right at his own Secession rally. Maybe Deacon hadn't seen it.

Deacon went on, "I believe it was Charlie Douglass who put that babble on my wall."

Again Ben knew better. Charlie Douglass might be a capable heckler, but he could never compose a rhyme or paint it neatly on a wall in the dead of night. Furthermore, Charlie had gotten himself into a fistfight with another drunk the day before and spent the night in the local jail, so he couldn't have been the nocturnal poet. But Ben had no interest in correcting Dr. Deacon, the most generous supplier of free whiskey he had ever met.

Deacon went on: "Charlie Douglass . . . that's the culprit. Put his own name in the verses to taunt me! Well, I intend to settle that score. You might be able to help me."

"I don't know how I could help you."

"Maybe you will be able to help more than you know . . . later on."

Such cryptic talk, which Deacon provided almost as liberally as his whiskey, always mystified Ben and he did not reply. Emptying his glass, he looked meaningfully at the doctor, who picked up the bottle and handed it to him. "Take all you want," he said, voice slurred. "You are a good companion, Ben. Do you know why? Because you listen and you understand. A man needs someone who will listen to him. Give him heed. Not pretend to listen while really betraying him on the sneak, like Amy did. Not shout back disrespectful bilge and paint vile rhymes on a man's wall, like Charlie Douglass does. No sir, you know how to listen.

You may be a vagrant and a town drunk, but you are becoming my good friend, Ben Scarlett. You are indeed my good friend, and faithful. Faithful to me. Right?"

"Right, Doc." Ben swallowed more whiskey and sat thinking how Dr. Deacon's slide into misery and drinking, though unfortunate for him, was good fortune for Ben Scarlett. Dr. Deacon was a moneyed man. He had good whiskey, was generous with it, and he was adopting Ben as a friend simply because Ben was willing to sit and listen to him and say what he wanted to hear. That kind of friendship was just the kind to suit Ben Scarlett. It didn't demand much from him.

They drank together for another hour, then Ben crawled onto a pile of rags in the corner and fell asleep. Dr. Deacon, very much drunk, picked up a pen and scribbled wildly on a paper, then stumbled across the room and tried to set it in type. He failed miserably. Swearing, he went back into his office, drank some more, and finally passed out in his chair.

Chapter 8

Hinton Helper's book served up enough controversial meat to keep Amy and Hannibal verbally fencing for days, but eventually—to the relief of Lena Deacon, who inescapably had to listen to these nightly sessions of "education"—they turned back to more general debate, going again over the same questions that had occupied them at the beginning.

The interview had reached its keenest point. Hannibal was leaning so far forward that Amy thought he might tip out of his chair and into her lap. His eyes, unblinking, bored into hers.

"Once more: Tell me, girl, why you believe the Union must be preserved!"

"Because it was bought with the blood of our ancestors, because without a Union in full vigor and cooperation the South cannot fully prosper, and because the South cannot continue to stake its life upon a system that enslaves other men. If the South breaks free from the North, the institution of slavery will live far longer than otherwise. That reason alone is sufficient to make me oppose Secession. Add to that the fact it is unconstitutional."

"Put that aside for now. Let's look at slavery. You believe all slaves must be freed, my dear?"

"I do, as I've told you night after night after night."

"And what of those who have invested in slaves, whose very way of life is dependent upon the continuation of the slavery system? What of them, hmm?"

"Their system must change, because to the extent it relies upon slavery, it is immoral. A way of life dependent upon the disregard of the rights of an entire race must yield in accordance with the moral law that guides this universe!"

"So you believe in freedom?"

"I do."

"Including the freedom of individual choice?"

"Yes."

"Fine. You choose individually to oppose slavery. Another man chooses to embrace it. Upon what moral grounds may you impose your individual, private view upon that independent man? Should he not have the freedom to act in accordance with his own conscience?"

"Not if acting in accordance with his conscience, or lack thereof, he inherently victimizes another. At that point a view held in private begins to affect the public welfare of others. I cannot with any intellectual consistency declare myself opposed to the enslavement of other human beings and yet be willing to stand aside in silence and allow them to be enslaved simply because others fail to notice the evil of it."

Hannibal lifted his hands, the image of an exasperated man. "But Amy, dear Amy, please get this into your mind once and for all: In a free society, no man who opposes slavery is forced to participate in it. He is free to reject it utterly, while those who favor its practice are free to follow their own moral lights. What is wrong with such a scheme as that? Is it not the very essence of freedom to leave slavery to the choice of the individual?"

"Uncle Hannibal, you are a man of keener mind than that! Under the logic you just presented, one would have to abolish *all* prohibitory law! I can picture you legalizing robbery in this fantastic little world of imagination you seem to live in. Then, when someone is robbed in this little world, and the robbery generates protest, you have only to answer: 'In my free world no man who opposes robbery is forced to participate in it. He is free to reject it utterly, while those who favor its practice are free to follow their own moral lights.' "

"Ah, but you miss the key point! Robbery bears the most obvious impact on the welfare of the person who is robbed," Hannibal objected.

"Just as slavery bears the most obvious impact on the welfare of the one who is enslaved," Amy shot back. She smiled coldly. "Rather than me missing the key point, Uncle, I think that you have just now found it! So let me be the first to welcome you to the abolition movement!"

He frowned, and for once seemed to be at a loss as to how to respond. Amy took advantage of the moment to reiterate a point she had been making in various ways for many nights now. "Uncle Hannibal, no society can wink forever at a system that ignores the fundamental rights of any of its members. To favor the continuance of the right to enslave on the grounds of 'freedom' is ironic and absurd. And it is merely another way of saying that slavery is a permissible option at some time or at some place or in some circumstance. But in *any* time, *any* place, *any* circumstance, the one who is enslaved has suffered the theft of a fundamental, natural, irrevocable right. Thus slavery must be opposed in all its forms at all times, and cannot be baptized with the false sacrament of 'freedom' when that freedom refers only to the freedom of one man to violate the freedom of another by force. Slavery cannot be allowed to stand as an option for anyone, anywhere. It is not a victimless institution. It is wrong, and it must be abolished."

Hannibal Deacon did not instantly reply. He stared at her very deeply. "Spoken with conviction, I must say!" he replied at length. "Tell me, Amy: This viewpoint of yours, there is no shaking you from it?"

"No."

"Not under threat, not under torture, not under any condition at all would you alter your convictions?"

"Under no conditions at all."

Suddenly he smiled, and that unnerved her more than any argument he had put forth anywhere along the way. "And of your belief in the necessity of maintaining the American Union of states: Is that belief just as firm as your hatred of slavery?"

"It is. You need not try to argue me out of it. You are wasting your time. I cannot be swayed."

His smile grew. Shadows that danced in the room, cast by the feeble flame of the too-small fire, played over his features and gave them a pixilated, mystic quality. She thought: *What is happening here?*

He said, "Yes, my dear girl, I believe that indeed you *cannot* be swayed."

Lena walked in so quickly that Amy was startled. "Hannibal, come here."

He rose; he and his wife went together into the front hall and spoke in whispers. A moment later Hannibal thrust his head back into the parlor. He looked very solemn. "Go to your room, Amy."

"We're through?"

"For tonight, yes. Good night."

"Uncle Hannibal, is something wrong?"

"Good night, Amy."

"But why did Aunt Lena—"

"Good night," he said again, very firmly.

She went up to her room without another word or a single look back.

Amy paced, unable to relax, bare feet wearing a path into the huge rag rug that covered almost the entire floor of her room.

There is something odd going on in this house tonight. I can feel it.

She glanced at the clock on her wall. A few minutes after twelve o'clock. Late for the Hannibal Deacon household; most of the time they were in bed by ten. But tonight all had been astir long after eleven, and since her abrupt ouster from the parlor there had been odd reverberations in the atmosphere, a sense of something either impending or perhaps already happening. Amy paced and wondered, and strained her ears to hear. But now the house was quiet and she believed she was probably the only one awake.

Earlier she had heard Hannibal and Lena continuing in deep and earnest conversation and had been tormented by her inability to understand what was said. Then their talk had come to an abrupt end with the seeming arrival of someone at the house. There had been a bustling and rush downstairs, multiple footsteps hurrying across the floor, doors opening and closing, then silence that held for half an hour. Then more voices, Lena's and Hannibal's alone this time, still talking in a hushed manner.

Amy was being eaten alive with curiosity.

She went to her window and looked out. By moving to the far right side of the window and peering around the rear of the pantry extension on the back of the house, she could see part of the wall of the little rear room where Rufus slept. To her surprise, a light burned there. Perhaps he was restless, too. Perhaps he sensed the same altered atmosphere that filled this house tonight.

Resolve filled her suddenly: *I'm going down there and talk to Rufus. We haven't had a good chance for talking since we came here. Maybe he knows what's going on here tonight.*

Pleased with her inspiration and enjoying the defiance in it, she wrapped a cloak over her nightgown, went to the door, cracked it open and looked into the dark hall and over to the landing. No light, no sound but the ticking of the big century-old oak grandfather clock in the sitting room downstairs and Hannibal's snores rising from his and Lena's downstairs bedroom. He snored just like her father. Amy put a bare foot into the hall and crept out, softly clicking her door shut behind her. She moved stealthily down the hallway, grateful that she was the lone occupant of the second floor. She reached the stairs. Try as she would, she could not descend them without making plenty of creaks and pops, but as she went lower she heard Hannibal's snores continuing; he did not hear her. She could only hope Lena was sleeping as soundly and that Hannibal's snores masked any of her own noise that might reach Lena's ear.

Amy left the house and crept around through the yard toward the rear of the house and Rufus's room. She heard a sound, very muffled and seemingly human, and froze. The autumn grass was cold beneath her feet; it was far too late in the year to be outside barefoot, and she wished she had taken time to put on her slippers. Listening, she heard nothing but the distant barking of a dog. Then suddenly she heard it again—a muffled but distinctly human voice, seemingly a child wailing mournfully.

The wail seemed to be rising from the ground itself.

Amy cast a nervous eye toward the little grave in the far corner of the yard, where her long-dead cousin lay buried. . . . *No!* She had never been superstitious and would not begin to be now. Amy Deacon did not believe in ghosts. She stood stock-still a few moments more, listening for a repeat of the sound, and did not hear it. Imagination, she decided. Or the cold wind.

She went around to Rufus's room; the light still burned inside. Softly she rapped on the door. "Rufus! It's me—are you awake?"

A moment later the door opened. "Miss Amy!" Rufus said. "Is everything all right?"

"Yes. I think so, at least. I'm cold. Let me in."

"Well, surely so, Miss Amy . . . if you don't think we'll be in trouble for it."

"Nobody saw me come out here. And I don't care if I get in trouble. With everything so changed I've just got to talk to somebody familiar. I've missed being able to talk with you. They've been keeping us apart on purpose, you know."

"I know. And Mr. Hannibal, he's been working me like a plowhorse down at his store. Got me doing things that don't seem to have no point other than wearing me out. I'm so tired this evening I can't get to sleep. You ever been that way?" He paused. "And besides that, things just . . . *feel* different this evening. Like something's a-going on. And I've heard sounds. Movements and maybe voices, and something like a thump down in the ground."

That his intuition and experiences so closely matched hers made the skin on the back of Amy's neck grow taut. She pulled up a footstool and sat down upon it. He sat on the end of his narrow bed, looking simultaneously uncomfortable with and glad for this visit, which both knew would be strictly forbidden by Hannibal had he known of it. "Rufus, I'm scared," Amy said. "I wish I were home. I even miss Father."

There was fire in his eye when he looked at her. "Don't you miss him, Miss Amy. Don't you never miss him. If there's anything good in what all's happened to us, it's that we ain't with him no more. I been with the Doc since him and me was young men. I know even better than you the things he can do, the kind of anger and madness that can be in him sometimes. He always hid that part of himself from his womenfolk. He never hid it from me. And it's been growing and festering in him the past year or more. I been afraid of him for a long time now."

"What do you mean?"

Rufus looked ill at ease. "I don't want to say."

"Rufus, in the name of heaven, tell me! There are too many mysteries in this house already, and I'll not stand for you being another one! For years you've implied all sorts of terrible-sounding things having to do with my father, and yet you'll never tell me. Well, this time I want you to tell me, *now*."

He looked at her. "There's things that ain't easy to know. Sometimes it's best *not* to know."

"Rufus—tell me."

"Miss Amy, please."

She said something very odd for an abolitionist: "Rufus, I am white, you are Negro. I have authority over you, and I'm *ordering* you: tell me!"

She watched him weighing his thoughts, deciding whether he should express them. "Very well, Miss Amy. Very well." He looked her in the eye, drew in a deep breath and said: "Your father, I believe he kilt a man once."

"Killed a man!"

"Yes'm. Kilt him in jealousy. It was because of your

mother. The man, he'd acted . . . forward. Tried to take her away from the Doc, and she—well, I hate to say it, but she seemed willing to be took away, and I don't blame her, the way she was treated. The Doc, he left the house one night, and next thing you know they're finding a dead man on the road. Cut all to pieces with a butcher knife, and the blade broke off in his ribs. It was the very man who'd cast his eye on your mother."

"But that doesn't mean Father did it!"

"I found the burnt handle and blade stub of a butcher knife in your father's fireplace ashes the next day. And a scorched-up man's money purse, bills still inside it, and the dead man's name writ on the lining. The Doc, he'd took them off the man to make it seem it was a robbery, you see. He'd tried to burn them but the fire had gone down before everything was gone. I lit it up again, burnt that stuff to a crisp. I didn't know what else to do. Next day, the broke knife blade was gone from the ashes. I reckon the Doc took it out and got rid of it. The Doc is a hard man. He won't stand for betrayal, or having something took from him— whether that be his wife, or his public standing, or his pride. He kilt that man, Miss Amy. I know he did. And your mama . . . he beat on her. Called her terrible names, and beat on her."

Amy felt sickened. Her mother . . . beaten. It seemed impossible—but memories came back from girlhood of unexplained bruises on her mother's face, unexplained pain visible like fire in her mother's eyes. . . .

"Rufus, why didn't you tell me this before now?"

"Oh, I couldn't have said nothing, Miss Amy, not with us still living with him. How could you have gone on with him, knowing that kind of thing? But I watched out for you with him. I was ready to protect you from him if ever he threatened you. He never did beat you, did he?"

"No."

"I thank the Lord. It was only your mama he beat, then. There's some men like that. They'll beat their wives, treat them like dogs. Sometimes they beat their little ones, too . . . but I'm glad he didn't beat you. If he had, I'd a-killed him, and I mean it. It wouldn't have mattered what they would have done to me for it. I'd a-killed him if he'd hurt you."

"Oh, Rufus . . ." She didn't know what to say.

"Miss Amy, I'm glad you ain't on Secession Hill no more. You're better off here, even with Mr. Hannibal and his odd ways. And I'm glad to be here, too. When the Doc learned that I'd been helping you and Mr. Eaton, I really figured it would be the death of me. 'Nother unsolved crime, like that rival of his dead on the roadside. I figured he'd make a corpse of me, just like them I used to haul for him."

With her mind already reeling, Amy required a moment to take in and digest Rufus's final comment.

"You hauled corpses? What do you mean?"

His mouth pinched shut and Amy knew he had said something inadvertent. "Nothing, Miss Amy."

"Don't tell me that! When did you haul corpses for my father? And why?"

He rubbed his hands together, long fingers entwining. "It was when he was young and studying to be a doctor. The schools for doctors, they used to use the corpses of darkies to study on. *Study* . . . that's what the Doc called it. What it was was cutting up on them, looking inside, pulling out the innards . . . a dead slave, that was something them schools wanted. And the Doc, he loaned me out to the school's use while he was a student. Had me haul in the bodies of my own kind of people from the farms and plantations, or out of the hospitals. You know what the darky folk call hospitals, Miss Amy? Dead houses. I used to have to go to the dead houses, and take out the dead slaves and haul them off to be cut upon—God!" He put his face into his hands and abruptly began to cry, surprising Amy even through the shroud of numbness that had oversettled her as he spoke. "It seemed wicked and wrong to me, but I had to do it. I carried many a dead man and woman up to be cut on like beef, Miss Amy. Oh, God, I even carried in the corpse of my own father! The Doc made me do it, and I've hated him for it ever since. He told me it was a good thing, that my pap would have wanted his corpse to be used so, if it would help doctors learn how to be better doctors. . . ."

Amy stared at him, stunned, realizing that she was the receptor of burdens Rufus had carried in secret for years, unwilling until now to cast them off and thereby burden her, too.

He wept a few moments, then regained composure. "I never intended on telling that to you, Miss Amy. No reason you need to know."

"I'm glad you told me," she said, though unsure that was really how she felt. "Now I can take comfort in being away from him. And you, too. We're free of him now." She reached out and patted Rufus's knee—a vaguely uncomfortable act. Despite Amy's abolitionism, despite her hatred of slavery and love for Rufus, she was yet a product of her time and society, and to touch a black man even in so vaguely intimate a way as a pat of comfort on the knee was not done without great self-consciousness. And her words and tone belied how she was feeling besides. What Rufus had told her was stunning—her father a likely murderer, a man cruel enough to beat his own wife, and to force a helpless slave to deliver up his own father's corpse for medical dissection—these were revelations that were too much to take in. She wished she hadn't come to this room after all, and rose to go.

"I'm sorry I had to tell you, Miss Amy," Rufus said. "But maybe it's good that you know the Doc for what he is, so you won't go back to him if the chance comes. You've growed up. You've broke free, even in such a way as this, and you ought not go back to him, never." He paused. "I'm sorry I said I hate him. I ought not say such as that to you 'bout your own pap."

"It's good you told me everything. I needed to know. Now I'd best go back to my room before I'm missed. Good night, Rufus."

"Good night, Miss Amy." He went to the door and opened it for her. Glancing out, he said, "There's something going on at this place that's peculiar."

"I know," she said. "Good night."

She slipped around to the kitchen door and opened it slowly. Pausing, she looked back toward the little grave and remembered that imagined subterranean wail. Chilling at the unearthliness of it, she couldn't help but listen for it again. Just when she was finally assured that there was nothing at all to listen for, she *did* hear it—the same fine, muffled child's wail.

She entered the house in a cold fright and ran upstairs as quickly as she could, creaking stairs or not.

Chapter 9

Disturbed by Rufus's revelations about her father and also the eerie and unexplainable wailing she had heard, Amy tumbled restlessly more than half the night, and wakened feeling tired. She went downstairs to find Lena Deacon very distracted and nervous, not at all her usual cheerful self.

"You'll be going to town today," Lena told her over a breakfast of atypically burned pancakes and sausage. Hannibal had already gone to the store, and taken Rufus with him. "Yesterday Hannibal promised Mr. Robertson at the *Democrat* that you'll help him operate his press today, but he forgot all about it until this morning. Mr. Robertson's son usually helps him, but he's under the weather, and you do have experience with presses. He asked Hannibal about it yesterday and he agreed."

"But I don't want to—" One further look at Lena hushed her. Amy knew she was in no position to protest or argue much of anything in this household.

"Are you going to take me to the newspaper?" she asked. "Uncle Hannibal specifically said that I wasn't to leave this property unless accompanied by you or him."

"Young lady, you'll take no wiseacre tone with me!" Lena snapped. Amy was so surprised she dropped her fork. Lena was eternally kind and meek, incapable of raising her voice, as far as Amy had known. "I am busy here today and I have full authority to be as firm or as lenient as the situation demands concerning your freedom to roam. You will go to the *Democrat* office on your own, you will do so without back-talk, and you will introduce yourself there to Mr. H. G. Robertson, and you will work hard for him and show him respect, whatever he may say or write that you disagree with. I'll send you a food pail for your luncheon."

"Yes, Aunt Lena." She dared say no more. Lena had made her feel like a chastened little girl.

She finished her breakfast, readied herself a little further, and obtained directions to the newspaper office. As she left the Deacon lot and headed in toward the main portion of town, she felt a thrill at even so minor a freedom, and fantasized about running away. Wouldn't *that* put Hannibal and Lena into a tizzy! But it was a cloud castle, and she knew it. Carrying her lunch pail like an obedient schoolgirl, she walked through the town— feeling abundant stares and hearing whispers that no doubt focused on her infamy as the betrayer of the famed George Deacon. Hannibal had been right about people knowing her story.

She found Robertson to be a very kind and pleasant man, easy to work for. He was curious about her father, whose journal he had frequently read, but Amy said as little as possible about George Deacon because it reminded her of the terrible things Rufus had told her the night before, things that now haunted the back of her mind every moment and which, despite her lack of doubt about Rufus's truthfulness, hadn't yet been fully accepted by her reluctant mind. Robertson apparently sensed her lack of desire to talk about George Deacon and was kind enough not to push the matter for long.

The workday passed quickly, and in the end Amy was glad she had come because otherwise she would have sat home all day, brooding over Rufus's revelations. She received her pay in cash and started home, then on impulse diverted toward her uncle's store. Freedom was too enjoyable to give up just yet, and she wanted Hannibal to see that, despite the stares and whispers she occasioned, she was capable of moving about Greeneville with nothing dire resulting. Perhaps, if she were friendly and pleasant and spoke positively of her day's work, he would loosen his hold on her a little.

It had been many years since Amy had seen Hannibal's store, which stood on a rear corner of the same block as the county courthouse, facing a big forested hill, and in easy walking distance of the house Andrew Johnson had lived in until 1851, near his tailor shop. Johnson's current residence, a much bigger and finer dwelling he had obtained from one James Brannan in trade for the smaller first house plus $950, was on Main Street, facing the opposite direction from Hannibal's store.

Amy walked onto the porch of the store and was reaching for the door when it opened quickly and a tall, very slender young man emerged, the same nondescript fellow who, like handsome Pleadis Mundy, had eyed her in the church service Sunday. He was carrying a wooden crate, whistling through his teeth, and clearly not thinking at all about the possibility of someone being on the other side of the door. Amy received a full-body bump, was knocked back and almost fell. Her empty lunch pail clattered loudly against the porch column.

"Pardon me for being in your way, sir!" she said with mild sarcasm.

The offender, who looked about twenty but had a slender, boyish face, looked at her with widening eyes as he recognized her. His words spilled out in a fast and uncontrolled babble. "I'm sorry—I didn't see you there, Miss Deacon . . . ma'am—I didn't hurt you, did I? I'm sorry—I wasn't trying to touch no bosoms or nothing, I swear!" And at that last unfortunate comment, he reddened severely and said, "Oh, Lord. Oh, no. I'm sorry. I didn't mean to say that . . . I just was . . . Oh, Lord." He trailed off, mercifully.

Poor fellow! He's like a spider getting tangled in its own web! Amy knew she was in the presence of a young man who was painfully, gratingly shy, probably mostly so in the presence of young women. "I'm fine, sir," she said.

"Accidents do happen." She went past him as quickly as she could and into the store, feeling embarrassment glowing off him like heat off a stove. Amy felt sorry for him; there was nothing more pitiful than a radically shy young man, and this one exuded a shyness she could all but smell.

"I'll be—it's Amy!" Hannibal's voice boomed from somewhere inside with a friendly tone that sounded a bit artificial—adopted, no doubt, for the sake of any customers who might be present. *He wouldn't want his patrons seeing how rudely he usually treats his niece,* she thought cynically. She tracked his voice and saw him coming around the rear of a long counter that ran the full length of the building. He was wiping his hands on a cloth, smiling, looking about to see if any extraneous parties were present. None were, and his smile vanished. He reached her, head tilted back a little to compensate for the fact his spectacles had slid down his nose. "I didn't expect to see you here, Amy. Where's Lena?"

"At home."

Eyes burned angrily behind spectacle glass. "I distinctly told you you were to remain at home unless Lena or myself was with you, Amy."

"I lent a hand to Mr. Robertson at the *Democrat* today, Uncle. You arranged it yourself, or so Aunt Lena told me. She told me to go there alone." Amy glanced around, looking for Rufus but not finding him.

"Oh, yes. Yes. I'd forgotten about that ... yes." He cleared his throat. "Did Lena also ask you to come by here when you were finished?"

"No ... should I not have come?"

"With no permission to do so, no. You should've gone directly home."

"Oh." Amy was stung by the rebuke, insulted at being ordered about like a slave, and also disappointed. She had hoped for some show of cordiality and lightness on her uncle's part. But he was so much more like her father than she had imagined, refusing to give or receive affection. "I'll go on, then," she said, turning.

"Yes. Do that."

He's a cold man. How can he stand to be so cold? Amy turned without a word and went back toward the door, there to run face-to-face into the same young man, just reentering without the crate. She moved to the left to let him by, but he moved in tandem with her. She corrected to the right; he did the same, his face going crimson.

She heard Hannibal laugh, but it sounded as false as that earlier short-lived tone of friendliness, and no doubt was forced so the young man would not see his harshness with her. "I didn't know you were so fine a dancer, Sam!" he boomed out. "Sam, meet my niece, Amy Deacon, from Knoxville."

"Pleased," Amy said curtly.

Sam said nothing at all, but nodded a greeting very fast and nervously, mumbling, making himself even more pitiful than before. Amy bypassed feeling sorry for him and went straight to being annoyed. Pushing past him, she left the store and strode toward the Deacon house as fast as she could go.

Amy was relieved to find Lena in a mood much improved since morning. Lena asked cheerfully about the day at the newspaper, her opinion of "kind Mr. Robertson," and so on. Amy gave minimal answers, then mentioned her brief visit to Hannibal's store. Abruptly, anger came. "Hannibal treated me like I was a child, Lena. He seems to despise me. I believe he hates me for what I did to Father. My own father hates me, and now my uncle as well—and all I've done is to take a moral stand that doesn't match their own!"

Lena went to Amy and put her arms around her. She hesitated almost guiltily, then said, "Amy, there are things you may come to know, very soon . . . things I wish I could tell you now. . . . But I shouldn't be speaking this way. Hannibal wouldn't be pleased." She withdrew her embrace.

"Wouldn't be pleased with what?"

"I can't say. I've promised Hannibal."

"What is it I'll come to know soon?"

"I can't say anything more—except this. Don't judge anything yet. Not anything, not anyone. Not even your uncle. Things are not always what they seem, Amy. Nor are people."

"Tell me what you mean, Aunt Lena!"

"I've said too much already. It's up to Hannibal. He'll tell you when he decides to . . . *if* he decides to. I'll do all I can to see that he does, and soon. I promise." She paused, then said more despite herself. "He's a good man, Amy. A kind and gentle and loving man, not the man you have seen since you came. There is a reason he is behaving like he is. . . . Just bear up, and hold true to what you think and what you are. Then things will be made clear to you. Trust me."

Frustrated yet intrigued, Amy went to her room and lay down on her bed, idly examining her ink-stained fingers. She closed her eyes and dozed off, awakening as she heard her uncle's voice outside, coming into the yard through the back gate. She went to her window. Rufus was walking in beside Hannibal.

And smiling, broadly. Amy was astonished. Hannibal said something and Rufus laughed, a loud, joyous, heartfelt laugh.

Rufus, laughing? Walking like an old friend beside a man who was his imprisoner, his taskmaster, his punisher? It made no sense. And why was Hannibal so light in manner, so cheerful? In her presence he was either chiding, cold, or professorial. She remembered Lena's obscure exhortations and wondered what in the name of heaven was going on in this place and with these people.

This was the oddest, most unexplainable scenario Amy had ever encountered. Nothing but mysteries and peculiar behaviors and questions. She was ready for answers, and it frustrated her greatly that she was not likely to find them until Hannibal Deacon was ready to provide them. She hoped it would be soon. *Hold to what you think and what you are,* Lena had counseled. *Then things will be made clear to you.* Very well. Amy would do just that. It was no more than she would have done anyway, but if along that path lay answers, she had all the more reason to hold her course.

* * *

Hannibal took her back into the parlor again that night after supper. This time, oddly, the fire was high and the room was warm. Only Hannibal's eyes were cold; they studied Amy intently. She expected him to scold her for coming to the store earlier, but instead he went straight to the topic usually discussed in this room.

"The last time we sat here, I asked you if there was anything that could sway you from your points of view, both Unionist and abolitionist. You said there was nothing. Now I ask you again."

"And I give you the same answer. I believe what I believe because I find it reasonable. I am persuaded by the force of logic and moral instinct. And I can't cease to believe, by a simple act of will, in what I see as virtually self-evident truths."

"Tell me again why you believe the Union must stand."

Amy's frustration mounted. How many times would he require this of her? But she drew in a deep breath and again laid out her Unionist views and why she held them. Hannibal listened closely, his face unreadable, stopping her only occasionally to challenge her at this point or that. She answered each with the ease that comes from much practice, and went on.

"Now tell me why you believe in the abolition of slavery."

She had known this question was coming as soon as she heard the first one. Another deep breath, another explanation, another meeting of challenges.

But this time there was something different besides the larger fire and the warm room. It took her some time to notice what it was, but when she did, she was intrigued: Hannibal's cold stare was gradually warming. The longer she talked, the more his look changed. When she was done, he leaned forward, very close.

"Is there nothing, nothing at all, that would make you falter in your beliefs?"

"I've told you many times: no."

"Not even threats? Imprisonment? Abuse?"

She shook her head. "No. Not even that."

Silence . . . and then he rose, his arms came up and out, he leaned his tall, broad form down and hugged her where she sat. At that moment, and for the first time since she had come to Greeneville, Hannibal Deacon was the man she had known in her older girlhood, when she had put her childish fears of him behind and come to know him as a happy and jovial man. "God bless you, girl, God bless you. I had hoped and prayed you would hold true to your conviction, and you have."

She was baffled. Pulling back, she looked up into his face and saw both a beaming smile and streams of tears. "Amy, my dear niece, I am proud of you. You are a young woman of immense intelligence. My poor brother, as wrong as he is about so many things, has always been right in what he used to say of you: 'three-quarters grit, one-quarter pride.' You are a rare human being, child. You are indeed a treasure who has come into my home."

"Uncle Hannibal, I don't understand."

"Haven't you learned it yet, Amy? Not all things are as they seem. Oh, my dear girl, it's been hard to treat you so coldly! But there's been good reason for it. We had to know just what kind of substance you were made of, didn't we!" Just then something moved in the doorway of the room; Amy looked and saw Lena Deacon there, smiling and tearful just like her husband, and behind her the dark face of Rufus, beaming with that same joy she had detected earlier as he crossed the yard with Hannibal. She looked more closely and saw tears on his face, too.

"Someone tell me what is going on here!" Amy demanded. She pulled away from her uncle, putting on a show of determined anger, but it fooled neither herself nor the others. A sense of something wonderfully good and unexpected had descended upon the little parlor, and though Amy could not imagine what it could be, she felt it strongly.

"*I* can tell you, Miss Amy," Rufus said. "They done told me the truth of the matter, just today. It's a wonderful truth, Miss Amy. Just wonderful."

"Rufus, if you would, please allow the pleasure of enlightening this young lady to be mine," Hannibal said. "After all, it is me who has put her through evening after evening of mental torment. Just testing your mettle, my dear, as I said, and it is indeed as strong as I hoped it would be!"

For some reason Amy suddenly wanted to weep. She had never been a crier, but over the last few days she had cried in bursts several times. All the stress of days of study and nights of interrogation, of being away from her home on Secession Hill, of being estranged from the father she loved despite all, of being confused by the odd transformation of character being displayed at this moment—these things together were too much even for her formidable will, and the tears came.

"Please, Uncle Hannibal. I don't understand what is happening here."

He went to her and put his arm across her shoulder. "Come with me, dear. We'll answer all your questions."

They left the parlor and went to the big door that led into the cellar. In her days here, Amy had never seen that door opened, though a time or two she had heard the creak of it from elsewhere in the house. "The lamp, Rufus," Lena said, and Rufus stepped into the main room long enough to fetch a hurricane lamp, which he handed up to Hannibal.

The lamplight across Hannibal's face made him look ruddier and broader than ever. "Come to the cellar, Amy. You'll find your confusion clearing."

They descended, Hannibal in the lead and Amy just behind. The cellar was dark and cold and smelled of musty earth. Shelves lined it, filled with cans and jars and wooden crates and rusted old tools. Hannibal led the group toward one of the shelves.

"What was it that I told you, Amy?"

"That my questions would be answered down here."

"Yes . . . but also . . ."

"That not all things are what they appear to be."

"Clever girl. Very clever. Observe . . ."

He reached to the top shelf and tugged at what appeared to be a loose, short piece of lumber lying on it among boxes of nails and scraps of metal. But the lumber piece didn't move. He grasped it and pushed it to the right, like a lever, and Amy heard a click from somewhere behind the shelf.

"And like Ali Baba of old, we enter!" Hannibal declared in showman's tones. His tears were gone and now he seemed in a playful mood. He dramatically put his hand on the shelf and pushed. "Behold! The mysterious cavern!"

The entire shelf moved, and Amy realized that its wood backing was in fact a door. Behind it an opening gaped, so dark it swallowed what little light could enter it from Hannibal's lamp.

"It's a hallway, a tunneled-out hallway, Miss Amy," Rufus said excitedly, unable to restrain himself. "It leads to a big room, with beds and a table and food and such, and beyond it there's another hallway—"

"Rufus! Having been the man who labored to build this underground marvel, I'd like the privilege of showing it," Hannibal remonstrated gently. Rufus, humbled but not chided, smiled and nodded. "Come!" Hannibal beckoned.

Hannibal had to duck his head to clear the somewhat low doorway. Amy and the others followed. Once inside, Hannibal's lamp illuminated the scene much more effectively.

"Uncle Hannibal, why is this hallway here?"

Lena, just behind Amy, touched her elbow and leaned up to her. "Think a moment, Amy. Can you not figure it out?"

"The only thing I can think of doesn't match what would be possible if in fact you believe what you claim to believe, Uncle Hannibal," Amy said.

"Not everything is what it seems! Always remember that. Live by it." Hannibal grew suddenly serious. "If affairs progress in our nation as I fear they might, it will become essential for many of us to live by that scrap of wisdom. Perhaps life-or-death essential. Now, come on. And be careful; right about here the tunnel slopes off like a Secessionist's forehead." He smiled at his own joke and winked at Amy; the somber moment had passed, but it had left a chill that Amy still felt.

They advanced another dozen feet, the tunnel descending sharply, and then the lamp spilled light out into a big chamber. Amy walked into it, looking around. The earthen walls were shored up with timbers, like those of a mine, and a big table filled much of the center of the room. Two unlit lanterns sat on it; two more hung from beams above. Cots and shelves lined the walls; the shelves bore containers of vegetables, preserved sausages, and the like. A little window that opened only into blackness was high on the wall to Amy's left. The opening of a ventilation shaft, probably.

"Not at all nice, but livable, eh?" Hannibal said. "It stays right about this temperature the year around, too. That little window there, it's the end of a ventilation shaft. The other end is hidden in the wall of the old dry well between this house and Mark Key's place next door. And see there"—he held up the lantern and pointed toward a closed door on the opposite side from which they had entered—"that opens into another branch of the tunnel and leads over to the Key house next door. He's in with me on this, you see. Mark is a staunch Union man and a despiser of slavery. Mark's a good fellow. Serves as postmaster over in the old Colter community post office east of town. Named after some of Sam Colter's ancestors, by the way. Used to be called Colter's Station."

Matters were coming clear now. Amy looked her uncle in the eye. "You, I believe, are one of those things that is not what it seems. Am I right?"

"I'm full of surprises, no question about it." He chuckled.

"This room . . . slaves?"

"Indeed, Amy. Slaves determined no longer to be slaves." He paused, then spoke lines Amy and every abolitionist knew by heart. " 'I would not have a slave to till my ground, to carry me, to fan me while I sleep . . .' "

Amy finished for him: " '. . . And tremble when I wake, for all the wealth that sinews bought and sold have ever earned . . .' William Cowper. Great and beautiful words. Uncle Hannibal, do I dare believe this means what I suspect it means?"

"If you suspect it means that I am an abolitionist, and that you now stand in one of many 'depots' along the Underground Railroad, then indeed it does, my dear."

Amy looked around the dark chamber and spoke in a whisper of awe. "The Underground Railroad. The road of hope. The way to the Promised Land."

"Yes. I see it gives you a shiver to think of it. It's the same with me. This chamber is a refuge for those who suffer, for those who have had taken from them the right that God Himself gave for each of His human creations to be free. Awesome, isn't it!"

It was. Amy felt overwhelmed. She looked around the room and loved it for what it was. Then she looked back at her uncle and loved him, too.

"This room housed three runaways last night, Amy. A father and mother, and their little baby, running away from slavery in North Carolina. They were here only a few hours, then moved on before daylight to catch a certain well-covered wagon heading for Kentucky. There's a web of us slave-spiriters spread across this land. We've smuggled many a soul to freedom, we have. Many who have spent nights in this chamber now walk on free Canadian soil."

"My temper was bad with you this morning because I was worried about our runaways," Lena said. "I'm sorry I spoke so harsh to you. I calmed down some as the day went by."

But Amy was not paying attention to Lena. She was looking about, thinking, her mind in a swirl. "We're beneath the yard . . . Uncle Hannibal, I heard the baby! I heard a sound like crying from under the ground! I looked over at Marie's grave in the yard, and . . ." She burst out laughing. "I feel a superstitious fool!"

At the mention of his daughter's grave, the briefest flash of pain whispered across the features of Hannibal Deacon, and Amy regretted her careless reference. But the moment passed and Hannibal spoke on: "This room and others like it may well become all the more important if war breaks out. There'll be white men as well as Negroes flying north. These mountains and valleys could become hostile country to those who hold to the Union, should Secession come. Many will flee, and if we and our secret room here can help them, we will." He looked around, proud of the place. "No one knows any of this is here except those of us here now, my employee Sam Colter down at the store—Sam helped me build it—and Mark Key."

It seemed to Amy that she had been living in a world of pure illusion. "Why did you wait so long to tell me, knowing that my views were the same as yours? Why did you pretend before me to believe what you don't?"

"I had to be sure of your conviction. Of your devotion. I had to know that you truly believed in the things Lena and I believe in so strongly. It is vital, you see, that this secret remain a secret. I had to know I could trust you."

"You can. You could have trusted me from the beginning."

"I know that now, but I couldn't know it if I hadn't put your will to the test." He put his arm on her shoulder. "Amy, Lena and I are perhaps not the most educated and intelligent of people, but we do hold strong convictions of what is right. But very few of our neighbors, very few, hold to the full abolitionist views that we do.

"Not so concerning the preservation of the Union, though. You'll find abundant disdain for the 'Secesh' crowd in these parts, more in the county than in the town, perhaps. Yet it all could change. So many factors can affect the public mood! Even now the young men are swayed toward rebellion. Sam Colter has friends who attend Tusculum College, and tells me the student sentiment is almost entirely disunionist. And should the Federal government call up arms to put down any part of the southern rebellion, you may find more than hotheads and college students taking up the Secession cause. And so Lena and I have maintained a neutral public posture. It has seemed the expedient thing to do about it. It is much the same as your situation in Knoxville: In order to preserve important secrets, one presents a false face before the public. Do you understand?"

"Of course."

"By the way, Amy, I know your father despises my neutral public stand. He believes that I'm simply a timid Secessionist who ought to get over his timidity and come out for the great and noble cause! If only he knew my *true* viewpoint, eh?"

"Yes," Amy said, smiling. "Oh, yes."

"Now that you are with us, it's more important than ever to maintain our public neutrality for the time being," he said. "If George knew he had sent his daughter into a den of abolitionists and Unionists, he might take you back."

"I wouldn't go. I want to stay here."

"And we want you to stay. But no point fighting battles

sooner than need be. We'll maintain our show of neutrality—
and you'll maintain a low and calm profile. Agreed?"

"Agreed. But will you ever let the truth be known?"

"One can't pretend forever. Someday we'll show our
true colors in public. But not yet. When the time is right."
Again a somberness invaded his manner, changing the tenor
of his voice. "There are wars of all kinds, Amy, and wars
within wars. Some of them are fought openly in battlefields
by warriors with ranks attached to their names and rifles
in their hands. Other wars are fought in the shadows, by
those who wear no uniforms and are often not what they
seem to be, and whose names seldom go down in history
books. And so many times, the great difference is made
by them. The hidden ones, the shadow warriors. Like me,
and Lena, and Sam. Like you. People doing their part in
secret, moving outside the official channels, seldom seeing
the light, and seldom being seen by it."

"Shadow warriors," Amy repeated. "That's what I want
to be. A shadow warrior."

"It's what you already are, my dear. Through your writing
and labors, you've been waging a war in the most shadowed
place of all: the human mind."

Amy smiled at him. "I'm glad I'm here. I was afraid at
first, but now I'm glad."

"So are we, Amy," Lena said.

"Indeed, and we'll keep you out of your father's clutches,
whatever it takes, Amy," Hannibal said. The lightness had
returned to his voice. "And in the meantime, you can begin to
help us. You can commence by seeing off our friend Rufus
when he makes his own flight to freedom."

Amy turned and faced her old friend. Rufus smiled and
nodded. "Unless you want me to stay, Miss Amy. If you
want me about, I'll stay. I won't run."

"No, Rufus," she said. "No. You make your flight. Go
north and find your freedom."

Hannibal said, "I don't believe I'll be in too great a hurry
to let poor George know his Negro has given me the slip. If
he finds out too quickly, he'll have every slave catcher north
of the state line scouring the country for him, just for spite.
We'll wait until Rufus is safely long gone before we let

George know a thing about the 'unfortunate escape.' And won't George bust his britches! Won't he just absolutely bust his britches!" He laughed his booming laugh; it echoed in the subterranean hallway and made the lamp in his hand shake and light dance along the walls.

Chapter 10

Hannibal Deacon penned and mailed a letter to his brother the next day, telling him carefully worded news of himself and his family, and particularly of Amy, though almost all the "news" concerning her was fabrication. He told her brother that Amy was doing well physically and mentally—true enough—and that under his tutelage she was slowly beginning to show some sign of "reforming" her earlier erroneous viewpoints—this, of course, being utter falsehood. What was needed, Hannibal wrote, was much more time. With continued cajoling and education, with more time away from Knoxville and the corrupting influence of Horatio Eaton's journal and the like, Amy might eventually make a full conversion in favor of Secessionism and even renounce her heretical abolitionism.

For a few days after the letter went out, life settled into an almost dull routine, but then came the month of November and the onset of a flurry of events that would shape the future like a sculptor gone mad.

On the sixth, Abraham Lincoln was elected president. Hannibal and his household heralded the election in secret, but not without some trepidation. The election of a man

seen as a northern regionalist had been the great looming
fear of those leaning toward Secession.

Hannibal watched the newspapers and read the public
sentiments, and was pleased to see that most people seemed
to hold to a wait-and-see posture. Despite the best efforts of
the rabid Secessionists, most Tennesseans seemed reluctant
to see the Union dissolved yet. Perhaps Lincoln would act
with restraint. Perhaps the issues dividing the nation could
yet be settled without disunion and the warfare that would
be a likely result.

Hannibal expected that Lincoln's election would generate
a particularly fire-breathing edition of *The Secession Advocate*, but none appeared. Ironically, Hannibal began to
worry. What had happened to his brother? Had he lost fire
for his cause? That seemed unlikely. Or might it be that
without the ghostwriting of his estranged daughter, he could
no longer find the words to express his views? Hannibal
waited and worried, and began to think of making a journey
to Knoxville to assess his brother's situation firsthand.

Amy, meanwhile, returned to writing, but this time in the
form of a private journal. She wished she could send her
commentary to Horatio Eaton for publication in *Reason's
Torch*, but Hannibal urged her not to do so. Her father was
surely watching Eaton's publication, looking for any clue
that she was still contributing. He might recognize her writings should they appear, and this would give the lie to Hannibal's claim that Amy was "reforming" her viewpoint. It
was best for her to remain quiet and mostly unseen. "Content
yourself to remain a private person for now," Hannibal urged
her. "The time may well come when you can make contribu-
tions of more importance than you can know just yet." So
Amy satisfied herself with her journal-keeping and watched
emerging political developments with great interest. Hannibal Deacon was her mentor and guide now. She would
trust his judgment and follow his guidance.

A runaway slave came via the Underground Railroad,
and Amy had the frightening but gratifying experience of
helping hide and feed the man in the subterranean shelter.
Out of all her efforts in abolitionism, this was the most ful-
filling, the most exciting. Before, all had been theory; this

was *real*. The man went on after one night and Amy found herself eager for the next Canada-bound "passenger" to arrive, whenever that would be.

On November 24 a mass public meeting occurred at the Greene County Courthouse. Amy longed to attend but did not. Hannibal, however, did, observing rather than participating, still hiding behind his public veneer of neutrality. He returned encouraged. The regional leaders who led the meeting, including James McDowell, T.A.R. Nelson, and Andrew Johnson, took a decidedly Unionist posture, and the voting delegates at the meeting adopted a series of resolutions encouraging patience, diplomacy, and a peaceful attitude. All in all the meeting was calm, conservative, and pleasing to such as Hannibal Deacon. Amy read the extensive coverage of the meeting in the November 27 edition of *The Greeneville Democrat*, scouring and analyzing the various resolutions passed and discussing them with her uncle.

Unionist though the meeting's tone was, there was certainly no call for abolition of slavery, and indeed, the passed resolutions included a declaration of support for the rights of states and territories to decide the slavery question for themselves. None of Hannibal's household had expected anything different. Despite the claims of some radical Secessionists that East Tennessee's Unionist enclaves were, in Dr. George Deacon's ghostwritten words, "cursed abolition hellholes," the fact was that the abolition viewpoint was often as despised by Unionists as by Secessionists. Many influential Unionists, such as Virginia's John Minor Botts, strongly opposed abolitionism on the grounds that it gave disunionists fuel for the Secession fire. To the extent that Secessionists could tie together Unionism and abolitionism in the public mind, the more support they could muster in a public that, the nation over, generally held the black race in low regard.

"We must realize that attitudes change very slowly," Hannibal counseled his abolitionist clan. "It will probably be years before we see any substantial positive change on the slavery matter. The Unionism of the people here, unfortunately, has mostly to do with politics, heritage, and economics. Abolition is not even on the table in most minds.

These affairs require more than a change of law. There must also be a change in the hearts of individual men, and there is no stone more resistant to alteration than the stubborn human heart." Amy copied that latter line into her journal, underlining it twice. She was young, restless, full of zeal, but she would try to be patient, as her uncle instructed.

In Knoxville, a meeting similar to that in Greeneville took place late in the month, and there the tide seemed to be flowing in the Secessionists' direction. Unionists managed to keep a vote from being taken, so the issue was left undecided. The Unionists, perhaps frightened by the apparent rising strength of the disunion element, realized they had work to do to keep the public rallied to their side. They went at it with vigor.

The odd thing about it all was that George Deacon, who had always been at the heart of every Knox County debate over Secession, was still nowhere to be found.

In Greeneville, Amy's life went on, falling into a pattern of journal-writing, Sundays at the Presbyterian Church—where she sat sometimes beside Pleadis Mundy and felt both pleased and uncomfortable with his attentions, conscious all the while of Sam Colter staring at them with a resentful look that Amy knew could only indicate he was infatuated with her, too—and occasionally working at the local paper when Robertson needed a hand.

December brought startling news. Amy wrote concerning it in her journal: "The state of South Carolina has at last broken through ice that I had hoped would remain intact and strong. A convention in that state has voted in favor of Secession from the American Union. I fear deeply that militarism can only follow, deepening the threat of war and the division of our nation." Then, as an afternote: "This news certainly puts a dark cloud over the celebration of Christmas, as has the fact that I have yet to hear anything from my own father, even at this holiday season. I believe he has rejected me more fully even than I had dreamed."

Just after Christmas, which Hannibal managed to make a relatively bright holiday despite Amy's pessimism, Sam Colter arrived at the Deacon house for a supper and discussion of plans for Rufus's escape to the North and freedom.

She learned that while most of the slave refugees who passed through by way of Hannibal's house traveled alone, at times Sam served as an escort and guide. He was to do so for Rufus.

Amy was excited on Rufus's behalf, but she had dreaded this moment, too. Rufus was a lifelong friend, a man with whom she had shared secrets and adventures and rebellion against the system in which both had lived. She knew that when he was gone, she might never see him again. He was talking of Canada, "the promised land" for slaves, where there was freedom and slave-catchers did not roam.

Hannibal urged immediate action. "I believe we must not delay Rufus's escape any longer. If Tennessee secedes, doors will close. We may be unable to get him out. I've already talked to Sam about this. He's ready to serve as Rufus's guide to a certain safe house where others will take him under wing. Rufus, are you ready to go?"

The slave looked aghast. "Tonight?"

"No. Tomorrow night."

Rufus seemed unable to speak. Hannibal chuckled. "Rufus, you seem struck ill."

"It's fearsome, thinking of it really happening."

"It is. But less fearsome than staying. If you want your freedom, now is the time to seize it."

Rufus thought deeply. "I do want it. I'm ready."

"Tomorrow night it will be, then. Sam, you've prepared yourself?"

"Yes, sir, Mr. Deacon."

Hannibal turned to Amy. "And what about you? Are you ready to part with Rufus?"

"I'll never be ready to part with him," Amy replied. She looked at Rufus. "But I wouldn't stand in his way for anything."

"Don't worry about Rufus, Amy. Sam is a capable fellow. The best refugee pilot I've ever run across. You could take him out in the remotest country, blindfolded, turn him around seventeen times and set him loose, and he'd not only find his way out, but he'd do it without being seen, heard, or smelled by anybody. Right, Sam?"

"I do well enough, I reckon." He reddened at the praise and was unable, as usual, to look at Amy.

"Sam will be following a well-established course, Amy, one we have used several times. There are stations all along the way, houses where Rufus will be safe.

Parting with Rufus the next night was difficult. There were tears and many embraces; Rufus himself rebounded between excitement, sorrow, and outright fear. When he and Sam made their departure in the dead of night, Amy wept alone in her room for hours, fervently praying for Rufus's safety, and fell asleep only an hour before dawn.

The next day, Hannibal received a letter from his brother, a reply to the one he had sent earlier. Both its form and content startled him. The letter was scrawled, rambling, filled with unfinished sentences, repetitious thoughts. Most of all it was scathingly hateful. Hannibal's first thought was that surely George must have been fiercely drunk when he wrote it; his second was that the mindset it reflected was chillingly reminiscent of his and George's father after he went mad. There was even a similarity in the circumstances. Their father had suffered some deep blows just before his breakdown—familial, personal, financial. The mental illness had set in quickly afterward. George had suffered some painful blows as well, and Hannibal feared the same result for him as had come for their father.

In the letter, George Deacon informed his brother that he had no interest at the moment in what his daughter was or was not doing. She had betrayed him, and a long time would pass before he would consider any kind of reconciliation. For the time being, and perhaps for good, Hannibal could simply consider Amy his own child. Then the letter veered off into political diatribes, and ended with a long section condemning "all those who have shamed me," particularly the man who had been the instrument of it all, Charlie Douglass.

Hannibal was deeply disturbed. He had not entertained any notion that his brother was in such an obvious bad state, and was stunned to think he would waste such venom on such as Charlie Douglass, by all accounts no more than a vagrant with a talent for crude humor. Hannibal hid the letter, not wanting Amy to see it, and decided that an investigative journey to Knoxville was in order.

By chance a friend came by Hannibal's store the afternoon after the letter arrived. The man was somber and said he had news concerning George Deacon that he believed Hannibal should hear. Dr. Deacon, he said, had ceased publication of his newspaper, had virtually withdrawn from practicing his medicine, and was rumored to be drinking heavily and acting irrationally. "I was told that Dr. Deacon has become something of a public joke," the man confided. "And he's making it all the worse for himself by the way he is behaving. He's lost all credibility that he once had, and those who used to back him are staying far away from him now. They view him as an embarrassment. And there's a rumor that he's taken up a close friendship with one of the town drunks. Even has taken the man in to live in his house. Hannibal, I'm not trying to intrude into your family affairs, but if you care about your brother, you need to go see him. They're starting to call him the 'Madman of Secession Hill.' "

January of 1861 came, heralded in Greeneville by a New Year's Eve mock dress-up party in which the boys of the town put on outlandish clothing, gathered before the courthouse, and called themselves by the names of prominent citizens, much to the amusement of almost all. Amy enjoyed the performance, but Hannibal was not there to see the little fellow who stood on short stilts with his hair combed up wildly, calling himself "Mr. Hannibal." The real Hannibal was at home, preparing for a trip to Knoxville.

Hannibal boarded the train and left Greeneville the next day. A business-related journey, Amy was told by her aunt, but she had learned to read Lena Deacon by now and could see that she was worried. She wondered if the trip had anything to do with her father, from whom she hadn't heard even an indirect word since her banishment back in October. She quizzed Lena without result.

Hannibal returned a couple of days later, smiling and

cheerful around Amy, but somber when he thought she wasn't looking. He told her in a forced offhand manner that he had tried to call on her father while in Knoxville, but the doctor was out of town, away on a business trip of his own.

"Why hasn't he answered your letter?" Amy asked.

"I don't know," Hannibal replied, and felt guilty for the deception of keeping Dr. Deacon's scathing letter a secret.

That evening Hannibal privately told Lena the truth. George Deacon had not been away from Knoxville at all. He had simply refused to see his own brother. "I visited Secession Hill, pounded on that door until my fingers were blue. At first George wouldn't answer at all, and when finally he did, he was cursing and swearing and telling me to go away. He said he had a gun and would use it.

"Merciful heaven! George threatened you?"

"He did. He's in a bad state, Lena. But after that experience, I think it's best I leave him be. This business of being 'betrayed' by Amy, and humiliated before his public, has destroyed him. It's sad. God knows I don't believe what George believes, but right now I'd like to see nothing more than a new copy of the *Advocate*, breathing fire at full steam. It would at least let me know that George was back to his old self again."

The advancing New Year brought more disruption to a troubled nation.

Following South Carolina's lead, other states held conventions and voted to secede: Mississippi, Florida, Alabama, Georgia, Louisiana. The pattern momentarily reversed with the admission of Kansas into the Union as a slave-free state—a move that greatly displeased Secessionists.

In Tennessee the strong state's rights governor, Isham G. Harris, called a special session of the General Assembly that resulted in the authorization of a state vote on the Secession issue. Specifically, the act authorized the voters of the state to vote yes or no on the question of whether to call a convention at which Secession could be mandated. The date for the vote was set for February 9.

Opinions about the advisability of such a convention were divided in Greeneville's predominately Unionist population. Some, including Hannibal, feared the very idea of such a convention; others saw it as a chance for Tennesseans to firmly put down the Secession idea. Amy did not know what to think, and awaited the balloting with much trepidation.

The Confederacy grew. Texas voted to join it at approximately the same time a "peace conference" convened in Washington City with the worthy goal of finding an acceptable, nonviolent compromise between North and South. The conference achieved little.

Meanwhile, a provisional Confederate government was formed in a meeting of delegates from Secession states, held in Montgomery, Alabama.

Hannibal Deacon joined the flood of voters who went to the polls across Tennessee on the ninth, and Amy sat home, wishing she were a man just so she could vote. Hannibal spent the day at his store, listening to endless discussions among his customers about how the vote would go, then returned home to await the count.

The outcome pleased him. When all the state's ballots were in, Tennesseans had voted 69,387 against Secession, and 57,798 for it. The anti-Secession vote out of East Tennessee had made the crucial difference. For now the state would remain in the Union.

The Confederacy, determined to advance with or without Tennessee, got on with its business, electing Zachary Taylor's former son-in-law, Jefferson Davis, a Mississippi planter, former United States Secretary of War, and senator, as president. He was inaugurated in the Alabama city of Montgomery to the tune of a song called "Dixie." Amy read about it in the *Democrat*.

Sam Colter had by now returned to Greeneville, looking moody and casting many poorly hidden glances at Amy as he reported back to the Deacons that he had left Rufus safely in an Underground Railroad "depot" near Philadelphia. Their flight had been difficult but successful, and Rufus, when last Sam saw him, was joyful at having his freedom and declared that he might forego Canada and take the risk of remaining in the United States in hopes that he could join the Union Army and help fight against the South, if war broke out and Negroes were allowed to enlist.

"There are plenty of former slaves just like him," Sam said. "All this trouble may be about states' rights to some folks, but to the slaves it's about slavery, pure and simple." Digging in his pocket, he turned to Amy and for once managed to look her in the eye. "Rufus told me to give this to you," he mumbled, handing her a carved wooden doll so small it fit into the palm of his hand. "He said it would be something for you to have to remind you of him. He said he's kept it for years because it was yours." Sam fidgeted and cleared his throat. "He got right teary when he give it to me. Told me he'd have give it to you himself, before he left, if he hadn't knowed he would break down weeping if he'd tried."

Amy took the doll, which she recognized as a tiny figurine Rufus had made for her when she was a child. Eventually she had outgrown her interest in such items and, in one afternoon of a growing girl's disdain for relics of early childhood, had disposed of it, along with most of her toys. Obviously Rufus had secretly retrieved this doll and kept it for a moment such as this. She nodded and thanked Sam in a muted voice.

"Rufus says he'll see you again, someday," Sam said. "He said he'd be sure to find you, whenever all the trouble is over and the slaves are free."

"We can only hope that day will come soon," Hannibal said.

With the doll standing on the desk before her, Amy secretly wrote a letter to her father that night, and mailed it the next day. She sensed that there were things Hannibal wasn't telling her about Dr. Deacon. And though she felt estranged from her father, despising and fearing him because of the things Rufus had revealed to her about him, it seemed absurd that months had passed and she had not had any contact with him. She could not overcome the compulsion to write him.

While she waited for a reply she continued to watch the advance of events. March saw the creation of two new territories, Nevada and Dakota, taken out of what had been the massive Utah Territory. It also saw the inauguration of Abraham Lincoln, with his vice president being one Hannibal Hamlin, declared by Hannibal Deacon to surely be a fine man, considering his name.

The Confederate effort advanced further during that month. The Confederate Congress adopted a constitution similar to that of the United States, but with clear protections of slavery and an emphasis on states' rights. And everywhere signs of impending war grew. Eager young rebel volunteers, still hopeful for Tennessee's ultimate Secession, began forming themselves into units and taking on names like the "Squirrel Shooters." Soldiers and would-be soldiers mobilized and drilled in Greeneville to the delight of every small boy in town. Amy witnessed one full-scale "battle" between two armies of juveniles who took sides based on their fathers' sentiments. They "shot" and "bayoneted" one another with stick rifles, the slain falling, then rising to fight again, and in the end to walk off as friends. Amy shook her head, wondering if these boys really comprehended that when their fathers and older brothers took up the fight for real, the dead would not rise again and the grievances of war would not be so quickly forgotten.

Amy grew increasingly more pessimistic about the chances for a peaceful resolution to the national division, and sensed similar thoughts on the part of Hannibal Deacon. Sam Colter, who she held in much greater esteem because of his successful piloting of Rufus, still struggled for optimism in those times, less rare now, that he managed to carry on a conversation with her. Tennessee might be able to function as a neutral buffer state between North and South, he said. Or perhaps, if Tennessee seceded, East Tennessee could break off and form a Unionist state of its own. Maybe, somehow, terms could be reached and war avoided. Amy listened but did not believe it.

Time passed. Pleadis Mundy increased his attentions to Amy, but she kept him at arm's length, unable to overcome her dislike for his Secessionist views. Meanwhile, no reply to her letter to George Deacon came. She grew more worried, feeling that something was wrong.

April brought conflict centering on a South Carolina Federal fort called Sumter, which had been threatened since December by South Carolina state soldiers. On the eleventh South Carolina demanded the full surrender of the fort, which was to be reprovisioned by orders of President Lincoln. On the twelfth a South Carolina general ordered his soldiers to fire upon Sumter, and the next day the fort's commander, suffering from lack of supplies, was forced to surrender.

The news about Sumter reached Greeneville and staggered the populace. At once the prospect of war seemed much more real, and both Unionists and Secessionists alike reexamined their views. Men stood in clusters on the streets, talking quietly and somberly, and on this day not even little boys played war.

Right after the Sumter episode, however, news came out of Washington that carried an even greater impact, and further enfeebled hopes for peace.

Abraham Lincoln, stung by the bombardment of a Federal installation, declared a state of insurrection and called for 75,000 military volunteers to sign on for three months' service to put it down. When the news reached the South, outrage rose in response. A United States president had called for soldiers to attack their southern brothers on their own soil—and on top of it, seemed to believe that the South would crumble in only three months, at the hands of only 75,000 soldiers.

Hannibal Deacon was crushed. "There is very little hope now," he said. "So many people have been sitting on the fence, sympathetic to the South but willing to support the Union as long as no coercion against the South was raised. Now Lincoln has brought on the coercion. He's pushed a lot of people who have supported him right into the arms of the Secessionists. God only knows what will happen now. God only knows."

Chapter 11

Hannibal Deacon's gloom was vindicated as days passed. In Chattanooga, Lincoln's call for troops evoked a fierce surge of anti-Federal feeling marked by the lighting of a bonfire outside a huge hotel on Lookout Mountain. Schools were dismissed and crowds gathered at a rally celebrating the coming of southern independence. The rally featured speeches, songs, and fiery talk of punishing the Federals for their effrontery. Similar spontaneous celebrations took place all across the state. Sam Colter, who had gone to visit friends over at Tusculum College, came to the Deacon house and reported that the campus was in an uproar. The young men of the old college had been mostly pro-Secession all along; now they were virulently so, parading about the grounds, cheering for the Confederacy, and making life miserable for the two or three students they suspected sided with the Union. Sam found himself unwelcome among former friends at the college where he himself hoped to study one day. Despite his professions of neutrality, they asserted they could see his true colors, and declared them red, white, and blue. He had almost been beaten at one point by a rowdy "Secesh" gaggle, and finally fled the campus for his own safety.

Amy saw how shaken and infuriated Sam was by the incident and felt great empathy with him, in the process realizing how much she was coming to like the reticent young mountaineer. How could she not admire a young man so brave and capable as to escort slaves to freedom? But her liking for him was different from his for her, she told herself. Despite her limited acceptance of Pleadis Mundy's attention, right now she wasn't interested in a romantic relationship with any young man . . . but of course, if Sam wasn't so shy, and wasn't so plain to look at, and if he would do more than just sit there *looking*, then maybe . . . She wrote the thought in her journal, then read it and laughed. Sam Colter getting up the courage to actually approach her romantically? Not likely.

Lincoln's call for arms generated a great increase in political rhetoric across the state, as leaders on both sides of the Secession issue toured each county, speaking from every stump, arguing their causes. In East Tennessee the will to remain in the Union was still strong, but Lincoln's call to arms had weakened it. Many declared that they had been willing to abide the Union as long as it showed itself to be operating in good faith, something destroyed as soon as Lincoln made his appeal. Many believed that Lincoln had directly violated his own government's constitution.

In Knoxville, bombast was high and the Secession cause heartily promoted in a climate of public outrage. But Dr. George Deacon was nowhere to be seen. Since his failed rally the prior fall, there had been no further editions of the *Advocate*, no more spontaneous speeches from the steps of public buildings, no more evident participation at all in a cause of which he had once been a symbolic leader. Unionists in general, Charlie Douglass in particular, continued to make a joke of Deacon's discreditation, but the populace as a whole seemed to be simply disregarding him. The rush of events, the swirl of rhetoric, the stark, prestorm tension of an atmosphere crackling with war—these things made it easy to forget the milder days when such matters had remained mostly theoretical, more nebulous ideas to be batted back and forth between name-calling, partisan editorialists in the public journals and disagreeable neighbors who sparred over back fences and on street corners.

In Greeneville, Hannibal faced a new kind of pressure. With issues polarizing, it was increasingly hard to pretend neutrality. How could anyone be neutral in such a climate as this? Before long he perceived that to cling to his feigned neutrality was pointless. For the first time, Hannibal declared himself a Unionist, and it was a great relief to be honest about it at last. Once in the open with his views, he became one of the most vocal public opponents of Secession, and was swept with great enthusiasm into the fold of Unionist leaders. Hannibal was a popular and persuasive man, and the fact he was brother to one of Secession's original and most controversial proponents didn't hurt, either. Before long Hannibal was taking part in rallies all over East Tennessee, urging the Unionist cause.

There was a price to pay, naturally, with the Secession faction in Greeneville. Hannibal suffered some loss of business, a few taunts, even a threat or two. But his neighbor and fellow abolitionist Mark Key got it worse. Once Key became open with his Unionism, calls for his ouster as Colter postmaster became frequent, and one fierce fellow even struck him in the nose with a well-aimed punch through the little countertop opening by which Key conducted his business. Key managed to laugh it off and pressed no charges, but he and all others knew that far more serious violence was bound to come soon, the kind no one would be able to laugh at.

In Amy Deacon's former bedroom on Secession Hill

Ben Scarlett lay on his bed, frowning at the dark ceiling above him. He knew the old adage about never examining a gift too closely, and generally followed it. But at times, when he would awaken as he had tonight, he would wonder just why Dr. Deacon was presenting a no-account drunk like him with such a fine gift as residency on Secession Hill.

It was one thing for Dr. Deacon to have shared his troubles with a stranger when he was distraught with fresh pain, as he had been that day when he splinted up Ben's injured arm. It was quite another for him to have extended and nurtured their relationship, plying him with liquor, taking him deeper and deeper into his confidences, and eventually allowing him to move into his own home. At Secession Hill, Dr. Deacon had allowed Ben every privilege he wanted. Plenty of liquor, food. New clothing. Pocket money. Ben found it a fine gift indeed, but puzzling. There was something at work here, something Dr. Deacon was up to, and Ben was growing curious about what it was.

Most of what he knew he'd surmised from the doctor's subtle but increasingly frequent hints that he had a task Ben could do for him. The implication was strong that this task, whatever it was, would constitute Ben's payback for all the kindness he was accepting. Ben was growing wary. Whatever the task would be, it must be big and important. Maybe a secretive and dangerous one. Why else would the doctor be so generous? Why else would he give free lodging and board to a common vagrant?

Dr. Deacon was an unusual man, no question about that. But unstable, too. Ben moved in a world of unstable men and knew how to spot one. He had not expected to find such in Dr. Deacon. But the doctor yielded up surprising and often troubling aspects of himself all the time.

His political aspects, for instance. In recent weeks the very developments Dr. Deacon had been hoping for over the past few years had finally begun to come about. States were seceding, and now that Lincoln had taken a militant stance on the issue, Tennessee's secession looked more likely. Ben expected Dr. Deacon to be elated. But when the doctor read his newspapers, he did so with a dark glower and many mumblings. Why? Ben guessed it was because the juggernaut was moving ahead without the involvement of George Deacon. Promoting disunion had been the force driving Deacon's life for years. Now that it was occurring, Deacon was left behind. He cursed the names of Charlie Douglass and Horatio Eaton again and again. He murmured continually about having been humiliated, discredited. He completely withdrew from medical practice. That was another surprise. Ben didn't think doctors acted that way. They were supposed to be solid and reliable, dedicated to the welfare of others. They weren't supposed to behave like men going mad.

Ben rolled over on his side, the mattress making a soft rustle. He thought over Dr. Deacon's obsession with having been "discredited." It didn't seem to Ben that it really was as bad as Deacon perceived it. Douglass's revelations certainly had embarrassed the doctor, and political foes and anonymous doggerel-writing Unionist wags had certainly made hay with it all—but was that so intolerable? With a more restrained response, Dr. Deacon could have regained his credibility. Men involved in public arena controversies often overcame far worse blows than Deacon had suffered. Ben supposed that the doctor's own daughter being at the root of the betrayal accounted for his extreme reaction. And the situation was made no better by the fact that Birch Lewis, obviously resentful of being fired by Doc Deacon, kept showing up on the street below Secession Hill, sometimes watching the house silently, other times yelling vague threats. Deacon seldom replied, though a couple of times he had gone onto the porch with his shotgun and sent his former editor scurrying like a roach for safety.

There was yet another thing to worry about. A couple of days before, Deacon had written a letter and taken pains to make sure Ben didn't see it. But Ben had seen it, just for a moment, and though he wasn't sure, it looked like Deacon had signed the name "Ben Scarlett" at the end of it. It was very worrisome. Why would Deacon be forging his name, on a letter to . . . whom? Ben wanted to know but hadn't asked. Asking might rouse anger, and anger might get him tossed back onto the streets again.

Ben closed his eyes, sleep beginning to descend. "You'll be performing that task for me very soon," Dr. Deacon had told him today. "You're just the man for it, and I know you won't betray me."

Ben slept, but not well. All through the rest of the night he tumbled in nightmares that he couldn't remember when the morning came.

* * *

During the next week it looked all the more likely that Tennessee's lot would be cast with the Confederacy. The Tennessee legislature heard a plan put forth by the governor to place the state within a "Military League" with the Confederacy. The League would effectively exercise a military rule over the state, and begin heavy recruitment of volunteers for the Confederacy military. The legislature approved the League, and in that action effectively made Tennessee a Confederate state even though no actual Secession had occurred. That triviality, however, was expected to be settled the next month in a public referendum to be held June 8. Again Tennesseans would be asked to vote yes or no on Secession, and this time pro-Confederates were far more hopeful of victory.

The Military League immediately began a public relations effort, particularly in Unionist East Tennessee. Unionists countered with rallies of their own. The hated Charlie Douglass did his part in his own colorful way, sitting on Gay Street and pounding a huge bass drum, yelling Unionist slogans and making a mockery of the Military League representatives who had come into Knoxville and set up camp near town. Douglass's unique activity made the newspapers, and Ben watched Dr. Deacon literally shake with fury as he read about it, then cast whatever newspaper he was reading into a fireplace, light it, and watch it burn.

Ben was dozing one morning in his favorite chair on Secession Hill when Dr. Deacon burst into the room, a wild light gleaming in his eye.

"Up from there, Ben! Our opportunity has come!"

"Opportunity for what?"

"The task I've been talking about! Our opportunity is at hand!"

Confused, Ben stood. "What is that task, Doc?"

The doctor stood before Ben and put his hands on his shoulders. He beamed the brightest smile Ben had ever seen him generate. "Evening the score, my friend. Setting right the balance. And you will be the instrument! You should consider yourself honored! Get your coat now. It's cool today."

"We're going somewhere?"

"Yes."

"Can I have a drink before we go?"

"No! No liquor! You'll need a steady hand and a clear eye. But afterward, you'll have your liquor. All you want. We'll celebrate together, you and me."

Ben was bewildered and a little frightened. But obediently he fetched his coat, threw it over his shoulders, and followed the doctor out of the house. "Where are we going?"

"We're checking you into a hotel, Ben. I've already reserved a room."

"Why?"

"One thing at a time, man! Go get in the carriage."

Ben walked down the steps toward the waiting vehicle and wished he hadn't been forbidden that drink. His heart pounded.

Dr. Deacon whistled as he guided the carriage down the street. Ben leaned out to examine other traffic on the street, and Deacon said, "Sit back, Ben. Don't let people see you with me."

"But everybody knows that I've been living on Secession Hill."

"Don't argue with me! I've been generous and good to you, haven't I?"

"Yes, sir."

"I've not asked a thing of you in return, have I?"

"No, sir."

"Well then, you owe me a favor or two, correct?"

"Well, I reckon so."

"Indeed you do. And now you'll repay my kindnesses by doing just what I ask of you—correct?"

"Well, I'll do what I can."

"You will indeed." He veered the carriage to the right and into a broad alley. He pulled to a halt behind a big hotel. "Get out, Ben. Go inside and tell them you are William Smith. You got that? William Smith. They'll give you a key. Don't mention my name—I paid one of your fellow vagrants to go in and make the reservation for you under that name. This task, you see, requires some discretion on my part."

It was growing evident to Ben that what Dr. Deacon had in mind for him was something that required hiding. That implied danger and illegality. He began to tremble. "Doc, I don't know that I like all this. What is it you want me to do?"

Deacon closed his eyes and shook his head in exasperation. "I want you to go into that hotel, tell them you are William Smith, take your key, and go to your room."

"But after that, what?"

"You'll learn soon enough. I'll be in to see you later."

"But how will you get in with no one seeing you?"

"See that adjacent roof? I'll come across it to your window. No one will see. You be watching for me. You stay in that room until I come. And no drinking! If I find you've gotten your hands on liquor, I'll make your life mighty hard."

Ben didn't like any of this, but he was not a strong-willed man and was greatly intimidated by the doctor. Silently he climbed out of the carriage, looked back uncertainly at Deacon, then walked slowly to the back entrance of the hotel. Another glance at Deacon, and he went inside.

For two hours Ben sat in the hotel room, longing for liquor and growing more nervous about whatever mysterious task lay before him. He thought about leaving the room and vanishing, leaving Dr. Deacon to do whatever the deed was on his own, but he was afraid the consequences of running would be worse than those of staying. And he kept remembering Deacon's promise of all the liquor he wanted just as soon as the task was done. If he ran there would be no liquor. Probably no more living the good life on Secession Hill. He sat, fidgeted, worried . . . but stayed.

A commotion arose outside on the street. He went to the opposite window and looked out onto the street corner below. A group of men were clustered around a flagpole; among them he recognized individuals he had seen frowning at that decorated Secession dog that day a few months back when Daniel Baumgardner had run him out of his store shed. In fact, there was Baumgardner himself, among the group at the pole. A flag was being attached, and raised—an American flag. Onlookers cheered as the colors rose. A few cursed and jeered, and one boy threw a rock, but hit no one.

"I'll be," Ben said to himself. "The Unionists are having theirselves another rally."

A booming noise erupted down the street, prompting more jeers, some cheers, and plenty of laughter. Craning his neck, Ben watched Charlie Douglass come marching down the center of the street, wearing a red, white, and blue hat and pounding his now-famous bass drum with vigor. "Hail to the Union!" he shouted, doffing the hat at a group of derisive pro-Confederates. The rock-throwing boy lobbed a stone at Charlie but only hit the drum, generating an extra beat. "Why, thank you, son! You're a fine Union drummer, you are!" Charlie said at the top of his lungs. "Hurrah for the old nation! And to hell with the Secesh!"

Ben grinned. One thing about old Charlie—he could put on a show when he wanted. Good thing the Doc wasn't hear to see this one.

A rap at the window behind him made him jump. He turned to see Dr. Deacon peering in. Rising, he went to the window and opened it.

"I told you to be watching for me," Deacon said as he crawled in. He was carrying something long, wrapped in an oiled cloth. It looked worrisomely like a rifle, and Ben eyed it nervously.

"I was watching the Union folk outside," Ben said. "They got them a rally going."

"Indeed they do," the doctor said, smiling. He laid the long object on the bed. "And I do believe I hear a drum beating."

"It's Charlie Douglass, Doc."

"Ah, yes. Charlie Douglass." The smile grew broader, and Ben grew more nervous.

"What's that on the bed?"

"Never mind that. Not yet. Let's take a look outside."

They went to the window. Douglass stood near the flagpole, beneath the flapping Old Glory flag, and was divesting himself of his heavy drum. A group of his fellow Unionists clustered close around him, protecting him as they had at Dr. Deacon's Secession rally.

Someone came walking up with a barrel and placed it in front of the assembled group. Another man, well-dressed and with a chin covered by a nicely combed and trimmed beard, climbed atop it and began to speak. "You know who that is, Ben?" Dr. Deacon asked.

"I believe that's Mr. Trigg, ain't it?"

"Connelly Trigg. Yes. Another loudmouthed Unionist."

Trigg's booming voice carried well on the street corner. In silence Ben listened to the usual Unionist arguments, but his mind was on that object on the bed. "Doc, is that a rifle you've brought in?"

"Look!" the doctor said excitedly, pointing. "Look coming there! That's Major Morgan."

Ben peered out and saw a man wearing a fierce frown, uniform, and holstered pistol approaching the assembly. "Who's Major Morgan?"

"He's with the state troop of the Military League," Deacon replied. Suddenly he looked worried. "I wonder if he's come to break up the rally? Blast! I hope not."

George Deacon didn't want to see a Unionist rally broken up? Ben was more confused than ever.

Still gnawing his lip and looking very worried, Dr. Deacon watched the activity outside for a minute more. Morgan, arms crossed, now stood at the rear of the group, listening to Trigg. "He doesn't seem like he intends to stop them," Deacon said.

"He ought to," Ben said. "Shouldn't have Unionists out bellowing on the streets." He had grown accustomed to saying anti-Unionist things to please his benefactor.

"This is one time I don't agree, Ben. This is one rally that I want to see go on." He turned and faced the other. "Ben, the time for your task has come. I want you to go back to the bed there and fetch—"

Commotion outside. Shouts and yells. Ben and Deacon looked. Morgan had pushed his way into the group and was facing off with Charlie Douglass, who was cackling and mocking and literally dancing derisively before him.

"What's this?" Deacon muttered.

Morgan spoke into Douglass's face, the words not loud enough to reach up to the hotel window. Ben knew Douglass as a man who managed to make his opponents furious while maintaining his own mocking control, but this time it was different. Obviously Morgan had said something that had infuriated Douglass, because he stopped his dancing, cursed loudly at Morgan and shoved him. Morgan shoved back, and Douglass jumped on him, kicking and seemingly trying to bite. The fight was so sudden and unexpected that all those around jumped back away from it rather than trying to break it up. Morgan, rolling on his back with Charlie atop him, screamed as Charlie managed to sink his teeth into an ear. He kneed Charlie hard in the groin. Ben winced. Charlie grunted and rolled off, then came to his feet and staggered away toward the far side of the street.

"Confound it!" Deacon spat. "Of all the bad luck—"

"Oh, God, he's going to shoot him!" Ben exclaimed.

Morgan was up, his pistol drawn. Men and women screamed and scattered. Charlie headed for a store across the street. The boom of a shot abruptly echoed between the buildings. Ben watched, horrified, as Charlie jerked and fell; another man just beyond him, standing just outside the doorway of the store toward which Charlie had been heading, also grunted and doubled over, falling, writhing, then lying still.

Deacon stared at the fallen, unmoving form of Charlie Douglass. He chuckled. "I'll be! The deed has been done for us!" And with that Ben understood. The fear that had nagged at his mind since the doctor entered the room was confirmed.

"Merciful Lord, Doc," Ben said, "you intended I should *shoot* Charlie!"

"Doesn't matter now what I did or didn't intend, does it?" the doctor said cheerfully. "Good Major Morgan has evened the balance for me." He laughed and shook his head. "It seems I've wasted much effort on you, Ben Scarlett. Not to mention much whiskey. Fate has stepped in for me! Could you have guessed it? Sometimes life can be sweet, eh? Sweet indeed."

Chapter 12

Outside and below, people clustered around the fallen men at the storefront, but Ben's attention was all on Dr. Deacon. "You *did* want me to shoot him!" he bellowed, rising and backing away from his companion. "You would have made a murderer out of me!"

Deacon quirked his brows as if Ben's reaction was quite an unexpected novelty. "And what if I had? What does that matter to a man who is no more than a common drunk anyway? You think your hellfire would have been all that much hotter for the killing of such a piece of Unionist rubbish as Charlie Douglass?"

"Was that what it was all about, Doc? All the liquor, the room, the food—working me around to be no more than a slave who does a murder for you?"

"My, listen to the moralist! Listen to the drunken, worthless, thieving moralist!"

Ben had no idea what a moralist was. But he knew what Dr. Deacon was, and was repelled. This doctor was surely a madman, and if not that, then something far worse: a man of pure, unapologetic wickedness.

There were more shouts outside, tumult. A woman yelled, "Oh, God, he's dead!"

"I ain't a murderer, Doc. I wouldn't have done it."

"You would have. You would have picked up that rifle, aimed it, and shot Charlie Douglass. Because you are a weak man, Ben Scarlett. You are controlled by liquor and therefore can be controlled by others. What? You thought I was doing all those kindnesses for you out of charity?"

"How long had you planned it, Doc? How long did you have it in mind to make me kill a man?"

"It came to me that day in my office when I was binding you up. I realized I had before me a man I could put to good use in a good cause."

" 'Put to use'—that's how it is to you, is it? 'Put to use!' Put to use to kill a man who has shared his soup with me, shared his flask!"

Deacon had lost all good humor. "You sicken me, Scarlett. Get out of here. I've wasted enough of my time with you, and I have no further need of you. Go! Get out of here, and don't let me see you again!"

"You're mad, Doc. Mad as you can be!"

"You dare insult me! *You?*" Deacon lunged toward the bed and wrapped rifle on it. Ben felt a sudden bolt of pure fear. Warm liquid spread down his legs, soaking his trousers, but he was unaware of it. He turned in a panic, jerked open the door and bolted out into the hall. He heard Deacon burst into laughter inside the room. Ben ran down two flights of stairs, knocking over a maid on her way up with a mop and bucket. Soapy water cascaded down the steps, making him slip and slide on the landing below as he rounded it. He fell down the final flight of steps, came to his feet on a roll, and charged out the back door of the hotel. He did not stop running until he was three blocks away. He saw a woodshed, door standing ajar, and entered, slamming the door shut behind him. Collapsing in the corner, he broke into sobs.

He eventually fell asleep. When he awakened, it was dark. He rose and left the woodshed. A clear sky arched above, and the breeze had turned warm, bearing hints of approaching summer. All was peaceful, serene. Crickets chirped, hiding away in the secret places they could always find and searching children could not. Ben let the breeze sweep across him, and slowly played his mind over the day's events.

He stood in the silence, thinking. His emotions had been settled by rest, and though he retained a deep, underlying sadness, he also felt relief. He finally knew the terrible thing that George Deacon had expected of him, but he had *escaped* it. Closely, to be sure, but he had escaped. He wondered if Deacon really would have shot him had he not bolted from the hotel room. Maybe not. He had laughed at the flight, after all. Toyed with him. Mocked him. Deacon had been, in effect, mocking him all along with his shows of kindness. It had all been a sham, a means of bringing him under control so he could be used for a task Deacon didn't want to be sullied with himself.

Ben thought about Charlie Douglass, and his sadness deepened. Douglass had not been a true friend—Ben had no true friends—but sometimes he'd gotten on well with him. Douglass hadn't deserved to die, and even though his death came at Major Morgan's hand, Ben considered Dr. Deacon morally guilty of it, even more so than Morgan. Morgan's act obviously had been impulsive, and probably Douglass had threatened him to provoke it. But Deacon had nurtured his plan. Over a long span of time he had conceived and strategized the death of a man, and only the intervention of fate had altered the scenario.

I wonder if I would have shot him, if things had gone different? It was a terrible thing to wonder, but Ben couldn't avoid it. Though he had denied to Deacon that he would have shot at Douglass, the truth was, he honestly didn't know. Deacon had possessed him very thoroughly—he knew that—and maybe he would have tremblingly gone along. God in heaven, he hoped not. But maybe . . .

Right then Ben Scarlett hated liquor. He hated what it had done to him, how it had weakened him and enslaved him. Deacon had been right. Because he was a slave to liquor, it was a short step to becoming a slave to other people. Ben's sadness grew.

He wandered out onto the closest street and made his way past dark buildings and houses in which people slept in warm beds. He envied them. He had become accustomed to comfort on Secession Hill. It would take effort to accustom himself to woodsheds and barn lofts again.

He didn't want to do it. He didn't want to go back to the empty life he had led. He wished he could throw aside liquor, get himself work, and make a life for himself. A *real* life. He hadn't lived a real life in years.

He stopped, realizing which street corner he had just reached. The flagpole around which the altercation had occurred thrust skyward. No flag flew now. Ben walked to the porch of the store where the second victim of Morgan's bullet had fallen. There was enough moonlight to let him see the bloodstains that darkened the wood. One bullet, two victims. The shot that felled Douglass must have passed all the way through his body and struck the other man.

"Hello, Ben."

Startled, Ben turned. It was Daniel Baumgardner, underbite and all, looking at him with some measure of friendliness and equally as much wary disdain. "Hello, Mr. Baumgardner."

"Ben, have you got over that cough you had last time we met?"

"Yes, sir."

Baumgardner said nothing. Stared at the bloodstains at Ben's feet.

"Why are you out so late, Mr. Baumgardner?"

"Couldn't sleep. I saw a terrible thing happen here today."

"I seen it, too."

"Did you? Terrible. Terrible. A foreshadowing of things to come, I'm afraid. One man dead, another wounded."

"Wounded?" Ben had assumed both were dead. "Which one?"

"Hm? Oh, Charlie Douglass."

"You mean Charlie ain't dead?"

"No, he's alive. The bullet grazed him through the side. Very painful, I suppose, because he passed out. The other man—I didn't know him—he took the bullet square in the gut. Died right there on the doorstep."

"Charlie Douglass ain't dead!"

"No. I just told you that."

Ben laughed. "Thank God. Thank God."

"Friend of yours, Charlie Douglass is? I suppose he is one of a kind with you."

Ben was too happy about Douglass's survival to pay heed to the hint of insult in Baumgardner's comment. "I know him some. You hate to think of somebody you know getting killed, you know."

"I gather you must not have stayed around to see the aftermath today."

"No. I ran off right after the shots were fired." No reason to say more than that, Ben figured.

"Well, it got worse after you left. It's a miracle more weren't killed."

"What happened?"

"Morgan went back to the Military League camp and—"

"He wasn't locked up in the jail?"

"Him? No! Acting in an official military capacity, he said. No crime committed. Charlie Douglass had threatened him and was heading for that store, or so Morgan claimed, to get a gun and shoot him. I don't believe it. But Morgan got off free as a bird, went straight to his camp and came back with nigh an army of Military League soldiers. They marched up the street here, threatening folks, all but daring somebody to try and engage them. Some of our local folk, Secesh and Union together, got up a little delegation and did some peacemaking, and finally the soldiers marched back to their camp. For a time there I thought they'd shoot half the city and burn down every building on the street."

Ben was astonished. "This here Secession thing, it's getting right serious, ain't it?"

"Mighty serious, Ben. You realize that today was the first bloodshed here in Knoxville over the Secession crisis? It won't be the last. When war comes, things will be ugly indeed." He paused, looking at Ben with distaste. "I believe you're Secesh yourself, ain't you, Ben?"

"I ain't nothing. I talked Secesh that day at your shed 'cause Charlie Douglass had told me you thunk along them lines."

Baumgardner flipped up a brow. "I see. You were misinformed, I'll have you know."

"I do know. Hey, where's Charlie Douglass now?"

"Somebody took him to a doctor for patching. Don't know which one—I can assure you it wasn't Doc Deacon, though!" He laughed without a trace of real mirth.

Right then Ben almost told Baumgardner what he knew. An impulse to lay out before Baumgardner the whole sordid scheme of Deacon's rose and almost became words on his lips. But something restrained him, and Baumgardner spoke again.

"Speaking of Doc Deacon, I hear you been staying at Secession Hill, Ben."

"Some. I been there some," Ben mumbled. "Not no more." Abruptly he wanted to be away from here and Baumgardner.

"Seems odd, him taking a common drunk in, if you don't mind me saying it."

"It was odd, I guess. He's an odd man. Mighty odd. Good night to you, Mr. Baumgardner." He turned and began to walk away.

"Where you sleeping tonight, Ben?"

"I'll find me some place."

"In other words, you're on the streets again."

"Yes, sir."

"Well, you stay out of my shed—you hear me?"

"I hear you. Don't worry. I'll stay out of your dang shed."

But he didn't. He went across the street and watched until Baumgardner was out of sight, then headed straight to the dry goods store, around the back, and into the forbidden shelter. He lay down and tried to sleep, but because he had slept during the day, he didn't really need sleep now. Finally he got up and poked around in the fenced rear yard until he found one of Baumgardner's tossed-out cigar stubs. He had nothing to light it with, so he chewed it and waited for dawn. When the sun came, Ben left and went out to the street. He headed toward the meat packing house, figuring that when it opened, he could get himself a goat's head and make some soup. There was good food in the pantry on Secession Hill, but no longer was that a place he would be welcome, or would want to go even if he were.

* * *

Charlie Douglass rebounded from his physical wound very quickly, but was a changed man. No more beating a bass drum, no more heckling of Secessionists. Ben saw him only once, about three days after the wounding, sitting on the porch of a house somebody was letting him live in. He said hello, but Charlie made no reply. He simply stared past Ben, lost in some world no one else could enter. It made Ben sad. Ben happened to have a little bottle of whiskey—stolen— and he gave it to Charlie and walked away.

Two days later Charlie Douglass was shot to death on that very porch by a party unknown. Investigation failed to turn up a clue. But Ben Scarlett knew who had done it. He knew that Dr. George Deacon had surely been furious when he learned that Douglass's first wounding hadn't killed him. Maybe he had taken care of the matter himself. Maybe he had found himself another vagrant like Ben Scarlett to do it. Either way, he was guilty, and Ben seethed with a fierce but fear-tainted anger.

Ben attended the funeral, as did most of Knoxville's residents, regardless of political sentiments. The funeral procession threatened to turn ugly, several radical Unionists bitterly desiring to use Douglass's murder as a grounds to instigate a fight, but peaceful men intervened and violence was avoided.

Ben had nothing to drink that night, though he felt the need of it more than usual. It would take courage to do what he felt compelled to do, and courage for him usually came from whiskey.

Somehow he managed to make himself act even without alcohol. He walked through town like a man going to face his executioners, and reached Secession Hill. A light burned in the front room. Shaking and even managing to pray, Ben climbed the stone steps to the porch and knocked on the door.

Dr. Deacon opened it and stared back at him without a word.

"I know you done it, Doc," Ben said. *God, don't let my voice tremble so!* "I believe you ought to go and confess it."

"Confess what, Mr. Scarlett?" The way Deacon said his name dripped with contempt.

"You murdered Charlie Douglass."

"No I didn't. You did."

Ben gaped. "That's a lie! You know it's a lie!"

"Well, it's just what I intend to say if you decide to get high and holy on me and go firing off your mouth. I intend to say that Ben Scarlett, whom I had taken in out of the goodness of my heart in an effort to help him shake off his liquor habit, ended up threatening me, telling me that if I didn't give him money and whiskey, he would go kill poor old wounded Charlie Douglass and then try to blame me for it. I'll say that when I refused, Ben Scarlett carried out his threat."

"Nobody will believe that."

"Oh? You think they'll believe you above me? You're a common drunk. A street vagrant. I'm a medical doctor. A man who has published the finest newspaper in Knox County. Now ask yourself, Ben: Which of us do you think is more believable? Hm? Oh, and by the way, there's that threatening letter you sent to Horatio Eaton, too. Some very terrible threats in that letter! I suspect that the great abolitionist is already packing his bags to get out of this town. For all his big talk, Eaton always has been nothing but a pitiful coward."

Ben stood silent. He feared he might cry.

Dr. Deacon went on: "Ben, I suggest that you leave this city. Go away and never come back. Because if I see your face again, I may just go make my report to the authorities. And then they'll put you on trial and hang you. So I suggest you leave Knoxville at once. Do you understand me?"

"I understand."

"Do you doubt I would do what I just said?"

"No."

"Then be off with you. Go wherever you want, as long as it's away from here. Go to hell, for all I care." He slammed the door.

Ben stood on the dark porch of Secession Hill. He had just looked pure wickedness in the face and heard it ringing in his ears, and for a moment it left him too stunned to move. Then he turned and hurried down the steps.

He hid in town for a while, wondering what to do. Finally he found a pencil stub in his pocket. He tore down the tattered remnant of one of the broadsides he had helped Amy Deacon hang before the fated rally, and on the back wrote the following:

Deer Mr. Eaton,

You have got a letter with my name on it that thre-tanned you, but I did not rite it. It was rote by Dr. G. Deacon and he sined my name on it without me saying he culd do it. I thenk Dr. Deacon is the one who has kilt C. Douglass and you should be careful of him becawse he blames you over his dawter riting for your paper. He is trying to make you leeve town and if you dont he mite hurt you or worse and will probly blame it on me. He is a bad man and you should be ware of him.

Very truly yours,
Ben Scarlett

Ben folded the paper and took it to the small frame house where Horatio Eaton lived. Sneaking to the porch, he quietly put it under the door and left.

He kept walking until he was out of town, heading west, not knowing or caring where he was going as long as it was away from Knoxville and Dr. George Deacon. He could find only two things to be happy about: He had gotten away without becoming the criminal tool Dr. Deacon had obviously intended him to be, and that terrible cough that had plagued him since the prior year was gone. Life in the warm house on Secession Hill had cured it.

Now that he was back on the road again, Ben doubted he would enjoy another warm house anytime soon. It would be sheds and stables and such for him, and stolen food, begged money, purloined whiskey. But at least he would be free, not locked up in the Knoxville jail as George Deacon's scapegoat.

He slept in a rural barn that night. He waited and watched the farmhouse the next morning until its occupants left. Praying no one still remained inside, he entered through a window and stole food, clothing, and half a bottle of homemade wine. Then he left and continued traveling west. He didn't know how far he should go. If he could find enough travelers willing to let him hitch wagon rides and such, he might go all the way to Nashville. He had never been to Nashville and had always wanted to see it.

He was near Kingston when he found a man moaning in a ditch by the road. He was in a bad way, bruised and bloodied. Ben knelt beside him. "What happened to you, mister?"

"I wath beaten," the man replied. His front teeth had been knocked out and his speech was muffled and distorted. "Beaten becauth I wouldn't thay a prayer for the Confederathy."

"Somebody was trying to make you say prayers?"

"I'm a preacher. It happened after thervitheth thith morning. Thomebody followed me, and here I am."

"Oh." Ben would have not even been aware it was a Sunday except for having heard church bells ringing across the distance that morning. "My name's Ben . . ." He paused. Perhaps it wouldn't be wise to advertise his true name very much, considering Deacon's threats to link that name to the Douglass murder. "Ben Kirby. I'm afraid I ain't a good man. I'm afraid I ain't much 'count at all. But I'll help you if I can."

"God bleth you, Mr. Kirby. God bleth you. My name ith Mainard. Lucath Mainard."

"Well, I'll help you up, if you can stand, Preacher Mainard. You live around here?"

"No. I travel. They took my horth, though."

"Anybody live hereabouts that would take you in?"

As best he could, the lisping, damaged man directed Ben toward a farm about a mile distant. The family there, church folk who knew Mainard and were aghast at what had happened to him, took him in and offered to take in Ben as well. Having no better prospects in the offing and hoping maybe there was some whiskey about the place, Ben accepted.

That night he slept again and awakened once in the night, thinking he was back on Secession Hill. When he realized he was not, he was intensely relieved, and slept peacefully thereafter, suffering only for lack of liquor.

Part III

SKAANTEE'S RIDGE

Chapter 13

Miles apart, two men moved through the mountains, one descending, one climbing.

The descending man, bearded and lanky-legged, was about forty years old, though he himself neither knew nor cared about his exact age. His race was white, his skin far from it: Weathered, battered, creviced, it was tanned to the color of a beech leaf in winter. Those who knew him thought him odd and dangerous. His name was Dabney Sloat, and the mountains had been his home all his life.

He seldom left the mountains. He found all he needed to survive right there in the forests, among the balsam and laurel, on the flint- and mica-strewn ridges, in the briar-filled valleys, beneath the surfaces of the rivers and creeks. There was little to draw him to any town, which suited him. He had hated every town he had ever visited, all three of them.

The one he hated most happened to be the very one he was descending to today: Marshall, a meager strip of a village Sloat still thought of by its original name of Lapland. It was the governmental seat of Madison County, and the only reason Sloat was visiting it now was that he had to do so in order to cast his vote in the day's North Carolina balloting to elect delegates to the convention on Secession. Before dawn Sloat had risen, said good-bye to the somber but devoted Cherokee wife he called Kate, and begun the long trek toward the town.

Nearing Marshall, he paused on the mountainside to look through a gap in the trees and examine the narrow little town below. Making do was a way of life in the western North Carolina mountains, for towns as well as people, and Marshall made do with what little slice of relatively flat land the French Broad River and mountains had decided to allow it. It was a squalid-looking place, made up of a few houses, stores, a jail, a courthouse. Marshall was tiny by the standards of most towns. Even so, it was the second-biggest town Dabney Sloat had ever seen. Plenty big enough in his estimation.

He scratched his beard, shifted the weight of his ancient flintlock long rifle in his right hand and briefly closed his eyes. "Lord God," he intoned aloud, "I'm going into that town yonder, and out of these your hills. There are them there in that town who hate me, and who I hate with the pure hate of the righteous. I don't go seeking trouble with my enemies, but if it comes, let me be square and true and do what is righteous. Ride on my shoulders, Lord, as I descend down among the wicked. Ride on my shoulders, and speak in my ear so that thy servant will hear."

He lifted his head, opened his eyes and continued on down toward the town.

Many miles to the southwest of Marshall, the climbing man was doing battle with wind and gravity on a steep ridge side in the country of the Oconaluftee Cherokee. About twenty years younger than the distant Sloat, he was Jim Matoy, a Cherokee of the little band called the Oconaluftee Citizen Indians. As Sloat was saying his prayer, Matoy was gasping for air, thoroughly winded. It was not easy for even a strong, fit young man to ascend to the mountaintop known as Skaantee's Ridge, and for most people there was little reason ever to try. Skaantee's Ridge was barren and windswept and unhospitable, almost as unhospitable as its only resident, old Skaantee himself.

To most of the Oconaluftee Cherokee, Skaantee would never be known as anything more than an eccentric,

unfriendly, somewhat tragic mountain hermit who rarely
left his isolation except to sell his ginseng root at Will
Thomas's trade store. Scaantee's name was seldom invoked
without shakes of the head, clicks of the tongue, rolling of
the eyes. He lived in a well-chinked cabin among the few
wind-battered, stunted trees that managed to survive on the
ridge's exposed crest, and was known as an onerous man
who made few exceptions to his sweeping dislike of human
company.

Jim Matoy was one of those exceptions. To Matoy,
Skaantee went by the name of Grandfather, a title that was
symbolically and reverentially accurate, if not literally so.
There was no blood kinship between the pair, only the kinship of mutual affection. Skaantee was Matoy's friend, his
storyteller, his ginseng-hunting partner in season, and most
of all his mentor, a source of counsel always worth the difficult climb to the top of the ridge.

As Matoy caught his breath he looked out from the ridge
side across the seemingly endless balsam and rhododendron
mountains. From the valleys fogs rose, fingering skyward
like the smoke of a miraculously frozen forest fire. Once,
the Cherokee had lived in great numbers in these mountains,
which they called the Land of the Blue Smoke. Now there
were fewer than two thousand of them in all of the western
North Carolina mountains. A mere remnant of the great
Cherokee society of old. That society and the numbers of its
people had declined slowly since the first inthrusts of white
settlement a century before. And just before Matoy had
been born, it had made a further, more severe and sudden
decline through the government-forced removal of most of
the Cherokee to a distant place far to the west. Only a few
had been allowed to stay behind. Among them had been Jim
Matoy's parents, and Skaantee.

Jim, born after the removal, had been told that the few
Cherokee remaining in the western North Carolina mountains were, like Skaantee, only a shadow of what they had
once been. The removed Cherokee now lived far away in a
very different kind of land. The fortunate among them had
left their homeland by riverboat. The more unfortunate ones
had been forced to trudge overland along the Trail of Tears.

Jim was glad his father and mother had not been among them. Many Cherokee had died on that sorrowful journey.

Jim's father and mother, childless at the time of the removal, had been among the seventy or so families making up the Oconaluftee Citizen Indians, a group whose cooperative behavior had won them favor and excepted them from removal. Now, among that Oconaluftee remnant, Jim lived a quiet life on the mountain farm of his parents, hunting the rugged woodlands, gathering ginseng in the fall, and hearing tales of the old days from Skaantee whenever he climbed the mountain to see him. Jim's father didn't talk of the past like Skaantee did. The past is gone, he would say. It was more important to live in the world that was than to dwell in phantom memory in a world that would never return.

But Matoy liked hearing of the old days, spoken of so vividly by Skaantee. The old man had lived in these high mountains far longer than Jim Matoy had been in the world. He was weathered and ancient, with a face like worn leather and a voice decayed into a whisper by the erosion of time. People told Matoy that Skaantee had once been the greatest, most vigorous hunter among the mountain Cherokee, boasting the wisest and most beautiful wife, the strongest sons, the prettiest daughters, the most productive lands. He had been sociable then, living in the valley, his door open to all. But his wife and all but one of his children were dead.The lost ones had been killed by disease except for one son, murdered by a white man. Skaantee's one surviving daughter was married to a white man named Dabney Sloat and lived miles away.

Skaantee's youth, vigor, and sociability had died like his family. But the man himself lived on, leaving the valley and moving high onto the lonely mountain, where he could look down upon a world in which those he had most loved no longer breathed and moved.

Matoy stood silent, gazing across the mountains until his breathing slowed and his muscles ceased to burn. Then he turned and began to ascend again, striking the foot of the final stretch of trail that led onto the white rocks of Skaantee's Ridge. He hoped he would find Skaantee at his cabin. If not, he would wait for him. There were difficult matters to be discussed, hard questions to be asked, a crushing weight of indecision to be lifted from the shoulders of Jim Matoy.

Dabney Sloat looked about in honest but well-concealed astonishment as he strode onto Main Street in Marshall. He had never seen the town this busy, this full of people. It cut very much against his grain to come into the midst of such a bustle. Made him edgy, crowded, nervous. He tried to ignore the claustrophobic feeling and walked with his big stride right down the center of the street, eating up more than a yard of ground with every step.

"Lord have mercy!" he heard a woman's voice declare in a near whisper. "It's Dab Sloat! Who'd a thunk *he'd* be coming in today!"

Nothing in his expression changed, but hearing that made him more ill at ease, more irritated to be so deeply among obnoxious humanity. Eyes staring, tongues wagging ... towns pressed people together and brought out the wickedness in them. Sloat perceived towns as inherently evil places. Didn't the Bible itself support that? When the Lord brought down fire and brimstone, it was always upon a town. The hills and mountains and wilderness he spared. In the wilderness there was safety, refuge, righteousness; in the towns, concentrated evil, enemies, wicked humanity in general.

Sloat looked at a certain two-storied hotel building on down the street to his right. A big sign above the door read COLTER HOTEL. Below it, in smaller letters: *Rooms for Rent at Good Rates*.

Sloat knew this hotel and the man who owned it, Wilton Colter. Colter wore the brand of enemy in Sloat's mind and contributed to his loathing of Marshall. There was a time he had sworn to kill Wilton Colter. Passing years had worn the cutting edge off that desire ... but he had never recanted his oath. If the opportunity came, Sloat might fulfill it yet. God rode his shoulder; he would tell him what should be done. Sloat studied the little hotel with fierce-looking eyes, then turned and headed toward the courthouse.

* * *

Wilton Colter, like Dabney Sloat, held deep religious convictions, but of a far less sinister variety. He was a gentle man, and kind; the God he believed in was not the unloving, harsh avenger of Dabney Sloat's conception. Wilton Colter's God, though awesome and to be feared, was also a forgiving God, a God who loved, a God a man could love in turn.

Wilton made it a habit once a week to spend part of the morning in prayer in a little Marshall church house. He found that in the empty, tiny sanctuary he could focus his thoughts— and nobody was there to laugh at him for praying the way his father had taught him to do it: out loud. His prayers were unvarnished and straightforward, spoken with the typical mountain disregard for proper grammar. Though Wilton Colter was not only literate but quite well self-educated, his speech was mostly untouched by his learning.

"Lord God," he said, seated in the midst of the row of benches that served for pews, his eyes open and fixed on the unoccupied pulpit and his hat resting on his knees, "I'm coming to you again with prayers for the well-being of them I love. I thank you for having give me loved ones, for there are some who have nary. I thank you 'specially for my nephews, who are, as you know, like sons in my eyes. Lord, I lay them out before you like Abraham laying out Isaac on the altar, and give them up to you for you to watch over and guide through life.

"Lord, I'm going to pray for both of them right now. I thank you for Sam, and that you helped me find him a place out of these Carolina mountains, for I believe you have give him talents and such that can make him a better life elsewhere. I thank you for my friend Mr. Hannibal Deacon, who has been so kind to take Sam in and give him work and a good place to live in Tennessee. Lord, Sam is a good boy and can do much with himself if you'll guide him, but he's way too bashful, Lord, and I fear he'll never be able to find himself a woman if he don't get over it. Make him be not so bashful, Lord, I ask you. And help him to get educated, too, there at that college if ever he'll get into it. A man needs an education to make good of himself in the world outside these hills.

"And Lord, I pray for Sam's brother Joe. He's a strong and hardworking young man, and a fine help to me here with farming and helping me run the hotel and café you give me, but he's headstrong, Lord, and way too fast of temper. It will get him in trouble someday if he don't change, so I pray you'll help bring that change about, if you would. Lord, Joe ain't like Sam, and he don't care nothing for the world outside these mountains, so I figure he'll probably stay here for good. I hope you'll smile on him and give him what good he can find in so small and cut-off a place as this.

"Lord, I pray for Cora, my hired gal, and thank you for the help she gives me in my business. She's got little sense, Lord, so she needs your hand of guidance even more than most. Be with her and help her stay straight, Lord, because she's not got much will and could be talked into bad things by the wrong kind of man, and there's plenty of them about.

"Now, Lord, I pray for this country. As you have probably heard, this state is taking a vote today on whether to sesh off from the nation or stay part of these United States. I don't know for sure where you stand, Lord, but I'm Union and hope you are, too. My ancestors fit off the heathen Indians to make this place part of the free United States, and I see no reason to go ruining what they did here not even a full century later.

"Lord, I don't understand all the reasons for the distress this here country is in at the moment, but I know that a part of it has to do with slavery, and you know where I stand on that. Maybe things was different in the past, or maybe not, but I do not believe, Lord, that in this age you intend one man to own another. I've raised my nephews as best I can to think the same way, and I know Sam is true and square on it, but I ain't sure about Joe. Anyway, Lord, I hope that if it is in your will, you'll make this vote go the way it should. And if we can be spared war, Lord, then please spare us. Please do. I know these mountain folk, Lord, and how deep and harsh they think of things. If there's war to divide us, there'll be blood all over these hills. There'll be hate and unforgiveness and men destroying one another, and hate running from father to son and son to grandson. We need men of peace in these mountains, Lord God. We don't need warriors. I lift up mine eyes to the hills, Lord, from whence comes my help, and my help comes from you who made the heaven and the earth. Give us all your help, Lord, that we may keep the peace and live as brothers together." He paused. "Again, Lord, I thank you for them you have give me to love, and to love me. I could be no richer, not with a king's palace. In Jesus Christ's name I pray. Amen."

He rose, turning his hat in his hands, and went to the door. Pausing, he turned back toward the pulpit. "Lord, I'll ask one thing more: Help us all to remember that we are but pilgrims and wayfarers here, each of us bound one day to find either the glory river or the river of darkness. Help us to shun the darkness, Lord." His voice quavered and eyes moistened; emotions always flowed easily for Wilton Colter when he was alone. "Help us to be men of peace. Help us to always seek the glory river."

He left the little church house, put on his hat and walked back toward his hotel on the long main street of Marshall.

The Colter Hotel had only three rentable rooms; two smaller ones below, one big one above taking up the entire second story. In that upper room a young woman named Cora, slightly simpleminded since falling from a high feeding chair as a baby, paused to look out the window, then let the curtain fall from her fingers. Eyes wide, she dropped her broom, hiked up her dress and headed for the stairs on a run.

"Mr. Colter, sir! Mr. Colter!"

Wilton Colter, freshly back from the church house, was kneeling behind the front desk, picking up the registration book he had just dropped. He rose. "What's wrong, Cora?"

"Mr. Colter, I just seen Dabney Sloat, walking right through town. Right up to the courthouse."

Wilton frowned. "Sloat . . . you're sure?"

"Yes sir. It was him."

"At the courthouse . . . he must have come to town to vote." He scratched at his chin. "Well. I didn't expect *he'd* show up."

"Mr. Colter, you ain't going to let him see you, are you?"

"Well, I have to vote."

"But he hates you, Mr. Colter. He hates every Colter they is."

"Not so loud, Cora! There's a guest still in Room One. I don't want him to hear this."

She softened her voice. "If he sees you, sir, he'll shoot you. I know he will. He had him his rifle with him."

"He always does, anytime I've ever seen him." Wilton brightened his expression. "Don't worry, Cora. I can handle Mr. Sloat. But thank you for the warning. Now if I run into him—which I probably won't—at least I won't be surprised."

"Don't go over to the courthouse till he's gone, Mr. Colter. I hope you won't."

"The poll isn't even open yet," he replied. "Don't worry. I'll watch out for him. But you understand, Cora: I'll not hide from him. Ours is not a spirit of fear, just like the Bible says."

Cora went back up the stairs and in a moment Wilton heard the whisking of her broom above him. Alone now, he glowered in concern. Merely having Dabney Sloat in town was reason for worry. Sloat lived by the harsh feud-code of the mountains, and held Wilton punishable for an offense Sloat ascribed to Wilton's father: the murder of his Cherokee wife's brother. Wilton's father had gone to his own grave without ever confessing or denying that murder. As much as Wilton despised to think it, he, like the Sloats, had always believed his father guilty. Micah Colter, though devoutly religious and a good man in many ways, had always hated Indians, particularly Cherokee.

Even earlier there had been far more nebulous troubles between the Sloat and Colter families. Wilton's grandmother, the Sloats had claimed, was a witch who through spells had caused Dabney Sloat's father to be accidentally shot to death during a hunt. Worst of all, the Sloats believed she had cursed the family to die away, and indeed they had died, one by one, until now Dabney Sloat was the last Sloat remaining in the mountains. The three children he had sired had all died. Wilton Colter had never known what to make of the witchcraft tales, but Dabney Sloat believed them to the heart and framed his hatreds around them, hatreds he veneered and vindicated with his own version of divine righteousness. Dabney Sloat was the kind of mountaineer, not at all rare in that time and place, who truly did believe that God rode on his shoulder. Such men made the most dangerous and unforgiving of enemies.

Wilton looked out the front window of his little hotel and pondered the mountains. There were two worlds within these mountains, populated by two different kinds of people: the mountaineers and the townsmen. Though the rest of the world might see little difference between the two, Wilton knew from his own experience that the differences were tremendous. Wilton had made the uncommon transition from mountaineer to townsman, moving out of the hills into Lapland before it became Marshall. He had learned something in that transition: the great extent to which the rural people of the mountains were a world apart from the world, a population cut off from society at large, many of them living, growing, fighting, marrying, giving birth, and dying within the same narrow valley or on the same thicketed mountainside where they had been born. Some spent entire solitary lifetimes in one tiny cabin.

The townsmen were different, even in such a remote and small town as Marshall. Rough-cut and uncultured though they seemed to those from the outside, they still were men of commerce, of politics, of courts of law, men with limited but significant contact with the world beyond the mountains. The townsmen tended to see the mountain people as cloistered, stubborn, often willfully ignorant. The mountain people in turn saw the townsmen as would-be aristocrats, borderline outsiders, people in touch with an unknown and probably wicked outer world. Many mountain folk perceived the townsmen as self-serving conspirators, using their laws and courtrooms to dole out an alien justice that often didn't seem to be justice at all—a perception Wilton Colter had to reluctantly admit was not fully inaccurate. Thus mountaineers often chose to dispense justice in their own private ways. The same man who sang hymns to God in some tiny log church house in a smoky hollow might dispense fatal justice to some enemy on a mountain trail, and never sense the slightest moral difficulty in it. The mountain folk worshiped a God of harsh justice, who punished sins for several generations. In their cloistered, seldom-changing world they had a far stronger sense of otherwordly eternity than of earthly time. Neither favors nor grievances were forgotten over passing years.

Wilton had grown up in that kind of world and had not much questioned its presuppositions until an unusual opportunity arose and he found work in the resort town of Warm Springs, some ten miles northeast of Marshall. A foot injury and subsequent inflammation had sent him to Warm Springs to bathe in the healing, hot natural springs there. He was amazed by the village's huge, popular hotel, operated by a family named Patton and served by stagecoach lines that ran on the Buncombe Turnpike. At first sight of the two-story, 250-foot-long brick hotel with its thirteen big porch columns and 240-seat dining room, he was struck with the realization that there was much more to the world than he'd imagined. While at Warm Springs, he saw men and women of wealth who came from long distances to bathe in the therapeutic waters and to vacation along the banks of the French Broad. He found work at the hotel for almost a year, then returned home knowing he would never be able to go back to the stifling, hidden mountain life he had grown up in. Not forever, at least.

Thus, when he was grown, he came to Marshall, and eventually opened his hotel and a small café next door. He married a Knoxville girl he had first met at Warm Springs; their marriage, though childless, lasted seven years, and then she died. He had no interest in a second marriage. He was content to operate his café, do his bit of farming on the side, run his meager hotel, pray and worship in his little church. His hotel was a far cry from the spectacular Patton hotel, but he was proud of it. Though even yet no railroad reached Marshall, he still saw people from places far away. After opening his hotel, he had done some traveling himself, as an adult, visiting Atlanta, Savannah, Knoxville, and the smaller towns in East Tennessee. In Greeneville he had met Hannibal Deacon and struck up a strong friendship.

When Wilton's brother and his wife died, leaving Wilton to raise their two sons, Joe and Sam, he eventually arranged for Sam—who, despite an intense shyness, had a hunger for a bigger and better life—to go to work for Hannibal Deacon's grocery in Tennessee. With Hannibal's help, Sam was saving money toward a college career, the first Colter to aim for a good education.

Wilton didn't believe envy was right, but he couldn't help but envy his nephew's chance at education. He had high hopes that through hard work, education, and escape from the isolating mountains, Sam would make a place for himself in the world.

Outside, the streets were more abustle than ever. Wilton had never seen so many people in Marshall at one time. The café would do brisk business today. With that in mind, he went up and fetched Cora, telling her to go to the café to cook. She promptly put away the broom and went out the rear door, heading around to the café, giving him one more admonition to please, please avoid Dabney Sloat. He smiled and nodded.

He went to the window and watched the streets a few minutes longer. No sign of Dabney Sloat. He hoped Cora had been wrong about seeing him. He intended to vote over at the courthouse, and didn't want to run into Sloat. One could never know what would happen where that man was concerned. Sloat was dangerous, and even though Wilton would never admit it to anyone but himself, he was afraid of him.

Wilton busied himself around the hotel for another hour, still watching for Sloat but not seeing him. Cora must have been mistaken, he thought hopefully. He put on his hat, paused to send up a whispered prayer of petition, walked out the door and headed for the courthouse. It was a beautiful spring day, the sky clear and blue. Wilton Colter admired it for a moment, then joined the crowd on the street and headed at a quick pace over toward the courthouse.

Chapter 14

Skaantee's Ridge, North Carolina

It was not clear to Jim Matoy how an old man with fading eyes and a back stooped like the hump of an ancient mountain managed to survive on the ridge that had come to be called by his name. Yet Matoy had never found Skaantee wanting for any necessity. The old man hunted with his bow and blowgun, trapped, basket-fished the mountain streams, and harvested the natural foods provided by the forest itself, as he had since his boyhood. And like Matoy, in the early autumn he hunted the roots of the mountain ginseng plant, which Will Thomas, whom the Cherokee called Wil-Usdi, paid for in his store. One of the few times in a year that Skaantee left his ridge was to make that autumn pilgrimage to Wil-Usdi's store with a basket filled with gnarled ginseng root riding on his shoulder.

It was the hunting of ginseng that first brought Jim Matoy and Skaantee together. They met by chance while scouring the same mountainside for the telltale yellow-leafed, red-berried plant whose tan-white roots contorted in the hard forest soil until they were mangled, striated, semi-human shapes. Under Skaantee's tutelage, Matoy had progressed from a mediocre to a skilled ginseng hunter. He and the old man now hunted ginseng together every autumn until the hard frosts came, and Skaantee had taught Matoy much beyond the right way to hunt a medicinal root. Their friendship had grown naturally, without cultivation, just like the hermit plant that forged the initial link between their lives.

As Matoy and his friend conversed now, they spoke in the old Cherokee language. Skaantee spoke only that tongue; Matoy spoke it along with English, having been taught the latter by a father who strongly believed the Cherokee could only find their place in the world as it was now by adaptation to the ways, language, and customs of the dominant white society. Perhaps that was true, but it was a pleasure to talk the traditional language with Skaantee, for it was a beautiful and musical language when spoken by his wooden old voice.

"You tell me you are worried?" Skaantee asked him. "What are you worried about?" They were seated by the fire in Skaantee's low-roofed, sturdy cabin, listening to the wind, eternal on this ridge, howling around them. It did not touch them; the log walls of Skaantee's refuge were thick and impenetrable.

"Yes, I am worried," Matoy answered. "There is going to be a war, they say."

"I've heard that myself, down at Wil-Usdi's store."

"Wil-Usdi says that the war will affect all of us. The Cherokee along with the whites."

"If he says that, then that's probably what will happen. Wil-Usdi is a wise man, I've found. He knows better than you or me what the white people are likely to do." Wil-Usdi—or "Little Will," the name that the diminutive white trader Will Thomas had been given years ago by Yonagushka, departed chief of the Oconoluftee Cherokee— shared with Matoy himself the honor of being one of the few persons the antisocial Skaantee called friend. Wil-Usdi, in fact, was called friend by almost all the Cherokee in the region. He had lived among them since the age of twelve, and had developed a friendship with Yonagushka that grew even closer and deeper, perhaps, than the friendship now shared between Matoy and Skaantee. Yonagushka, who also had been a close companion of Skaantee in younger days, had given Will Thomas his Cherokee name, even declared him his adopted son. When Yonagushka had died at the end of the 1830s with eight decades of life behind him, he passed the responsibility of seeing to the welfare of his people to Wil-Usdi, and in the estimation of almost all the Cherokee, the white trader had lived up to that trust. He advocated for them with the government, working with legislatures and lawyers to do what he could for their benefit, meanwhile carrying on a successful series of business enterprises in their midst, including the trading post where he purchased the ginseng root that Matoy, Skaantee, and other Cherokees brought in. And at the time of the Removal, it was substantially because of Wil-Usdi that the Cherokee renegade named Tsali had come into custody and been executed, an event that helped ensure that a remnant of the Cherokee would be allowed to stay in North Carolina. Occasionally some mistrustful Cherokee whispered doubts about some aspects of Wil-Usdi's dealings with them, but all in all he held a position of great respect among the tribesmen. What other white man had done so much for the Cherokee? Who else had traveled to Washington City on their behalf, time and again, for the last twenty-four years?

"Here's what I don't understand, Grandfather. For years now, Wil-Usdi has told us that we must look to the United States government in Washington to make sure we are treated well. He has encouraged us to cooperate with them, to believe them. But now, as I understand it, Wil-Usdi is taking the side of the states that have rebelled against that same government. He believes there will be war, and that when it comes, the Cherokee should fight against the United States government."

"Have you heard him say that yourself?"

"No. I haven't talked to him. But it's what I am told by my father and mother, and my friend Nikatimsi also says it's true."

"And why are you worried? Are you afraid to go to war?"

This was a question Matoy dared not answer honestly. In fact he was afraid, and ashamed of it. He came from a people who historically prized bravery and battle prowess, but in his lifetime Matoy had not known war and had never developed any ambition for it, as had his friend Nikatimsi, who was eager to take up arms and go to battle as soon as he could. Matoy would not want Skaantee to know he was afraid. "I'm not afraid of war, Grandfather. But I don't know which side is right. Wil-Usdi has always told us to cooperate with the Washington government. Now he is saying to fight against it. I don't know what to think."

"When a man doesn't know what to think, he can only put his trust in those who have shown themselves to be wise in the past. If Wil-Usdi is for this new rebel government, then I will be, too. So should you."

"Nikatimsi says that Wil-Usdi wants to make an army of Cherokee to show the Confederate government that we are strong and worthy people."

"Do you want to join his army?"

Matoy did not want to join any army, but he said, "I will if it's the right thing."

"You worry very much about right and wrong, don't you?"

"Yes. I want to do right. I want to be a man of honor."

"Honor is a good thing. But tell me, do you see much sign that the Washington government has worried nearly so much as you about what is right or wrong or honorable in how they have treated the Cherokee?"

"Not much, no."

"Do you believe that Wil-Usdi has tried to do what is right and honorable for us?"

"Yes, I think he has."

"Then if the Washington government tells you it is the better way in this great war that is coming, and Wil-Usdi tells you that no, the rebel government is better, which do you trust, if you don't know what is right or wrong yourself? Who do you listen to: the Washington government that hasn't done right in the past, or Wil-Usdi, who has?"

"I would listen to Wil-Usdi."

"Then you've answered your own question, Jim Matoy. If war comes, and the Cherokee are involved, you should fight on the side that Wil-Usdi says is the right one."

After that there was no more discussion about war and

honor and Wil-Usdi. Matoy and Skaantee talked briefly about other matters, and then Skaantee fell into a familiar silence that told Matoy it was time to go. He said his good-bye and left the cabin to begin the long descent from Skaantee's Ridge.

It had been a somewhat anticlimactic visit. Now that it was done, Matoy knew better what he had been hoping to hear: that the war was a white man's war, not the concern of the Cherokee, and there was no reason he should involve himself in it. If Skaantee had said that, Matoy would have gladly followed that counsel. But Skaantee hadn't said it. He had said the same thing, in fact, that Matoy's father was saying, and that Nikatimsi was saying. . . .

By the time Matoy reached the base of the ridge and took the foot trail toward his home, he had resigned himself to the inevitable. War was indeed going to come—he could feel it, all but smell it—and when it did, and Wil-Usdi gathered his Cherokee soldiers, Jim Matoy would be among them, assuming Wil-Usdi would have him. It would be the only right and honorable thing to do.

Jim Matoy, it appeared, was soon very likely to be a warrior, even if a reluctant one.

When the people of Marshall looked back on what happened in their town that day, most were inclined to blame the whiskey, which loosened an avalanche of personal and political emotions that had been barely restrained to begin with.

The loudly pro-Confederate Madison County sheriff, of all people, started the trouble. Already drunk before the day lost its morning freshness, he stood in the street, waving his hat and shouting cheers for the Confederacy and its president. A jeering countercheer arose—"Hurrah for the Union and Abe Lincoln!"—angering him. He located the heckler, advanced upon him and, to the shock of all, drew his cap-and-ball revolver from its holster at his side.

At that moment Wilton Colter was emerging from the courthouse, having just voted. He saw in one glance two situations that seemed designed to chill his blood: the sheriff moving forward with pistol in hand, a threatened citizen backing away from him while the crowd gave way—and off to the side, none other than Dabney Sloat, looking, as always, like a piece of the mountains themselves come to life, and holding his ancient long rifle and slumping against a porch post, having not yet noticed Wilton.

Heart pumping wildly, Wilton faced a dilemma. He wanted to slip back into the courthouse to avoid Sloat, but he couldn't do that, because the citizen upon whom the sheriff was advancing was none other than Wilton's own nephew and employee, Joe.

There was only one thing he could do, Dabney Sloat or not. Wilton steeled himself and advanced toward the crowd, which at sight of the sheriff's drawn firearm had broken itself into two rough lines of humanity on either side of the street. The sheriff and Joe Colter faced each other between them. The degree of silence that had suddenly descended upon the previously boisterous conglomeration of people evidenced the surprise and fear roused by the sheriff's unexpected, extreme action.

"Sheriff!" Wilton said as he pushed through the nearer line of people and into the center of the street. "Wait, there, sir. That's my nephew."

"He's a damned Lincolnite, Mr. Colter. He made mock of me in public. It ain't the first time I've took lip from him. I ain't taking no more. I'm an elected official and ain't got to." The sheriff was so drunk his words were all slurs and jumbles.

Wilton could not deny that his nephew had antagonized the sheriff before. Joe Colter was vocally pro-Union, had been for months, and had antagonized the emotional sheriff several times with a typical lack of restraint. "I take responsibility for him, sir. I apologize to you. Now, please, put away your pistol."

"Your nephew is a growed-up man, Colter. He can answer for hisself."

"Please, Sheriff. Please."

"Listen at you whine!" the sheriff said. "I ought to—hey there, you! That's right, you!" He had abruptly turned away from both Colters and was now looking toward the far side of the street—straight at Dabney Sloat. "What are you doing in town, toting that rifle? You coming here looking for trouble?"

The crowd broke its silence with a collective, fearful murmur. Most of the people there knew Dab Sloat, knew his reputation, his temper, his habit of carrying his rifle everywhere he went, and his willingness to use it if provoked. They also knew that Dab Sloat held a long-standing personal grudge against the Colter family, and Wilton Colter in particular. The sheriff, apparently, either did not know what the rest knew, or was too drunk to care. The explosive situation suddenly developing here burned with not two, but three fuses.

Sloat, who had locked a cold stare upon Wilton Colter as soon as he entered the street, now shifted his gaze to the sheriff and blandly raised his flintlock. "I'll shoot you dead if you come a step farther," he said in his flat monotone grumble. Wilton hadn't heard that voice in years. He didn't like hearing it now.

But the sheriff's distraction was convenient. Wilton slipped over to his nephew, grabbed his arm and pulled him toward the far side of the street. Thus he wasn't looking when he heard another voice besides Sloat's spout an abusive comment at the sheriff, cursing him as a traitorous "Secesh." Then there was the sheriff's voice, swearing, but drowned out in mid-cuss by a terrific boom. The crowd shouted as one, and Wilton and Joe both ducked to the ground by instinct.

Turning, Wilton saw smoke rising from the cap-and-ball revolver pistol of the sheriff, who stood near the crowd on the other side of the street, a crowd now breaking up and running in all directions. "Who's shot? Who's shot?" Joe asked wildly.

As the crowd gave way Wilton saw a boy lying on the street, writhing and moaning, already drenched in fresh blood still gushing from holes in his arm and side. Kneeling beside him, yelling wordlessly in fury, was a big man whom Wilton recognized as a farmer and friend of Joe's, who like Joe was an outspoken Unionist. It was his voice, Wilton realized, that had last challenged the sheriff just before the shot had boomed. What had happened was obvious: The overwrought sheriff tried to shoot the man but instead hit the son standing beside him. The ball passed through the boy's arm and into his torso.

Wilton looked for Sloat, but he had vanished. Terrified now, Wilton said, "Up, Joe! Let's get away from here!" Joe obeyed, and together they scrambled back toward the courthouse and around the back of it, not pausing to see what else transpired on the street.

The sheriff turned and ran as well, as a substantial portion of the men in the crowd, made brave by fury, chased recklessly after him. The pursued man bolted into a nearby house. The door slammed shut behind him.

A quarter of a minute later he appeared again, at an upstairs window overlooking the street. He kicked the window out, waved his pistol over the yelling, angry crowd and shouted, "Come up here, you damned Black Republicans! Take a shot about with me, if you have the grit!"

The man whose son lay bleeding back on the street stepped to the front of the crowd. "I'll take my turn, damn you!" He reached beneath his coat, produced a pistol and fired. The sheriff grunted and fell back away from the window, a hole in his chest.

Another man ran up to the door of the house—this was the town constable, only now arriving. The door was bolted, so he went to a nearby window, broke it open, slid it up, and entered. Unseen by the constable, the man who had just shot the sheriff followed moments later.

The constable reached the room upstairs and found the sheriff on the floor, bleeding profusely. He knelt beside him, reached down to cradle his head. The man who had followed entered the room and without a word put another ball into the wounded sheriff, striking him in the head and killing him instantly.

Wilton and Joe Colter, meanwhile, had managed to work their way through yards and back lots until they came to Wilton's house. Turmoil was breaking out on the main street of Marshall, people on both sides of the Secession issue and on both sides of the bloody altercation that had just finished, going at each other like savages. Wilton ran to his front door and bolted it shut. He jerked shutters closed and locked them. Then he and Joe collapsed into chairs in the front room, panting, sweating, pale with fright. They sat in silence for a minute, listening to the sounds of brawling outside.

Joe was the first to speak. "That was Dab Sloat out there, Uncle Wilton."

"I know," Wilton said.

"He's the kind who might just shoot you down. Or me. Shoot down any Colter."

"You don't have to tell me that, Joe. I know it all too well."

Joe closed his eyes, still panting. "This has turned into one hell of a day."

"Don't curse," Wilton said. "You know I don't allow it in this house. I invited the Lord to live in my house years ago."

"The Lord may soon have the chance to return the favor, if Dab Sloat comes after you," Joe replied.

Joe Colter remained with his uncle the rest of the day, though there was plenty to be done on his farm. Wilton encouraged him to go ahead and see to that work, but Joe stubbornly refused. "After what has happened today, and with Dab Sloat in Marshall, I'm going to stay close by you until we know there isn't any danger."

"You think you could best Dab Sloat if he came after me, do you?"

"I don't know. But two would have a better chance than one."

"Dab Sloat came to town to cast his ballot," Wilton said. "I doubt he's got plans for me, as long as we stay away from him. Hang it, he's probably long gone, anyway. Back to the hills and that squaw of his."

"Maybe. But until we know, I'm staying with you."

And he did. After the brawling in the street was broken up and the town constable had restored order and the voting resumed amid wagging tongues that recounted again and again the bloody events of the morning, Wilton returned to the hotel with Joe at his heels. They found Cora red-eyed and frightened; she had observed all the bedlam on the street and was very upset to have seen the boy shot by the sheriff, and the fighting that had followed.

"Did the poor boy live?" she asked.

"I don't know," Wilton answered. "I haven't been out asking. And for the time being, I think I'll keep it that way."

The balance of the day went remarkably well considering its turbulent first half. The polling place closed and what crowds had remained after the terrible altercation broke up, the town beginning to empty. Wilton Colter almost ceased worrying about Dabney Sloat, ate supper at his own café, and headed to his hotel, where he checked on the welfare of the two guests now there and told them to ring the bell that hung between the hotel and his house if they needed anything in the night that Cora could not bring to them. She had a small exterior room at the rear of the hotel, near the pantry and back entrance.

He left the hotel to go over to his own house. Joe was at his side, still concerned about the possibility of Sloat being around, but that fear was put to rest when they encountered a neighbor just outside the hotel.

The man said: "Just wanted you to know, Wilton: I seen Dabney Sloat heading back up into the hills after all the tragedy this morning. Not that I figured you was fearful or nothing. I just thought you'd like to know."

The news was far more welcome than Wilton allowed himself to show. Joe, just as relieved, was finally persuaded to return to his own house. There, he cleaned up a bit, then went to visit a girl he had been seeing lately. Wilton went into his home, dressed for bed, drank a cup of water, and began to relax at last. His nerves had been on edge since the tense encounters of the morning.

He made a habit of going through a chapter of the Bible and a chapter or two of some volume of good literature each night before falling asleep. He was about to doze off in the midst of a lengthy Hawthorne chapter when he heard a knock at his back door and was startled into dropping the book.

"I thought I told them to ring the bell," he muttered to

himself. He threw a robe over his nightshirt and headed to the door.

When he threw it open, Dabney Sloat stood there, rifle already leveled. Wilton stood looking at him blankly, incredulous. Ludicrously, he thought about slamming the door in Sloat's face, as if that would somehow stop whatever was going to happen from happening.

"Hello, Colter."

Wilton stared at the rifle. "Dab Sloat, why are you here?"

"I come to town to vote. Did you vote, Colter?"

"I did."

"Which way?"

"Union."

"I figured. I voted Secesh."

"I heard you'd left town. Why have you come back?"

"Well, Colter, I didn't aim to. I left town today after all the trouble, heading back for my home. This is a wicked place. I don't favor towns."

"Then why are you here?"

"The Lord has brought me back, Colter. I was heading back toward my home, but the Lord kept reminding me of things. Old wickednesses done to mine by yourn. When I seen you on that street today, right then the Lord had whispered in my ear, 'I have sent him unto thee this day so that thou mayest slay him and set even the balance that his father before him did set awry.' I heard them very words as clear as you can hear my voice right now."

"Dabney, put down that rifle."

"No. Because I've come to use this rifle to set right the old wrongs. You see, Colter, when I heard the Lord's voice I didn't listen to it like I should have. No, I kept on traveling away from this cursed town, and the Lord, he plagued my conscience over it for miles up into them hills. So finally I stopped and says, 'Lord, I'm ready to obey,' and come on back."

He's come to kill me. He really intends to murder me, right here in my own house! Wilton Colter responded slowly, choosing his words carefully. "The God I know of says, 'Thou shalt not do murder.' "

"He also says, 'Vengeance is mine, I will repay.' "

"Then leave that vengeance to Him. He can achieve His ends without you committing murder. And I've done you no wrong that I know of, Dab. I've never lifted a finger against you or yours. But if you have aught against me, I ask your pardon and will do anything I can to set it straight. I mean that, Dab." Wilton was beginning to tremble, finding it harder to speak, but he managed to extend his hand to Sloat.

Sloat did not even look at the offered hand. "The sins of the fathers are visited upon the sons, Colter. That's Bible." He steadied the rifle. "I ain't an unfeeling man. You can pray if you want to. You can kneel and be praying as you go out of this world, asking the Lord to forgive the sins you and yourn have done against me and mine for so many years."

"Don't shoot me, Sloat. This is wrong. You know it's wrong."

Sloat ignored him, lifting his eyes heavenward for a moment. "Lord God above, direct my rifle ball straight and true. Amen."

Wilton reached out an entreating hand. "Please, Dabney, please—"

Sloat pulled the trigger. The flint-bearing rifle lock snapped down. The rifle belched fire, smoke and noise that echoed down the narrow street and off the side of the nearby dark mountain.

Sloat stood for a moment observing what he had done through the cloud of acrid powder smoke. "Amen," he said. "Glory be to God."

As lights filled windows, hands fumbled at shutter latches and muffled voices rose all around, he turned and quickly vanished into the dark, bound for the mountains.

Chapter 15

Though business was often at its best in mid-afternoon, the door of the Deacon Grocery was shut tight and locked. Curious would-be customers frowned at the sign on the door glass and peered inside. They could see no one. They mumbled and frowned and speculated among themselves about why Hannibal was closed down at such an odd time, then went on their way.

Hannibal Deacon was back in the store's rear ware room, talking quietly with Sam Colter, whose eyes were reddened and moist. Sam held a letter in hand, written by Joe Colter and posted to Greeneville from the little Carolina town of Marshall in neighboring Madison County, and had just described the letter's contents to Hannibal.

"It's purely awful," said Hannibal in reply. "I can scarcely believe it. Thank God Wilton's still alive!"

"Yes," Sam replied. "If it's right to be thankful that a man is still alive when he's reduced to blindness and lying in his bed, not able to say nothing."

"Joe knows for certain that it was this Sloat fellow who shot Wilton?"

"No. There were no witnesses of the shooting and Wilton's not able to talk. But Joe writes like there's no real doubt it was Sloat. Sloat was in town that day. He carries on a feud with the Colters. He had seen Uncle Wilton . . . but here. Read it for yourself." He handed the crumpled sheets to Hannibal, who adjusted his spectacles and read. Joe Colter was neither a penman nor a wordsmith, and it was slow going. The grandfather clock in the rear of the store ticked softly in the silence, and back among the stacked bags of grain a mouse scampered and gnawed. Sam stood rigid, staring unblinkingly at a copy of a newspaper lying on the floor. Its first column carried a headline reading: BLOOD-SHED IN MARSHALL, followed by three other decks of smaller headlines describing the carnage in the tiny town. The newspaper had come in almost simultaneously with the letter.

Hannibal finished reading, folded the letter, and handed it back toward Sam, who shook his head. Hannibal put the letter into his own pocket. "Joe wants you to come to Marshall. Will you?"

"I reckon I have to. For Wilton. I can't just not go when he's hurt so bad."

"Of course. Would you like me to go with you?"

"The truth is, Mr. Deacon, I believe I'd like to make this trip alone."

"I fully understand. You tell Wilton that I'll be over to see him soon, though. Tell him to get well."

"It sounds as if it may not do no good to tell him. I'm worried for him, Mr. Deacon. Joe says he's blind, and he doesn't speak. He lies there in his bed and looks up at the ceiling without even seeing it."

Hannibal nodded. "It's a tragedy, Sam, and I'm sorry. I know he is like a father to you. This kind of cursed thing is probably a foreshadow of far worse to come, if the war machine keeps grinding along. Well, when will you be leaving?"

"I'd like to go tomorrow, if that won't inconvenience you. I'd leave today if the hour was earlier."

"Tomorrow is fine." Hannibal paused. "Sam, pardon my intrusion, but I hope you and Joe won't try to punish this Sloat yourself. I hope you'll leave that to the law."

Sam felt a stab. Hannibal had just touched on a matter he

anticipated would soon generate strife between himself and Joe. Joe was a mountaineer in body, heart, and soul; he would assert that punishing Sloat was his personal duty, and Sam's, not that of some abstract system of laws and courts. The letter itself contained subtle hints that Joe was already making plans for revenge.

Sam didn't answer Hannibal directly. "The main law in Madison County happens to be dead at the moment. The sheriff was killed the same day as Wilton was shot."

"That's true. But whatever the situation, you leave this Sloat to those in authority, you hear?"

"I hear."

"And don't let your brother talk you into anything otherwise. You understand? There's a vengeful tone in this letter I don't like."

Sam wished Hannibal wasn't so perceptive. "I don't want you to worry over me, Mr. Deacon. I'll be fine."

They reopened the store a few minutes later, but Sam Colter didn't work out the full day. He was distracted and tense; after he snapped rudely at a customer who complained about being inconvenienced by the store's brief earlier closure, Hannibal excused Sam for the afternoon and told him to go up to his room above the store to get ready for his journey.

Amy Deacon, at that moment, came walking around the corner of Main and Depot streets, close beside a very handsome, beaming young man. Hannibal, watching, didn't recognize him, though he seemed familiar. She was smiling politely and talking with apparent interest to the fellow. Hannibal was stunned; obviously Amy had gained herself an admirer, one he hadn't known about.

Sam, exiting the front door, also saw Amy and her companion, and stopped abruptly. Looking on, Hannibal saw Sam go tense. His hands clenching and unclenching, he pulled his head down between his shoulders like a fighter about to butt his opponent. He remained in that posture only a couple of seconds, then broke loose and strode quickly away toward the alley stairs leading up to his room. Amy looked over just then and waved cheerily. Hannibal waved

back, but Sam was no longer looking. Hannibal heard him
stomping very hard up the stairs a moment later.

Hannibal mentally revised the realization he had just
experienced: Amy didn't have an admirer, she had two—the
handsome young fellow beside her on the street, and the
much less handsome Sam Colter. Hannibal shook his head
and sighed, wondering how he could have failed to observe
before that his niece's charm and beauty had vanquished his
shy young employee. Maybe Sam had hidden it, or maybe,
Hannibal thought, with all the press of a world falling apart
around him, he had just been too busy and preoccupied to
notice something so unobtrusive and private as a quiet young
transplanted North Carolina mountaineer falling in love.

That night, Hannibal described the events of the day to
Lena, who was sobered by the tragic news about Wilton
Colter, but amused by Hannibal's prior failure to notice
Sam's infatuation with Amy.

She was lying at his side, her arm across his broad chest.
"Hannibal, are those spectacles of yours failing you? You
haven't noticed the way poor Sam looks at her? You haven't
noticed his nervousness, the way he stammers about when
she's near? Poor fellow! It's made me downright forlorn,
sometimes, just watching him suffer."

"I confess I hadn't noticed. Distracted, I suppose.
There's so much going on these days."

"You wouldn't have noticed anyway. Men seldom do."

"Perhaps not. Let me ask you something else: Who was
that buck she was with? He looked like what every man
wishes he had looked like at that age."

"I'm sure it must have been Pleadis Mundy. You should
know him, Hannibal—he goes to church with us."

"Well, I suppose that's why he looked familiar. I've not
met him, though. What the deuce kind of fool name is
'Pleadis'?"

"I would think that anyone named Hannibal would be
slow to make a mockery of anybody else's name. And if
you've never met Pleadis Mundy, as many times as we've

sat within ten feet of him on Sunday mornings, all I can say is that I'm married to an unobservant man."

"Concerning romantic affairs of the young, and handsome young Adonis types with silly names, I suppose I am on the unobservant side. I've got far too much to do and think about to pay attention to trivialities." He held thoughtful silence a moment. "Even so, I feel bad for poor Sam. First his uncle is shot, then he sees the girl he is smitten with walking down the street with a handsome buck at her side and a big smile on her face. Two hard blows, one after the other, and him such a fine boy."

"Yes. Though the fact is, he should have never let himself be taken with Amy to begin with. Amy likes Pleadis, but she's not interested in being seriously courted by anyone at the moment. She's told me as much. She's so caught up in everything that's going on around us, you know. I never saw a young woman take such an interest in politics—more than she should, if you ask me. But even apart from that, I just can't picture Amy taking a shine to somebody like Sam, even if Pleadis wasn't around."

"Well, she could do worse. Sam might not be fine to look at, but there's depth in that young man. Spirit. But bless his soul, he'll never be able to turn her head away from that handsome gent she was with today. Now, just who is this Pleadis Mundy, anyway?"

"Well, he's originally from somewhere near Mossy Creek, Amy says. He's a student at Tusculum. His father owns a fine, big farm. He has an eye on a medical career."

"Really? Just like my brother, eh?"

"Yes. In more ways than one."

"Meaning?"

"He's strongly in favor of Secession. Quite a rebel."

"I should have known. Most of the young students are. Well, that won't stand with Amy, eh? Handsome or not, no Secesh will ever win that young woman's heart."

"So she tells me. But she is flattered by the attention, and he is handsome! No woman could fail to notice that."

"Oh? Are you peeking around window shutters and watching young men these days, wife?"

"Every chance I find."

He laughed and gave her a squeeze. "Can't blame you, with a fat old bear like me for a husband."

"I'm fond of fat old bears."

Another squeeze. They lay silently beside one another, thinking their own thoughts.

"You know, I hope Amy doesn't get too close to this Mundy fellow. Him being a Secessionist, he might sway her mind in wrong directions."

"Hannibal, I don't know what to make of you. Do you not know your own niece by now? Don't you remember that this is a young woman who grew up under the influence of one of the most radical, overbearing Secessionists you could find anywhere, and still managed to think for herself? You should know by now how much iron is in her."

"I suppose you're right." He pondered it a few moments. "Yes. Yes. You are certainly right. But why is she keeping company with a rebel? It doesn't fit her."

"She doesn't take him seriously, Hannibal."

"So if he should propose marriage, you don't think that—"

"For the love of heaven, husband! Of course she wouldn't!"

Hannibal smiled, embarrassed slightly by his wife's chiding.

Lena went on, "Amy told me something a day or so back that makes me sure she'll not become involved with any love affairs anytime soon. She said she's glad she has no husband or beau. She says that this is no time for love affairs. People who are in love stand to lose the ones they love. . . ." She paused, thinking. "Oh, Hannibal. I feel afraid for you when I think about the future." She hugged her husband closely.

"Lena, I'm an old man. Not likely I'll be a soldier. Nobody's going to be hurting your old husband." He gave her a reassuring pat.

"You're a Unionist in a state that just seceded from the Union. Union men are already starting to slip north. Andrew Johnson himself has moved on. Eventually there may be arrests, or conscriptions."

"Or the moon may fall on top of our house before

morning. Let's take this one day at a time, dear. It's true we have seceded, but there is still majority Union support in our part of the state. Perhaps we'll be able to break free from the rest of the state and stay within the Union. That's being seriously talked about among some very prominent Union men."

"I hope something works out. I don't want to see war at our doorstep."

"Go to sleep, wife. All your worrying won't change a thing in this world. And the only thing at our doorstep tonight is that stray cat I've been trying to run off for three weeks."

A few minutes later she was asleep, her arm still across Hannibal's chest. Despite his encouraging words, he too was worried. So far events had progressed along the lines he had most feared. When true war swept in, his situation might indeed be dangerous. Especially when the secret work began, the covert activity that Unionists would be forced into, the espionage, the guerrilla warfare. He remembered atrocities from the Mexican War, men not merely killed but killed without mercy, made to suffer for suffering's own sake. There was the capacity for such in the human soul, even in those who seemed utterly peaceable and kind in days of peace. He dreaded to think of what ugliness might reveal itself in darker days to come.

He gave his head a sharp little shake, and himself an inner scolding. *Too early to be thinking that way yet. Maybe we will scrounge up a way out of war even yet. I pray that we will.*

Hannibal lay with his wife close beside him and wondered what the future held.

Chapter 16

In the mountains of Madison County, North Carolina

An old half-breed Cherokee had taught Sam Colter how to ride in the mountains when he was barely old enough to sit a saddle. He had become adept at riding on the steepest of mountain trails and the narrowest of cliffside ledges without worry or hesitation. When Sam was in the mountains on foot, he was happy and comfortable; when he was in the mountains on horseback, he was happy, comfortable, and fearless.

Until today. As Sam Colter rode along now, he was shaking fearfully, and his horse—Della, the sixteen-hand-high strawberry roan mare that was his proudest possession—was just as nervous. Thirty minutes before, traveling along a lonely stretch as a summer storm gathered, horse and rider together had experienced the incomparable fright of seeing a tree splintered by lightning no more than fifty feet away. Sam had felt the heat of the crackling blast and the electric tingle in the atmosphere, and yelled in fright at the splintering snap of the tree, half of which fell directly toward him and his horse, crashing to the earth just a few feet behind them. Della bolted, and for the first time in his riding career, Sam almost failed to bring a mount back under control. He was almost swept off Della's back by a low-hanging oak limb before he finally managed to stop and calm her.

Shaken, he had dismounted, found shelter at the base of a hillside, and waited for the storm to come and go. It never came. Instead a strong wind erupted, dispersing clouds and moisture. Sam led his mare out onto the road again, mounted and rode on.

But now it appeared that the passing storm had been a mere prelude to an even larger one that would not merely pass over. The air felt crisp and tingly, the wind carried a cutting chill, and thunder-grumbling clouds roiled thick and inky in a darkening sky. Sam paused, looking up, wondering what to do. He had gotten off late and made far slower time than anticipated. Night would catch him still traveling—a stormy night at that.

"Della," he said, "we've made a mistake. And if we don't get burnt up alive by lightning, we're going to get drowned by rain."

Della, quite naturally, had no reply. Thunder rumbled. Lightning flashed again, this time about two ridges over, and the clap that followed shook the hills. Della quivered her ears; Sam fancied he could feel her big heart throbbing somewhere deep in her big strawberry roan equine form. Come to notice it, his own heart was pounding pretty hard, too.

"Reckon you'd not complain if we found shelter for the night, would you, girl?" Sam said. "Though God only knows where it'll be. Maybe we can find a cave."

As the lightning and thunder grew closer and more disturbing, and another lightning bolt struck a tree perhaps a mile away, Sam began to worry quite seriously. He looked around in a mild but growing desperation, and in the quickly fading light saw the mouth of a path leading off the road and into the woods.

"Paths go somewhere," he said to Della. "Maybe that one goes to a house or something. I don't like being under trees in a storm, but if there's shelter at the end of that trail . . ."

He took it that Della was agreeable. Dismounting, he led her into the woods, where the light level fell instantly to about half what it was on the road. He could still see the path, though, and followed it at a good pace. A few drops of rain fell, rattling among leaves that turned pale undersides up and out into the moist wind. A squirrel scampered off for shelter.

The path was ever more difficult to see as the darkness grew. The rain and lightning increased, and Sam had begun to lose hope of finding shelter when the smell of wood smoke reached his nose, bearing with it the scent of roasting meat.

Smoke meant fire—maybe fire from a chimney, with walls and a roof to go with it. Encouraged, he went on, pulling the skittish horse along behind him.

A turn in the path revealed a cabin ahead, its dark, bark-bearing logs barely discernible against the forest backdrop. Smoke spilled out of the chimney, breaking and swirling downward in the wind so that it poured over the cabin like water overflowing a glass. He looked at the chimney and saw that it was scorched and oddly ruptured, as if from the inside out. He had never seen a chimney in such a condition before and could not imagine how it got that way. This was clearly an old cabin; the log walls looked substantially rotted around the door frame, and the shutters that swung back and forth in the breeze were very much decayed.

"Hello the house!" Sam hollered. The rain pelted harder, more of it striking him now that he was in a clearing and out of the shelter of the trees. "Hello the house! Can you spare me shelter?"

There was no response, which was confusing and troubling in that obviously someone was in there. If not, who had started the fire?

"Della, I hope that whoever he is, he ain't getting us in his sights while we stand here." This he said very softly. Then, loudly: "Hello there! Is anybody at home?"

No reply. Sam stood there, growing drenched, while the horse snorted and acted nervous at the rumbles of thunder still rolling over the mountain forest. A searing lightning bolt flashed down and splintered a tree on the nearest ridge top; it fell with a mighty crash, just like the one that had almost struck Sam earlier.

That event made him move. Still leading his skittish horse, he advanced toward the window. "Hello in there! I'm coming friendly, just looking to get out of the storm!"

Still silence. The smoke continued to pour out of the ruined chimney—and out of the window, too, Sam noticed now that he was closer. "Hello?"

He reached the window and put out a hand to stop the swinging of the shutter. It was very dark now, and rain began to fall in sheets. He peered inside and saw nothing but a seemingly empty room, a very sparse, scattered fire burning in the fireplace, and odd, red glowing chunks all across an uneven floor.

"I'll be!" he muttered. "Looks like that fire's been kicked out across the room." Yet he still saw no sign of anyone inside.

The horse snuffled and knickered. Noticing a lean-to on the rear of the cabin, tall enough to accommodate Della, he led her there to stable her—and was surprised to look into the long, big-eyed face of a pale-colored horse already there. Lightning flashed and illuminated the interior of the lean-to long enough to reveal a saddle placed over to the side.

So there *was* someone here at this obviously abandoned old cabin. Someone who had stabled his horse, built a fire— but who was not answering his call. Someone, perhaps, who didn't want to be found. And therefore, it seemed reasonable to assume, someone who had *reason* not to be found.

"Maybe we ought to go, Della," Sam whispered. *Lord have mercy!* he thought. *What if it's Sloat himself, hiding out?* Then he scorned the idea. Sloat lived far from here.

Sam felt inclined to leave anyway, but the lightning still flashed all around—the worst lightning storm Sam Colter had ever seen, and in his many hunts in the mountains both alone and with his older brother, Joe, he had seen aplenty of them—and he couldn't get it out of his head that something was amiss here. Maybe dangerous, maybe not, but definitely amiss.

Why was that fire scattered over the floor? And that chimney all broken and—

Suddenly he knew, or at least suspected. Lightning must have struck that chimney, shattering its top. It might have run down the chimney itself and set whatever wood remnants were in the fireplace ablaze even as it scattered them. That would be an odd event, surely, but lightning did odd things sometimes. Growing up, Sam had known a man in Marshall who had been struck and who had never had to wear a coat ever after. Even the coldest of weather didn't chill him. Lightning was a mystery, an almost magical thing, and it was a known fact it sometimes ran down chimneys.

So maybe there was no one inside at all. Maybe this horse had strayed here on its own and come into the lean-to to get out of the wet. *And brought its saddle with it, and put it away all nice and neat?* Not likely. No, somebody was here . . . and if whoever it was had been working on that fire at the time the lightning struck the chimney . . .

Sam stabled his horse hurriedly beside the other, leaving them crowded in the leaky lean-to, and went to the door. "I'm coming inside," he said loudly. "Don't go shooting. I want to make sure you ain't hurt by—"

A lightning flash lit the interior of the room, and Sam's voice choked off in shock. In that fleeting half moment of pure white light he saw the form of a man, lying on his back amid the hot cinders that had made the scattered red glow on the floor, head turned to the side and facing Sam and eyes wide open. And it seemed to Sam that smoke was rising off his body.

Burnt to a cinder! Surely he is! Sam was repelled—he smelled again that scent of roasting meat and felt sickened—but he had to go in. If the man were by some chance still alive, he would need help.

With everything dark again the cinders again glowed red, and the fire, which had risen a little over the past minute or two because of wind down the chimney, was flaming up and casting some light into the room. Sam could make out the man's dark, unmoving form on the floor. He went inside, fighting nausea because of that roasting meat smell, and knelt beside the man. Sure enough, smoke was rising from him—but now that he was close, Sam realized the smoke came not from the man himself, but from ashes that had scattered across him, probably at the same time the lightning hit the fire. They were hot and smoldering and about to set the man's clothing afire. Sam brushed them off, then teetered back in surprise and almost fell on his rump when the man let out a moan.

He was alive. Sam could hardly believe it.

"Sir, sir? Can you hear me?"

Another moan.

"My name's Sam Colter, Mister. You lie still. I'll build up some light and have a look at you."

He rose and began kicking some of the glowing chunks of wood together on the floor, then toward the fireplace. Once back in the blaze they flamed up nicely. He added more sticks from a pile of them beside the crude mantel of rounded river stone, and the room filled with a yellow, shadow-casting glow.

The man moaned now even without being jostled. Sam rose and went to him, just then noticing that a hunk of meat of some sort, almost thoroughly roasted, lay on a spit stick between the man and the fireplace. So *that* accounted for the roasting smell!—a smell repellent when he thought of it as the smell of lightning-roasted human flesh, but deliciously appealing to a hungry traveler now that he knew what it really was. Sam was struck by how easy it was for a man to misinterpret a situation if he didn't know all the facts.

He knelt beside the man, who was moving now and groaning all the more. "Mister, you rest yourself. You've been hit by lightning, I believe, but you're alive, and we'll see that—I'll be!" He gazed in astonishment at the man's face, bathed in firelight and now clearly seen for the first time. "Greeley Brown? Is that you?"

The man, whose eyes had been open the entire time Sam was with him, only just then seemed to regain the control of them. Sam watched them move, come into focus, then fix on his own face.

"Caesar Augustus!" the man said in a very tight voice. "I'll be sure danged if Saint Peter ain't got the face of little Sam Colter."

"Hello, Greeley Brown," Sam said. "I ain't Saint Peter, and I ain't little no more, but I am Sam Colter, and I'm glad to see you."

The meat, which was pork that Greeley admitted came from a hog he had killed in the woods—an obviously farm-raised hog that must have broken out of its pen and had the misfortune of running across the wrong man—wasn't bad fare at all with the grit and ashes brushed off it and the roasting completed. As the storm continued outside the little cabin—the lightning was much lessened and farther off—Sam Colter and Greeley Brown sat eating together, and talking and drinking coffee that Sam had brought with him and boiled up in the little travel pot he carried on many a mountain hunt and many a run north with some of Hannibal's escaped slaves in tow. Sam had been only ten years old when he and Greeley had last laid eyes on one another, and there was much to talk about. Greeley was a Marshall native, but had moved to Tennessee years ago, settling in the mountains around the town of Elizabethton in Carter County. But he still loved Carolina. Greeley swore that the hunting in Madison County beat anything he'd found in Tennessee, and sometimes he came all the way here just to get a taste of it. That was, in fact, the reason he was in the area at the moment, he told Sam.

Sam had gotten it mostly right about the lightning running down the chimney. Greeley explained it all. "I'd finished my hunting when the storm commenced to rising. I knowed this old cabin was here, and made for it. Already had my hog meat and was ready to cook it and eat it, so this place was just the thing. I put my horse back in the lean-to, built me up a fire and had it roasting good, and the next thing I knew I was looking at you. Lord have mercy! That bolt must have been fierce. I got only the vaguest notion of a memory of it—just light and heat and feeling like God's own foot had squashed me. And then you. I really did think there for a second that you was Saint Pete."

"I doubt Saint Pete would put up with looking like me."

"You know, Sam, I'm lucky. Could have been much worse. I had an uncle who was once struck when he took to a tree in a storm, and it left him with no control of his bowels for the balance of his days. Lived the rest of his life shunned by all others, that poor man did. His wife never laid with him again. Old Uncle Poot. I'll never forget him."

Greeley's still the same, Sam thought. *Same big lies.* "You are lucky not to be dead, no doubt about it," Sam said.

"The Maker was with me, He surely was. Hey, Sam, why you in North Carolina? Last I heard you were store-clerking in Tennessee."

"I still am. I'm heading for Marshall. My uncle Wilton is in a bad way, Greeley. He was shot, most likely by Dabney Sloat."

"Sloat! Caesar Augustus, I remember that devil. What happened?"

Sam told the story as best he could, based on his brother's letter and what he had read in the newspaper. Greeley listened intently, his lean, whiskered face glowering. Greeley Brown, about thirty-five years of age, was a good friend of all the Colters. He knew about the old feud between the Colter and Sloat families, and what a dangerous man Sloat was. It felt good to Sam to tell his tale to Greeley, because Greeley responded with just the right measures of rage and consternation. Further, he felt that providence had sent his path across Greeley's, anyway. Greeley Brown was a wise fellow, or so Wilton Colter had always said. He could be trusted to give a good judgment on difficult matters—and Sam felt the need for a bit of judgment just now, having a notion of what he would face in his brother Joe once he reached Marshall.

"You know what Dabney Sloat's problem is, Sam?" Greeley asked when Sam was done. Just then a lightning bolt seared down about a mile away and made Greeley flinch, which in turn made Sam grin because there were few people alive who could say they had ever seen Greeley Brown flinch at anything. "You know his problem?" Greeley repeated. "He finds a way to justify every foul spirit he finds in him as righteous. It's easy to do that, you know, and too many folks do. A man who gets to thinking that his every thought comes straight from on high can justify no end of evil to himself. Even murder, though it seems old Dab missed out on that, leaving poor Wilt a-lying there still alive. He must not have known Wilton was still living, else he would have finished him off."

"I figure the same. He probably ran right after he shot."

"Dabney Sloat is a wicked man. I'd like to be there when

his due finally comes." Greeley took a bite and chewed thoughtfully, then poured himself the dregs of the coffee and took a sip to wash down the unseasoned meat. "How's Joe taking it all?"

"I don't yet know. All I know is what's in the letter. But I'm glad you asked that. I expect Joe will have it in mind to go after Dabney Sloat. Joe's that way, you know."

"I do know, yes. Joe's got a temper and old-time notions about justice. Them kinds of notions get people killed. It's something, ain't it! All them folks shooting at each other there in Marshall!"

"Think there'll be a big war, Greeley?"

"If the sorry old Seceshes are bound and determined, I surely do."

"So you ain't Secesh?"

"No. Are you?"

"No."

"Good. I'm a Union man to the bone. My grandfather fought redskins and British to see the United States of America brung into being, and I'm loyal clear through."

"I feel the same. Most folks in these mountains do. Same's true in East Tennessee—I guess I ain't telling you nothing you don't already know, Greeley—though there's a good number of Confederates around, too. The newspaper in Greeneville is leaning Confederate. But a lot of the people, 'specially out in the counties, they're strong Union."

"God bless them all, then, because we'll need them."

"Greeley, let me ask you about Joe, and going after Sloat, and all that. If Joe does want to, should I do it?"

"Why you asking me?"

"Because I covet your opinion."

"Well, Sam, it may cause Joe to call you something you don't want to be called, but I wouldn't do it if I was you. These here are different and new times. Men have to follow law, even in the mountains. If they don't, well, then there *ain't* no law and we're no more than savages." He paused. "Besides, the chances are good that you'd just get yourself killed. Sloat's nobody to mess with. Let the law handle him. If they can't, *then* maybe it would be up to you and Joe. But not to start off, no sir."

"That's my own thinking," Sam said. "Thank you, Greeley. I'll do it just that way, if the matter should come up."

"I hope that Wilton makes it through and gets well."

"So do I. He's been like my father. Just like Hannibal Deacon in Greeneville is now. Hannibal's who I work for. Wilton set me up with him because Hannibal's a friend of his."

"Sounds like a good situation."

"How about you, Greeley? You like living in Carter County?"

"I do, and I'll like it even better once I'm married."

"Married! You're getting married again?"

"If she says yes, I am. I aim to ask her as soon as I'm home."

Sam recalled that Greeley had been married once before. According to Wilton, Greeley's wife had been a slip of a girl he had hitched up with when he was hardly more than a boy himself. She had died in childbirth, the child dying, too. Wilton had said that Greeley took it harder than most and swore never to marry again. Shortly after that, he moved to Tennessee, a lonely and sad man, though his good nature often hid the evidence of it. Greeley also had sorrow in his background beyond the death of a wife. He had lost a sister and two brothers in a cabin fire during his childhood, and his father was killed a year later in a hunting accident said to be the fault of Greeley's only surviving sibling, a younger brother named Thatcher. He had dropped his rifle, simple as that, and the ball had found his father, who lingered in suffering for three days before dying. Whispers among the mountain people had it that Greeley's widowed mother lost her sense in her grief and held the accident against little Thatcher, whom Greeley had to protect from abusive treatment for a long time thereafter. Eventually Thatcher was sent out of the mountains and up to a small town in New York to finish his raising in the home of a cousin of his father. Sam had heard that Thatcher had become a newspaper correspondent in New York City and was doing quite well for himself, wandering about the nation at newspaper expense and writing travel stories. It was perhaps no accident that one area where Thatcher Brown had not paid a journalistic visit was his native Carolina mountain country. Too many painful memories among these ridges and valleys, Sam figured.

Sam was pleased to hear Greeley was thinking of going back on his pledge of perpetual bachelorhood. He figured Greeley would make a good husband for any woman. He was a well-liked man still in his prime, cheerful and friendly despite the losses life had handed him, and though Sam would never say it to Greeley or anyone else, Greeley had been quite a boyhood inspiration to him before he moved to Tennessee. Through Greeley Brown he had come to see that the mountains could belong to a man without the man belonging to them. Greeley was one of those rare individuals who was, as Sam had come to think of it, "bigger than the mountains." Wilton had wanted Sam to be that way, not tied for life to these isolating ridges and peaks; thanks to Hannibal Deacon, that scenario had come about.

He knew that most mountain folk weren't like Greeley and himself in that regard. The mountains overwhelmed them, hemming them in, blocking the world from their eyes, making them turn in and in and then in some more, until they became captives of the mountains themselves, unable to break free. Here in these wild hills there were people who, like Dabney Sloat, had never set foot elsewhere. Many were born and lived and someday would die within the same little world. They would know every tree within miles, every twist of the mountain stone and every curve of the creeks, every whorl and crevice and shadow pattern on the logs that made the walls they had studied as infants and would study again as they lay on their deathbeds—but they would never know what they might have seen if they had just let themselves look beyond the hills.

Such people clung to the land they possessed, and which possessed them. In most cases that land had been claimed by an ancestor, and probably wrested through violence, or treaty, or both, from the hands of the Indians. Once claimed, it remained in one family, passing from one generation to the next. These mountaineers were as rooted as ancient oaks. They weren't going anywhere. And even when they were dead, they would lie in the same family soil until their bodies decayed and they became part of the land itself, in the most literal sense. Such might have been the life and eventual death of Sam Colter, had it not been for the liberating influence of his uncle and Hannibal Deacon.

"Well, who is it you're going to marry, Greeley?"

"Her name is Martha. Martha Lou Fellers. Lives near the Carter Depot. Her pap farms, does blacksmithing work. She's been married once before, but her husband died. Just up and fell over across his plow one day, and left her widowed."

"She have children?"

"No. But if she marries me, I'll make every effort to give her a houseful."

"All the best to you, Greeley. I hope she says yes."

"Thank you. You got you a lady, Sam?"

Across Sam's mind flashed the image of Amy Deacon's face. Pretty enough in reality, it was enhanced to goddesslike perfection in his mental vision. "Well . . . no. Not really."

But Greeley was perceptive and read his expression. "One you have a shine to, though, eh?"

"Maybe so."

"I wish you luck with her."

"Thank you. Likely I'd need a lot of luck to catch her eye. A lot of luck and maybe a new face."

"Women care less about looks than men do. Lucky for men, huh?"

"I don't know. This girl sits in church with a fellow who looks like one of them statues of naked men you see in the books."

"Sits in church naked, does he?" Greeley grinned and took another bite of pork.

"Greeley, I swear, you ain't changed a bit. Always joshing."

They finished eating, and Greeley produced a pipe and tobacco. He gave Sam a smoke, then took one himself, and they talked more about the terrible thing that had happened to Wilton. Then the subject turned again to war.

"Greeley, you figure to become a soldier?"

"I don't know. If I have to be. Don't want to, but it may be my duty."

Sam was thoughtful a few moments. "Greeley . . . I don't know if I could ever kill nobody. Not even in war."

"Well, maybe it's something a man is able to do when he has to, even if he can't see it beforehand."

"I don't want to be a soldier. I don't want to have to shoot at folks." *Or get shot at myself,* he thought, but without speaking it.

"There's others ways to serve without being a straight-out soldier."

"What do you mean?"

"These mountains are full of Union folk, Sam. I have a feeling that before this is over there'll be plenty of reason for them to want to leave. Some already are. Some'll want to go fight for Lincoln. Some'll just want to be away from here, where it'll be safer for them and their families. But if the rebs try to make it hard to leave—and they will—it'll mean escaping by way of the mountains. Folks doing that will need guides."

"I reckon they would."

"I believe I'm well-suited to guide folk. Come to think of it, you might be, too. You know these mountains well. Not only in Carolina, but Tennessee, too, and you have to pass through Tennessee to get into Kentucky."

"You really believe Union folk will be leaving in big numbers?"

"Whole herds of them. Stampeders everywhere. You wait and see."

They relaxed quietly a bit longer, then went out and fed grain to the horses from the small supplies they had carried with them. They brought in their bedrolls and spread them on the floor near the fire. Even in early summer the mountains had a nighttime chill, especially in the wake of a drenching storm.

Sam thought about what Greeley had said as he fell asleep that night. The rain abated to a steady patter, peppering the leaky cabin roof and sizzling in the fireplace. Greeley's talk of becoming a guide for stampeders touched a responsive chord in Sam, who had already done plenty of surreptitious guiding on his own on Hannibal's behalf, spiriting escaped slaves to free soil—not that he was about to reveal that to Greeley. One didn't talk about the Underground Railroad to most anybody.

Maybe I could be a Union guide, too. Maybe I could help Greeley. Guiding refugees was something he could do well.

He rolled over in his blankets, staring at the banked fire, and thought deep thoughts far into the night.

Chapter 17

Sam Colter stood beside his uncle's bed, hardly recognizing the man upon it. Wilton Colter lay pale and listless, staring up with eyes that did not see. A bandage covered the left side of his head, hiding the ghastly wound that had made a living corpse of him. Sam wondered how it could be, and why, that Wilton Colter had survived the shooting at all. Surely death would have been preferable to this condition.

"He ain't said a word since it happened, and I don't expect he'll speak ever again," Joe Colter said to his brother. "I was relieved at the first that he lived. Now I don't feel that way."

"Joe, can he hear us talking?"

"No. I'm sure now he can't. Lord knows I've spent enough time speaking into his ear, trying to get some motion out of him, some finger wiggle or twitch of the eyebrow. Nothing's happened. Wilton is as close to dead as a man can get without being dead. The bullet went right through the side of his skull and lodged in that wall yonder. I've already covered the bullet hole in the wall. It plagued me to have to see it."

Sam wanted to speak, but no words emerged. His eyes grew wet and he turned his head away so Joe wouldn't see.

"Don't be ashamed of tears, Sam. I've shed plenty of them since this happened."

Sam collected himself nonetheless. "What will happen now?"

"For the moment, nothing but waiting for Wilton to travel on. I believe he'll have his time soon, though you can't know. Sometimes folks go on for years like this."

"What about the hotel, the café?"

"Closed up for now. I'll run them myself later, I reckon. They'll pass on to me, you know, by terms of the will. Wilton showed me that himself years ago."

"To you?"

"Yes . . . but don't be fretful. He's leaving you a spot of money, instead of property. You know why, don't you? Because he figured property might make you come back to Marshall and stay. He never wanted you staying here. He always said you were better suited to life out there." Joe gave a general wave of his hand, his expression hard to read. Sam knew that Joe had never understood him or his desire to build a life beyond what was close to home.

Out there, Joe had said. Typical mountaineer's way of viewing the rest of the world, and Joe was truly a mountaineer. He was one with this lush land of mists and ridges.

Sam said, "Seems wrong, talking about Wilton like he's already dead."

"He is already dead, for all purposes. Look at him, Sam. He'll never be back with us like he was. Thanks to Sloat."

"You don't have proof it was Sloat, Joe."

"Who else would it have been? What other enemy did Wilton Colter have? Everybody else thought the world of him. Sloat's the only one who had a thing against him, all for things that happened years ago if they happened at all. Sloat did this, and I intend he'll pay."

Here it comes, Sam thought. "By way of the law?"

"By way of the feud law. The law that no man ever wrote and no man can unwrite. That's the law Sloat believes in, and that's the law we'll see him punished by."

Sam did not reply. Joe's words had just confirmed the

warning given both by Hannibal Deacon and Greeley Brown. Sam did not miss the fact that Joe had indicated both of them, as brothers, would be involved in seeing Sloat recompensed. So far everything was falling out just as he had anticipated.

For now the matter went no further. Sam remained at Wilton's bedside. Joe left, tending to whatever business there was at a hotel and café that had been closed since Wilton's shooting. Cora came along after a time and took over the tending, and Sam took a long, thoughtful walk around Marshall.

The next two days passed in a sort of haze for him. Joe talked more about going after Sloat, even began gathering ammunition. He did not ask Sam if he intended to come along; he assumed it. Sam kept his silence, intimidated by the surety of his brother's preparations and attitude. He knew the only reason Joe had not already set off on his vengeance quest was that he didn't want to leave with Wilton lingering between death and life. Meanwhile, the people of Marshall brought food and words of encouragement and prayer. The Colter brothers accepted it all in somber resignation to the inevitable.

Surprisingly, Wilton did seem to get better the fourth day after Sam's arrival. He moved his eyes, made noises in his throat. Cora was thrilled, believing he was about to come around fully, but Sam had his doubts. By now he had changed the dressings on Wilton's wound many times and knew how bad it was.

On the fifth day, Wilton spoke. He said only one word: Sloat. Joe was there when it happened and was a man vindicated; his fury redoubled and he talked incessantly of seeing Sloat dead for his crime. Sam still held to his determination not to be involved in punishing Sloat, but he had not yet dared to tell Joe. It was keeping him awake at night, worrying.

The sixth day, Wilton Colter died. It was a quiet passing that occurred with nothing dramatic to herald its approach. Wilton Colter simply drew in a final breath and was gone.

The funeral drew a large crowd, was lengthy, difficult, and capped by a graveside service conducted by a preacher who warned that there would be far more funerals to come before long, that a wicked rebellion was arising in the nation. Sam left feeling very low and alone, grieving for his lost uncle and knowing with dread that he could not put off any longer telling Joe that he wanted no part of chasing after Sloat.

The subject did not arise that night, to Sam's relief. The next morning he got up, ready to give the dreaded word, but before he could a letter arrived. It was from Hannibal Deacon and said that Lena had suffered a stroke and was very ill; Sam should return at once to Greeneville if he wished to see her. The letter did not speak directly of death, but it was strongly implied.

With letter in hand, Sam went to Joe. "I'm going to have to leave, Joe. Mrs. Deacon is sick. Maybe deathly sick. I can't stay. She's been like my mother."

"Like your mother? And wasn't it Wilton who was like a father to you and me both? You can't leave now. It's time you and me went after Sloat."

Sam summoned his strength and made himself say the dreaded words. "I'm not going after Sloat."

The look on Joe's face was indescribable. Sam's will shriveled and grew small. He qualified his statement. "Not while Lena Deacon is sick."

Immediately he was ashamed, knowing he was merely seizing on Lena's illness as a conveniently timed justification for a decision he would have made anyway.

Joe didn't give the excuse credence in any case. Iron-cold eyes locked on his brother's face, he said: "You leave, Sam Colter, and every step you take you tread on Wilton's grave."

"Don't talk to me that way, Joe. I'm doing what I have to do. And don't you go off after Sloat while I'm gone. You leave him to the law."

"You're a coward, Sam. I never thought I'd have to say that about any Colter. But it's true. You're a damned coward, running from your duty because you're scared."

One part of Sam wanted to rise and with his fists show Joe Colter that he was not in fact a coward at all. He wanted to tell him about the dangerous days and nights he had spent in the company of fleeing slaves, hiding in huts and safe houses, and sometimes in roadside brush while dangerous men rode by, their eyes sharp for refugee slaves. He might have his fears, but he knew he had proven himself to be no coward time and again along the invisible tracks of the Underground Railroad. Yet the very secrecy of that freedom route made it impossible for him to say what needed saying. Though Wilton had raised them both to disbelieve in slavery, Joe held tight to the typical mountaineer view that black men and women were inherently inferior, beings to be despised even if not enslaved.

So Sam said the only thing he could. "I'm no coward. I owe Hannibal and Lena Deacon too much to go off on some wild vengeance hunt while she may be dying, that's all."

Joe ground and popped his teeth under his rough beard. He had done that as long as Sam had known him, whenever he was angry.

"Tell me the truth, brother: Would you have gone with me after Sloat if that letter hadn't come?"

Sam faltered, wanting to speak the truth—but he couldn't, not in the heat of that glaring, judgmental face. "You know I would have, Joe."

"No," Joe said, shaking his head. "I don't. I heard you say just now I should leave Sloat to the law. That's coward talk, brother. It ain't the law who owes a reckoning to Dab Sloat. It's me and you."

"I have to go back to Greeneville, Joe. That's all I can say about it."

"Then you'll come back, will you, and go after Sloat with me?"

Sam had hoped Joe wouldn't ask that question. He could not answer. Joe looked at him and shook his head like Sam was something contemptible and small.

"It don't matter. I wouldn't have waited on you no-how. Sloat's gone unpaid long enough. You go back to Tennessee. I'm going after him alone."

"Don't do it, Joe."

"Why the dear devil not? I'll not be a coward, like you! I'll not turn and run tail-tucked from my duty!"

"He'll kill you, Joe. Then who is avenged?"

"What's happened to you, Sam? Whatever became of honor? Whatever happened to doing right by them who've raised you?"

"I can't do a thing for Wilton now. Neither can you. But I can go be with the folks who's give me a home and living and the chance to make something of myself. That's what I owe to honor right now, Joe."

Joe's narrowed eyes studied him for the longest, most discomforting time. "When your inheritance money comes free, I'll have it sent to you." He turned away and began to stride off, then turned again. "Sam, if you do leave here—don't come back. You understand me? You run away, and you're my brother no more."

No knife could have cut Sam more deeply.

When Sam began his frantic ride back across the mountains to Greeneville, he did so with tears on his face. He cried for Wilton Colter and out of fear of what would happen to Lena Deacon. But mostly he cried for Joe, the brother who would be his brother no more. And he cried for himself, one condemning word ringing in his mind, not losing its force even though he tried to deny its validity.

Coward.

Hannibal Deacon home, Greeneville

"It's apoplexy, Sam. So the doctor says. It struck her out of the blue. She collapsed at the top of the stairs and fell all the way down. That's why she's so bruised."

"Mr. Deacon, will she—"

"She'll live, Sam. She'll live," Hannibal said quickly, not letting Sam finish the question. He ran his hand through his graying hair. "She has to live. She must live."

Sam didn't have to inquire further to know that the situation was not hopeful. He felt an overwhelming sadness. He had just lost an uncle, and, in another way, a brother. Now it seemed he might lose the beloved Lena Deacon as well.

Fearing he might cry and shame himself, he excused himself quickly and went into Hannibal's yard. Wandering about, he wound up beside the grave of Hannibal and

Lena's long-dead daughter. He looked at the tombstone, which heightened his morbid mood. He had always thought it odd that the Deacons had buried their daughter so close to their home, where they would constantly see the grave and be reminded of their loss. He wondered if Lena would soon be buried beside her child.

He heard someone behind him. Turning, he saw Amy. On the verge of tears, he swallowed hard and forced a smile. Oddly, he didn't feel his usual burst of shyness in her presence. Other emotions ran strongly and had overwhelmed bashfulness for the moment.

"Sam, I wanted to tell you how sorry I was to hear about your uncle," Amy said. "He raised you, Hannibal told me."

"Yes. He was a good man. I thought of him sort of like I think of Hannibal now. And Lena."

Amy nodded. "I've begun to feel the same way about them. I don't really have a parent at the moment. My father has cast me aside."

Sam thought about his own severed relationship with his brother. "It's hard when your own people do such a thing to you. My brother, he doesn't have any use for me now."

"Why?"

"He wanted me and him to go after the man who killed my uncle. I told him I wouldn't do it, that the law ought to deal with him, not us. He told me I was a coward, and that if I left Marshall and came home, I needn't come back."

"I'm sorry. I didn't know."

"I haven't talked about it. Not even to Hannibal; he's got enough to think about with Lena being sick. I ain't sure I'd talk to him about it anyway. Ever since it happened, I've been wondering if maybe Joe was right and I really am . . ."

"A coward?" Amy finished for him. "Oh, Sam, I know you aren't a coward. No coward guides runaways on the Railroad. No coward could have helped Rufus like you did. You're as courageous a man as I know."

Warmth filled Sam and showed itself in a blush across his lean face. *She called me courageous . . . called me a man.* He smiled just a little. "Thank you for saying that."

Amy looked back at the house. "I hope Lena gets better."

"So do I."

"Hannibal says he's going to stay at her side until she's well."

Even in his despondency, Sam was finding it thrilling to be talking so easily with Amy. "I'd expect he would . . . I reckon I'll be running the store for him, then."

"Yes. And he's asked me to help—I hope you won't mind it."

Mind it? Sam couldn't have heard better news, and good news was something he could use a dose of at the moment. "Why, of course not. I'll be glad for your company."

"You'll have to tell me what to do. I've never done store work."

"It ain't hard. I'll let you help with sales and such. I'll handle anything to do with the commission agency. That takes a bit more experience."

"I'll do the best I can."

When Sam walked back a little later toward his room above the Deacon store, he struggled not to grin. It wouldn't be seemly, walking through town with a big smile with so many people knowing that Lena Deacon was sick and that he himself had lost an uncle. But it was hard not to smile.

Amy was going to be with him every day, working within the same walls, under the same roof. It was too good to believe.

Fortune had smiled on Sam Colter. The way things had gone for him lately, it seemed to him it was about time.

On a western North Carolina mountainside

Joe Colter stood outside the remote cabin, rifle in hand and an expression of fury on his face. Dabney Sloat's cabin was empty! Sloat had fled! And not just for the moment, it appeared. There were no weapons inside, no clothing, no food. Sloat and his wife obviously had vacated this place and gone elsewhere, if not for good, at least for the long term.

It was terribly anticlimactic. Traveling here, locating and reaching the cabin, preparing himself for the experience of killing Sloat or being killed . . . it hadn't been easy. And then to find this!

"The bastard has run off," he said aloud. "He knowed I'd be coming for him, I'll betcha. He knowed it, and he run off."

He paced around the barren dirt expanse in front of the cabin, which was hidden away in a high hollow with ridges rising almost all around. It was the very kind of place he would have expected human vermin like Dabney Sloat to occupy. It fit the character of rats, after all, to hide.

The more Joe Colter paced, the more furious he grew. Did Dab Sloat believe he could escape punishment by fleeing? Joe Colter would show him different! There might be one coward in the Colter clan, but it wasn't Joe. He'd find where Sloat had gone, somehow, and he'd track him down and mash him like the roach he was.

But how? Sloat might have gone anywhere.

Joe vented his frustration to some measure by burning the cabin down. A little well-placed kindling, some flares of gunpowder, and he got the cabin to burning quite well. He stood back, enjoying the baking heat and the sight of the cabin being reduced to cinders. It was nearly dark by the time the fire had mostly burned itself out. Too late to head home. Joe went back to the place he had left his horse, rode the homeward direction a mile or so, then found a good place to camp.

He slept comfortably that night, accustomed to rough conditions and hard ground. When he awakened the next morning, he sat up with a bolt of excitement, realizing abruptly where Sloat had probably gone.

That wife of his was Cherokee, and as Joe had heard it, her father was still living. What was his name? It slipped his mind for the moment . . . but he did recall having heard that the old redskin resided on a high ridge in the Cherokee country, a ridge that was named for him. . . .

Joe Colter smiled. He had remembered. *Skaantee.* The old man was named Skaantee, and lived on Skaantee's Ridge.

"Went to pay call on your pappy-in-law, did you, Sloat?" he said to the forest. "I believe I'll make the same journey. If you're there, Sloat, I'll find you. And if I do, you'll never leave that ridge. I vow you that. You'll never set foot off that ridge again."

Joe broke camp without pausing for breakfast. He was too excited to eat just now. He had a journey to make, and a man to kill.

Chapter 18

Greeneville, Tennessee

Sam Colter shaved his face carefully by the light of an east-facing window, squinting into a tiny standing mirror and trying to avoid nicking himself. He had never enjoyed shaving and usually got by with two or three shaves a week, and even those he would gladly dispense with had not nature cursed him with bristly, multihued whiskers that made the fashionable full beard of the day no desirable option for him. Besides, he couldn't grow a decent full beard even if he wanted to. The one time he had tried, his chin sprouted like a fertile, tricolored field while his moustache area remained a barren and growthless desert.

Sam finished his shave and washed the soap from his face in the basin, noting to himself that this was the first time in his life he had been so concerned about grooming. Of course, it was also the first time he had ever had inspiration to do so—a beautiful, pulse-quickening reason who would greet him with a smile in mere minutes down in the store below his room. He was eager for it. Recombing his hair for the fourth time, he smoothed his shirt with his hands and stuck a piece of mint candy into his mouth to freshen his breath. He gave no thought to breakfast; his appetite was much lessened this week.

He was almost ruined from working beside Amy
Deacon. The experience had been as gratifying and exciting
as he anticipated, but he hadn't expected it to render him so
worthless. He was now ineffectual at everything he tried.
Didn't seem to hear a word customers said to him and
couldn't care less what they had to say anyway. All this distraction was novel to a young man who had always striven
to be the best worker he could, and would have worried him
if it were possible to worry with Amy nearby.

But worry, like everything sorrowful or bad, faded into
unimportance when she was close. In her presence he forgot
all the things that had distressed him before: his uncle's
death, his disagreement and estrangement from his brother,
even his concern that maybe he was a coward, like Joe said.
Forgotten were politics and war. He had even substantially
ceased to think and worry about the health of Lena Deacon,
who had not improved at all since her apoplectic attack.

No bad things could penetrate his bewitched mind. Sam
Colter was in love, and falling in deeper every moment he
was near Amy Deacon.

What was more, he believed that just maybe she held
some reciprocating feelings—perhaps not as strong as his
own, but at least a liking and respect for him. Things she had
said, the way she smiled at him . . . he struggled not to make
too much of such small things, yet dared to hope despite
himself. Apparently, in piloting her beloved Rufus northward, he had earned more respect and admiration than he'd
realized. His ego, never large, was growing fast. It felt good.

He checked himself in the mirror one last time, scratching
at his teeth, rubbing out the corners of his eyes, digging at his
ears to make sure they weren't waxy, tilting up his nostrils to
see if any nasal hair needed clipping—he went through the
full range of undignified hygienic rituals practiced by the
human male about to be ushered into the presence of his
beloved. It was never this hard to get ready for work before.

He stepped out onto the landing at the top of the exterior
staircase and looked up and down the street. It was a lovely
morning, the kind that made him curse the prospect of a day's
work indoors when the fields and forests beckoned beneath

an arching blue sky. Young townsman though he now was, Sam Colter had the mountains in his blood and eternally felt their call, especially on such days as this. At least this time there was extra compensation for a day at work. There was Amy.

He descended the stairs and circled around to the front of the store, then stopped.

Amy was on the porch, standing with arms wrapped tightly around herself and tears in her eyes.

He did not even have to ask what had happened.

They hung the store with black crepe, mourned and prayed over the remains of Lena Deacon in the same parlor where Amy had received her interrogations from Hannibal, and then memorialized her in a funeral service in the sanctuary of the Presbyterian Church. They buried her beside her daughter in the yard of the Deacon home, and Hannibal stood by, tears streaming down his wide face. He looked old and tired, and Sam could find nothing to say to him. Amy stood nearby; beside her was Pleadis Mundy. Sam watched him from the corner of his eye and despised him—but noted at the same time that Amy's posture and manner revealed no affection for the handsome young man. She seemed alone in the midst of the crowd of mourners.

Sam looked at the grave. It was hard to believe Lena was dead. She had always seemed strong and healthy. He became all the more aware of mortality. His uncle, and now Lena . . . Death seemed to him like a vulture hovering above, descending without warning, and with alarming frequency.

Perhaps, he thought, *it smells war and is growing hungry.* It was a dark thought and made him shudder.

The black crepe soon came down from the front of the Deacon store and life resumed. Hannibal returned to work, but to Sam's pleasure, Amy remained as well, working in the afternoons and spending the rest of her time tending to Hannibal's household affairs.

Hannibal was thoroughly changed. Gone were the smiles and joviality. He seldom spoke and seemed distracted all the time. Sam, sobered by all that had happened, broke through his own love-inspired complacency and compensated for Hannibal's ineffectiveness by working twice as hard.

Sam wondered if his mentor's devotion to his beloved Union would lose or maintain intensity because of Lena's death. He had begun to suspect the former until Hannibal announced that he would be making a journey to Knoxville to attend a Unionist convention on the thirtieth of the month, where efforts would be made toward trying to keep Tennessee from seceding. The Secession matter was to come before Tennessee's voters again on the eighth of June, in reaction to Lincoln's call for volunteer soldiers. Tennessee's governor was taking the stand that Tennessee would send no soldiers to fight for an aggressive North, but would gladly raise any number to defend its homeland, should Federal soldiers pass through Tennessee in an invasion of the Confederacy.

"Is there any hope for us at all if Tennessee secedes?" Amy asked Hannibal.

"The only hope would be a division of the state. Perhaps East Tennessee can sever itself, remain Unionist . . . I don't know. It will be one of the matters discussed at the convention."

"I want to go with you," Amy said.

"No," Hannibal replied, so firmly that even stalwart Amy dared not argue. "I'll need you here, helping Sam with the store."

Hannibal returned to his house early that day, feeling tired and too full of grief to work. After he was gone, Amy said to Sam: "I'd like to be at that convention. It's hard, not being able to take part in such things. Sometimes I wish I were a man."

I for one am mighty glad you ain't. Trying to be encouraging, Sam said, "Maybe the whole state will vote to stay in the Union, like before."

"I doubt the vote will go so well," Amy replied. "Public sentiment seems to have turned toward the Confederacy, especially in the middle and west of the state. Or so

Hannibal says." She stopped, frowning. "What in the world is that ruckus?"

Sam had heard it, too—a wild horse squeal out on the street, then a man's shout: "Watch where you're going, man!"

Sam went toward the front of the store, Amy following. Squinting through the front window into the brighter outside light, Sam assessed the scene on the street and said, "Looks like a man's nearly been trampled by a horse."

"Great merciful heaven!" Amy whispered. "Is that—"

"Oh, don't worry. He ain't hurt, Amy. See? He's coming this way." Sam chuckled. "Look at him—I believe he's skinnier than I am. And that's the reddest hair I've ever seen." He glanced over at her and was surprised to see that her eyes were wide and her face slightly pale. "Amy, are you all right?"

"Oh, it *is* him! I thought it was!"

She bolted around Sam and ran to the door, energetically throwing it open and startling the already alarmed near-victim of the horse, whose equally unnerved rider was heading on down the street toward the little clapboard-covered log building where Andrew Johnson had operated his tailor shop for many years. The rider cast a dark glance back at the carpetbag-toting man who had almost walked into the horse's path. Amy rushed out the door and threw her arms around the man, who dropped the carpetbag, stumbled back and almost fell.

"What the devil!" Sam mumbled.

Outside on the porch, Amy and the redheaded man, whose expression had gone from one of bewildered fright to one of happiness as soon as he saw who had embraced him, talked fervently. Amy hugged him again and he patted her shoulders, beaming. Unnoticed, Sam glowered at the man through the window, overwhelmed with curiosity and actually jealous that this fellow, whoever he was, had stolen all of Amy's attention. *I sure wish she'd hug me like that.* Then another thought: *Lord! I wonder if that's her father?*

Amy pulled away from the man and stuck her head back through the door. "Sam, I have to go home. Can you stay and close the store alone? Oh, thank you! I do appreciate it."

"Amy, wait—who is . . . what's going on here?"

"An old and dear friend of mine is here from Knoxville, Sam. It's Horatio Eaton!"

Eaton . . . the abolitionist? Publisher of the widely read and mostly hated *Reason's Torch*? Sam looked at the newcomer in a fresh light, remembering that this was the man for whose journal Amy had written in secret—the very offense that had caused Dr. George Deacon to banish her to Greeneville. *I reckon that in a way I owe you a debt of thanks, Mr. Eaton,* Sam thought. *If not for you, Amy probably would have never been exiled from Knoxville, and I'd have never known her.*

He watched them stride together up the street and around the corner, heading toward the Deacon house on Main Street. He wished he could go with them, not only because he liked to be with Amy as much as possible, but also because he was quite curious about what had brought Eaton to Greeneville. Given Eaton's former association with Amy, Sam supposed the visit had something to do with her. Whatever it was, he hoped it wouldn't be anything that would take her away. The way he had come to feel about her, he wasn't sure he could stand that.

They sat in the parlor. Hannibal had changed to his house robe after returning home and had dressed again very hurriedly when Amy arrived with her unexpected and notorious visitor, and he now looked very rumpled. He had apparently shed some tears while alone, because his face, already broad, looked puffy and blotched. He made for quite an odd-looking host as he sat heavily in his big overstuffed chair.

No more odd, however, than his visitor, a man he had never met, though he read his writings extensively. Eccentric and unusual at any time, Horatio Eaton was all wild red hair, twitches, sputters, fidgets, and fragmented sentences spoken either too softly or too loudly. He was obviously edgy, perhaps fully terrified. He sat, or rather, twisted about, on a chair that creaked with every movement, wringing together hands with nails chewed to the quick. It was troubling merely to watch him.

And more so to hear what he had to say. He got to it with few preliminaries, being in no condition to make small talk.

"I've been threatened, Mr. Deacon. Only yesterday it happened, and I'll admit to you that I'm frightened out of my wits."

"Frankly, Mr. Eaton, I would have expected that a man who has taken the controversial public stands you have would have received threats before," Hannibal replied. Though he obviously was trying to put spirit into the conversation, he sounded listless. As Amy watched Hannibal and saw his manner, the absence of Lena was palpable in the little room.

"I have, sir. It is indeed part and parcel with the nature of my work." Eaton paused for a couple of seconds to nervously gnaw a thumbnail. "But threats are something you learn to interpret. You can tell when they are truly serious, and most I've received aren't. Just trifling. The threat I got yesterday was very serious, and Mr. Deacon . . . it was made by your brother."

Amy almost came out of her chair. "Father threatened you?"

"Yes, Amy, he did. To my face. And he was armed. I found him in my yard, carrying a pistol, and he told me that if I didn't leave him alone, I would be dead. It was obvious he had been there outside my house since sometime in the night before. Me inside asleep, him out there with that pistol . . . brrrr!" He shivered visibly and gnawed his thumbnail again.

"What did George mean about you leaving him alone?"

Eaton shifted postures again and looked toward the floor. "This, uh . . . this is difficult for me to say, considering the kinships to Dr. Deacon represented here. The fact is, Mr. Deacon, under the encouragement of the former editor of the *Advocate*, I've been doing some investigation of the murder of Charlie Douglass, and—"

Amy did rise this time. "Charlie Douglass was murdered?"

"Why, yes, he was," Eaton said. "You hadn't heard?"

"No."

"Who is Charlie Douglass?" Hannibal asked. "The name is familiar."

"He's a vagrant of Knoxville," Amy replied. "A rather loudmouthed Unionist who enjoyed harassing my father in public. He's the one who revealed all the things at that rally that got me in trouble with Father." She peered closely at Eaton. "Mr. Eaton, are you about to say that you believe my father had something to do with Charlie Douglass's murder?"

The abolitionist looked sorrowful. "I'm afraid so, Amy, I'm sorry."

Amy sank back into her chair, stomach suddenly aching and burning, her mind echoing back words Rufus had spoken to her: *Your father, I believe he kilt a man once. . . .* And if he killed one man, he might have killed another, particularly one he hated like he had hated Charlie Douglass.

Hannibal, though, bristled slightly at the accusation. He spoke coolly. "Perhaps you should begin at the beginning, Mr. Eaton."

"Yes. Yes, I should." Eaton gnawed a nail, twisted in his seat. "All of you know very well, of course, what happened at that Secession rally back in November, how Charlie Douglass humiliated Dr. Deacon, revealed that Amy had been writing for me in secret, and so on. Well, after Amy left Knoxville, *The Secession Advocate* ceased publication. Vanished like smoke. Dr. Deacon fired his editor, and without Amy helping, he must have found he couldn't write. Such seems to be the conclusion most have drawn, at least. In any case, Dr. Deacon withdrew from public life. Stayed closed up in his house up on Secession Hill. Not only ceased his newspaper, but ceased his medical practice as well. They say he was drinking heavily . . . there were rumors he was behaving oddly, as if the strain and embarrassment were taking a toll on his mental condition. I don't know. I'm no judge of lunacy—"

" 'Lunacy' is a harsh word, sir," Hannibal said icily. The matter was delicate to a man whose father had spent his final days in an asylum, and who suspected his own brother might be following a similar grim course.

"Yes, I'm sorry, sir. I should watch my words more

closely. In any case, Dr. Deacon ceased to be a public man. Eventually he took a town vagrant in at Secession Hill. Gave him room, board, and no doubt lots of liquor. The vagrant's name was Ben Scarlett."

"Ben Scarlett!" Amy exclaimed. "I know that man. He helped me hang broadsides for the very rally where . . . where everything fell apart. Father took *him* into his home?"

"Yes. I see your quizzical look, Amy, but believe me, I couldn't explain it any more than anyone else. It was a very curious situation, to say the least. That's when the rumors about Dr. Deacon's lunacy . . . Dr. Deacon's mental state, I should say, began to circulate at their strongest. People began talking about—and I apologize for this phrase—the 'Madman of Secession Hill.' Mad or not, you must admit it was bizarre for a noted man like Doc Deacon to take a town drunk into his own home. The Unionist camp had quite a spree of spreading tales and speculation—the discreditation of such a noted Secessionist as Doc Deacon was no small coup, you see. In any case, none of this involved me except to the extent that it was I who had published Amy's secret writings, but I knew that surely Dr. Deacon must especially despise me, and I admit I had the occasional fearful thought about what he might do to me if ever he had the chance to retaliate. I . . . I'm not a brave man, you must understand. Bold at times, when it comes to my cause, but not brave. I'm ashamed to say it, but it's true."

"Tell us about this Douglass murder," Hannibal urged.

"Yes. That was earlier this year. In . . . let me see, in May. Right about the time I received a letter signed with the name Ben Scarlett. It threatened my life. It was worrisome, but I didn't take it too seriously. There was something odd about it. . . . I kept the threats in mind, believe me, but I didn't really think anything would happen. Why, after all, would anyone write a threatening letter and then sign his own name to it if he really intended to go through with the threats? I recognized Ben Scarlett's name as that of the drunkard who was living with Doc Deacon on Secession Hill, and figured he must have written it while he was drunk, maybe after listening to Dr. Deacon complaining about me making his daughter 'betray' him, or whatever. The letter also mentioned Charlie Douglass's name, in no flattering terms, let me tell you. And another thing about that letter . . . it didn't seem the kind of letter someone like Ben Scarlett would write. It was too neatly written, spelled correctly for the most part, but with a few misspellings thrown in that didn't have an authentic feel to them. Like they were deliberate.

"Shortly after that letter came, Charlie Douglass was shot by an officer of the Military League during a rally in town. Not killed, just wounded. Then, just a few days later, Douglass was shot again. No one knew by whom. And this time he died—and I started to worry. What if the letter I had received was real after all, and Ben Scarlett had done the killing? The letter implied that he was angry at Charlie Douglass as well as me. What if I was to be the next one killed?

"Then . . . I found another note at my door one morning, signed with the name of Ben Scarlett, like the first one, but this time in a different handwriting, and with all kinds of misspellings and so on—the kind of letter a drunk really would write. It said that the first note I had received was a fraud, that Dr. Deacon had actually sent it and signed Scarlett's name . . . but here, let me show you. I've got both letters with me." He reached into his carpetbag and pulled out two folded papers. Spreading them open, he handed them to Hannibal. Amy rose and went to her uncle's side, peering down.

"That's my father's handwriting," she said, pointing at one of the letters.

"Is it? I expected you would confirm that. That's the first letter I received," Eaton said. "The second one, as you can see, is scribed out very differently. I believe it is from the real Ben Scarlett—who, I might add, has vanished. He hasn't been seen since about the time of Charlie Douglass's funeral."

"So your theory is that my brother sent you a threatening letter, but signed it with the name of a vagrant he had taken in . . . and then the vagrant himself caught onto the scheme, left you a second letter disavowing the first one as George's work, and claimed that George murdered this Douglass fellow and might kill you as well. Quite a theory," Hannibal said.

"I'm sorry to be the source of such terrible allegations," Eaton said.

"You've done right in coming here," Hannibal said. "Mr. Eaton, I apologize to you. You were absolutely right to use the word 'lunacy' in talking about my brother's behavior. If I reacted strongly to it, it's only because there has been some instance of that earlier in my family line, and I admit a certain sensitivity about it. And there's the fact that—I may as well confess it—I'd come to have similar thoughts about George's mental state myself." He looked at his niece. "Amy, I'm going to come clean with you. I have received one letter from your father since you came here, and it was so garbled and raving that I didn't show it to you. Instead I took that trip to Knoxville at the first of the year to see George for myself and find out what was wrong."

"I remember . . . and you came home saying that Father wasn't there and you didn't get to see him."

"It was a lie, my dear, told to spare you from worry. George *was* there. And he threatened my life right on the porch of Secession Hill."

"Threatened you!"

"That's right. I should have told you before, but I didn't want to lay the burden on you. But I came back to Greeneville glad that you were here and not there. I'm afraid that George has truly broken down. He's a dangerous man at the moment, and I'm glad you're out of his reach."

"He *is* dangerous," Horatio Eaton said after spitting out a newly chewed-off fingernail. "Remember that he was in my yard yesterday morning, threatening me with a pistol. That's when I knew the time had come for me to leave Knoxville. For that matter, to leave Tennessee. I'm going to meet a cousin of mine, in Kentucky. His name is Jonathon—a good man, right-thinking, working for . . . never mind that. I almost say too much sometimes. Suffice it to be said that I believe Tennessee's secession will come next month, and I'm not about to let myself be trapped in a seceded state with a crazed man after my life."

"I don't blame you," Hannibal said. He was actually beginning to show some of his old spark. "I believe you are wise to leave. But why did you come here?"

"To warn Amy. If Dr. Deacon hates me as much as he obviously does, then there is no assurance he might not be a threat to his own daughter. He's already rejected her and put her in exile. And there is you, too, who deserve warning, sir. It's well known in Knoxville that you, the very brother of 'Madman' Doc Deacon, have come out in favor of the Union. In fact, knowing you have declared for the Union is the only thing that made me feel free to come here and find you. If you shared your brother's point of view, I'd have been afraid to come. But come I did, and asked about on the street until someone pointed me to your store. I was so eager to get there I almost ran under a horse, and imagine my surprise when none other than Amy herself appeared at the door and—"

"Never mind that just now," Hannibal said, irritated by Eaton's rambling. "What were you saying about me needing a warning, too?"

"Oh, just that your brother is bound to be well aware of your declaration of Unionism, and no doubt resents it. If he should decide to punish you for opposing his pet cause ... well, let me just say that you might consider doing what I've been doing since yesterday morning, and carrying a pistol with you at all times." He nudged the carpetbag with his foot.

Amy went back to her chair and sank down in it, feeling broken and sad. Horatio Eaton watched her and said, "I'm sorry, Amy. This is to a large measure my fault. If I hadn't drawn you into writing for my journal, most of this, maybe all of this, would not have happened."

"I don't blame you," she said. "I made my choice freely, and I can't regret it. But I'm shocked, and astonished at myself. How could I have lived all my life with my father and not seen this violent side of him? Hannibal, Rufus told me that he beat my mother. I never knew. He told me that once he even might have murdered a man, and hidden the evidence."

Pallid and shaken by the things he had heard, Hannibal

shook his head. "George was always able to wear a mask. Even when we were boys he could hide his feelings, put on false shows, better than anyone I knew. And I saw evidence from time to time of how hard and cruel he could be. But I ignored it. It was too frightening to think about, so I just ignored it."

"Mr. Deacon," Eaton said, "far be it from me to be a fear monger, but might it be wise for you and your own family here to leave? Come north, resettle yourself before the Secession comes and the Confederacy closes the doors around us."

"I can't flee," Hannibal said. "There are things that will need doing here, should war come to Tennessee. I won't go."

"But your brother may be a danger to you."

"There will be many dangers to us all, very soon," Hannibal replied. "George will be just one more. And in any case, I'm not inclined to simply sit here, waiting for him to show himself, if that is even his intention. Better to go to him and get this dealt with than sit here fearing every noise and shadow. Otherwise I'll be worried for Amy, not to mention myself. And besides, he is still my brother. If he's not well, he'll need help."

Amy said, "But if he's dangerous—"

"He's still my brother. I owe it to him to see what state he's in and help him any way I can. I won't be careless. There's more danger of harm from him if I don't go find him. I'm sure he knows of the Union convention coming up. I'm sure he'll expect me to be there, which indeed I intend to be. I can hardly hear this kind of news about my own brother and then go all the way to Knoxville and yet not look into the matter. It would be foolish and irresponsible of me."

Amy said, "I'm going, too."

Hannibal said, "You are not going."

"He's my father! I will go!"

"You will not, and there will be no more argument about it." He said it very quietly, in that listless way in which he said most things now, but still the words carried force. Amy glowered in silence, resenting his authority.

Hannibal said, "Mr. Eaton, you said you had been investigating the question of my brother's involvement in this Douglass fellow's murder. This is based, I assume, on the allegation in the apparently authentic Ben Scarlett note?"

"Yes."

"Have you found anything further to back that allegation up?"

"A rumor . . . I was told by some of the vagrants that there was one man who said he actually saw Dr. Deacon shoot Douglass from hiding. But the man is nowhere to be found. The vagrant population moves and shifts, and this man was apparently a transient. No one has been able to attach a name to him, much less tell me where he might have gone."

"And Ben Scarlett is absent, too, you say. Well, that complicates matters. But maybe that note would be enough to have George brought in for questioning."

"You want to have him arrested?" Amy asked.

"Yes, for the sake of his safety as well as ours. If he has broken down to the point of threatening a man's life in that man's own yard, he needs to be removed from society for his own good. Mr. Eaton, would you consider going back with me to Knoxville and telling the police the origins of those notes and so on, just like you told us here?"

The abolitionist looked from face to face, mouth quivering. He began to shake more violently than ever. "I can't, sir, I can't. I'm too afraid. I'm not a brave man. My health is poor these days . . . the strain . . ."

"Very well," Hannibal said after a pause, a look in his eye that might have been veiled disdain. Eaton had done great things toward the cause of abolition, but at the moment he seemed meek and pitiful, even to Amy, who had admired him for years. "Then at least let me have the letters. I'll do the best I can without you."

"I want to go with you," Amy dared to say again.

"You'll stay here," Hannibal replied. He paused, then decided to be blunt, even painfully so. "I don't think my chances of success will be helped one bit by having you confront your father right now. That letter he wrote back to me, the one I didn't show you—he all but disowned you. As far as he is concerned, you are a traitor he wants nothing more to do with. If he sees you, it might cause serious trouble."

She turned her face away; Hannibal perceived the emotional struggle within her. He wanted to tell her not to fight, that it was permissible to cry. But to prideful Amy Deacon one did not say such things.

She won the struggle. No tears came. "Perhaps it is best I stay behind, then."

She is strong. The strongest young women I have ever known. "I believe it is, Amy. And I'm sorry."

"You have nothing to be sorry for," she said. "Good-bye, Mr. Eaton. Best of fortune to you." She left the parlor, ascended to her room, and closed herself in.

Amy was watching out her bedroom window when Eaton left about an hour later. From dish-clinking sounds she had heard below, she surmised that Hannibal had fed him.

On impulse she left her room, descended the stairs, passed through the house without encountering Hannibal, and ran outside and after Eaton. She called to him; he turned and looked surprised to see her approaching.

"Why, Amy, I thought I'd seen the last of you."

"Mr. Eaton, Horatio, I just wanted to tell you that . . ." She realized that for once Amy Deacon, the master manipulator of words, didn't know what to say. Yielding to another impulse, she went to him and quickly kissed his cheek.

"Amy . . . oh, my . . . thank you. What a kind thing to do."

"Horatio, I owe you so much. Because of you I was able to learn better what I believed and to do something about it. It's very much because of you that I was able to come here and find Hannibal. He's one of us, you know. Not just in his Unionism, but about slavery, too. Did you know?"

"No, I didn't. He's an"—Eaton glanced about and lowered his voice—"an abolitionist?"

"Yes. Very active, too. The Underground Railroad. He even helped Rufus escape."

"Praise be! I was wondering just moments ago why Rufus wasn't about today."

"You mustn't say it, of course, about the Railroad and Hannibal. It would be dangerous to him."

"Of course. Of course. Have you become involved in that effort with him?"

"I have. It was wonderful. Just wonderful."

He looked at her more deeply than he ever had before. "Amy, you are remarkable. I've never seen anyone so devoted. And so brave." He looked around again and spoke even more softly. "Might it be that there would be other ways you would be willing to serve, here in the rebelling country?"

"What do you mean?"

"I can't say much . . . I'm talking of giving service to the Union through means that would require the utmost courage and sacrifice. Ways that would be . . . important. But not safe, not safe at all."

She was chilled by his tone, but intrigued. "Yes. Oh, yes. I want to serve. I *want* to do important things. Even if they are dangerous."

"Amy, I'll be meeting my cousin Jonathon. I can tell you nothing about the specifics of his situation, but suffice it to say that he is situated to provide opportunities for important service to a select type of individual. Not my type . . . I'm far too timid. But your type—yes, yes indeed. Would you allow me to recommend your name to him?"

"What kind of 'service' are you speaking of?"

"I wish I could say. Yet I can't. Will you trust me?"

"Of course I will."

"I'll tell him about you. Recommend you. Perhaps nothing will come of it, but on the other hand . . ."

Amy longed to know more, though clearly Eaton had said all he would. She kissed his cheek again, making him blush.

"Good-bye, Horatio. God go with you."

"And you, too, my dear Amy. God go with us both, wherever we may be."

He strode off, a funny little man who mixed courage and rabbitlike timidity in the most unique way. Amy watched him go, then returned to the house. Hannibal's bedroom door was shut; she heard him moving about inside. Climbing the stairs as softly as she could, she reentered her bedroom and lay down on the bed, staring at the ceiling and wondering what was the mysterious work that Eaton had spoken of.

Chapter 19

Despite his insistence that Amy not come with him to Knoxville, Hannibal missed her as he slumped back in the rumbling train, staring out the window as he raced toward his destination. It would be gratifying at the moment to share company with someone who understood his situation like Amy did. There were plenty of men he knew around him on this same train, all Unionists bound for the Knoxville convention, but he kept apart from them and did not tell them that his journey involved more than merely attending the convention. The matter of Dr. George Deacon, the "Madman of Secession Hill," was a burden Hannibal was not free to share, a burden doubled by the grief of his recent bereavement. He gazed through soot-dirtied glass at the rolling landscape of roads, fields, hills, occasional towns, and distant mountains, and remained locked within himself, missing Lena, thinking that the world even looked different now, empty and lonely. Wherever he looked, she was not, and her absence loomed more immensely than the presence of all else.

He detrained at Knoxville and turned his eyes toward Secession Hill, clearly visible from the train station. Even over a considerable distance he saw that the yard was overgrown, the walls of the house crawling with uncontrolled ivy, the rose trellises broken down, and even the well-known SECESSION HILL sign half covered by tall, swaying weeds. The exterior of the house reflected in a frighteningly apt way the deterioration he expected to find in the person of the man living inside.

"There's where your famous brother lives, eh, Hannibal?" one of his fellow Greenevillian travelers said, coming up behind him and talking in a booming voice. "Secession Hill! One thing you must say for your brother: Wrong-headed though he may be, he's certainly put the Deacon name into the public eye! Why, the very fact he is so rabid a Secessionist only makes your support of our side all the more valuable. But your brother must be quite a man in his own way. How many of us have a house with a name everyone in the state knows, huh? Not many, no sir!" Laughing, the jovial man slapped Hannibal on the shoulder and wandered off, so enveloped in his own good cheer that he did not see that Hannibal had not responded to him at all.

"Do you have a place to stay, Hannibal?" another man called from the other end of the platform.

"I'll find a room," Hannibal replied.

"If they're in short supply, maybe we can put up together."

"Maybe so."

In fact Hannibal was determined to room alone, but it took great effort to find such quarters. The Union convention had drawn a sizable contingent of visitors to the town even beyond the usual traffic of travelers who filled the hotels and rooming houses, and Hannibal had to wander with bag in hand all the way across town until he finally found a little hotel near the East Tennessee College with a single room available. It had two beds in it, so he paid a double price to ensure no one else came along later to claim the spare bed. He wanted solitude. Once booked in, he paced about between the beds, realizing how much courage it was going to require to go face a potentially dangerous brother on Secession Hill. A brother, he reminded himself, who had already waved a shotgun at him once before.

What will I say to him? Hello, George. Good to see you. By the way, I hear you've been threatening people and mur-

dering vagrants, and maybe you and I should take a walk down to visit the local law enforcement folks. . . .

Hannibal honestly didn't know what he would say or do. He lay down on the bed to think it over and fell asleep, and when he wakened it was about suppertime and he was hungry. He left the hotel and walked to the nearest café, where he ordered a steak and vegetables and coffee. He ate slowly, dreading to finish because that would leave him with no excuse for not going to Secession Hill. He drank cup after cup of coffee and had two desserts, stretching the meal out as long as possible. He looked at the empty chair across from him and wished Lena were in it, alive and healthy and his again. *I hate death,* he thought. *I hate the loneliness and seperation it brings. God, I believe that surely man was not truly made for dying, else it wouldn't seem such an alien thing to him when it comes.*

When he left the café, he wandered very slowly through town, making himself take interest in every store window, every porch, every garden, every cemetery. Anything to delay the dreaded meeting.

Within an hour he was back in his room again, never having reached Secession Hill. His courage had failed him. He told himself he was weary from his journey—despite having napped part of the afternoon away—and would do better the next day. He would attend the convention, then go to Secession Hill. Yes, that would be the best way. Relieved at the self-imposed delay, he went to bed, read a bit from a book he had brought along, and went to sleep.

The convention the next day was fiery and intense, filled with discussion of what to do should Tennessee vote for secession on June 8. Hannibal took little part in all the talk, however, still preoccupied with his brother, and in the early afternoon he left the convention in secret, steeled his courage, said a prayer for strength, and made his way toward his brother's big house.

He strode up the walk and stood looking at the big structure. No sign of life presented itself. All of the windows were shuttered except for one in the third-story attic, and it was covered by a curtain. *Well, here I go.* He drew in a deep breath and walked up the stone steps leading up the hill to the porch.

He knocked sharply at the door, then stood back, straight and tall and trying to look confident and imposing, but not threatening. He waited for an answer, but none came. He knocked again, even more forcefully. Still no reply.

Either Dr. Deacon was not home or was hiding away inside and refusing to answer. Hannibal went to the shuttered window and tried unsuccessfully to look in through the slanted slats. He cupped his hands around his mouth and put them against the shutter.

"George? Are you there? It's Hannibal! I've come to visit you."

No reply. He called again, still without success.

"You won't get an answer."

Startled, Hannibal turned. A man stood at the base of the stone steps.

"I beg your pardon?"

"You won't get an answer. Doc Deacon don't answer the door for nobody no more." To Hannibal's surprise, the man looked up toward the attic. "That's right, ain't it, Doc! You just sit and fester in there, ashamed to face the world."

This man is drunk. "Who are you, sir?"

"My name's Lewis. Birch Lewis. Former editor and pressman for *The Secession Advocate*."

Hannibal recognized that name. This was the fellow whose indiscreet talk in the taverns had armed Charlie Douglass with the information with which he had discredited Dr. Deacon at that infamous November rally.

"Wait—are you saying that my brother's inside this house right now?"

"Your brother! I'll be! You must be the one from Greeneville . . . what is that name . . . Hannibal. Are you Hannibal Deacon?"

"I am."

Once again Lewis looked toward the attic window. "Hey, Doc! Your brother's out here to see you! Ain't you going to let him in?" Lewis looked back at Hannibal. "He won't let you in. Doc Deacon wouldn't let God himself in if He came knocking on the door."

"You seem to have quite a cynical attitude, Mr. Lewis."

"Your brother fired me. Cut me loose from my job, and I ain't been able to find no other decent work at all. I live from hand to mouth, working whatever job I can find. Thanks to your brother, sir, I've been down to shoveling manure out of horse stalls. But I ain't cynical about the Doc, no sir. I just plain old hate the man."

Hannibal did not like this fellow at all. "Why are you here, Mr. Lewis? Have you come to see my brother?"

"Nobody sees the Doc. He don't leave that house at all"—Lewis raised his voice to a near shout and aimed it at the attic again—"unless it's to go out and threaten folks he don't like. Like Horatio Eaton! That's right, Doc! I been watching you! I know about you and your shotgun paying call on old Eaton the other morning! I watched the whole thing! I've watched you a hell of a lot more than you can know! By the by, Doc, Eaton's gone now. Run off from town. You scared him bad, real bad."

Hannibal trotted down the steps and faced Lewis. "Sir, I don't care for what you're saying. And you're drunk."

"I'm drunk quite a lot, Mr. Hannibal Deacon. That's about all that's left for me since your madman brother cut me loose." He yelled up at the attic again. "I ain't forgot you, Doc! I'm going to even the score with you yet! I know it was you who shot Charlie Douglass, and I'll prove it one of these days!" He laughed, then said to Hannibal, "Did you know about that? How your brother murdered an old drunk? He did. And somebody saw it, too, or so I hear. Once I find that man, I'll see your brother hauled before the law."

"I asked you already: Why did you come here today?"

"I come by here quite often, just to send up a word or two to the Doc. Just to let him know that not everybody's forgot him. Why, even before I was fired I used to come by and watch this house. Had me a different reason then. A real pretty reason name of Amy Deacon. I used to watch her almost all the time. There's an old barn over yonder, that if you get up in the loft you could see right into her window. She wasn't always as careful as a proper and pretty young woman ought to be about making sure her curtain was plumb closed, either! But old Doc, he took that pretty show from me, too. Sent that pretty little peach away. Lord knows I've thought a time or two about following."

Hannibal hit him. His fist caught Lewis on the side of the jaw and knocked him to the ground. The former editor crabbed back a couple of yards, sputtering, then got up, gripping his jaw. He fired a string of obscenities at Hannibal, a few more up at the attic window, and turned and ran clumsily away, still holding his face. When he was a safe distance off he turned and yelled, "I'll see your brother in jail before I'm through! Or maybe I'll just take care of punishing him myself!"

"If you continue to make those kinds of threats, it will be you who goes to jail!" Hannibal yelled back.

Lewis cursed him again, then ran drunkenly on and was gone. Hannibal looked about and was relieved to see no one close by to have witnessed the altercation.

He stepped back from the house another step and looked up at the attic window. "George! Are you up there?"

No reply.

"George, I've come to see you! Won't you let me in?"

Nothing. Discouraged almost to the point of tears, Hannibal sighed and turned away. He walked on down the street, glancing back from time to time. He thought once he caught a tiny movement of the attic window curtain, but was too far away to be sure.

He didn't return at once to the convention, but wandered the streets, letting his emotions calm themselves. His right hand hurt and tingled from having struck Lewis's jaw. Not a pugilistic man by nature, Hannibal was surprised at his spontaneous violent action. But as he thought about the ratty editor lewdly spying on Amy in her own room, he couldn't regret having hit him, whatever the consequences.

He finally rejoined the convening Unionists, but took no part in the proceedings and hardly heard a word that was said. He would return to Secession Hill in the evening, he decided. Maybe George would let him in this time. After that, he had no idea what would happen.

When the convention day closed, however, Hannibal had lost his will. He was depressed and fearful, deeply wearied by the stress of the afternoon's events. He walked by Secession Hill but found himself unable to summon enough courage to go to the door. Intriguingly enough, the house was completely dark except for a dim light that illuminated the drawn attic curtain. Birch Lewis must have been right about Dr. Deacon's habits. Hannibal stared at the dim light for a while, then shook his head and moved on, returning to his room and pledging that he would come again to Secession Hill first thing in the morning.

Early the next day

Hannibal stood quietly at the base of Secession Hill's stone steps, tears streaming down his face, and listened as a man beside him explained what had happened in the night.

"We were notified right about midnight and came out with every man in the fire company, but it was too late already when we got here. The whole house was flaming, so hot you couldn't even get near it. We did what we could, but all we could hope for was to keep it from spreading, which we did. It seemed to have started in the attic, best we can tell. Probably from a lamp being kicked over or something."

Hannibal stared at the ugly, smoking ruin of charred timbers, roped off now to keep the morbidly curious out of the still-hot remains of the house. "Where did you find the body?"

"Well, the house had fallen in, but from where we found the corpse, I'd say he'd been in the attic, near where the fire began. They say he'd been living up there, hiding away. Doc Deacon has gone through some hard times, I hear, these past few months. They say he wasn't the man he once was."

"Yes. So I understand. I came to visit him yesterday. He wouldn't let me in. I wasn't even sure he was inside."

The fireman scratched at his beard. "Uh, sir . . . you'll be hearing this from somebody soon anyway, so I reckon I ought to just go ahead and tell you. It looks like the Doc might not have died from the fire."

"What do you mean?"

"Well, there wasn't much left of the body, hardly a thing at all, but it appeared there was a bullet hole through his skull. It may be that he . . . that he had shot himself. And maybe it was him jerking or something that knocked the lamp over and started the blaze."

"Killed himself . . ."

"So it appears, sir. I'm sorry. Maybe it ain't my place to be telling you these things. I'm just here to watch the ruins and make sure no blazes start up again."

"It's all right. Like you say, they would have told me anyway."

"There'll be somebody talking to you about what to do about the funeral and burying and such. You're his next of kin?"

"He has a daughter."

"Oh, yes! I should've remembered. It was her who used to write for him in his newspaper, and was sneaking on the side to write for that abolitionist. Is that right?"

"That's right. She's in Greeneville now, living with me. I suppose I'd best wire the news."

"I'm sorry about your brother, sir. He was a great man before he lost his . . . before he changed and started hiding away. Very tragic. Very tragic. I used to enjoy reading his paper. He made a rebel out of me, the Doc did. He was a great man. Used to be, at least."

"Thank you. He would have liked knowing you felt that way. George enjoyed being admired. It was always very important to him."

"You and all the other bereaved have my sympathies, sir. Now if you'll excuse me, I see a little flame starting back up there, and I'd best go douse it."

Hannibal left while the fireman was busy, pushing his way through the slow-moving crowd of onlookers ogling the ruins. He wiped off his tears, forced control upon his emotions, and strode toward the telegraph office at the rail station, trying to compose in his mind the best way to word the wire. News of the death of Dr. George Deacon would spread quickly, and he didn't want Amy hearing it from some other source before he could let her know himself.

He glanced back and took a final look at the smoldering

heap of timbers. Nothing remained of what had been there before except the defiant sign George had placed in his yard to mock his critics. SECESSION HILL. For some reason that struck Hannibal as sadly ironic. He looked away and walked on, more quickly now.

Chapter 20

They buried the remains in Knoxville's Gray Cemetery at about the same time, over in western Virginia, Union General George B. McClellan drove a Confederate contingent out of a stronghold at a mountainous place called Philippi. The body took its resting place among many of Knoxville's most prominent and revered citizens. Hannibal was glad his brother's corpse would lie in such soil; it would have meant much to George Deacon's massive but tender ego to know he shared company with the great and admired. The funeral itself had been something of a spectacle, attended not only by those who had admired Dr. Deacon before his decline, but also by members of the press, gawkers, and old political enemies who took a morbid delight in seeing the old Secessionist laid away at last. The graveside service, kept private, was much more restrained and dignified than the funeral itself, and provided Hannibal the chance to say a proper good-bye to a brother to whom he had never been close, but still loved.

Amy kept a stoic face throughout the funeral and burial, but Hannibal sensed the pain she felt. Life as the daughter of Doc Deacon had been an odd and often straining affair, particularly at the last. Hannibal knew how mixed and confused her feelings about the man had become upon learning details of his life and actions that no daughter would want to know.

Yet even in all this grief, Hannibal felt a certain private relief. The more he had learned about George Deacon's final mental decline, the more afraid of him he'd become, not only for himself, but especially for Amy. Had George Deacon lived on with his mental health declining and his paranoia about his "betrayers" growing, he might have hurt her. In one way, it was for the best that he was gone.

They went back to Greeneville and sought to get life back onto as normal a track as possible. Hannibal returned to his store, and on June 8 joined the flood of voters who went to the polls to again face the question of Secession. This time the vote, as Hannibal feared, went opposite from before. More than a hundred thousand Tennesseans voted to join the Confederacy, with only some forty-seven thousand voting to remain in the Union. Of that number, most were East Tennesseans.

The Union convention that Hannibal had attended in Knoxville reconvened in Greeneville on June 17. Hannibal heralded it. With so much grief and death in his recent experience, he was ready to throw himself all the harder into the Unionist effort, if only for the sake of distraction.

From counties all across East Tennessee the convention delegates gathered, a somber but determined group, almost every man of them knowing that this convention represented the last feeble hope of East Tennessee loyalists to avoid being finally swallowed and digested by the whelming Confederacy. At the Knoxville session some hope of an anti-Secession state vote had lingered, but June 8 shattered it. Now matters were murky indeed for the Unionists of East Tennessee.

As Hannibal Deacon made his way up Main Street toward the courthouse, he wondered if the population as a whole understood the precariousness of the situation nearly as well as the convention delegates themselves. East Tennessee's predominate Unionism in itself tended to distort the picture as seen by the average citizen. Surrounded by loyalists, and out-of-touch with the rest of the far more heavily Secessionist balance of the state, it was relatively easy for an East Tennessean to believe that nothing of consequence was really going to happen, that life would go on as before.

Hannibal knew better. Before seceding, Tennessee loyalists had been free to air their views freely as citizens of the United States. Now matters had changed. What was mere political dissent before was now potential sedition. Already the undercurrents of Unionism that had flown in the more heavily pro-Secession middle and western regions of the state, encouraging and supporting the much more open Unionism of East Tennessee, had been substantially dammed off. There were widespread reports, seemingly reliable, that many polls in Middle and West Tennessee had been manned only by Secessionists back on June 8, and that some locales had forced ballots to be placed in the collections boxes unfolded, so the loyalist votes could be exposed to view. Prior to the election, Unionist newspapers had been suppressed, advocacy of Unionism forbidden, and loyalists intimidated by threats.

The unfairness of it all rankled Hannibal and his fellow Unionists. But unfair or not, the result was clear: East Tennessee's Unionists now stood almost alone in opposition to a Confederate state government that would not allow them free rein for long. Soon the vise would close and tighten. Whatever could be achieved to keep East Tennessee in the Union would have to be achieved now. Hannibal could think of only one way to achieve that: East Tennessee must form its own state.

That conviction was shared by most others at the convention. T.A.R. Nelson submitted a lengthy "Declaration of Grievances" against the Confederacy, and a series of resolutions that in effect declared East Tennessee independent of the rest of the state. Speaking in favor of this radical move were influential loyalist leaders, including Thomas Arnold and Robert Johnson, the latter a son of Greeneville's own Senator Andrew Johnson.

Other voices raised unwelcome doubts, however. Joseph Cooper, of Campbell County, forced the more overwrought

Unionists to face an obvious fact: If East Tennessee withdrew from the Confederacy, it would bring warfare right to its door. East Tennessee would become, Cooper declared, "a hell."

Eventually almost all saw the merit in Cooper's objections. Though there was an excess of support among the delegates to pass Nelson's defiant declaration of East Tennessee independence, the resolutions were sent to a committee for study. Hannibal's feelings about this were mixed. He sensed that there was no time for committee deliberations and continuing debate; to fail to act now might mean losing the chance to act at all. Yet to actually declare independence . . . that was a frightening notion. Who could say what would be the response of the Confederacy to such an uprising?

Before long an event occurred that hinted at the answer to that question. A Confederate band calling itself the Louisiana Tigers came riding pell-mell into town in the midst of it all, shooting off pistols, threatening citizens, slashing down the American flag that had been hoisted by the conventioneers, and committing a few blustering acts of vandalism. The convention attendees spilled into the streets while this occurred, and some were angry enough to take on the rebels then and there. But saner heads prevailed and no real violence erupted, to Hannibal's relief. The Louisiana Tigers, whooping and yelling, galloped on out of town, leaving the convention delegates unmolested, unarrested, but very sobered.

Hannibal would not forget the incident. As he thought it over he found his spirit for a rebellious response to Tennessee's secession fading fast. An immediate Unionist rebellion in East Tennessee would have consequences far more serious and bloody than a mere flag-slashing display by a gaggle of out-of-state, high-spirited Confederates—a display that Hannibal felt sure was not coincidental in timing nor spontaneous in generation. Confederate authorities were sending a message to the East Tennessee Unionists: Do not defy us.

The convention, shaken by the intrusion of the rebel soldiers, ended with the passage of a "Declaration of Grievance" that fell short of the more fiery Nelson resolutions.

The declaration merely aired loyalist doubts about the veracity of the June 8 election and requested, though six calmly worded resolutions, that the state legislature allow East Tennessee to begin the process of becoming a seperate state.

Hannibal did not expect the resolutions to bring results, but perhaps their peaceful tone would at least cool any immediate Confederate desire for stern punishment of recalcitrant East Tennessee. He left the convention with the feeling that it had been anticlimactic. The resolutions seemed little to show for a gathering that had begun with fire, bluster, and talk of armed resistance. But they had done the best they could, and for now would simply have to wait and see what would follow.

What followed was not encouraging.

On July 16, Union General Irvin McDowell, acting under orders from President Lincoln, marched his soldiers out of Washington as bands played and crowds cheered. They were headed for Virginia, anticipating a quick and easy routing of the Confederate armies there. With a big delegation of cheerful citizens following them, wearing their Sunday finest and boasting among their number congressmen, officials, and civic leaders, the army dragged along for two days, covering only twenty miles until it reached the town of Centreville and the winding Bull Run Creek. A Union division skirmished to its disadvantage with one of the Confederate lines of General P.G.T. Beauregard encamped behind the creek, resulting in a day's delay of the planned main attack.

The real battle began shortly after two o'clock on the morning of July 21, a Sunday. McDowell took the offensive and initially seemed destined for a sure win. Confederates fell back in great numbers, though one brigade, led by Brigadier General Thomas Jackson, would not be ousted. The sight of Jackson standing like a "stone wall" before the enemy cheered the faltering Confederates, and they turned back into the fight. Meanwhile, fresh rebel soldiers who had just arrived joined the fray. Also adding to the sudden Confederate resurgence was the fact that some of the rebels were dressed in blue uniforms, confusing the Union batteries and giving the Confederates a chance to move in close, open fire, and prevail.

The Union soldiers fell back, crossed the creek, then set off in a mad retreat that was witnessed by the many Washington citizens who had come out to observe the battle at their leisure. Panic struck all, and the road back to Washington became a morass of vehicles and pedestrians, all fleeing from the unexpectedly strong foe. When casualties were totaled later, it was found that nearly three thousand Federals were either dead, missing, or wounded; the Confederacy suffered about two thousand similar losses.

The North was stunned. Expecting an easy march into Richmond, they had instead encountered a fierce battle. The South, on the other hand, was thrilled, though the thrill was muted by the size of the casualty list. The Bull Run fight had proven something important: The North would not find the South an easy foe. Lincoln had called for war, and he was going to get it.

As news of Bull Run swept the South, Confederate spirits soared. The Union had been put in its place—a mere foretaste, jubilant rebels declared, of other victories to come. East Tennessee's loyalists felt the sting of Bull Run and knew their situation was becoming all the more precarious.

On July 26 the Confederate government in Nashville made a move Hannibal Deacon had anticipated since June 8, creating a military district in troublesome East Tennessee. Placed in command of the new District of East Tennessee of the Confederate Armies was Gen. Felix K. Zollicoffer, a well-known figure in Knoxville, where he had once been a printer. A veteran of the Seminole War, a former state comptroller, Nashville newspaper editor, and state senator and congressman, Zollicoffer was well-liked in East Tennessee. He was among those who had initially opposed Secession, but had changed his view after Lincoln's call for volunteers. He was tolerant, understanding, and as likely as anyone Hannibal knew of to successfully keep East Tennessee from running out of control.

A great unease settled on Unionists of the state's mountainous east. More and more of them "stampeded" out of

East Tennessee, running north either to join the Union Army or to avoid any future conscription into the Confederate forces. Hannibal encouraged Sam Colter to consider stampeding himself, but Sam firmly refused. Hannibal knew the reason was surely Amy. His devotion to her was obvious to all—except perhaps to Amy herself. Hannibal was finding her unreadable these days.

Amy had changed with the death of her father. Changed in ways that made Hannibal worry. She was somber, intense, possessed with political developments and war news.

She's becoming just like her father, he thought. *Obsessed, driven, caught up in herself and her cause to a degree that might not be healthy. And it may be that I'm unwittingly encouraging it.*

Pleadis Mundy visited Amy on a clouded afternoon and declared that he loved her and wanted to court her with hopes of marriage. She looked him in the eye and told him she had no interest in marriage to him, and that furthermore, she despised his political views and would have nothing further to do with any man who favored the Confederacy.

Stunned and broken, Pleadis Mundy walked out of her life. A day later he enlisted in the Confederate Army and was gone. Amy gave him not a further thought.

Sam learned of the event from Hannibal, and knew that the time had come for him to do what he'd wanted to do since the first. He approached Amy just as Mundy had, told her of his affection for her, and asked her in as formal a way as he knew for the privilege of calling on her. It was the most difficult thing the shy young Carolinian had ever done.

She had not been gentle with Mundy, but she was with Sam. It didn't matter. The result was the same, and it shattered him.

"I care for you very much, Sam," she said, holding his hand. "There might have been a time when I would have accepted what you offer, but not now. Don't you see what's happening around us? The world is falling apart. There will be war and death. It's best not to love in a time of war and death. Can't you see?"

"But I do love you, Amy. God knows, I never thought I'd have the courage to say it to you, but it's true, and has been almost since I first saw you."

She smiled, very sadly. "No, Sam. My answer has to be no. I don't think I can marry, not anytime soon. As long as this conflict holds, my only spouse is the Union and abolition."

"But no conflict holds forever, Amy. And one of these days abolition will come. When that happens, might you consider . . . ?"

"Maybe. But for now I can't think of anything beyond this war," she replied. "The future will have to be dealt with when it arrives."

He removed his hand from hers and looked away.

She folded her hands together. "It's no time to love anyone, Sam. There's just too much death. And there will be more. We'd best ready ourselves for it, and not waste our time with frivolous love affairs and so on."

Frivolous. He thought of the hours he had spent thinking about her, the effort he had gone through to overcome his own shyness in her presence, and the love and devotion he stood ready to give her if only she would take it. *Frivolous,* she had said.

If this was her feeling, there was no more to be said, and he left her where she was without even a good-bye.

The next day's newspapers carried the story. It came out of North Carolina and concerned the mysterious shooting deaths of a white man named Dabney Sloat and two Cherokees atop a remote mountain ridge in the Cherokee country.

As best could be told, the three had died at the hands of the same gunman; that gunman in turn apparently had been wounded, as surmised from spatters of blood found leading down the ridge. The blood trail at length dwindled away; whoever left it had not been found either dead or alive.

Sloat, described in the story as a "mountain dweller and recluse of ill reputation in the western North Carolina wilderness country," was found with a flintlock rifle in his death grip; it had been fired, and was presumed to be the weapon that inflicted the apparent wound on whomever had attacked the trio.

The Indians, a woman in her thirties and an old man named Skaantee, had no weapons about them and presumably were killed merely because they were present and could potentially identify the attacking shootist.

The matter was "of interest to authorities of the law" but was not expected to be easily solved, since there had been no surviving witnesses to the shootings. There was, however, a sideline matter of interest: The victim Sloat was suspected in the recent murder of a Marshall, North Carolina, hotel operator named Wilton Colter, whose family was "widely known to be despised by the unfortunate Sloat." Whether Sloat's death was tied to the Marshall shooting was unknown, but "officials of the law are said to be seeking two nephews of Wilton Colter" for questioning in the matter.

According to the newspaper, the bodies on the ridge had been discovered by a young Cherokee man named Jim Matoy, a reported friend of Skaantee's who had climbed the mountain to investigate reports of repeated gunfire heard on the mountaintop. Matoy, it was noted in closing, had been questioned but subsequently was not himself suspected of any involvement in the deaths.

Sam read the story, reread it, then tore it from the newspaper. Picking up a piece of foolscap and a pen, he scrawled a note, blew it dry, and folded it around the newspaper item. Leaving it in a visible place on the table in the corner of his room, he rose, gathered clothing, food, his old cap-and-ball rifle and ammunition, blankets, and various personal items he placed in a saddle pack. He carried them down the stairs and around to the stable where he kept his horse, Della. He saddled her, tied the blanket roll onto the rear of the saddle, mounted and rode out of Greeneville with a heart full of sadness.

Hannibal found the note late the next morning, after ascending to Sam's room to find out why he had not shown up at the store. He read it and the torn-out newspaper story, then returned home to give Amy the news it carried, afterward destroying the letter in accordance with Sam's own written instruction.

"So he's gone, though he doesn't say where," Hannibal said in an atypically weak voice, after telling her the main facts. "He says there is no longer anything in Greeneville worth staying for. And he doesn't want to be questioned about the shootings."

"I see."

Hannibal looked at Sam's note. "He writes that he doesn't know precisely what he will do, but that he does intend to find out, if possible, if his brother is still alive. He says he does not plan to return to Greeneville anytime soon, wishes us well, apologizes for leaving us in the lurch at the store, says for us to watch out for the rebs and that he will see us again someday, if he can. He says he . . ." A pause.

"What?"

"He says he loves you."

"Oh."

Hannibal stared at the paper in his hand.

"I don't understand why he doesn't want to be questioned about those shootings," Amy said. "He had nothing to do with them."

"Yes. But his brother almost certainly did. Sam doesn't want to have to inform the law that Joe Colter had vowed to kill Sloat. Brotherly loyalty. It's driven him away." He glanced at Amy meaningfully. "Or perhaps it is only one of the things that has driven him away."

Amy had nothing to say.

Hannibal crumpled up the pages.

Amy asked, "Will the store be open today?"

"No," Hannibal said, a deep depression sweeping over him. "Not today."

"Very well." She nodded, stood, and went up to her room. She remained in it all day, leaving for only moments at a time and locking the door behind her each time she reentered.

Hannibal spent the day in the parlor, sitting in a chair and staring out the window, a man very alone and sad. Wartime intrigue, danger, and loss were changing him, he realized, just as they were changing Amy. He felt depressed and doomed, as if fate was lingering somewhere in the shadows, making grim plans for him. Optimistic and cheerful by nature, he had never experienced any such morbid sensations before. But all of life was different with Lena gone.

Amy kept her light on late that night, and as he passed her door Hannibal heard the scratch of her pen. She was writing in her journal. For all he knew, she might have been writing all day, pouring out whatever feelings were in her. Her journal was her outlet. His outlet had always been Lena . . . but Lena was gone.

He tapped on Amy's door, told her good-night and heard hers in return, then went to his bed and the brief respite of a summer night's sleep in a world changing far too fast all around him, and taking from him, one by one and in various ways, all those he loved.

Part IV

THE BRIDGE BURNERS

Chapter 21

Late October 1861; a few miles east of Greeneville, Tennessee

A stockade had stood nearby many years ago. First called Haverly Fort, and later Colter's Fort after some of Sam Colter's pioneering ancestors, it had been the heart of one of the earliest settlements in the days of the Tennessee frontier. Raided by Cherokees in 1776, Colter's Fort had withstood and become the centerpiece of a community called Colter's Station. Eventually, as the dangers of Indian raids faded away, the stockade had rotted and crumbled, and Colter's Station had been quickly overshadowed by faster-growing communities such as Rheatown, Greeneville, and Warrensburg. The Colter community of 1861 consisted of no more than a few farmhouses, one small general store and post office, a mill, several private stables and barns, and one high, short railroad bridge spanning a deep gully that had been too long for the track engineers to merely go around.

Hannibal rode toward Colter under cover of a gloomy night. He halted his horse and dismounted about a half mile from the railroad bridge. Leading his horse down toward Sinking Creek, he tethered it in a clump of trees. Removing a small sack of oats from his saddlebag, he dumped it on the ground in front of the horse, then slipped off on a trail that wound through woodlands sparse in undergrowth because of the cattle that grazed here. The night was cool, the wind gusty, moving the trees and brush and often making Hannibal halt, frozen in place, listening to be sure that whatever odd sound he had just heard was not of human origin. The closer he drew to the railroad bridge, the more cautious he grew and the more often he stopped. There were others out tonight, wearing gray uniforms, carrying rifles, and under orders to guard the Colter railroad bridge. It would not do for him to be caught.

Hannibal stopped when the bridge came into view. He had moved up somewhat from the creek and into the woods between it and a small farm. He hoped no dogs were roaming very close by. His big form, unaccustomed to this strenuous and stressful movement, ached for rest. He gulped air, trying not to gasp too loudly. Squatting, panting, he peered through the autumn brush and saw the bridge dimly, a skeletal structure against a black-blue sky. A tiny light flared against that background, illuminating the face of a guard putting match to pipe bowl, then all was black again. Lord willing, he thought, there would be a far brighter light burning here before long.

He heard a voice, a laugh, and barely made out the black shape of a second man striding out onto the bridge to join the first. Hannibal shivered. There was danger here. *I'd best get on,* he thought. *Lena will be furious with me if she finds out I came this close to . . .* Then he remembered, and felt that now-familiar pang of grief that came with each fresh realization of bereavement. Remarkable, how easily he could forget for a moment that Lena was no longer with him, even after these several months.

He thought: *What does it matter if there's danger? It doesn't really make much difference what happens to me now. Lena's dead, Sam is gone, and Amy has her inheritance and her own strength to see her through if I don't come through this alive. No one is left who needs me.* He looked up at the bridge again. *Reverend Carter was right to select me. I am the right man for this job, for it doesn't matter if I survive or if I don't.* He was vaguely aware that such a morbid thought would have never crossed his mind before Lena's passing. He had never imagined how much the loss of the only love of his life would change him.

Rising, he headed back down toward the creek and back to his horse. Pausing for a moment, he rubbed his neck. For days now he had suffered sharp, abrupt headaches, sometimes accompanied by nosebleeds. He massaged the pain into submission, wriggled his shoulders, and swung heavily up into the saddle.

"Your turn to ache now," he whispered wryly to the horse. But he didn't smile. Hannibal seldom smiled now, and when he did, it was almost invariably forced and without feeling.

He rode back down the creek a quarter of a mile and then across a small footbridge, into a copse of maple trees, and at last into an open field. On the other side of the field, beside the shell of a farmhouse that had burned to the ground two years before, stood a crumbling log barn, covered with wild ivy. It was dark and as uninviting as a cavern, but he headed straight for it, hoping one of the others would already be there, for this was a gloomy, sad, haunted kind of night, and he was eager for company.

What meager light there was rose from a single lamp with the wick cranked low. It sat on a barrel in the midst of the largest stall in the old barn, and spat yellow light upward onto the faces of a circle of very nervous, intense men. They huddled close to one another as if to ensure the flickering glow didn't somehow penetrate the thick walls of the old barn and reveal their presence to the gray-clad patrols who moved up and down the roadways.

"The bridges are the key," Hannibal Deacon was saying, his voice held to a fraction of its usual booming volume as he laid out a plan that had been presented to him days before by a most remarkable Unionist preacher from Carter County. "Without the railroad, the rebels cannot possibly move enough men, arms, and munitions to respond to the kind of invasion we will be looking at. And the best way to shut off the railroad is to destroy the bridges."

"But the rebs know that as well as we do," said the most

nervous-looking of the dozen men present. His name was Henry Ross. "Hang it, there's been rumors of a Union invasion for weeks, and I heard it being talked up only three days ago that the sign of the invasion coming will be the burning of the bridges on the East Tennessee and Virginia. They're guarding most every bridge now. Ain't no way we can burn them."

"If you feel that hopeless, Henry, I suggest that you either stampede or go make your vow to serve, honor, and obey Jeff Davis. It won't be simple to burn those bridges, no, and it will be as dangerous an enterprise as any man among us is likely to face—but it must be done. The consequences of failure will probably be the subjection once and for all of East Tennessee. If we succeed, East Tennessee may be retaken for the Union. If that should occur, the Confederacy will be divided, right down its middle. The main line of supply will be closed off. The war could be ended much more quickly."

"It's risky."

"This is war, man! There's risk in taking a walk down the street! And it will only grow worse. Have you noticed how Zollicoffer's hand is growing heavier as weeks go by? He was easy enough with us at the beginning, letting us meet, letting Parson Brownlow keep publishing the *Whig*—but all that is changing. Did you know that Brownlow has been shut down? He's gone into hiding somewhere in the Smoky Mountains. With the *Whig* shut down, the last great Union voice is choked off. The rebs are guarding the bridges, the mountain passes, arresting men who try to leave the state—"

"Calm down, Hannibal!" scolded Jack McAmis, a bulky, red-faced, and wide-jowled Colter resident who owned the barn in which the clandestine meeting was taking place. "Nobody here needs to be preached at. We all revere the Union and we all know the stakes. Henry's point is that it may be impossible to burn those bridges if the rebels keep up a close enough guard."

"I know that, gentlemen," Hannibal said, forcing himself to calm. Since Lena's death, and since Unionists had begun to truly feel the Confederate vise beginning to squeeze, his emotions swelled and rose too easily. "But you must understand the level from which this plan descends. This is no mere local strategy. The burning of the railroad bridges has the sanction of Lincoln himself."

"Lincoln!" Henry Ross declared. "You mean it?"

"I do. The president has a deep and personal concern for East Tennessee. He knows we are a highly loyal area, and he knows we're beginning to suffer for it. For our sakes he considers the liberation of East Tennessee a moral obligation as well as a military necessity."

"How do you know all this?"

"I've heard it from the very man to whom Lincoln made the statement—and at the same time specifically sanctioned and financed the operation to burn the bridges."

"I had heard that this was no more than a Parson Brownlow notion being talked up by the preacher Carter over in Elizabethton," Ross said.

"It was a suggestion of Brownlow's, among others, to begin with. And it's the Reverend Carter I've spoken with, and who conferred with Lincoln."

"Perhaps you should begin at the first and tell us everything in order," McAmis said.

"A good suggestion," Hannibal said. "You gentlemen will have to pardon my struggles to communicate. I confess I'm rather wrought up over all this."

"You and me, too," Ross said.

Speaking in a soft but intense tone, Hannibal told the little Unionist cluster a story, at the center of which was a Princeton-educated Presbyterian preacher and businessman from the town of Elizabethton in neighboring Carter County. The preacher was William Blount Carter, a descendant of the prominent East Tennessee family after whom his county of residence had been named. The Secession crisis had drawn Carter into political advocacy. He took a visible and fervent public stand against the Confederatization of Tennessee. Well-known across East Tennessee, Carter had been an official representative of his county at the Union conventions in Knoxville and Greeneville. Already a friend of Hannibal's, particularly so after Hannibal openly declared his Unionism,

Carter had given Hannibal much comfort after the destruction of Secession Hill and the death of George Deacon.

Earlier in the year, Hannibal explained to the clustered group of Unionists, Carter slipped north to Kentucky to Camp Dick Robinson, the Federal recruiting center to which most East Tennessee "stampeders" went to join the Union Army. At the camp, Carter met with political and military authorities, including Generals William T. Sherman and George H. Thomas, Senator Andrew Johnson, prominent Unionist Horace Maynard, and Carter's own brother, Samuel Carter. The latter had, at Lincoln's personal direction, left a lieutenancy in the United States Navy to become an Army brigadier assigned to recruit and command volunteer soldiers for the East Tennessee Brigade, to be composed of East Tennesseans. At Camp Robinson, Carter promoted the proposal that the railroad be destroyed in a simultaneous uprising of East Tennessee Unionists, to be followed up immediately by a Federal invasion from Kentucky.

It was a bold plan, but won the favor of the Camp Robinson delegation despite some initial resistance from General Sherman that was overcome by supportive arguments from General Thomas. Carrying a letter of introduction from the latter, Carter had been sent immediately to Washington, where he conferred directly with President Lincoln and General George B. McClellan, general-in-chief. Both listened to and approved the idea of an East Tennessee Unionist uprising and invasion, and Reverend Carter came back to East Tennessee, by way of Camp Robinson, with a $2,500 Federal allocation to finance the plan. Carter had traveled about like a fast-moving shadow, consulting with Unionist leaders in communities across East Tennessee, describing the plan and entrusting selected ones of their number, including Hannibal Deacon, with the gathering of small forces of bridge burners to carry out the actual destruction on the night of November 8. "And that is my purpose here," Hannibal concluded. "Reverend Carter has given me charge of destruction of the bridge at Colter . . . and from our group here tonight, I want to raise the band who will actually do the work."

Silence followed. Out in the darkness beyond the barn a dog barked and an owl screeched.

Ross broke the silence. "You know what they'd do to us if they caught us?"

"If they didn't shoot us on the spot, they'd certainly arrest us, try us, and lock us up until the day of doom."

"Or hang us."

"It could be."

McAmis cleared his throat. "Hannibal, talk is easy. Burning guarded bridges isn't. How would we carry this out?"

"Very simple, Jack. Rifles, fuel, and matches."

"Simple? How do you suggest we deal with the guards?"

"That's an impossible question to answer in advance. Like any operation, this will have its risks, among them the possibility that any given bridge will be too heavily guarded to allow burners to reach it. But tonight I observed the Colter bridge before I came here. I saw only two guards, and they were fairly careless about exposing themselves to view. They were out on the bridge itself. One struck a match to his pipe. A good sniper could have dropped him then and there."

One of the men, Caleb Tweed, shuddered. "I'm a farmer. I'm a deacon in the Baptist church. I ain't never thought about shooting nobody. I don't know that I could ever do it, except to protect my own."

"Maybe we won't have to shoot anyone," Hannibal said. "And if we do, maybe you won't have to be the one to do it, Caleb. But as for protecting your own, that's exactly what it will be. It will be no easy matter to remain a loyal man in a rebel region as this war goes on. And war will go on a long time indeed, unless something intervenes—such as cutting the entire cursed Confederacy in half by bringing the Union Army into control of East Tennessee."

McAmis asked, "How many bridges would be destroyed, Hannibal?"

"As many as can be, out of what I take to be ten or so, though Reverend Carter told me only so much as I needed to know. In Greene County there will be two—the bridge here at Colter, and the bridge over Lick Creek. Our bridge is the smallest one targeted. The biggest prizes will be two big bridges over the Tennessee River, one at Loudon, the other down in Bridgeport, Alabama. Others that will be burned include a couple over Chickamauga Creek down about Chattanooga, some over the Holston, and one across the Hiwassee."

"Who'll destroy the Lick Creek bridge?"

"That group is being formed by others, and the less any of us know about who else is involved, the better. We cannot betray information we don't possess."

"Do you know who it will be?" Ross asked.

"I do. I'll bear the burden of that knowledge alone."

Ross eyed him closely. "I hate to ask this straight out to your face—but how do we know we can trust you?"

"You have a reason not to, Henry?"

"You ain't telling us everything."

"You don't need to know who will burn the Lick Creek bridge. Why would you want to?"

"Because you're asking us to put a lot of faith in you, but you ain't telling all the facts."

"I'm telling you as little as possible for your own protection. What you don't know you can't be forced to tell. I don't even know all the details of this, and don't want to."

"Makes sense to me," McAmis said.

"Spit it out, Henry," Hannibal went on, sensing that Ross was not yet satisfied. "You have some solid reason for distrusting me?"

"Maybe I'm just thinking about the fact you're the brother of a man who was as Secesh as they come. I'm thinking it's possible that maybe kin tend to think alike."

"Wait a minute, Henry," McAmis interjected. "If you're trying to say that Hannibal Deacon isn't a true Union man, I've got to speak against you. I've not seen anyone work harder for the cause than Hannibal. And as for kin thinking alike, you know as well as I do that this cussed Secession has divided families all over this state. Some of the strongest Union men in Greene County have sons and brothers who have gone for the Confederacy."

"I know that," Ross replied snappishly. "But when a man

has doubts, he ought to speak them, especially when he's being asked to put his neck on the chop block."

McAmis's face reddened and he opened his mouth to reply, but Hannibal cut him off. "Henry, you're right. If you have doubts about me, then I don't ask you to trust me. But I vow to you there's no duplicity in this. My brother, God rest his soul, thought his own thoughts, not mine. I've been a Union man all along."

" 'Tain't so," Ross replied. "You declared yourself neutral for the longest time."

"I'm a merchant, Henry. I do business with men of all political stripes, and I saw no cause to drive half of them away by coming out Union before it was necessary. But when the pinch got tight, I took my stand and meant it. I'll die before I'll betray the United States."

Ross paused, raising and lowering his brows. "I reckon I'll have to take your word for it, then. But you'll pardon me if I reserve the right to follow my own instincts."

"Enough of this," McAmis said. "We've got a proposition laid out before us and we've got to make up our minds. Hannibal, I want you to know I trust you completely. That's *my* instinct, Henry, and I'll follow it just like you follow yours."

"Suit yourself," Ross replied.

Hannibal looked around the group. "Well, who's with me? Who's ready to put action to his words, and burn that bridge with me come November?"

Caleb Tweed pulled his moustache nervously and said, "I trust you, Hannibal, but I'm going to have to think mighty hard before I get into this."

"There's little time for thinking," Hannibal replied. "The time will be on us soon. All I ask of you, if you don't agree to join this operation, is that you keep secret the names of those who have. Lives may depend on your silence."

Silence held a moment, then McAmis said, "I'm with you, Hannibal. I may live . . . or die . . . to regret it, but I'll be beside you."

"And so will I."

"Me, too."

One by one they agreed, all but Tweed and Ross. Eyes

turned toward them, studying but not condemning. To agree to Hannibal's proposal was no thing to be done lightly or halfheartedly.

"You can go home, if you like," Hannibal said after a few moments. "No one will fault you. I'll ask nothing of you but your silence." He looked directly at Ross as he said it.

Ross looked back, eyes narrowed, then around at the others. He shook his head, turned and was gone. They listened to his receding steps as he left the barn and headed toward his house, which stood less than a mile northward. Tweed looked after him as if he longed to follow, moved in that direction half a step, paused, then shook his head. "Aw, hang it all! It looks like I'm in, too."

"Good man, Caleb," McAmis said. He stroked his beard nervously. "I'm worried about Ross, though. I don't trust him."

"Maybe I shouldn't have called him here tonight," Hannibal said. "But he's been strong to speak for the Union among his neighbors, and I believe we can at least trust him to keep quiet."

"I hope so."

Hannibal raised his right hand. "Before your eyes, gentlemen, I swear my allegiance to the Union and my devotion to you as my brothers in arms. I cannot promise you we will not fail, but I do promise you that whatever may come, you will find me standing beside you."

"Or swinging beside us, as the case may be," McAmis said with a wry smile no one else seemed in a hurry to emulate.

"To the Union," Hannibal said, hand still lifted.

Hands went up all around, illuminated by the lamp, and voices rose in serrated chorus: "To the Union."

It took Hannibal much of the rest of the night to travel the approximately seven miles back to Greeneville. At every noise or unexpected movement he veered off the road and into hiding, to emerge when all was clear with his heart hammering and the sweat of fear drenching his thick brows and dripping onto his spectacles. He was discovered only once: Passing near a farmhouse, he was accosted by a man who leaped out his door with a shotgun, then lowered it as soon as he saw who it was. As a merchant, Hannibal knew almost every person in Greene County, and this fellow, Jim Harvey, was an aquaintance, frequent store customer, and fellow Unionist. "Sorry, Mr. Deacon," he said. "I thunk you was a rebel come to steal my boy off into the army."

"You 'thunk' wrong, Mr. Harvey," Hannibal said. "I don't blame you for caution, though. Tell me: Are the rebs stealing boys into their army?"

"Well, not yet that I know. But it'll come to that. You wait. It'll happen before long. What're you doing out away from Greeneville in the midst of the night, Mr. Deacon? Ain't safe."

"You're right about that. I'd best be getting home."

"You do that. By the way, sir, I ain't seen you since your brother died so tragic and all. I'm sorry for your loss. I never agreed with a word your brother put out, but a brother's a brother and you have my sympathy."

"Thank you." It seemed that Harvey hadn't heard about Lena's death, or he surely would have mentioned it as well. Hannibal was glad Harvey didn't know. Sympathy was appreciated, but also a reminder of loss.

Harvey pontificated: "This here Secesh business, it's going to split up more families than anything that's ever been. People's notions turning against one another and all. Just like you and your brother. My own boy, he thinks more Secesh than I wish he would, though he knows better than to say much around me. I'll never let him be a rebel, not while he's under my roof."

"Good for you. Good night, Mr. Harvey."

"Good night, Mr. Deacon. You be careful going home."

Amy was awaiting Hannibal when he finally reached his home. She came out to the stable while he dealt with his tired horse.

"Amy, I had thought you were asleep."

"I was. I woke up and didn't hear you snoring. I went to check on you, and you were gone."

"I had some business."

"At this time of night? What kind of business do you do at night?"

He smiled at her, but inwardly was a bit annoyed. He was in no mood to be interrogated. "My, you have a certain nosiness about you this evening, Amy."

"I want to be involved, Hannibal."

"In what?"

"In whatever plans you're making. We both know that you've been out tonight on Union business. What is the plan? Are you going to burn the bridges like the rumors say?"

He was slightly unnerved that she hit the truth so exactly, so quickly. But again, there had been widespread speculation about bridge burning among the populace.

"Amy, do we really have to talk about this now? I'm tired and hungry. Is there any food inside?"

"Where have you been, Hannibal? I'll not give you any peace until you tell me."

"Out. Taking care of some matters that require secrecy." He began walking toward the house.

Amy fell in beside. "So it's as I thought! Uncle Hannibal, you know how much I want to actually *do* something for the cause. Why won't you involve me?"

They went inside; he shut the door behind them and removed his coat and hat. "Isn't it obvious, my dear?"

"Because I'm female . . . is that it?"

"We all have our roles to play. Some things were meant for a man to carry out. War happens to be among them."

"I can burn a bridge as well as any man."

He looked at her more sternly. "Amy, I've said nothing tonight about bridge burning. And I wish you wouldn't try to speculate about strategies. Some conversations are best never held, so that if there are questions later, one can honestly say he, or she, knows nothing."

"But I *want* to know! I don't want to be left out."

"Amy, give me some peace long enough to at least put something under my belt. I'm half starved."

She plopped down in a kitchen chair, arms crossed and a sullen look about her. He sat at the table, eating cold ham and biscuits left over from a supper that seemed a distant memory, thinking that if Amy were trying to impress him with her worthiness for the involvement in Unionist sabatoge, she wasn't doing much of a job of it by putting on such a childish demeanor.

When he had finished eating, she said. "*Now* may I talk to you?"

"I doubt I could stop you."

"Uncle Hannibal, I want to know what my role will be in this war. I know that you and other Unionist men are making strategies. I can even guess what some of them might be. Is there no part I can play? You don't know how frustrating it is to believe so strongly in something, but to be left to do no more than write about it in a private journal."

"I can indeed know, Amy. Remember that for the longest time I was an ardent Unionist and abolitionist in a town where I had to play neutral. Even now I can't discuss my abolitionism, even among fellow Unionists. I'm very familiar with frustration." He paused. "And about that journal, Amy . . . I'm thinking that perhaps you should consider destroying it."

"Destroy . . . but why?"

"Tell me honestly: Have you written things in that journal that would be dangerous to anyone should the wrong eyes see it?"

She thought for a moment, and her face reddened. "But it's a private journal. No one would . . ." She did not finish, knowing better. Of course someone might read it. Would some rebel raider on a rampage through the house feel any compunction about reading a private journal?

"I believe you've answered my question," Hannibal said.

"I'm sorry," she replied. "I'll destroy it. I just never thought about the possibility that the wrong people might see it."

"And there's a point that needs making, Amy, even if you don't like hearing it. You didn't think about the possibility, you say. If one is to do the sort of surreptitious things you speak of—and in no way am I confirming that I am involved in anything surreptitious—then one must always think of every possibility. To fail to do so can be, quite literally, fatal. Not only for yourself, but also for others." He paused to let her think about that. "Eagerness and devotion you have in abundance, Amy. But those are not enough. Alone, in fact, they can be dangerous. There is another ingredient needed, but which you lack."

"What is that? The correct gender?"

"That wasn't what I was speaking of. You lack experience. Maturity."

She had no answer for a moment, then said, "But wait! What about Sam Colter? He's no older than I am, yet you've let him guide refugee slaves! And I never heard you tell him he was disqualified for lack of experience or maturity."

It was Hannibal's turn to be left wordless. She had him on that one. Sensing his disbalance, she went on. "You are right about the journal, Uncle Hannibal. I'll grant you that, and I'll destroy it this very night in the fire. But you know as well as I do that the problem isn't my age. There are plenty of young men no older than me, some of them younger, in fact, who are signing on as soldiers on both sides. They lack maturity, they lack experience, and they'll be thrown into many situations that will involve endangerment for themselves and others around them. But no one turns *them* away! Uncle Hannibal, my problem isn't immaturity, and you know it. My problem is that I am a girl—no, a *woman*, and on that point you hold exactly the same kinds of backward views my father held."

Hannibal surprised her then. His eyes reddened and his voice grew choked. "Amy, don't stand in judgment of me. Maybe to you it seems foolish, me trying to hold you back and keep you away from danger. But please understand, Amy. I've been in war. I've seen danger. I know what a hell it is. And I also know that I've just lost the only woman I ever loved, and I couldn't bear the thought of losing my dear niece as well. You're all that's left to me, Amy. In the time you've been here, I've come to love you like you were my own dear lost daughter, come back to life again and with me."

Amy pulled back, unable to speak. Hannibal wiped tears away, then pulled a handerchief from his pocket and blew his nose. Sniffing, recomposing himself, he said, "I'm sorry. I didn't mean to become emotional."

Amy stood. "Maybe I should go on to bed. I'm tired all at once."

"Yes. Well . . . good night, Amy. Sleep well."

"Good night to you, Uncle Hannibal. Are you staying up for a while?"

"I hadn't planned to . . . but I think I will. For a little spell. I have a bit of thinking to do." He rubbed his neck. "And my head is hurting tonight. Headaches and neckaches. That's all I have anymore. Headaches and neckaches. I'll sit up until I feel a little better, then I'll go to bed."

They both know that when morning came, he would be asleep, not on his bed, but on the parlor sofa. Since Lena's death it had been difficult for him to rest in the bed he and his wife had shared so many years.

"Good night, then. I hope your headache goes away." She walked away, up the stairs and into her room.

He was already awake, dressed, and cooking breakfast when she came down the stairs again the next morning. She knew from his manner that there was something to be said, and she had already guessed what it was.

Thus she showed no reaction when at the close of the meal he said, "Amy, I don't anticipate you'll like what I have to say, so I'll put no pretty face on it and say it squarely. I've decided you should go north. Get out of Tennessee for now, and stay out until this cursed war is settled. I have a cousin in Barbourville, a fine woman, a widow, who lives alone in a fine, big house. No doubt arrangements can be made to place you with her. Even in Barbourville the situation may become tense, but Kentucky is at least officially neutral soil, and I believe you will be far safer there than here. I don't think it would be wise for you to be too close to me in the coming days."

He sees me as a child, Amy thought. *He's even assigned a nanny to me.*

"Her name is Mrs. Jerome. Mrs. Cynthia Jerome. She is as staunch a good Union woman as you will ever meet. She doesn't know about my abolitionism or the Underground Railroad activity, by the way, so you'll need to keep quiet as to that. Otherwise I think you'll be very happy there, and safer."

What could she say? What he presented sounded intolerable, but after last night she understood at least the sentiment behind his ideas and couldn't fault it. He saw himself as protecting what remained of his small circle of loved ones.

"Well, Amy, what do you think? Would you enjoy being a Kentucky girl? I believe you would."

He seems so changed now, she thought. *It's sad. Lena, why did you have to die?* "Well, Uncle Hannibal, I suppose I'll have to adjust to the idea, but—"

"Adjust, yes. Yes. And I'm sure that adjust you will, quite well. And believe me, I'll be much happier down here in Tennessee knowing that you are safe in Kentucky with dear old Cynthia Jerome."

He seems so distracted, like there is so much on his mind. "But what about the house, and the store? Who'll help you run your business?"

"Hmmm? Oh, I'll hire some help. Don't worry about that. I'll even hire a housekeeper, if need be, to keep this place clean. No problem there."

"I doubt there is any point in arguing with you."

"No," he said, smiling. "I doubt there is."

"When will I go?"

"As soon as possible, Amy. I'll begin the arrangements today. My! Don't I feel relieved, seeing you take it so well, and knowing that you'll be on neutral soil!"

"I'm glad," she said, telling him what he wanted to hear. "I want you to be happy, Uncle Hannibal. And if it makes you happier for me to be in Kentucky, then there I'll go."

"Good girl, Amy. Good girl. I'm so pleased. If Lena were here, I know she'd be pleased, too. Not only that, but she'd be going with you. East Tennessee is simply no place for a good Union woman to be at the moment. Don't you think?"

She smiled. "It appears that good Union women are quite unwelcome in East Tennessee. Listening to you, I'm beginning to see just how unwelcome."

He nodded, smiling, utterly missing the sarcasm. "Good girl, Amy. I'm glad you see the matter as I do." He dug out his pocket watch. "Mercy! We'd best hurry, Amy, or we'll be late. I do miss having Sam around to get the store open. Come on now, hurry up! We've got a full day's work ahead, and we'd best enjoy what time of normalcy we have left. I wish we could just go on forever with . . . but never mind that. What is, is, and what is not, is not. Let's go, my dear."

Chapter 22

They passed the day of November 8, 1861, in their own assorted ways. Some paced in silence in their rooms, some traveled, some prayed, some drank, some jested, some carried on the business of a normal day, and some removed themselves from the company of their fellows and spent hours in silent, tense contemplation. Then night fell and one by one they came together in their designated bands, some small and others large, and moved out in silence to burn the bridges and clear the way for the anticipated Federal invasion of East Tennessee.

Hannibal Deacon was among them. He joined his hand-picked little band in the same barn where they had first discussed the plan. They waited until deep night, took big tins of fuel, weapons, and several blocks of matches, and headed on horseback toward the Colter bridge, riding on the happy wave of a fact one of the number had brought in with him: There was no one guarding the bridge this night.

It is as it should be, Hannibal thought. *The bridge is unguarded, my raiders are ready and willing, and there is no one at home to grieve me if the worst happens.* Amy was gone for days now, up in Kentucky with Cynthia Jerome. He was gratified that she had gone along with it all so willingly. He hadn't expected that from Amy. Had he not been so preoccupied with the arson work at hand, he might have wondered why she had been so atypically unargumentative.

Perhaps it was simply that things sometimes worked out as they should. If providence smiled this evening, the destruction of the Colter bridge would work out just as well.

Elsewhere there were other raiders with much bigger targets in their sights than the little Colter span. The bridge over the Tennessee River at Bridgeport in Alabama was the largest and most important on the list of destruction because of the great difficulty and expense that would be involved in replacing it. Two men rode out to assault the big structure, but when Robert W. Ragan and James D. Keener saw the long line of rebel soldiers guarding it, they had no choice but to turn away and leave the job undone. They had ridden eighty-five miles from their homes to burn the Bridgeport span; now they rode the same miles back again, hoping that the other bands of burners would have more success than they.

At the town of Loudon, they did not. The burners assigned to destroy that structure found it, too, so well guarded that any attempt was pointless, and turned back.

In Marion County, Tennessee, some thirty miles to the northeast of the two unsuccessful Bridgeport raiders, two others rode in the night. They were W. T. Cate and W. H. Crowder; their mission was the destruction of two bridges across Chickamauga Creek, the first on the East Tennessee and Georgia line, the second east of Chattanooga and on the Western and Atlantic. Cate and Crowder fared much better than had Ragan and Keener, and left both bridges, each near to the other, in flames, and headed home without having been seen or harassed.

Meanwhile, miles away near the Hiwassee River on a public road brilliantly lighted by the moon, yet another pair of men sat on their horses, waiting for a third man. The two were brothers, A. M. and Thomas Cate, siblings of W.T.; the man they awaited was one Adam Thomas. The task they faced was the destruction of the intricately built, roofed railroad bridge over the Hiwassee River, near the town of Charleston on the Bradley County side of the river, and the community of Calhoun on the McMinn County side. Though they had examined the bridge covertly days before and knew it would burn swiftly once ignited, they did not anticipate firing it would be an easy accomplishment. Indeed, the man who was to have led the raid, William Stone, had turned away from the job at the last moment, overwhelmed by it, and left it in the hands of A. M. Cate.

Now, as they waited, A. M. Cate felt something like cold fingers around his spine as he saw two full squads of Confederate soldiers come marching into view in the moonlight, led by an officer. To move now was pointless; they had already been seen. So he and his brother took the opposite tack and rode directly toward the approaching rebels, acting thoroughly casual. Slumping in their saddles, nonchalant, they revealed none of the anxiety they felt as the gap between them and the approaching rebel squads narrowed. The officer eyed them; pleasantries were exchanged.

The rebel squads marched on. The Cate brothers continued riding the other way until the soldiers were out of sight, then rode back to the spot where they had been before, and found Adam Thomas awaiting them.

The three rode on down the road to a place where two others, Jesse F. and Eli Cleveland, a father and son, waited for them with unlighted pine torches, matches, and turpentine. With miminal words or noise, they gathered all their supplies and began the journey toward the long, beautiful bridge over the Hiwassee and whatever end fate held in store for them there.

Some fifteen miles east of Knoxville, a good-natured, devil-may-care Sevier County man by the name of William Pickens rode along back roads in the company of about fifteen other men, bearing weapons and fuel. Unlike A. M. Cates's band near the Hiwassee, they enjoyed the benefit of some moon-obscuring clouds. Any worries among the group didn't seem to be shared by their leader, Pickens, but he hadn't worried about much anything in years, as far as anyone knew. A former county sheriff, Pickens was known for his recklessness. He advanced now toward the railroad bridge at Strawberry Plains in an attitude of high sport, anticipating that all would go off without a hitch and the Strawberry Plains villagers would soon enjoy the spectacle of quite a nice bridge fire along the East Tennessee and Virginia line.

They abandoned the road and progressed through a field, then dismounted, tied their horses, and left them to the care of a few of their number. The remaining dozen or so went toward the Holoton River on foot. Reaching a fence, they worked a board loose and crept through, went a little farther, descended the riverbank and slipped along it toward the abutment of the bridge. Pickens peered along the dark line of the trestle and, though it was too dark to be certain, saw no sign of guards. He grinned. It appeared this was going to be even easier than anticipated, and no doubt quite a lot of fun.

With whispers and motions the group improvised a simple plan on the spot. With part of the group keeping watch and the rest ready to follow momentarily, Pickens and a companion made their way to the base of the bridge. The second man began climbing the trestle, carrying a tin of turpentine and an unlighted torch with them. He clambered atop a beam about halfway up the structure and paused a moment to pant for breath, then reached into his pocket, pulled out the single block of matches the bridge burners had brought, broke off and struck a match, and applied it to a pine torch dipped in turpentine.

He might as well have applied the match to dynamite, considering what followed just thereafter.

The yellow glow of the torch revealed a large wooden shelter box built up into the understructure of the bridge, and inside that box, an armed man. Yelling in surprise, the man with the torch dropped it; it sputtered on the ground below, giving only the most feeble illumination to the stunning fight that commenced.

The relative darkness was broken by the flash of a firing

pistol; the man who had dropped the torch fell almost atop it, badly wounded.

A wild, scrambling fight in almost total darkness followed. Pickens himself ascended to do battle with the bridge guard, a scrappy, wiry man to whom the darkness lent a demonic quality. There was slashing, shooting, screaming, and when it was done, the guard was gone, having either fallen or jumped from his perch, bearing on his person many wounds. He managed to get away in the night and make his way toward a nearby house for medical help, his left hand almost severed and gushing blood.

The bridge burners were hardly better off than the guard, with many assorted wounds among them. Pickens had suffered multiple stabs and a gunshot wound, and was fast losing blood.

Worst of all, the matches were gone, lost in the darkness, and the torch that had fallen to the ground was burned out.

"There's a house yonder," someone suggested. "Let's go see if they'll lend us some fire."

"Are you a fool?" another replied. "You want to shove your face up in front of some stranger and say, 'Pardon me, I want some matches to burn yonder bridge, thank you kindly,' you go ahead. Not me! I don't want to hang!"

Argument lasted only moments more before the obvious was accepted: If the bridge at Strawberry Plains was to be burned, it wouldn't be tonight. An entire gang of men against one bridge and one guard—and they had failed, all for lack of planning, the bulldog tenaciousness of a single rebel, and a shortage of matches.

They abandoned the bridge, making for the place they had left their horses, managing somehow to keep the bleeding Pickens conscious. Mounting up, they rode off as others converged on the bridge to investigate the gunfire they had heard and to puzzle over what had happened to the wiry little rebel who'd been guarding the bridge.

In a stand of pine less than a mile from the Hiwassee River bridge they were determined to burn, the Cate brothers, Adam Thomas, and the two Clevelands listened closely, and for the first time in some two hours heard no sound of human activity. Since eleven o'clock they had hidden in this thicket, hearing noises of merrymaking from the nearby towns. Such a babble could only indicate that many soldiers were present, enjoying a Friday night's fun. But surely others were stationed at the bridge, guarding it. There had been many rumors about bridge burning, after all, and the rebels could scarcely afford to lose the Hiwassee bridge. Initially, A. M. Cate had been dismayed. Would they have to turn back? He was resolved to do so only if essential.

The decline of noise from the towns indicated that the revelry had broken up for the night, so Cate felt slightly more optimistic. He turned to the others and suggested they go have a look at the bridge.

Jesse Cleveland was hesitant. The bridge would surely be well guarded, considering all the bridge-burning rumors. And they already knew rebels were out on the roads tonight, meaning flight would be dangerous even if they got the bridge aflame. Maybe the best thing would be to turn back.

A. M. Cate was not surprised by this loss of nerve on Cleveland's part; the time of waiting had given the men time to consider what a dangerous situation they faced, and hesitation was natural. It was up to him to revive spirits. He shook his head and told them he would not go back, even if they did. He had come to burn the bridge, and would see it done at any risk. All he would ask of them was that they keep his identity secret should any rebels come inquiring afterward.

Silence . . . and then the men looked at one another and rose, gathering their fuel and weapons. A.M. was going on, and so would they. He smiled to himself. A good and brave band, this one.

They went to the tracks and headed along them toward the bridge, keeping a watchful eye all the way. The bridge was quite a structure, several hundred feet long, and with a pitch-covered roof. One of them commented on what a shame it was, having to burn such a fine structure.

Contrary to expectation, there were no soldiers visible at the bridge. But a guardhouse stood nearby, dim light spilling from its window. Tom Cate sneaked to the window and looked inside; the single guard was fast asleep. He was relieved; the men had been prepared to kill the guard if need be—a distasteful job—or offer him a hundred-dollar bribe, which would be the more palatable approach but leave open the possibility of a betrayal later on. A sleeping guard was the best scenario, the very one they had hoped for. At that moment they all felt sure of success for the first time since the venture began.

The actual destruction of the bridge and the simultaneous cutting of the nearby telegraph line was performed by Tom Cate, Adam Thomas, and Eli Cleveland. A. M. Cate and the elder Cleveland stood guard, hoping not to awaken the rebel sentinel but ready to kill him if they did.

The fire, ignited by torches put to turpentine spilled along the bridge, was as much like explosion as mere flame. A. M. Cate watched with a thrill of awe as the fire shot up the dry wood of the bridge and ignited the pitch roof with astonishing speed. Fire raced at demonic pace down the bridge top. It was one of the most striking sights he had ever seen.

There was no time to linger to admire the spectacle. In minutes the bridge would be surrounded by confused and furious Confederates. At top speed the raiders made off, the bridge flaring behind them, sending flames and light high into the sky.

A. M. Cate was satisfied. Whatever success or lack of success occurred at the other bridges, there was at least one major span that had fallen to the torch. It would be quite some time before the rebels would run supply trains across *that* bridge! The Cate brothers and their cohorts had done their job, and now wanted nothing more than to put miles behind them as quickly as possible until they were safely out of range of discovery and retaliation.

Across East Tennessee other bridges burned that night.

The bridge over the Holston at Union Depot in Sullivan County was burned by a band under the command of Daniel Stover, son-in-law of Andrew Johnson. Among Stover's bridge-burning band was Greeley Brown.

Yet another bridge, crossing the Watauga River at Carter's Depot, would have been torched by Stover's band had not a company of Confederates under Captain David McClelland, stationed nearby, rendered it inaccessible.

One bridge that did go up in flames was the long and spindly one spanning the marshy Lick Creek in Greene County, destroyed by a substantial and rather rowdy group of bridge burners led by the appropriately named Captain David Fry, who was a Greene County native out of Company F, Second Regiment, East Tennessee Volunteers.

And a few miles beyond Greeneville, the bridge at Colter was lost to the torch, destroyed without opposition by the group formed and led by Hannibal Deacon. Everything had gone well for Hannibal's group. If not for the fact that he suffered throughout the entire event with one of those now-frequent nagging headaches of his, and a nosebleed besides, he would have found it all very nearly exhilarating.

All in all, the operation seemed to have been a moderate success. Though several targeted bridges had not been destroyed, enough were now gone to hobble the rebels for the moment. And if all went as planned, a moment would be all that was needed. The bridge burners had been assured that the Federal army was poised to sweep in through Cumberland Gap, spill across East Tennessee, and divide the Confederacy down the middle.

The Unionists of the mountain empire could hardly wait to see it happen.

For those involved, the immediate aftermath of the bridge burnings varied from man to man.

Captain David Fry, destroyer of the Lick Creek bridge, headed for Union service within Georgia, while several of those who had helped him sought refuge among the hidden Unionist bands ranging the country. A. M. Cate stampeded north for Kentucky with his eye on the Union Army. The wounded Pickens of Sevier County, smarting not only from his wounds but also from his failure to destroy the Strawberry Plains bridge, was hauled on horseback to a home some miles from the bridge, treated there by a physician, then placed on a sled and covered with fodder, beneath which he was hauled to Wear's Cove, a remote section of the Smoky Mountains that was becoming a hiding place for Unionist refugees. He would never be captured as a bridge burner, but his aging father would be arrested in his place and die in the Confederate prison at Tuscaloosa.

The bulldog of a Confederate guard who had fought with Pickens also survived the damage he received at the bridge—though he lost most of his left hand—and would become a hero among Confederates by merit of a lurid, gory pamphlet about the Strawberry Plains incident that was published some months after the event by a Smoky Mountain postmaster named Gatlin. The failed Strawberry Plains bridge burners would find themselves mortified by their characterization in that pamphlet as bumbling, immoral, damnation-bound fools, and by the presentation of the guard, a sprightly little man named James Keelan, as a virtual minor god, bound for eternal glory. The gushing title alone was rankling to those Keelan had bested: "The Parentage, Birth, Nativity and Exploits of the Immortal Hero James Keelan, Who Defended Successfully the Bridge at Strawberry Plains, and Alone, Put to Flight Fifteen Lincolnites on the Night of the Eighth of November, A.D. 1861."

As for Hannibal Deacon, he headed back to his home in Greeneville—a lonely home now, but a welcome sight for a man who had enjoyed no assurance that he would live to come home at all. But all his concerns, realistic though they had been, had thankfully come to nothing. He couldn't have been more pleased with the outcome of the burning of the Colter bridge. No resistance, no guards, no difficulty at all. He was grateful all had gone so flawlessly.

He rose early the morning of November 9 eager to get into town and watch reactions to the spreading word about the burned bridges. He knew only of the success of the Colter bridge burning; if fortune had smiled, all the other operations had gone just as well, and the Confederate railroad system in East Tennessee was gravely damaged. He anticipated the likely immediate result if in fact all the burnings had gone off as planned: panic among Confederates and joy among Unionists in expectation of Union invasion. Hannibal walked through Greeneville toward his store, feeling more youthful and vigorous than he had in months.

News wasn't long in coming. The bridge burnings had caught the Confederacy by more surprise than they should have, and near panic ensued in some quarters. Hannibal learned through the flying gossip which bridges had been destroyed, which had survived, and feigned great surprise at all he was told. Secretly he assessed the overall effort: not perfect, since several bridges had survived, but probably sufficient. The ruling Confederacy was reportedly livid with anger, and also worried. It had long been spread about that the burning of the bridges would be the signal for both internal Unionist revolt in Tennessee and a Union military invasion out of Kentucky by way of Cumberland Gap. In the wake of the burnings, leading Confederate citizens began looking for havens of safety for their families and themselves, anticipating warfare on their doorsteps.

Indeed, Unionists did rise up across the mountain country, eager to meet and join the anticipated Federal invaders. Great bands of Unionist men swiftly gathered at various points in East Tennessee, ready to help reclaim their homeland. A Union force of some five hundred came together near Strawberry Plains, and in Hamilton County upward of a thousand Unionists took up arms. A thousand men came together at Elizabethton in Carter County, armed with old rifles, shotguns, and in many cases pitchforks, hoes, and the like. Fired with anticipation, this ragtag army set out to attack McClelland's rebels at Carter's Depot, though at length some wise counsel from some of their level-headed leaders made them change their minds. Best to wait for the regular Federals to arrive before pitting an army of poorly equipped farmers, merchants, and mechanics against a trained and well-armed rebel force.

They did not anticipate having to wait long. The plan had been too carefully made, the invasion too firmly promised. Now that the bridges were burned, the end was near. Surely nothing could go askew.

* * *

The rebel panic continued apace. Telegrams crackled along the wires that remained uncut by the raiders. John R. Branner, president of the East Tennessee and Virginia Railroad, wired Judah Philip Benjamin, Confederate secretary of war, news of the bridge destruction on his line, adding that there was "great excitement along the whole line of road and evidence that the Union party are organizing and preparing to destroy or take possession of the whole line from Bristol to Chattanooga, and unless the Government is very prompt in giving us the necessary military aid I much fear the result." Failure to act, he warned, would mean that "transportation over my road of army supplies will be an utter impossibility; it cannot be done."

General A. S. Johnston, in Bowling Green, Kentucky, wired Tennessee Governor Isham Harris that the state government should "use every exertion to ascertain the extent, power, and organization of this insurrection if, as I fear, one exists, and most urgently I press your excellency to leave no means untried to put arms into the hands of your unarmed levies."

Though he was not positioned to see the full extent of the uproar, Hannibal enjoyed very much that which he could see, and waited eagerly for the Union force to break through. For the first time since Lena's death he felt truly invigorated. At last something good was going to happen. At last sanity was about to return to a region that had seen too little of it lately.

But days dragged by, no invaders in blue appeared, and news of high-level Confederate determination to find, convict, and hang all involved with bridge burning spread wide. The makeshift Unionist armies that had gathered the day after the bridge burnings either dispersed or, as in Carter County, took to hiding in the mountains. Though Hannibal himself had felt relatively safe, there now grew a nagging fear that perhaps all might not go as well as he had hoped. One idle word, one rumor of his involvement, and he might be arrested. He grew distressed and ever more eager for the planned Federal invasion, thinking that if it did not come soon, he would be forced to consider stampeding himself.

Then matters grew worse. He began to feel very odd. Sickly. Easily winded, and sometimes dizzy. Occasionally his chest gripped him with sharp pain and he broke out in sweats.

Coming down with something, I suppose, he thought. *Well, it will pass.*

A grim rumor arrived, the grimmest yet of many beginning to travel down the Unionist grapevine: There would be no invasion at all, prior plans to the contrary. A Zollicoffer-led Confederate foray into Kentucky had slowed General Thomas at a place called Wild Cat, only forty-five miles south of Camp Dick Robinson, as Thomas advanced toward Tennessee. Shortly beyond that point, the rumor had it, General Sherman had ordered Thomas to halt and return to his base. There had been a change of strategy. Sherman decided that the Union army was too scattered, and the rebels too much in force in areas nearby East Tennessee. So the Federal invasion of East Tennessee was for now called off.

As for those who in good faith carried out the bridge burning, it was simply too bad. The change of strategy had come about too late for word to be sent to call off the operation.

Hannibal was bewildered to consider that all they had done, all the risk they'd taken, had been for nothing. For the first time he could remember, he felt stung and even betrayed by the government to whose preservation he had devoted himself.

Hannibal's arrest came unexpectedly as he walked from a café on Main Street back toward his store, his chest hurting him again and his forehead wet with a sweat he couldn't account for. He was surrounded, chained, and shoved into the back of a closed wagon, where he sat, stunned, under the guard of a stern Confederate with widespread eyes and so narrow a chin that he looked like a cat.

"Where are you taking me?" Hannibal asked.

"Knoxville."

"Why?"

"You've been accused of burning the bridge at Colter, or so I hear."

Hannibal's chest hurt worse, and he felt he might become sick, but he forced a defiant expression. "On what evidence am I charged?"

"I'm just a guard. I don't know about evidence. All I know is that the big men are eager for a few bridge-burner convictions. Want a few examples to set for others who might think of taking up the torch. I hear they see you as a likely one. That's why they're hauling you all the way to Knoxville. You're special, my friend, because of who you are. I hear there's a man who says he can testify he was present when you planned the burning of the bridge." The guard clicked his tongue reprovingly and shook his head.

Ross! Hannibal's stomach lurched with an acidic, burning pain. It had to be Ross. No other present for that initial meeting would have betrayed him.

Hannibal, fighting to keep his composure, kept silent a few moments, then said, "They'll not be able to convict me."

"You'd better hope not," the guard replied. His slick smile widened and he looked more like a cat than ever. " 'Cause if they do, they'll hang you." The grin lingered. "I'm glad I ain't you, mister. It ain't no way to die, dunging up your britches right in front of everybody, stretching your toes trying to find the ground. . . ." He shuddered. "No way at all for a man to have to die. Yes sir, I'm mighty glad I ain't you." He reached in a pocket. "Hey, Lincolnite, you look peaked. Downright sickly. Maybe you need a smoke. Want you a cigar? If you do, sing out, for there ain't likely to be nobody else offering you one."

Though Hannibal hadn't smoked in years, he accepted the offer. "You're a true Christian, sir," he said with all the sarcasm he could muster."

"I try," the cat-faced guard said. "I do try. One wants to be assured of heaven when death comes calling. And for some of us, sorry to say, it comes calling before our time." He leaned back and laughed.

Hannibal did not join in. A new headache stabbed through his skull, and when his upper lip moistened unexpectedly a while later, he touched it and saw blood come away on his finger. Another nosebleed. He pulled a handkerchief from his pocket, pressed it to his nostrils and sat in glum silence, feeling vaguely faint. He pictured himself being hanged and found the image intolerable. He shoved it from his mind, but it reentered at once and would not be expelled again.

Chapter 23

A few days later, just below Cumberland Gap

The rider, though slender and light, was having quite a hard go of it. Astride a mare and enduring a worn-out saddle that fit neither horse nor human particularly well, the rider jolted along uncomfortably, the beast barely under control and increasingly skittish as the wind rose and dusk approached.

Ahead, lights began to appear in the windows of the scattered cabins and houses of the valley. On the hills and rolling farm country north of the Powell River, distant flickerings rose from cook fires. There was an occasional crack of a distant rifle, and the frequent clatter of military drumbeats from someplace far away. Occasionally an isolated laugh or shout would ride the wind and reach the ear. The rider, seemingly alone, was far from it. The valley was filled with Confederates.

In the late afternoon the changing wind had generated fear that rain would come, but now what clouds there were did not seem likely to precipitate and the wind no longer had a moist feel. The rider was glad. Enduring a storm on a night with no available shelter would not be pleasant.

A quarter of a mile on, the rider jerked the horse to a halt suddenly. The horse nickered and stamped. The rider peered through the dwindling light toward a hillside ahead, down which a road meandered. A sizable body of Confederate soldiers was approaching along that road, perhaps three-quarters of a mile away. The rider turned the horse at once and left the road, heading across a field toward a stand of woods.

By the time the Confederates passed it was almost completely dark on the open land, and very dark indeed in the copse. Initially worried that the horse would make some noise and draw the attention of the soldiers, the rider now knew this had been a vain worry. The soldiers had made such a racket as they passed that they wouldn't have heard it anyway.

Rising, the rider stood pondering whether to go on or to remain here for the night. There were dangers either way. Traveling by day, one was easily visible and subject to being stopped and questioned. By night, travel bore overtones of secrecy, of spying, of having reason not to be seen. Night was the time of the stampeders, men moving like phantoms through mountain hollows and over high passes in a quest for escape from a rebel government. But this rider moved in the opposite direction, back deeper into Tennessee.

I'll go on, the rider thought. *Safer by night, and surely no one can mistake me for a stampeder while I'm moving south.*

Pausing to let the cramps work out of weary legs and a saddle-jolted spine enjoy a welcome stretch, the rider reached up and yanked away a broad-brimmed hat. Long brunette hair spilled out like a flood, and the rider ran her fingers through it, enjoying the feel of letting it fall free instead of being stuffed up inside the hat as it had been all day. It was a risky ruse, this dressing as a man, but it had worked, and Amy Deacon was proud of herself for having pulled it off.

She had traveled from Barbourville and a brief but frustrating bondage endured in the house of Hannibal Deacon's widowed cousin, the meek, worrisome, eternally dispiriting

Cynthia Jerome, whose prattling and nervousness had been almost impossible to bear and whose lack of pleasure at having Amy about had been evident from the outset. Only Amy's plan for escape—a plan that began to take shape from the moment Hannibal announced he was sending her away—had given her the patience to endure the old widow for a while.

Amy Deacon had suffered quite enough of being sent here and sent there. Shipped off to Greeneville by her father, then to Kentucky by Hannibal, she would put up with such treatment no more. From now on she was deciding for herself where she went and what she did—and what she was going to do now was return to Knoxville, take up some sort of lodging there, and then . . . she wasn't quite sure beyond that. Whatever she did, it would involve serving the Union cause and advancing abolitionism, the two driving forces of her life.

It hadn't been particularly hard to get away from Cynthia Jerome. Amy had put up with the disagreeable widow for just long enough to appear settled and content, and one day handed Mrs. Jerome a letter she said she had just received from Hannibal. Amy secretly watched while the trembly old widow read the letter, moving her lips with each word.

"Why, Hannibal says he's changed plans concerning you, Amy," Mrs. Jerome said once the letter was read and reread. Mental digestion of new ideas was a slow process for Cynthia Jerome. "He writes that he's made plans for you to go to Hazel Patch and join a Mr. Harold Burke and his family, some old friends of his."

"Yes, I know. Uncle Hannibal says he's come to think I'll be a burden on you in these hard times, and I must say I believe maybe he's right."

"Why, no, of course you haven't been a . . . I mean, you're quite welcome and such a fine guest . . . but oh, well, we must do what Hannibal wants, mustn't we? May I help you with your packing, Amy?"

Amy had fought to squelch a smile. "No, Mrs. Jerome. I can see to it myself."

Once alone, and as she folded her garments into her travel trunk and gathered her other personal possessions,

Amy let the smile beam. She was proud of how cleverly she had worked everything out. The letter was her own work, a careful forgery she had written herself and signed with Hannibal's name. Mr. Harold Burke and family were fictional, and she had no intention of going to Hazel Patch. Amy had known that Mrs. Jerome, slow and unsophisticated, would take the letter at face value, not question how it had come or demand to see any postmarked envelope. Amy knew she was an unwelcome houseguest, and had counted, rightly, on Cynthia Jerome leaping at the opportunity to be rid of her.

Mrs. Jerome offered to make arrangements to hire a buggy to carry her to Hazel Patch, but Amy quickly said she would handle that matter herself—no need to trouble Mrs. Jerome, who had already "been so very kind." The only driver Amy could locate was a seedy-looking fellow who grinned and winked at her from his perch and smelled worse than his dirty, broken-down horses. She directed him to leave town as if bound north for Hazel Patch, then to swing about and head southeast along the Cumberland instead. Her intention was to leave him near Cumberland Gap, change into rugged male garb she had privately purchased as part of her escape plan, and cross the mountains on foot through one of the lesser passes downrange from the Gap.

Here, for the first time, the plan had gone awry. The driver lived up to the impression he generated and made unwelcome advances once they were away from town. Amy had been forced to leap out of the carriage, tearing her dress badly and abandoning her luggage. By good fortune she had retained most of her money in a hidden pocket sewn inside her skirts.

Shaken by the driver's mistreatment, unwilling to return to Mrs. Jerome, and not wanting to delay her homeward journey by having to give explanations and pleas for help to some stranger, Amy turned thief for the first time in her life. Having lost the male clothing she had planned to wear over the mountains, she dared to steal some from a chest in the back room of a stranger's house. She was terrified the entire time, taking the garments at the rear of the house while listening to voices in the front. Finding a hiding place, she transferred her money from the dress pocket to the trousers, stuffed her hair into a purloined hat, and smeared her face with dirt to give it a whiskery look at least from a distance. She then resumed travel on foot and managed to avoid directly encountering anyone at all.

The trip over the mountains was terrifically difficult and filled her with appreciation for the trials endured by those Unionists on Confederate soil who had to flee through the wilderness to reach friendly ground. She came down the southern slope of the Cumberlands covered with grime, her stolen clothes tattered and soiled. But she had made it! She had escaped her Kentucky exile, and now was ready to begin her great and still substantially unplanned adventure for the causes she believed in.

Having stolen clothing, Amy took a further step, quite a big one, and turned horse thief. She did this impulsively when tempted by the unexpected finding of a good mare in a stable hidden out in a big grove of woods. She supposed the horse was in such a remote place to keep it from being commandeered by soldiers, who were prone to take any good animal they ran across. Feeling guilty, but also secretly thrilled to be at such a dangerous and forbidden task, she took the horse along with an old saddle she found in the same stable.

She was proud of her escape, thinking that this was quite a fine adventure, even if it was worrisome and even if Hannibal was bound to find out about it sooner or later and be furious with her.

She couldn't worry about that kind of thing anymore, though. Hannibal's clear belief that she was less capable than a male of serving the great causes, and that she needed some mousy little guardian like Cynthia Jerome to "look after" her, had insulted her deeply. Amy did not bear insults well. She would show Hannibal Deacon who was strong! She would show him, the world, herself, that she was perfectly capable of forging her own destiny without anyone to "look after" her. She was on her own, and no one would stand in her way now!

* * *

After shaking out her hair and resting briefly, Amy steeled herself to move on.

"Let's go, old Dobbin," she said to the recalcitrant mare. "Let's see if we can shake a few more miles out of you tonight."

"Well, Jimmy!" said a male voice that came out of the inky darkness not three feet to her left, making her gasp and turn with a jerk. "I thought there was something a bit oddish about this here intruder!"

"I discerned just the same, Miles," a second voice said, also to her left and very near. "Our he is a she!"

Panic surged. Amy had stumbled into a hiding place already occupied! Her fresh experience with the carriage driver had left her skittish, and there was something in the tone and deliberately startling approach of these strangers that was particularly threatening. She yanked at her horse's lead and tried to bolt out of the trees at the same time. Then a hand reached out of the darkness and filled itself with her hair. The hand pulled back, hard, and she fell.

"Damn! I wish I could see her!" her captor said. "I'd like to know if she's pretty!" His hand descended to her face, tracing its shape. She was too frightened to scream.

"Here we go, Miles—take a look," the other said. They were kneeling beside her, knees jamming her ribs, foul breath from unseen faces stinking in her nostrils. A match flared; their faces, illuminated, were bearded and dirty and ugly. They looked down at her, the man with the match grinning a hungry grin, but the other puckering to blow out the match at once.

"You damned fool!" that man said. "You want them rebs to see a light?"

"They can't see nothing in these trees, and besides that, they've done gone by. Hey, did you see her? All smudged up, but pretty. Real pretty." Amy sensed his now unseen face lowering toward hers, felt the brush of his whiskers. She lunged upward with her head and bit his nose hard. The taste was oily and foul, repulsive, but she didn't let up until the salty taste of blood joined the other tangs already insulting her tongue. Her victim howled in agony.

"Jimmy, Jimmy—hush, Jimmy! The rebs—look out there! There's more of 'em!"

"God, she bit my nose, nearly bit it off!" Then something pounded hard into the ground beside Amy's head, and she knew he had tried to hit her but missed in the darkness.

"Jimmy, shut up and lie low!"

She screamed, "Help! Help me! Please!"

She jerked her head to the left; a fist again pounded the ground, this time right where her face had been. She screamed again, and felt a sudden sharp, stinging pain in her side, but it lasted only a moment.

The men swore, struggled a little more, then finally let her go. They got up and moved away, the more aggressive one managing to kick her in the side of the head as he went. It hurt, but did not stun her. She rolled away, got up and pushed into some brush until she could go no farther. She turned and looked back. It was ebony dark in the woods, but through the brush and trees she could see some of the field beyond.

She had dropped the lead of her horse when they pulled her down, and the horse had left the trees and gone into the field. The men went after it, but it ran. They chased it, finally caught it. Above, clouds parted and the field became more light. One swung into the saddle and the other came up behind him. They rode double toward the road and she lost sight of them.

Amy wondered who the men had been. Stampeders? Or might they have been rebels themselves, deserting? Amy expected there would be a lot of desertion before the war ended, but it was early in the war yet. So most likely they were stampeders. Or maybe mere criminals on the run, afraid of authorities in uniforms of any color.

Amy remained in the brush for a minute. Then she heard a yell out in the dark somewhere, from the direction of the road. "Halt!" Silence, then the identical call again, and then a crackle of rifle fire.

"Got 'em!" someone yelled. "Catch that horse, Private!"

Amy did something she had never done before: She inwardly cheered for a rebel soldier. Whatever Confederate sentry or patroller had shot down the two miscreants, he was a friend of hers.

She squeezed back out of the brush. Her face was scratched and she felt much abused and bruised. It was bad that her horse was gone, but at the moment she didn't much care. She was alive and not seriously hurt. . . .

She froze where she was. Her hand had just brushed her side at the point she had felt that sting in the mist of the struggle. Something warm and liquid covered her fingers and palm.

Oh, God help me, they stabbed me! She hadn't even realized it.

She had known a girl in school who had fallen against a scythe, passed out, and bled to death before anyone even knew what happened. Ever since, Amy had felt a horror of the idea of death by bleeding. To feel life draining away, to feel consciousness fading and knowing that when it was gone so also was any hope of staunching the life-draining flow . . .

Feeling weak and faint all at once, she made for the field. "Help me!" she screamed, staggering out of the woods and into the open. She could dimly make out men on the road, gathered in a cluster around the pair they had killed. Rebels. She did not care. They were soldiers and they would help her. "They stabbed me! Help me, please . . ."

"Sweet Moscs, that's a *lady!*" one of the soldiers exclaimed.

Amy stopped, swayed, and collapsed.

She sat on a folding stool inside a tent, a blanket across her shoulders and a cup of stew in her hands. Facing her was a kindly-looking soldier who had introduced himself as Lieutenant Dupont Reaves, and though he was doing his best to make her feel at ease, his gentle smile and soothing way of speaking only deepened the tremendous embarrassment that Amy felt.

The soldiers, a small band of scouts, had gotten her to their temporary camp in some manner—having fainted like a wilting flower, Amy had missed all awareness of being transported—and stirred back to life with much sincere concern. They had spoken comfortingly to her, placed her on a cot, covered her with a blanket, put folded blankets beneath her head, and brought in a fellow they all called "Doc" to check out her wound. It had turned out to be nothing major at all, not even a true stab. Somehow in the struggle with the two men in the grove, something had managed to lacerate her side. Maybe a knife, maybe just a sharp stick on the forest floor. The wound had bled quite a bit, but there was nothing threatening about it and certainly nothing that should have made her become weak and faint. "Doc" had offered to stitch it up for her, if she wanted, but said he figured it would heal just fine without stitching.

It was humiliating. She had set out on a great, idealistically driven adventure, determined to prove herself as worthy and capable as anyone—and what had she done so far but almost be molested by a carriage driver and two hidden stampeders, and then faint like a morning glory in the noonday sun because of a minor cut.

Maybe I should have stayed in Cynthia Jerome's parlor after all, she thought, self-disgusted and scared. *Maybe Hannibal was right about women and war.* She took another sip of the thin, brothy soup and swallowed sullenly. *Maybe he was even right about my maturity. This isn't a game. It isn't safe. I could be hurt, or worse. But I won't let that happen . . . I'll have to be cautious and clever to do it, but I'll make it through.*

Adding to Amy's tension was the necessity of lying to these rebels. She wasn't about to tell them who she really was or what she was up to—the Amy Deacon name was somewhat infamous among rebels now that the story of her "betrayal" of the famed George Deacon of Secession Hill was known by almost all—and so she had to come up with answers off the cuff as the well-meaning lieutenant asked them. She had worried that these soldiers might think her a spy because of her male clothing, but so far she had received nothing but rather syrupy sympathy from young men who seemed determined to make an instant company sweetheart out of her.

"And so them two made you come with them, Miss

Mundy?" the lieutenant asked, jotting down notes as she related the "facts" of her situation. Amy had contrived a cover story of kidnapping, making it up as she went along. Among the contrived details was that her name was Amy Mundy, and her brother, Pleadis Mundy, was a Confederate volunteer who, as best she knew, was now at Morristown. Amy claimed she had been on her way to Morristown from her home in Bulls Gap to tell her brother about the death of their grandfather, who had raised them after their parents had died of fever, when the kidnapping occurred.

"Those two terrible men came upon me while I was passing through Russellville and—"

"Why, that's my home, Russellville!" the lieutenant said, smiling. "Where exactly were you when they came upon you?"

"I was . . . just on the road there, you know. I don't remember quite where."

"I understand. You've been frightened, miss, and young women, they often get panicked and forget things when they've been frightened."

Patronizing, conceited fool, Amy thought. "Yes, you're right," she said, sniffing, voice quivering. "I seem to have forgotten so much."

"Just tell me what you can remember."

She went on, playing the role of the shaken and abused young innocent, concocting a tale of having been kidnapped by two men who were heading north to fight for the Union, of being forced by them to wear a man's clothing so as to not attract attention, and of being almost ravaged in that dark grove of trees, only to be saved by the timely arrival of the lieutenant and his fellow brave soldiers.

When the lieutenant put away his note-covered pad, he seemed quite proud to have been part of such a noble rescue. He rose. "Miss Mundy, I am pleased that us soldiers here have been fortunate enough to have helped you out when you needed it. And I regret that you've had to put up with such ill treatment from them two Union scoundrels— who will never hurt no other innocent woman again, thanks to the ready rifles of the sons of Dixie. And I want to tell you something. I intend to see you reunited with your brother. I'm going to arrange for some men to take you there. We'll get a carriage or at least a wagon for you—ain't got one at the moment, but we'll get one. We'll see you took safe and sound to Morristown, and put into the company of your brother. That's my pledge to you."

"Thank you, Lieutenant," she said. "You're far too kind to me."

"Not at all, miss." He touched his hat. "I'll leave you be for now. You can rest up and let that wound of yours heal. Meantime, I'll have a dress or two fetched for you and you can get out of them sorry man clothes."

"God bless you, Lieutenant. God bless you and the whole Confederate army."

"I believe he's going to do that, ma'am. I believe that the Yanks will find the men of the South ain't the kind to see their home overrun and their rights trod on and their women mistreated. Them two who mishandled you, that's typical of the Yankee-lover for you. Only thing worse than a northern Yankee is a southern Yankee-lover. Them's the worst kind, for they got no excuse for being what they are. Not a one. And they got no morals, neither. Well, good day to you, Miss Mundy."

"Good day, Lieutenant Reaves. And thank you for all you did for me."

He grinned. "It wasn't much, I don't reckon." She knew she had him under control. He would believe anything she said and probably leap any number of hurdles to do for her whatever she wanted.

She'd like to see Hannibal Deacon turn a rebel into a fawn! Obviously there were some things a woman could do better than a man, whatever Hannibal thought about it. She relaxed significantly.

The lieutenant was as good as his word. Within an hour Amy had been given two dresses, probably confiscated from the bureau of some local woman. They were plain and a little too large, but adequate, and the colors suited her complexion. When she came out wearing one of them, she sensed that she had an entire encampment of rebels instantly infatuated with her. For a young woman who had never played much on her charms, it was an interesting but uncomfortable feeling.

Lieutenant Reaves had clearly marked a personal claim upon her, and took it upon himself to give her a tour of the little camp, which was no more than a few tents, cook fires, and a rope horse pen. She put on a great show of interest.

Reaves chattered on, pointing out this and that, doing his best to make himself and his band of scouts sound like the future of the Confederacy lay with and in them alone. Being so absorbed with thoughts of her own, Amy had trouble paying attention to him, but masked her heedlessness by slipping her arm into his. She felt him tense at her touch, then relax. It was entertaining to watch him struggle not to grin.

Chapter 24

Near the Doe River, south of Elizabethton, Tennessee

Sam Colter, wirier than ever and with face covered by the multihued whiskers he hated, sat astride his big strawberry roan mare and examined closely a narrow road that led up a steep, forested hillside.

"This is it, Della," he said. "Or so I believe. Looks to match the directions that old Negro give us, leastways."

He turned her up the path, thinking of how it reminded him of the same path he had taken that day when he found Greeley Brown unconscious in the lightning-struck cabin. He intended to find Greeley again this time, though in a better situation: According to the directions he had received from a kindly old slave in Elizabethton, this trail led up to Greeley's home.

Sure enough, at the end of the trail he found a log and clapboard house in a woodland clearing. It was a plain structure, but on a beautiful site. A long, sloping meadow rolled down to the east and north, with a small creek at the bottom and another stretch of woods beyond. Above the treetops all around Sam saw the high, winter-brown mountains through whose gaps passed the trails and roads leading into North Carolina and the wild Blue Ridge Mountains.

The sun was just now touching the trees to the west, sending a pale orange light across the land and heightening an already stunning beauty.

"Greeley's got a pretty place here, Della," Sam said. "But I see no light in his house. I wonder if he's home?"

Riding into the front yard, he stopped and called, "Greeley? Are you home? Have I come to the right house?"

No one answered. He called again. "Greeley? It's Sam Colter, come to visit you!"

Still no reply. Sam sighed, dejected. It appeared Greeley was away, and that was a disappointment since he had hoped to be offered a place to sleep for the night.

He remembered Greeley's talk about getting married, and wondered if maybe Greeley's wife was in and unwilling to answer the call of a stranger. These days, people were much more careful about hospitality than they used to be, with the roads crawling with Confederate patrols and suspicions being cast all around, neighbor against neighbor.

He thought that perhaps he should leave, but his eye fell on a log barn to the rear and left of the house. Now, *there* was a place he could sleep, even if no one was home. But he wouldn't want to do it if Greeley's wife was huddling inside, wondering who he was. Being awakened with a shotgun stuck into his face by some overwrought woman would not be at all pleasant.

"Guess it can't hurt to knock at the door and be certain nobody's in," he said.

Dismounting, whistling loud and bright and leaving his rifle in its saddle scabbard so he wouldn't seem threatening, he strode to the door. "Hello the house!" he called, then knocked. "It's Sam Colter, come to visit my old friend Greeley Brown. Mrs. Brown, are you or Greeley home?"

No sound. He went to a window and peered in. The house looked empty.

Satisfied, he went back to his horse. "Della, we've got a barn to sleep in this evening. I just hope Greeley and his missus don't come in later and us give them a scare."

As tired as he was, that possibility didn't disturb him much. He led Della to the barn, removed her saddle, fed her from a supply of grain he found—Greeley wouldn't mind, he was sure—then took his pack, blankets, and rifle, and climbed up to the loft. Spreading one blanket on the hay, he lay down atop it and pulled the other over him. It wasn't even fully dark, but he was ready for rest. Digging in his pack, he produced some biscuits and jerked beef, which he ate, washing it down with water from the ancient canteen that Wilton Colter had given him as a family heirloom. Now wrapped in good cured leather to protect it, the canteen had once belonged to some British soldier back in the Revolution, and was taken as war booty at some time or another by Joshua Colter, a hunter, woodsman, and ancestor of Sam's.

Sam reflected that he himself was living something like one of his own pioneering ancestors these days. Since leaving Greeneville he had roamed the North Carolina mountains, cautiously searching for Joe or news of Joe, wary all the while of not being detected by anyone who might turn the law on to him. Joe was a murder suspect now, and Sam was unsure just where he stood himself in relation to the crime.

He was haunted by what Joe had done. Not so much the slaying of Dabney Sloat, which in the terms of moral equity as perceived by mountaineers held some justification. What haunted Sam was the killing of the other two, the old Cherokee man and Sloat's wife.

He hoped that Joe had held some reason for those slayings. He hoped they had threatened Joe and he'd been forced to kill them in self-defense. But Sam had heard nothing about any dropped weapons or other indicators that the two threatened Joe. Would he have killed them simply for being associated with Sloat? Or worse yet, simply because they were Cherokee?

Sam stoppered his canteen and put it away. He propped up and watched darkness descend, then rolled over and pulled his blanket up under his chin. It was going to be cold this evening and the barn was drafty, but the hay around and under him was warm and comfortable. He would sleep well.

He awakened to the sound of many voices and the trampling beat of horse's hoofs on the earth. Sitting up, he gaped into the darkness of the loft and tried to remember where he was. Then he saw light through the places in the barn's log wall where the old chinking had fallen out and left gaps. Flickering light, hot light . . . fire.

There were yells and whoops and curses. Below in the stall, Della stamped and snorted. Eyes widening with fear, Sam grabbed his rifle, crept to the edge of the loft, and peered over. Out the big barn entrance he saw riders in Confederate uniforms, and others on foot, running about with torches in hand. He couldn't see the house, but the rippling orange light illuminating the milling scene outside told him the house was ablaze.

He ducked back into the loft, thrilling with pure fright.

Confederate raiders . . . burning down the house of the Unionist Greeley Brown.

Paralyzed with fear, Sam sat on his haunches and wondered what to do. Then a dark thought came: *If they're burning the house, the barn will be next.*

He had to escape, but there seemed no way out. He wished now he had looked over the terrain a little more closely before dark. What was behind the barn? Woods, open fields? If he descended and ran, would he be seen?

Suddenly there were men below, carrying torches. Light struck him in the eyes and he sat like a rabbit confronted by the mesmerizing face of a serpent. He dared not move, for if one of them caught a flash of motion and looked up, he would be seen at once.

"Hey, there's a fine mare in this barn!" one of the raiders said. "I claim her! She's mine!"

"Dang and durn you, Willie, why is it you're always so lucky? What do you need with another mare? Let me have that one."

"You can have my old one. Here, help me get her out of here, then we'll set this barn a-burning."

Exposed to their view if only they looked, Sam had to sit and watch in silent misery as they took his beloved horse from the barn. He felt like crying; Della was his most dear possession. He realized, though, that Della was ironically saving his skin at the moment, because with her to distract them, the men did not look up and see him. He had his rifle in hand, but the thought of using it never crossed his mind. Even if it had, it surely would have gotten him killed by others who would respond to the shots.

When they were out of the barn, Sam rolled back, grabbed his blankets, and threw them into the corner. Sweeping up his canteen and keeping a grip on his rifle, he buried himself in the nearest pile of hay, then lay still as a statue as he heard them return.

As he had anticipated, they explored the barn before firing it. He didn't see, but heard and sensed one of them climb the ladder and peer around the loft. Seeing nothing unusual, the man descended. He heard them moving around below, laughing, and quickly the smell of smoke filtered up to him. He struggled not to sneeze from the stimulation of smoke, dust, and hay tickling his nostrils.

What to do now? If he remained here, he would burn. If he left, he would be seen and shot down. He squeezed his eyes closed, fought panic, and prayed.

The smoke thickened; it grew hard to breathe. The flames made a loud crackle below and Sam sensed their spreading. He couldn't restrain himself from coughing, and now he kicked the hay off him and came to his feet in a hell of smoke and heat. There was no one in the barn now to see him. They had been driven out by their own fire.

The loft ladder was flaming; he could not descend by it. Flames suddenly shot up behind him, climbing the wall. The hay caught and smoke billowed even more profusely. Sam took his only option: He went to the side of the loft, sat on its edge, then jumped off, canteen and rifle in hand.

It wasn't a long drop, but he anticipated being seen as soon as he hit the earth. A loud, collective whoop and holler from outside made him sure that had indeed happened, and he turned and ran out the rear of the barn, expecting to be pursued and shot at.

Outside, he gasped in fresh air, looked around a moment, and made for the closest stand of woods. As he ran he saw movement around the other side of the barn and heard more triumphant yells. Shots rang out and he winced, running harder. He made the trees and dove behind a log.

Peering up over it, he saw the truth. They hadn't seen him at all. They were riding off, back down the trail toward the road, leaving the buildings to burn. The shots he had heard were fired at the sky in celebration, not at him. The shouts had been yells of jubilation.

He lay back down behind the log and listened to the increasingly distant hubbub of the raiders. Closing his eyes again, he hugged his rifle and thanked his Creator.

He had survived, and had not been caught.

Sam didn't remain where he was very long. He suspected the raiders had hoped to find Greeley himself at home, and he figured they might have posted a guard to watch the road and wait for him to return.

Sam struck off across and down the sloping fields behind the house, leaped the little creek, paused to refill his canteen, and went into the woods beyond. He grieved for the loss of his horse, but was glad to still have his rifle, although it was a single-shot cap-and-ball weapon with only one load in it. Unwittingly, he'd left the rest of his meager ammunition supply in the burning barn. His food, too.

Sam found a thicket, crawled inside and settled down to sleep, if he could. He dared not show himself on any road tonight, and anticipated with dread the likelihood of having to spend the next day here, too. He was terribly unnerved, and it would take time to gain the courage to take to the open road again.

Finally he did doze off, though only fitfully. When he awakened it was early morning, and standing before him was Greeley Brown. Sam looked up, stupid with grogginess, and simply stared at the lean mountaineer.

"Caesar Augustus, Sam, it's a good thing I ain't a bear. I'd have eat you by now."

Sam rubbed his face and shook his head sharply to regain his senses. He stood, pushing up with his rifle. "Greeley, they burned your house and your barn."

"Yep. I discovered that here about ten minutes ago. I figured it prudent to take to the woods, and then here I've gone and found you." Greeley was leaning on his rifle. Tapping it with a finger, he said, "I was about ready to shoot you as one of the raiders until I seen it was you."

Sam stuck out his hand and Greeley shook it. "I'm sorry about what they did. I was sleeping in your barn when they came."

"Do tell! Well, that explains how you come to be here. Glad you didn't roast. But I thought you was still in Greeneville."

"I had to leave. My brother, he went and killed Sloat, Greeley. And not only him, but his wife and her father, too, them two being Cherokees. They're looking for him as a murderer, and they're looking for me, too. Wanting to ask questions I don't want to answer. So I'm on the open road now, moving around and trying to avoid the law, and the rebels, too."

"Right now the rebels *are* the law," Greeley said. "And they're looking for me."

"Why?"

"They say I'm a bridge burner."

Sam had heard about the burning of the bridges and the rumors that a Federal invasion was expected to follow—an invasion that obviously had not come about so far. "Are you a bridge burner?"

"I won't deny the truth to a friend. I helped Daniel Stover burn the bridge at Union. There were a couple of guards there. One got away, but the other we caught, and pledged him on his honor to keep our names secret. It wound up this bird didn't have no honor. As soon as we let him go, they identified every last one of us and the rebs took to searching for us. I ain't resided in my house for days on end, knowing they'd find me there if I did."

"So that's why there wasn't nobody home when I came knocking."

"Why'd you come to see me, Sam?"

"Well, no reason other than you being an old friend and me needing a place to sleep. I didn't expect to walk in on a house burning. Greeley, what about that wife you were going to take for yourself? Where's she?"

For the first time, Greeley looked truly somber. "I ain't

got a wife. She turned me down cold. I admit it surprised me. I really thought she would . . ." He shrugged. "Maybe it's for the best, considering. This ain't no time to be entangling oneself in love affairs and marriages and such."

Those words gave Sam a twinge. "Somebody else told me much the same thing here recently."

Greeley pondered a moment, then flicked his brows. "Ah! That girl you had an eye on?"

"Yes. That's the one. Lordy, I wish she'd told me yes! But she said no. Too many important things to do with the war on, all that kind of thing. But war or not, I'd marry her in a second."

"Well, we got more to think about than women who won't have us. Like staying alive. You're still Union, I reckon?"

"Yes indeed. I'll be Union until the end."

"You aiming to do any soldiering?"

"Well, I've had it in mind to do *something*. . . . I've been thinking along the lines of guiding stampeders, like you talked about before. I don't know that I could be much of a killer, even on a battlefield. I'd hesitate. I'd get myself shot by some rebel while I was wondering whether or not I ought to shoot him first."

"Well, being a stampeder pilot is a worthy goal. But even a pilot may have to fight. When you take men under your care, to guide them, you owe them protection."

"I know. Dang it, I don't know what I'll do. Maybe I'll enlist as a regular soldier after all."

"Don't give up the pilot notion. I'm glad to hear you talking about it. Maybe me and you could work together. But right now we'd best forget everything except getting to a safer place. I know such a place, if you're willing to make a hard wilderness journey come the next nightfall."

"I am."

"Won't be safe. If they find you with me, they'll arrest or shoot or hang us both."

"What the devil. I reckon I ain't safe anyway. I'll take my chances with you."

"Got any food?"

"It was all burned up in your barn."

"I got some victuals buried in jars over near the edge of the woods there. I buried them when I found out the rebs were looking for me, just in case such a situation as this came up. Ain't the best of provender, but it'll fill a belly."

"Sounds good to me. Let's go dig it up."

The day, so much dreaded by Sam earlier on, turned out to be one of the most pleasant he had passed in a long while. Greeley was fine company, astonishingly cheerful despite his circumstances. He and Sam rested and talked the day away, Sam telling more about the killings ascribed to his brother, Greeley talking about the bridge burning and the way the rebel government was responding, moving in to harass and arrest Unionists, haranguing citizens for any information about the identities of bridge burners, and pledging to execute any who were found.

When Greeley mentioned that one of the burned bridges was the small one over the Colter gulch, Sam wondered if Hannibal might have been involved. It seemed the kind of thing he would do. Involved or not, it was likely Hannibal was suffering in some way under the current Confederate harassment of Unionists.

Night came and they moved out, traveling remote trails and back roads that Greeley knew well. They hid three times to let Confederate troops pass, but were not detected. Soon they left anything resembling a path and headed into some of the wildest country Sam had ever wandered. It was just as well he didn't have his horse now; Della could have never penetrated this tangled country.

They moved up hills and mountains and Sam quickly lost his way in this unfamiliar Carter County wilderness, but Greeley traveled with confidence. At length Sam sensed from Greeley's manner that they were nearing their destination, and just as that feeling struck, there came a call from some unseen sentry in the trees: "Who goes there!"

"Two good Union men seeking haven from the rebs," Greeley replied.

"Greeley Brown, is that your voice?"

"It's me. Is that you, Claymore?"

"Indeedy. Come on, Greeley. We've been looking for you to come."

Minutes later, as dawn spread in the sky, Sam was seated in a mountain hollow in the cleared center of a monstrously big laurel and ivy thicket in which a big rough shelter had been built of logs, sticks, leaves, stones, anything at all the terrain offered. He and Greeley were surrounded by bedraggled but jovial Unionist men who seemed very happy to see Greeley in particular, and who welcomed Sam readily on the credentials of being Greeley's friend. Sam was introduced to many men by their names and ranks, and promptly forgot most except for Colonel Daniel Stover, whose rank, status as a bridge burner, and family connection to Greeneville's Andrew Johnson made him memorable. Listening to the men talk, Sam learned they were in the remote Pond Mountain region, near a stream called Elk Creek. These men had only recently come here after having determined that prior encampments were too exposed. This military band was from the group of Unionists who had gathered at Elizabethton the day after the bridge burnings, and had since taken to hiding.

The food at the camp at the moment was quite poor— mostly loaves of bread baked on slabs of wood leaned up near the fire—but Sam welcomed it and would have gladly eaten far more of it had it been offered, which it wasn't. He tried to make his last portion last as long as possible, nibbling small bites and listening to the men talk about the bridge burning and subsequent arrests. Meanwhile, weariness from his night-long wilderness trek was quickly overcoming the energy generated by its successful completion. He anticipated a long morning of sleep as soon as he was finished eating.

"So you're from Greeneville, are you?" one of them asked Sam.

"Originally from North Carolina, but yes, I've been living in Greeneville."

"They burned two bridges up near there," the man said. "Lick Creek and Colter. A good job of it was done, too, though I'm sorry to say there have been some arrests of a few of the brave men involved.

"Who are they?"

"Let's see . . . there's a man named Hensie, one named Fry—not David Fry, who led the group, but another fellow he ain't kin to, as I understand it, and a man last name of Self. All of them were in on the Lick Creek bridge burning. Only one arrested for the Colter burning, that being the fellow name of Deacon whose brother was sorry old Doc Deacon, the big Secesh."

The last bread fragment dropped from Sam's fingers.

"Hannibal Deacon is arrested?"

"Yes, that's him. Do you know him?"

"Yes. More than know him. I worked for him up until a few weeks ago. I lived in a room above his store. He's mighty close to me." Sam tried to take it in. "Hannibal's arrested . . . God, are they going to hang him?"

"They say they'll hang them all as soon as they're convicted."

Sam stood. "Where is Hannibal now?"

"Well, I don't know. Greeneville, I suppose. That's where he was arrested."

Sam turned to Greeley. "I've got to go to Greeneville. I've got to see Hannibal." He strode off.

"Wait, there, Sam! You ain't going nowhere right now," Greeley said. "We've been traveling all night and you're exhausted. And we can't risk you moving out in the daylight, anyway, not and giving the rebs a hint as to where we are."

"Greeley, didn't you hear him? He said Hannibal is under arrest, and that they're going to hang the bridge burners."

"And how do you propose you stop them, eh? You plan to walk in and knock down a jail wall with your fist? You plan to wrestle down the Confederacy single-handed?"

"What are you saying? That I ought to do nothing?"

"I'm saying there ain't likely a thing you *can* do."

"He's been family to me, Greeley. Just like my uncle Wilt was. Wilt's gone. I don't want Hannibal gone, too. I couldn't bear that."

"Sam, listen to me: There's nothing you can do. If he's a

prisoner, he'll face trial, and the only hope is there'll not be enough evidence to convict him. Maybe he'll be freed."

"Slender hope of that," contributed the man who had told Sam of the arrest. "As I understand it, Hannibal Deacon is quite a prize. Considering that his brother was one of the original Secessionists, it gave a lot of weight to the Union cause when Hannibal Deacon came out against the rebellion, especially after Doc Deacon became a public joke. The rebs hate Hannibal Deacon. They'll put on a show trial, then they'll hang him."

Sam swore loudly, then louder yet.

"Sam, calm yourself," Greeley admonished. "This is hard news, no doubt about it, but you've got to face the facts as they stand. There's probably no hope for Hannibal Deacon short of a pardon, and you and me both know that ain't likely."

"I got to go to Hannibal, Greeley."

"I'll go with you, then. You and me together—but right now we both need sleep. Let's rest, and this evening we'll head toward Greeneville, and if there is anything that can be done for Mr. Deacon, we'll do it."

Sam wasn't at all satisfied with that proposal. How could he sleep? How could he wait even one day? It was Hannibal they had, Hannibal his friend and mentor, Hannibal who had given him a home and work and a chance for a life far better than anything he could have otherwise hoped for.

But there was no other option and he resigned himself to it. Heartsick, he crawled into one of the shelters, lay down, struggled not to weep, and then somehow did manage to rest.

He awakened near sunset. Greeley was already up and eating. Sam ate, too, and accepted a supply of the fire-baked bread that was the staple of the encampment.

Greeley said, "Are you ready to leave now, Sam?"

"I am. And Greeley, don't take this wrong, but I been thinking, and I don't want you to come with me."

"Caesar Augustus! Why not?"

"Because this is my situation, and my duty, and I don't want to have to worry about somebody else as I deal with it."

"Sounds like you have rash plans, my friend."

"No. The fact is I don't have much of a plan at all. But

whatever I come up with, I want to feel free to do it without worrying that I'm endangering anyone else."

"Sorry, Sam. If you go, I go. You and me, we're partners now."

"We are, are we?"

"Yep. Whether you like it or not."

Sam smiled. "Partners it is, then. Just don't slow me down."

"I was about to make the same demand on you, my friend."

As darkness crawled up from the wooded forest floors and gradually obliterated the lingering sunlight glowing off the towering stone escarpments and wooded ridges all around them, they set off together, and despite what he had said before, Sam was glad that Greeley Brown was with him, for the country they would travel was full of hostile men, and there was no way to know what they would encounter.

Chapter 25

Near Bean Station, Tennessee

Amy Deacon was growing very weary of pretending fascination with the dull things being chattered at her in competitive spirit by two privates assigned to convey her to Morristown. Both were lanky country boys, lifelong friends and neighbors from some tiny rural hamlet in Virginia, and had signed on together to "whup the Yanks and have a lark." They were obviously having a lark at the moment, riding through the countryside in the company of the kind of young lady who would probably never give them a moment's attention in normal circumstances. It wasn't easy for Amy to give them attention even now. She had never met two less interesting fellows.

Dull though they were, however, they were also as chivalrous as they knew how to be, clearly regarding her as the epitome of all that was desirable, noble, and worthy of protection in a female. Amy, not much of a romantic spirit and never one to think much about the impact she made on anything beyond the cerebral aspects of other people, was amused at how charming she appeared to these fellows. That amusement was all the pleasure she found in this odd situation. A vexing and potentially dangerous problem would face her once she reached Morristown.

It was a problem she became cognizant of only after climbing into the carriage to begin the journey, and now she couldn't perceive herself being as clever as she liked to think. She had made a dire blunder in choosing the name of Pleadis Mundy for her fictional brother. Where was her foresight, selecting the name of a real person? If she had made up a false name for her "brother," she could at least have feigned mystification when she failed to find him in Morristown. But in the crush of interrogation, her old suitor Pleadis's name was the only one that came readily to mind, and she spewed it out unthinkingly.

It had been the worst of choices. Pleadis came from the Morristown area, out of a prominent family. When she showed up on his own stomping grounds, claiming kinship to him in a place where everyone knew there was no daughter in the Mundy family, it wouldn't take much investigation before her story would collapse around her. Worse, what if Pleadis was still about Morristown? She knew he was a Confederate soldier now, but not where he was stationed. Pleadis's father had wealth and influence. He might have manipulated a close-to-home military assignment for his son. The thought appalled Amy. She might be able to bluster her way through trying to find Pleadis Mundy and failing, but not through trying to find him and *succeeding*.

The best she could hope for was that Pleadis Mundy wasn't at Morristown at present, and pretend that the one she sought was some other fellow who happened to have the same name. But who would believe there could be more than one living being with the name Pleadis Mundy in the entire world?

No, that option wouldn't be best, couldn't be. . . . The best would be to get away from these two bumpkin soldiers she was stuck with, before she ever reached Morristown. But how?

Her escorts, oblivious to her tension, talked about every subject dear to young men of the southern rural world: farming, hunting, fishing, how to dam a creek, how to trap foxes, how to mend wagon wheels, how to deal with balky mules and Negroes who forgot their "proper place" in the scheme of life, and how terrible it was whenever a south-

erner had to deal with the astonishing stupidity of northerners who failed to realize that a single rebel soldier on his
own soil was worth at least ten Yankees. Amy had said
"Really?" and "Do tell!" and "My, oh my!" so many times
that those responses were coming automatically anytime the
soldiers paused in their chatter.

When Bean Station was left behind, the Holston crossed,
and the carriage rolling along the final stretch toward Morristown, the soldiers turned to the matter of the war in general, then the recent bridge burnings in particular. Amy had
missed news of this while in Kentucky, and for the first time
she became authentically interested in what was being said,
especially when one of the pair mentioned that two of the
burned bridges had been in Greene County.

"My, that's just awful!" she declared in the most
offended tone she could marshal. "Have they caught the
people who did such a wicked thing?"

"Some of them, and they'll catch the rest before they're
through," the soldier with the louder voice and the big pan-
cake freckles said. "And as I hear it, the Secretary of War
has done declared he wants every one of them strung up by
the neck from the very bridges they burned."

"That sounds purely terrible," Amy replied.

The softer-voiced soldier spoke next, and what he said
hit Amy like a blow from a hammer: "Did you know that
one of them they've caught is the brother of poor old Doc
Deacon, who died so tragic in Knoxville a while back? He
was a great man, Doc Deacon was."

Amy's heart palpitated. Blood drained from her face and
she felt faint.

"I knowed about that arrest already," the other said, not
immediately noticing her reaction. "The scoundrel's name
is Hannibal Deacon, and he's been one of the big Lincolnites who's stirred up the Union rabble all over East Tennessee. Rabble . . . that's like your common dumb kind of
folks, Miss Mundy. Anyway, they're holding him in
Knoxville and are all set for a big trial. With him being kin
to such a great man as Doc Deacon, they say he's sure to be
used for an example to make sure nobody else tries to burn

bridges or such. . . . Miss Mundy, are you feeling bad all of a sudden? You look peaked."

"I . . . I feel weak . . . vaporous . . ." She saw an old empty house ahead, and behind it a privy. Somehow, despite the grip of sudden nausea that was doing a quick chew through her insides in reaction to the news about Hannibal, the sight of those buildings brought an inspiration. "Can we stop here, so I can—"

"Can what?"

Amy feigned a look of self-consciousness.

"Merciful heavens, Lawrence!" the other chided. "Have you got no delicacy at all? There's some things that's *private* with a woman."

"Oh!" The other reddened. "I'm sorry, Miss Mundy. Having never had no sisters, I sometimes don't think of such things as quick as I should. Of course we'll stop."

The carriage halted in front of the house. Amy thanked heaven that from where the carriage sat, the house blocked the view of the privy.

"I'll only be a moment or two," she said as the freckle-faced one helped her down from the seat. "Thank you so much."

Trying not to tremble visibly as she walked, she rounded the house, went to the privy, opened and then loudly closed the door without actually entering, lifted her skirts to her knees and took off on a run across the overgrown lot behind the privy and into the woods. She looked back, saw that the soldiers were still out of sight around the front of the house, then redoubled her speed and made off as fast as she could.

Now reaching Knoxville was more than a goal. It was a necessity.

They had Hannibal.

Near the Watauga River

They came upon Sam Colter and Greeley Brown so quickly it was as if they had materialized from the barren forest itself. No sound, no hint of movement—yet there they were, three of them, dirty and grinning and ugly in the light of the new morning, one of them sticking a shotgun into Sam's face as another took his rifle and a third poked the point of a saber threateningly into Greeley's side. In half a moment Greeley was disarmed as well.

"Well, pilgrims, tell us straight out: You Secesh or Union?"

Sam Colter stared into the double-eyed, fully cocked shotgun. He glanced at Greeley as his mouth went dry. He knew the breed of men that these were—but of what stripe were they? He had no doubt that the continuation of their lives hinged upon how they answered the challenger's question.

"Talk up, pilgrims! Secesh or Lincolnite?"

Greeley answered. "I'm a Confederate, and proud of it—and if you're Lincolnite trash and aim to kill me for being a southern patriot, then go ahead and do it!"

Sam gaped at Greeley and wondered if he had taken a fool for a partner. But it proved out that Greeley had said just the right thing. The lead mountain ruffian, a lean, muddy-looking wisp of a man with a face like a wedge, lowered the shotgun—though not fully, and the saber tip held by one of the other two continued probing Sam's side. But at least Sam's and Greeley's heads hadn't been instantly blown off. Then understanding came to Sam: Greeley had figured out the fellow's own southern allegiance—if such a man really had an allegiance at all—because of his use of the word "Lincolnite," a term not used by Unionists. Sam saw that Greeley had the better grip on his wits, and so decided to hold his own silence, if their accosters allowed him to do so, and trust Greeley to handle this situation.

The seeming leader of the ambushing trio said, "Well, now! You spoke what needed speaking, for if you had declared yourself Yankee, you'd be dead this moment. I thunk you pilgrims had the look of southern patriots about you!"

"So you can let us go our way now?"

" 'Fraid I can't do that, pilgrim. 'Fraid not. We're soldiers of the South, and we got need of you pilgrims."

Sam knew these men were not soldiers of any kind. Their breed showed in their looks, their manner, their ambushing tactic. The war was still relatively new, and already human vermin like this ranged the mountain country, taking advantage of the war to raid, rob, rape, and kill. A similar breed of wicked men had ranged this same country in the days of the Revolution. Wilton Colter had told Sam many tales about the troubles his own ancestors had experienced with backwoods criminals of this ilk almost a century before in the old war. Now the war was new, but the human silt it stirred was just the same as in centuries past.

"What do you need from us?"

"I need your services, pilgrims, on behalf of Jeff Davis." The others chuckled when he said that.

"What kind of service?"

"We're going to punish us a bridge burner."

"Why do you need us?"

Greeley had asked one question too many. The man grew angry. "Put a cork on them questions. You'll know when the time's right."

"You'll sure 'nough know!" the one with the saber chortled. "Won't he, Tyler? He'll sure 'nough know. Both of 'em will!"

"Shut up, Rex," the third ruffian replied in a gravelly voice. To Greeley he said, "Rex there has a mouth like a loose bowel. Always running, all the time."

"I ain't a soldier," Greeley said. "Neither is my partner here. We got no authority to serve as such."

"We're authorized by Jeff Davis hisself to conscript. Ain't we, men? Got the authorizing papers right in my pocket. So I'm conscripting you pilgrims. You're soldiers now."

Sam knew there were not yet any Confederate conscription laws. These men were brash liars.

Greeley asked, "Can I see them papers?"

"What? You doubt my word?"

"No."

"Ain't no need for you to see the papers, then. I say I got them, then I got them. You're coming with us."

"What if I say no?" It was a daring question, and Sam wondered if Greeley would be shot for it.

"You say no, then we quit conscripting and go to executing. You understand me pilgrim?"

"I understand."

The bushwhacker turned to Sam. "You understand?"

"I understand." Sam was embarrassed by how his voice quivered in comparison to Greeley's firm and clear speaking.

"That's good. That's prime good. Now get a move on and let's take a walk together."

"Ain't you going to give us an oath?" asked Greeley.

"What?"

"An oath. Don't we have to swear oaths to be soldiers?"

"Ain't no swearing to it. You just do what I tell you."

"What's your name?"

"You can call me 'sir.' No . . . no, call me Captain. Yeah, I like the sound of that. Captain. That's all you need to know. Now get on with you."

The saber prodded and Sam walked. They kept him from getting too close to Greeley. "Captain" kept the shotgun trained alternately on him and Greeley all the time, and Sam did not doubt he would use it if he tried to run. Nor did he doubt that on the other side of whatever crime he had planned, Captain would use that shotgun on him whether he ran or not.

He couldn't accept this. It seemed too unreal and had come on far too quickly for his mind to accommodate it. But the saber prodding him was real enough, as was that shotgun, and Sam had no idea what was going to happen to him or his partner.

Alone in his cabin, the old man did not put up much of a fight. They had burst in on him in his tiny, dirt-floored, mountainside hovel, not two miles from where they "conscripted" Sam and Greeley, and dragged the old fellow from his chair with curses and kicks. Now, with his thin wrist in Captain's hand, the old fellow knelt weeping and trembling and drooling before them, filmy blue eyes looking from face to face and toothless jaw tremoring in terror while the one called Captain accused him of being a "damned Lincolnite bridge burner."

Bridge burner ... this ancient fellow was a bridge burner? It surely couldn't be. This man couldn't stand and hardly seemed able to see. One side of his mouth drooped in memorial of apoplexy long past. Sam was revolted that anyone so old and helpless—the fellow was eighty at the least—should be treated so badly when clearly he could not be guilty of what they accused.

"No ... bridge burner ... not me ..." The old man's words were hard to understand.

Captain grabbed the old man's left hand, shoved it to the floor and stomped it, hard. Bone cracked aloud, and Sam struggled not to retch there on the spot. The old man's scream was like nothing he had ever heard. Sam looked at Greeley imploringly, as if there was something his companion could do. Greeley's eyes fluttered, but remained locked on the old man and his tormentor, his face rigid, expressionless.

Captain said, "You *are* a bridge burner and a Lincolnite, and I'm authorized by Jeff Davis to execute you on the spot."

"Please, no, please ..."

"And I can do it any way I please. I can shoot you through the head or I can slice you in pieces, bit by bit, until whatever black Lincolnite soul is in you can take its choice of bleeding holes through which to fly out of your sorry corpse. How's it going to be, old man?"

"Don't hurt me no more, please don't!"

Captain's response was to stomp the hand again. The old man screamed once more and almost passed out, but Captain slapped him awake. Sam saw Greeley close his eyes a couple of moments, then reopen them.

"Only one way out for you, old man. You can buy your way out by donating to Jeff Davis's treasury. Everybody knows you got money buried hereabouts. You give it to us, we'll let you be. Otherwise that boy right there"—he pointed to Sam, and Sam's legs seemed to lose all their bone—"will take a knife and slice your throat from ear to ear. You hear me?"

The old man cried. Sam began to cry, too, inwardly and without tears, full of horror and seething with a deep hatred of these vile torturers. But he was helpless to intervene, as was Greeley; one of them had a long cap-and-ball pistol stuck against his spine. Greeley was being probed by the same saber that had been pressed against Sam earlier.

"Ain't no money . . . not no more . . ."

Captain lifted his foot to stamp the hand again. Sam could stand no more. "No!" he yelled, and no one was more stunned than he to hear his shout.

The man with the pistol against Sam's spine drew the weapon up and around and hit him across the forehead with it, not hard enough to knock him out, but enough to lay open a cut above his ear. Blood flowed profusely; Sam staggered. Greeley moved toward him a step, but the saber knicked him and made him stop.

"Don't you fall down," Sam's abuser said. "Fall down and I'll kill you. And quit that crying. You ain't no baby to be crying over seeing a damned Lincolnite get his due."

Captain stomped the hand. Sam knew now that they intended this old man to die whether he cooperated or not. He prayed that if there was to be no escape for the poor fellow, they would kill him quickly and quit making him suffer. He had never seen such cruelty. The crushing snap of those mashed fingers would surely ring sickeningly in his mind for a long time to come.

"Where's the money, Lincolnite?"

"There was others . . . they done took it. I swear! Dug it up and took it . . . See the hole behind the house? It was there, now it's gone. Oh, God, help me! Have mercy on me, God!"

Captain kicked the old man in the side. "You want to pray, you pray on your own time." He looked at one of his fellow demons. "Tyler! Look out back and see if there's really a hole. Old man, if you're lying, we'll quit breaking fingers and take to slicing off ears and noses."

The third bushwacker left the cabin and circled to the

rear. A couple of moments later they heard his muffled curse, then he came around to the door again. "There is a hole. Big one, and right fresh. Nothing in it."

Captain began to curse and kick the old man, again and again, as if he had committed some offense in telling them the truth. The old fellow, moaning, leaned to the side, and Captain let him drop. Sam thought for a minute the man was dead, but he moaned again and the dim blue eyes fluttered. The drool escaping the corner of his wrinkled mouth was tinged with blood.

Captain paced about the cabin, cursing and ranting, occasionally coming back to the old man to kick or strike him. Once he trod on the broken hand again, just to worsen the man's torment.

Sam didn't recoil now. His horror was no less than before, but his hatred had doubled, trebled, until it overwhelmed even revulsion. He gazed at Captain and saw a man whose life did not merit a moment's continuation and whose soul belonged not in a living human body, but in hell.

He had always wondered if he would have it in him to take another life if it ever came down to it. Looking at Captain, he knew he could. *Here is a man I could kill,* he thought. *Here is a man I could kill without a thought, and know that I was righteous for doing it.*

Captain stopped pacing at last, wriggled his shoulders like a man fighting a backache, sighed and shook his head. "Hell, boys, we've been outfoxed, and I reckon we'll just have to face it. Tyler, give the boy there your knife. And then, boy, I want you to cut the throat of our old Union mud puppy here. Cut it slow. You hear that, old man? You're about to give your life for Lincoln. You're about to be a hero for the Union!"

"I won't do it," Sam said.

"That right? Then we'll cut your neck, too. Tyler . . ." He made gestures to indicate the act should be done at once.

"Wait," Greeley said. "That old coot don't mean nothing to me. I'll kill him, if you'll just leave my partner be."

"Now, there's a man with some spirit about him!" Captain said. "I like you, pilgrim. What's your name?"

"Bowie," Greeley said. "Jim Bowie."

"Jim Bowie? Like the one what died 'gainst the Mexes at the Alamo?"

"That's right. It ain't my true name, though. They call me that 'cause I'm so good with a knife."

Captain grinned. "Well, Mr. Bowie, you just take that knife and show us how good you are by carving up our rooster-bird there."

"You ain't really going to do it, are you, Gree . . . are you, Jim?" Sam asked.

"What do I care about that old Unionist? Why, it'll ease his suffering to kill him. That crushed hand must hurt mighty fierce."

Captain seemed pleased by what he was hearing, but he voiced a firm warning to Greeley. "Mr. Bowie, you listen: Don't try nothing with that knife other than what I've told you to do. We'll shoot you if you try any tricks."

Grinning, the bushwhacker named Tyler drew a long, rusty blade from a scabbard on his belt. The knife was almost as long as the other bushwhacker's saber. He thrust it out toward Greeley, blade first. "Don't you try nothing—you heard what he said."

"I won't." Greeley looked at the extended blade. "Give me the handle. I don't want to grab that blade."

"Uh-uh. You take it by the blade or I'll lay you open with it."

Greeley closed his hand around the blade as Sam wondered if the bushwhacker would be able to resist the cruel joke of jerking it back and severing Greeley's fingers. With Sam breathless, heart pounding out of his chest, Greeley gripped the blade. The bushwhacker kept a grip on the handle, grinning wickedly—then lunged his body forward and yelled: "Whoooo!"

Greeley didn't let go of the blade, nor budge. Sam was filled with astonishment and admiration at his iron nerve. Not many men had such grit. Sam looked at Greeley's hand. Uncut. Tyler had moved his body, but not the blade. Still, Greeley couldn't have known Tyler wouldn't have cut his fingers off, and yet he hadn't flinched.

"Here, friend Bowie, take it," Tyler said, still laughing,

handing Greeley the knife again, this time by the handle. "You got the pluck about you, that I'll grant. Now let's see how good a butcher you make."

Sam took hold of the knife's handle and turned to face the pitiful fellow he had been told to kill.

The old man lay staring up at him, gripping his broken hand, looking back pleadingly but unchallengingly. He saw his death coming and knew he could not fight it. It made Sam's heart ache, and he wondered if Greeley was really going to go through with it. He hoped not. Surely Greeley had some plan up his sleeve.

But if he doesn't, and he does kill you, you fight him, old man, even though he's Greeley. You ought never to quit fighting. Any man tries to kill you, you make it hard as you can for him. If Greeley hurts you, you hurt him back. Don't ever just give up, never ever. But Greeley, don't do it. Please don't do it.

Greeley knelt beside the old man. The pale eyes shifted sideways and up, waiting. Greeley looked right back into his face, pulled the old man's shirt open at the collar and raised the blade.

The old man closed his eyes, moaning softly.

Greeley lowered the blade suddenly and peered at the old man's upper chest, just below the neck. "Caesar Augustus!" he said. "Look here at this!"

"What?" Captain asked.

"I ain't never seen such as this, that's all. Old man, you always hide your money that way?"

"Money?" Captain asked, still suspicious but also intrigued. "I didn't see no money on him."

"Ain't on him," Greeley said. "It's *in* him! I ain't never seen the like! This old Lincolnite has got sort of a natural pocket in his flesh! Gold coins in it! I ain't never seen such a thing!"

Captain swore and avowed Greeley was lying.

"Come look for yourself if you don't believe me."

Captain came forward a step, hesitated, then said, "You toss that knife away while I come over."

Greeley sighed. "Very well." He tossed the blade to the

side, well out of his own reach. Sam watched it all, intrigued, believing that surely Greeley was up to something but having no good idea just what.

Captain drew nearer, then knelt slowly beside Greeley. "Mr. Bowie, you'd best know that if this is a trick, your friend back yonder will be killed by Mr. Tyler."

"Well, Caesar Augustus! I can't be having that, can I!" Greeley said, and suddenly his right hand was flashing up, gripping a knife that had been hidden in his right boot. It caught Captain in the neck. Greeley gave it a twist and pull, and Captain went down, writhing, gurgling, neck spurting blood.

Greeley came up and moved toward the fallen man. "Mercy!" Captain begged. "Give me mercy!" Something about his blood-choked voice sounded vaguely like a gobbling turkey.

"No," Greeley said. "No mercy." He jerked Captain's hands away from his throat and slashed. The neck was laid open so far that Captain's head was almost severed.

Sam's guard, who had been as frozen as Sam at the sight of the unexpected bloody spectacle, now moved; Sam anticipated being stabbed or shot or struck, and so he pushed back bodily against the other, as hard as he could, and made him fall. Sam kept his own balance, however, and ducked away as a shot blasted up and went through the roof, whizzing mere inches past his face. Sam brought up his booted foot and came down with it, hammering his heel onto the fallen man's nose as hard as he could and caving in the face. The guard screamed a muffled, distorted scream and fired his revolver again, missing Sam by at least a yard. Sam grabbed the pistol, yanked it from the man's hand, and shot him through the forehead. He turned in time to see Greeley putting his knife into the heart of the the ruffian with the saber. The man had frozen in surprise a moment too long and allowed himself to be taken. The saber fell from his fingers as he collapsed, dying on the way down.

The room, filled with acrid, hanging gun smoke, was now as silent as a tomb. One of the dead, settling into the dirt floor, broke the silence with a faint, brief hissing sound. *So this is war,* Sam thought. *This is what war is. Old men getting their hands stomped. Men bleeding and gurgling while they die. A man who thought he'd never be able to kill anyone crushing the face of another man with his boot. This is war. Now I know. Now I've seen it. Now I'm part of it.*

He heard a strange sound—a quiet, spasmodic little vocal sound that he couldn't identify. Then he looked at the old man with the maimed hand and knew what it was.

He was laughing. The tormented old man, having seen death coming for him, only to turn and claim his torturers instead, was laughing. A finger of the bloody river forming in the worn-down center of the dirt-floor room touched the old man's broken hand, but he did not flinch from it. He just kept on laughing his harsh, jagged chuckled, blood puddling around his hand.

Sam looked at Greeley and said it. "This here is war. This here is really what it's like."

Greeley nodded. "Yes, Sam. This here is really what it's like."

Sam looked around the room. "I don't believe I care for it much."

Sam listened to the feeble laugh of the old man while his vision went white and he passed out on the floor, a crumpled heap of unconscious humanity among the bloody dead. And the ragged laughter continued still.

Sam and Greeley did not bury the dead. They took their weapons and ammunition, and dug some money from their pockets and food from a pouch one had carried. Then they dragged them out and threw their corpses over a nearby bluff into a brush-filled hole thirty feet below. Sam wondered if what he and Greeley had done made them murderers. No. No. If there was a moral line drawn on the fabric of reality, he and Greeley stood on the right side of it. They had killed to *stop* a murder, killed to protect not only themselves but an old man who would have been butchered. It was self-protection . . . wasn't it? Perhaps not fully. When Greeley had killed Captain, the man had already been rendered unable to do further harm and was pleading for mercy.

But he didn't deserve mercy. And he wouldn't have given it to whoever he next decided to torture and kill. These men had to be got rid of, and Greeley and me did it.

He argued the points forcefully in his mind, convincing himself, but aware quite keenly of one central fact: *I've killed a man. I'll never be just what I was before. I've got blood on my hands now.* He felt sick and shuddery inside to think of it. *This is war.*

When the bodies were dumped and out of sight, Sam returned to the cabin and the old man. Whatever qualms Sam felt about what had happened, the old man clearly felt none. To him, Sam and Greeley were heroes, scourges of the wicked, saviors of the abused.

But not really saviors, Sam could see. The old man, injured and shocked by his experience, was dying.

"They're gone," Greeley said to the old man as he entered the cabin, where the old man lay on a sagging bed in the corner. "We dropped them over the bluff."

"I thank you, thank you so much," the man said. "They'd have killed me."

"Would have had *me* kill you," Greeley corrected. "That way they'd have been able to lay the blame on me, if blame should have ever come about to be laid. That's why they forced me and my partner into this, I feel right certain."

"Bless you for what you done. Bless you."

"Don't bless me, sir. I should have found a way to do something faster, so we could have spared you such suffering."

"You done what you could, Mr. Bowie. And I do bless you."

Greeley grinned at Sam, who forced a grin back. *Bowie,* he mouthed, and winked. "Then bless my friend Mr. Crockett here, too," Greeley said. "He killed one of them. Stomped him right in the face."

Sam wondered how Greeley could play games with names and keep a smile on his face while talking about such a macabre thing.

"God bless you, too, Mr. Crockett." The poor old fellow was in no shape to comprehend Greeley's subtle joke.

"Thank you," Sam mumbled.

"What's your name, old fellow?" Greeley asked.

"Lynch. Jarrell Lynch."

"Well, I'm pleased to know you, Mr. Lynch. How old are you?"

"Know when I was born, Mr. Bowie? Same year as the United States. Seventeen and seventy-six. Born in Watauga, I was. I'm eighty-five-year old, son. Eighty-five. Just like the nation. And I ain't never been disloyal to the nation in all my years."

Sam looked at the old man's ruined hand. "Greeley, maybe we ought to bind his hand up."

"It don't matter about the hand, Mr. Crockett," the old man said. "I ain't going to live. I can feel things happening inside me. It's death a-gnawing my innards."

Greeley asked, "You want me to fetch somebody? A preacher or such?"

"I made my peace with Jesus long ago, Mr. Bowie. All I ask of you is to stay with me until I'm gone."

Sam looked at Greeley. There was no need to say anything; Greeley knew just what he was thinking, and responded to it in a near whisper. "You go on alone, Sam. You ain't got time to waste. Go find your friend Mr. Deacon. I'll stay with Mr. Lynch."

Sam thought about it only a moment, then nodded.

"Take that revolver with you when you go," Greeley further instructed. "It's a good one, and you may need it."

Sam found some food in a wooden box in the corner and took in unhesitatingly. Jarrell Lynch was clearly not going to need food any longer, but Sam had miles before him, and was hungry.

He ate. The old man declined even as he watched, and Sam doubted he would make it through another night alive. "Will you catch up with me later?" he asked Greeley.

"I will. You be careful, traveling alone. There may be others like them three, lingering about."

"I'll be careful." He walked over, extended a hand toward Greeley—he was embarrassed to see that it trembled—then, after shaking Greeley's hand, nodded a farewell to the old man. Lynch didn't see the gesture; his eyes were closed and looked sunken.

* * *

When Sam was gone, Greeley ate some food himself, then found a pen and ink bottle and tore a page from a thick old Bible on the stand beside the bed. Across the page he wrote: JARRELL LYNCH WAS KILLED BY MURDERERS, MONTH OF NOVEMBER, 1861. HIS SLAYERS LIE AT THE FOOT OF THE BLUFF AND HAVE PAID THE PRICE FOR THEIR CRIME.

The words weren't fully accurate yet. Lynch was still alive. But what remained of this old man's earthly life could now be measured in hours.

"Ain't none of us can count on our lives continuing much longer, Mr. Lynch," he said to the old man, who was now in a coma and uncaring. It didn't matter; Greeley's words were really spoken to himself. "All this cruelty like you suffered, this dying, this bleeding and turning hard and mean, Lord help us, we'll see much more of it before this war is through. You won't, I suppose. But I expect I will. Fighting, maiming, killing, stealing . . . and I'll wager you, sir, that a fair portion of us who'll be involved won't know but halfway what the whole confounded thing is about. Caesar Augustus, Mr. Lynch, we are a race of fools. We are indeed a race of fools."

Greeley dozed off about sunset. When he awakened, the old man was dead.

Chapter 26

Knoxville, Tennessee

In this town folks called the jail "Castle Fox" as a tongue-in-cheek tribute to a jailer named Fox known for lording over the place in monarchal style. Fox's little kingdom had never enjoyed such a high population of imprisoned peasantry as lately. Already it was filled beyond its proper capacity with arrested Unionists, and more were being rounded up every day, often on the thinnest of suspicions. An overflow facility had been opened at the corner of Prince and Main, but at the rate Unionists were being swept up, it too would soon be overrunning.

Amy Deacon walked between rows and clusters of cells and marveled in disgust at the crowded and unsanitary conditions. A deputy jailer with a youthful voice and pitted skin strode beside her, swaggering, proud to hold power above so many men older than he, proud to be doing the work of the Confederate government, proud to be at the side of so pretty a young woman, even if not by her choice.

"Ten minutes, miss. That's all I'm to allow you," he said as he put a key into the lock of one of the more crowded cells. "I'll be back to fetch you."

"Thank you," she said, already looking among the faces for Hannibal's. She did not see him.

She entered the cell, which was close and tight and stinking with the musky fetor of crowded and fearful humanity. The men parted, nodding solemn greetings, and on a bunk at the rear, hidden from her view until now, unveiled to Amy was Hannibal, lying on his back, face flushed and eyes marbled with pain, looking straight up.

She approached the bunk slowly, like a child walking for a last visit to an old grandfather's deathbed. "Uncle Hannibal?"

The glassine eyes turned her way looked at her blankly, but brightened. "Amy?" His voice was weak.

"You're sick, Hannibal."

"Yes, I am. Very feverish. And my head . . . oh, my head hurts so much now, hurts all the time." He frowned suddenly. "Amy, how did you get here? You're not supposed to be . . . Why have you . . ." He tried to sit up.

"No, Hannibal. Lie down. I came because I heard you were jailed."

"Cynthia brought you?"

Amy did not think it would be wise to admit she had deliberately fled the refuge to which Hannibal had sent her, so she said only, "Cynthia helped arrange for me to come."

Amy could imagine how astonished and angry Hannibal would be if he knew how she had really arrived here. After her escape from the two privates who had taken her nearly to Morristown, she went to the vicinity of New Market on foot, following a difficult route that avoided the main road. There, she bought a train ticket, since there were no burned bridges between that point and Knoxville to hamper the trains—thanks to the effective resistance of the Strawberry Plains bridge guard James Keelan, who was already being hailed a Confederate hero—and finished her journey.

Hannibal closed his eyes. "Cynthia shouldn't have let you come. You don't belong in a place like this."

"Neither do you. I want to help you get out of here, Hannibal."

"They'll never free me. My fate is sealed, my dear." He rubbed his head. Amy noticed a dried crust rimming his nostrils. Blood. She wondered if they had beaten him, but decided she didn't really want to know.

"Don't give up hope, Hannibal."

"The matter is out of my hands."

"Do they know you're ill?"

"What does illness matter when I'm going to be hanged? And there are plenty of sick men here. Our health is no great concern to the Confederacy." He drew in a deep, trembling breath and seemed very weary. "I have a prayer, Amy. I've been praying that I'll pass on and be with Lena again before they can get that noose around my neck. I'm a man at peace with God and the fate He has willed for me. I'm ready to die."

His hopeless manner made her mad. "Don't say that! You aren't dead yet. How dare you give up! You of all people!"

"I'll be tried this very afternoon, as I understand it. I have a lawyer, a local attorney, Unionist. Good man. Volunteered services. But it won't matter. I'll be convicted—as well I should be, considering that I'm guilty as sin. I'm too well-known as the brother of George Deacon, the great Secessionist, not to be dealt with. I'm too ripe a plum not to be used as an example. I'll be hauled back to Greene County and hanged at the Colter bridge."

"You won't. I'll do something . . . ask for mercy. I'll tell them I'll become a spokesman for the Confederacy, and take up my father's mantle, if only they'll let you go. I'll tell them I'll start his newspaper again, and call it *The Confederate Advocate*. I'll make a public repentance of the things I believe, and—"

For a moment all sign of Hannibal's sickness, all his weakness, all the pain that flickered in his eyes, was utterly gone. He was the Hannibal who had faced her in the parlor in Greeneville, stern and commanding. He sat up sharply and glared at her. "No. *No!* You will not do that. No matter what. And if you do, you are not the woman I believe you to be. You will *not* lend your voice and your name to . . . *them!* Never!"

"But it's your life, Hannibal. Your life!"

He sank back against his pillow, weak again. "Every life has to end at some time or another. Mine included."

"You talk like a man determined to die."

"As I told you, I'm at peace with my God and my destiny." He looked squarely at her. "It doesn't bother me, the thought of dying. Not even of dying by the noose, if it comes to that. I miss Lena, Amy. I want to go to her, to join her. Life hasn't really been life without her. The only thing that troubles me is the thought of giving the Confederacy the satisfaction of causing my death. That's why I've been praying that my death will come naturally, before they can get their hanging rope around my neck. I've prayed it, and I will it. All my will I've focused onto that one effort, the one way I can deprive them of their satisfaction."

Amy knelt beside the cot, leaned over and put her arms around him. She was empty, tired, too upset even to cry. But Hannibal did cry. She felt his chest heave beneath her, and he wrapped a big arm around her shoulders. "I love you, Amy. So much a part of me in this short time we've had together."

"I love you, Hannibal. I don't want you to die."

He patted her with his broad hand and said no more.

Minutes later the guard returned. "Time to go, miss."

Amy rose, then bent and kissed Hannibal's forehead, hot with fever. "You are so dear to me, Hannibal. You don't know how dear."

He smiled weakly. "I do know, dear girl," he said. "I do know. Good-bye."

The guard touched her shoulder. He was glad to have a reason to touch her. "Miss. Come on now." But she did not come until he began to tug at her arm and all but drag her away.

She looked back over her shoulder as she was removed. "I won't say good-bye to you, Hannibal. I won't. This is not good-bye! It *isn't*!" The cell door opened and closed, and she was gone.

"Yes, dear Amy," Hannibal whispered under his breath. "I'm afraid that it is."

She walked the streets, frantic and afraid, knowing that if Hannibal was to have any hope of a fate other than the one to which he was resigned, it would be up to her to bring it about.

I must think, think, think . . . I must think of a way. There must be something. . . .

Yet she couldn't think. She could only feel, and tremble, and move quick-pacing around Knoxville like a blind thing, unaware of all around her, feeling the passing of time and knowing that before this day was out, Hannibal would be tried and convicted.

Maybe she could testify for him. Intrude into the court and demand to be heard. . . . But what could she say? She knew nothing to help him. And why would the ear of the Confederacy turn favorably toward her, the betrayer of one of Secession's great and early voices? Could she betray her own conscience and turn advocate and apologist for the Confederacy, despite Hannibal's fervent reproachment of that idea? She could, but Hannibal would consider it no less than a betrayal.

Though she was too tormented to feel hunger, she realized that she hadn't eaten in a long time. Without food she could not hope to think clearly. And so she forced herself to become as calm as possible and bought a small meal in a café on Gay Street. She ate it not as food, but medicine. Fuel for the mind, to give rise to some idea for the salvation of Hannibal Deacon. Then she folded her napkin on her plate, left money on the table, and left the café. Walking down the street, she suddenly remembered the night she and that oddly likable town drunk had hung broadsides along this same street announcing her father's great rally. At the time she had been unable to know what great changes in her life would begin with that event. Now she felt caught up in a stream of events whose energy she could not subdue. She was being swept along, rudderless, out of control. She walked faster, head down, unobservant of the figure coming down the same walk from the opposite direction.

The voice brought her to a halt. "Well, hello there! Fancy seeing Miss Amy Deacon, of all people, walking these streets again!"

She looked up and was chilled. Birch Lewis stood directly before her, staring, smiling. He looked as sickly as

Hannibal had, but from the smell hanging about him, she realized he was merely drunk.

Oh, no. Why him, especially now? "What do you want, Mr. Lewis?" Hannibal had told her how Lewis harassed her father in his last days, and she despised him deeply for it.

"Why, Amy! Is that any way to greet an old friend?"

"You have never been my friend. Now let me pass." She headed around him, but he reached out and grabbed her arm.

"Let me go, Mr. Lewis, or I'll call for the authorities."

"Ain't you the priss! I ain't hurting you. I just want to talk. Want to tell you how sorry I am about all that's happened."

"As I have heard it from my uncle Hannibal, you have much to be sorry for. I know how you badgered my father while he was helpless and losing his sanity. I do not appreciate it."

"Your father wasn't 'helpless' by any stretch, Amy. He was threatening the lives of folks in this town. Why, he even showed up with a shotgun in the yard of your old friend Horatio Eaton! And he murdered Charlie Douglass, you know that? In time he'd have murdered me, too, if he had the chance."

"I told you to let go of my arm!"

Lewis suddenly grew whining, but he didn't let go. "Amy, there's no reason for you to despise me so. I've always thought the world of you. I'll admit it: I admire you. I'd like to know you a lot better than I do."

"There's no chance of that, sir, I assure you. Now: Let me go!"

He dropped his hand, looking angry. Her arm hurt where he had held it. "Very well, girl. If that's the way you want it, that's how it'll be. But maybe you'll see things different once times get hard for you and you're all alone. I heard about your uncle. They're going to hang him for bridge burning, you know."

"I have nothing more to say to you." She walked away.

He yelled after her: "You'll regret walking away from me, missy! Damn you Deacons! You've brought nothing but trouble and sorrow for me!"

She walked on, shoulders straight, acting like a woman

with a place to go though in fact she was merely trying to put distance between herself and Lewis.

"You ain't heard the last of Birch Lewis, you priss! I'll not forget the way you and your kin have treated me!"

He's demented, she thought. *Why did I have to meet him, today of all days?*

She went farther and glanced back over her shoulder, hoping he would be gone. He was following her, though at a distance. She felt the urge to run, but turned, stalked back and faced him instead.

"Why are you following me?"

Cowed by the confrontation, he went back to his sniveling persona again. "I'm sorry I shouted at you, Amy. I was wrong. I've been drinking and I don't think straight when I drink. Can I talk to you, just for a minute?"

She sighed. Maybe giving him that small satisfaction would be enough to send him away. "Have your say, then, and let me go about my business."

"Amy, I know I haven't done the kind of things to endear myself to you, and I admit I'm the kind of man who holds his grudges too long, but . . . but I haven't ever been able to put you out of my mind. Back when we worked together, I used to wish I could make you just *look* at me, and see something good in me, something you might find worthy and fine."

She said, "Mr. Lewis, I don't understand you. Before today I haven't seen you since the night of that rally. We were never more than two people who happened to be associated with the same enterprise. Yet now, after we meet by chance, you act as if you are some old suitor. Your behavior is offensive, and furthermore it makes no sense to me. I think you should leave me alone."

"Please, Amy, come sit down with me somewhere and we'll talk. I'll buy you some food, or something to drink."

"I've already eaten, thank you."

"Won't you spend at least a little time with me? I'll tell you how sorry I am about the way I've behaved. I'll prove to you that I don't feel about you the same as with your father and your uncle. He hit me once, you know, your uncle did."

Amy didn't know. Hannibal had told about his run-in with Lewis the day her father died on Secession Hill, but obviously had not given the full details.

Lewis went on. "But I don't hold that against you. And I don't hold anything your father did against you, either. Please, Amy, come be with me awhile."

"We've met today by chance, Mr. Lewis. I wish we hadn't. It would have been better. And I have no time to spend with you. My uncle is to go on trial for his life today, and I've got to find some way to . . ." She quit speaking when she realized she very well might cry, and she would not do that before Birch Lewis.

His look and voice took on a new and subtle quality. "Today, you say! Maybe it wasn't chance we met, then. Maybe we were meant to meet. When I looked up and saw you, that's how it felt to me. You and me, we were meant to meet today."

"Why should there be any purpose in us meeting? I came to Knoxville because of my uncle's situation. That's all that concerns me here. You have nothing to do with it at all."

He looked keenly at her. "You'd like to see Hannibal freed, I presume?"

"Of course I would."

"Maybe I know a way to save him."

Had he said anything else but that, she would have turned and walked away without another word. But in this desperate time, her emotions at full tide and rational faculties strained and poorly functioning, Lewis's unexpected comment struck her with surprise but also an absurd hope.

"You could save Hannibal?" If she had heard her own voice as Lewis did, she would have been ashamed of the plaintively childish way it sounded just then.

"Maybe I could! I've been a man of some influence in this town. I been a newspaper editor. I've stood up and introduced folks at rallies—you're own papa! Now, you just come put your arm in mine and let's me and you take a walk back to my room, and we'll work out a plan to get your uncle out of that dark old jail."

The alcoholic smell of his breath struck her, foully, and brought her back to her senses. The irrational hope Lewis had managed to spark revealed itself as the vanity it was. Birch Lewis was in no position to help anyone. His last sentences had reminded her that his life station had never been high, however he might have perceived it, and he had spiraled down even from there. He could do nothing for Hannibal. He was throwing out false hope merely as a way of trying to attract the object of his longtime lust to his room.

"No, Mr. Lewis. I won't go with you. There is nothing you could possibly do for me or Hannibal. Now please: Go away and leave me alone."

He looked so furious that Amy was afraid he would hit her. If that was his impulse, he restrained it. "You'll regret this, Amy."

She turned and walked away, taking the next corner to get out of sight of him. Walking fast, she turned other corners, tracing an evasive course just in case he had followed her. She ducked into another café and ordered a piece of cake and a cup of tea, just to get off the street for a time. When she was finished, she looked carefully about outside before leaving—and saw him. He had followed her again. He was on a nearby corner, talking with animation to a group of Confederate soldiers and pointing toward the café.

She went to the proprietor of the business. "Pardon me, sir, but have you a back entrance?"

"Yes, ma'am. Back yonder." He pointed.

"Thank you." She paid her bill and left that way, hurriedly, hearing the belled front door open and close simultaneous with her exit. *The soldiers . . . they're after me. What has he told them?* She was in an alley, and ran toward the street.

She heard noise behind her. Men coming up the alley. She panicked and ran harder. Rounding a corner, she pounded squarely into a uniformed soldier, knocking him flat on his back and tripping herself so that she fell sprawling onto the edge of the boardwalk and out onto the street.

"Here she is!" the soldier yelled. "I found her!"

They came as if from nowhere and surrounded her. One reached down and grabbed her arm, helping her to her feet against her will. "Miss Deacon?"

"Yes . . ."

"I'm afraid I have to ask you to come with us."

"But why?"

"We've been informed that you have made threats against the life of Colonel William B. Wood in retaliation for the incarceration of your uncle, Hannibal Deacon."

"It's a lie!"

"Come with us, ma'am."

"I tell you, it's a lie! Birch Lewis told you that, didn't he!"

"Come with us, please, or we'll be forced to take stronger measures with you. We have no desire to be rough with you."

"Birch Lewis is a liar! He's trying to cause trouble for me because I would have nothing to do with him!"

"If so, that should come clear with investigation. But we cannot take threats against military authorities lightly, you must understand. Now you will come with us, and there'll be no more protest about it."

"I will not!"

"Then we'll be obliged to carry you bodily."

She tried to run, but there was no hope of getting away, and she realized, too late, that it only made her look guilty. They grabbed her and hustled her off, as Birch Lewis stood watching on the street corner, arms crossed and a big smile on his face.

Everything happened after that in a kind of blur. She was taken before an officer and questioned. She was seated in the hall of the courthouse, guarded by one of the Confederates who had arrested her, then taken into a room and questioned some more by a different man. Out a window she saw soldiers leading Hannibal along, a stranger in a dark suit at his side, talking with his head thrust in close. Hannibal's lawyer, outlining his defense to his client, making valiant plans that both he and Hannibal knew had no chance of really working. The sight was overwhelmingly sad to Amy, and she collapsed in tears, unable to answer any further questions, though they put them to her for several minutes more, demanding answers.

"Please," she said. "Let me go to my uncle's trial! I need to be there with him. He has no one else. Please!"

They would not allow it. The interrogation broke down and she was taken back into the hall again and kept there by a guard. At length another man, a uniformed stranger, came to her and told her she was to be held until the matter could be "clarified to the satisfaction of the military authorities." It seemed, the man noted, that the fellow who had made the accusation against her had since vanished, and they felt the need to find and talk to him further before proceeding any longer with her.

"Are you taking me to jail?"

"No, ma'am. Not the jail as such. We've made arrangements with a private citizen of the city to hold you in a secure cellar room of his home, so as to give you the privacy and such you need."

She felt it was all a ploy, a grand conspiracy to keep her far from where Hannibal was. Birch Lewis, these strangers, the entire Confederacy—they were doing this in collusion, keeping her and Hannibal separated!

Rationality, in a far more muted voice, told her it was not so. There was no conspiracy here, nothing but the tragic outcome of a chance encounter with the wrong man, which generated hopeless hurdles at just the wrong time. Birch Lewis, in his fury, had gained his revenge on the Deacon family in a far grander way than he probably knew.

As they led her to the house that would be her prison, and locked her in a cellar room with only one tiny, narrow window, far too small to be squeezed through, and a heavy door barred and locked from the far side, she yielded to despair and a further cold, rational realization. It really wouldn't have mattered if Birch Lewis hadn't come along when he did. There was nothing she could have done to stop the machinations already at work to destroy Hannibal Deacon. He was right. It was his destiny to die.

Night came; she did not sleep at all. The trial was surely done by now. It would not have required long to convict a man whose condemnation was already all but sure. She wondered if Hannibal was still alive, or if the final deed had been done. Had he said they would take him back to Greene

County for execution? She thought so. The details of her last meeting with Hannibal were already growing murky in her weary mind.

Morning brought two men in uniform who questioned her again about her alleged threats. She denied it all as before, and begged to know the outcome of the Hannibal Deacon trial.

"He was convicted, late in the afternoon, and sentenced to hang," was the reply.

"Is he still alive?" Amy asked.

The uniformed men looked at one another quickly, oddly; she wondered what was at play here. "I've said all I should say," the man replied.

They've hanged him, Amy thought. *They probably hanged him right here in Knoxville, to get it done more quickly.*

She asked if Birch Lewis had been found. No. He was still being sought. And what will happen if he isn't located? Again she was told that enough had been said already. For now she must remain where she was.

A young soldier brought her food a little later and she begged for information about the Deacon trial. "I ain't authorized to speak of it as I know of, ma'am," he said nervously, looking scared.

She remained alone the rest of the day, every passing hour deepening her assurance that it was all surely over. Hope really was gone now. And the irony was that she had finally thought of something she might have done to make a difference. She could have telegraphed Confederate President Davis himself and put forth a plea for Hannibal's release. She could have begged the president to show mercy for the sake of Hannibal's kinship to Dr. George Deacon of Secession Hill, whose work had contributed so greatly to the Secession cause. She could have played out the forbidden hand of offering herself as a propagandist and spokesman for the Confederate cause, however much Hannibal would have despised her for it. Jefferson Davis might have responded to such an offer. But it was surely too late now.

But maybe not. She went to the door of her cellar room

and called for someone to come. No one did. She heard movement in the house above her, but no one appeared.

That evening the same young soldier brought her food, which she turned away. He looked at her as if wishing to speak, but held back. Lifting wet eyes to him, she said, "Is there nothing at all you can tell me about my uncle?"

He looked around, though they were alone. "I ain't supposed to say, but . . . no, no, I can't talk about this to a prisoner."

"Please! I beg you. I must know. Have they hanged him?"

He trembled like a child. "Yes," he croaked. "By now they'll have hanged him."

She bowed her head and cried a few moments. "So he's murdered. They've murdered him."

The soldier's face for a few moments was that of a man in moral struggle. She was a yielding, and his voice became a whisper. "No, miss. They didn't murder him. It wasn't the noose that killed him."

She looked up. "What did you say?"

"You can't let on to no one that I told. You got to promise."

"I promise. What do you mean, the noose didn't kill him? He's alive?"

"He's not alive. Your uncle, he was already dead when they loaded him up to take him up to the bridge he'd burned. They were going to execute him there, but they couldn't, because he was already dead."

"But how?"

"He just died. Right at the end of the trial. He declared that he had a sharp kind of pain in the side of his head, and his nose commenced to bleeding, and he slumped over 'gainst his attorney and died, right there. I didn't see it, but another fellow I know did and told me. It's supposed to be secret. They didn't want nobody to know. They want it believed that they hanged him, you see. They don't want the Union folk saying that he kind of got away without being punished for what he did, you see."

Tears streamed down Amy's face, but she laughed. Looking at the young soldier, she laughed convulsively.

"He did it. He died before they could kill him. He did it, just like he had hoped he would. He *willed* it! Do you see? He willed it, and it happened! He got away from them the only way he could!"

The soldier's eyes were wide. He backed away from her, leaving the tray of food, and got out the door as if he was running from a ranting demon.

Amy's laughter continued a minute more before it turned to sobbing. She lay down and cried until she was asleep. Sometime during her slumber someone came and took away the tray of untouched food, but she was never aware of it.

They set her free the next morning, with many apologies. Her accuser, they told her, had been found, hungover and maudlin, and had admitted he contrived the story of her threat-making because he was angry with her. The Confederate States of America, they said, deeply regretted any inconvenience her incarceration had caused, and handed her a letter to that effect.

She refused to accept the letter, and walked out of her makeshift prison without saying a word.

At the Colter Bridge, Greene County

Sam Colter walked slowly toward the bridge, not wanting to see, but feeling he must see all the same. He knew already that he was too late; he had met a hunter in the woods and asked if there was word of what had become of the man accused of burning the Colter bridge.

"You go there, and you'll see him," the hunter replied. "The traitor's already swinging from what remained of the trestle. They plan to leave him there a couple of days, I believe. To discourage any others from treason, you know. It was the oddest thing, in a way. Folks had got wind of the hanging and gathered to see it, but they wouldn't let them in close. They kept him hidden and did it all in a way that nobody could even see it going on until he was already hanging there. I can't figure it. If they wanted to make him an example of what comes of treason, you'd have thunk they'd want folks to see it all, beginning to end."

Treason. Sam filled with anger. Loyalty to the United States was now criminal; defending it against what Sam and myriad others believed was an illegal civil revolt was now treason. It was absurd. Infuriating.

There was a guard at the bridge, so Sam left his weapons hidden among the brush before showing himself. He was still alone; Greeley was either still back at the Lynch cabin or had not yet caught up with him.

The guard watched Sam approach. Sam felt his studying eyes, knew they were noting the raggedness of his appearance and the grime that his hurried, stressed journey had put upon him.

"That's close enough, young fellow," the guard said. He tried to sound strong and harsh, but it didn't come across. He seemed like the kind of man who used to loaf and whittle on Hannibal's store porch on warm summer afternoons. "You can see him from where you are."

Sam gazed for a minute or more at the still, hanging form of a man he had worked beside, admired, loved. He could hardly recognize the face at first, gray with death, but the longer he looked the more he saw the familiar features and felt the unspeakable pain of knowing that Hannibal Deacon was beyond any help he could have given. Not that there was anything he could have done anyway. The impulse that had driven him here was like the one that, unknown to Sam, motivated Amy Deacon to rush to Knoxville—the impulse to simply be with him, to respond in some way, futile or not, to his situation.

"He was a bridge burner," the guard explained without invitation. "He was tried and convicted, and hung up here to serve as a warning to folks not to perform acts against the Confederate States of America. We'll leave him here another day before we cut him down. There'll be others to die just like him. They're rounding up bridge burners right and left, and they'll hang. They'll hang all of them they can."

Sam stared on, unspeaking. A breeze stirred and the hanging corpse swayed back and forth, just a little.

Sam thought: *This is war. Just like all the hell that happened back at that poor old man's cabin, this is war. It's good men killed, and their very bodies hung up for ridicule. It's righteousness become sin, and patriotism become treason. This is war, and I hate it.*

"His name was Deacon, Hannibal Deacon," the guard continued. He seemed to have a need to talk; beneath the veneer of nonchalance the guard affected, Sam sensed a man filled with the same kind of horror Sam himself had brutally come to know within a span of mere days. When this guard had volunteered for service, had he envisioned such a gruesome duty as guarding a dead man who didn't deserve to be dead? Sam doubted it. The guard went on: "They say he was brother to George Deacon, who used to publish *The Secession Advocate* down in Knoxville. Odd, ain't it, two brothers taking such different sides, and now both of them being dead?" He looked over his shoulder at the hanged form. "Too bad, really. They say this fellow was a good man, even if he was a Lincolnite."

"Yes," Sam said. "He was a good man. A very good one."

"You knew him?"

"Yes."

"Hard kind of thing for you to see, then, him hanging there."

"Yes."

The guard frowned thoughtfully, glanced around, then said: "If it makes you feel any better about it, he was dead before it happened. I ain't supposed to tell it, but it's true."

"What?"

"He was dead before they hung him. He was sick all through his trial, they say, and he died in Knoxville. They brought him here anyway, so folks would think he died from hanging."

"He died in Knoxville. . . ." Sam remembered the hunter's description of the odd way they had conducted Hannibal's hanging. It made sense now. They had kept the process hidden so no one would realize they were merely hanging up a dead man. "I wouldn't have known about it myself if I hadn't have been called on to help."

Sam looked more closely at Hannibal. His neck, though

distorted and squeezed by the rope, did not look like it was broken.

It was true. They had hanged a dead man. Sam wasn't sure what to make of that, how to feel about it. He thought awhile and decided it was better this way. Hannibal was dead, lost to him forever, no more to give him counsel or make him laugh with one of his absurd jokes—but *they* hadn't killed him. For some reason, that made a difference.

You skunked them, Hannibal Deacon. You had one good chance to skunk them, and you did it. Good for you, Hannibal. Good for you.

"Why did they try him in Knoxville instead of Greeneville?"

The guard was quickly forgetting what little military aloofness he had been instructed to exercise. "Well, I ain't sure, but I believe it was because this one was special. In Knoxville they could make more of a show of trying him. They could control it all better there, hold him more secure. This one was prominent, you see, and he had used his name to support the Union heresy."

Sam wondered from what newspaper or stump speaker this bumpkin had picked up the phrase "Union heresy." "And that's why they hung his corpse, too . . . because he was 'special'?"

"I expect that's plumb right, young man. This Mr. Deacon was well-known. He had took a family name that had always been thunk of as Secesh and made it Union. So they strung him up, and we're to leave him until they tell me to take him down." The guard examined Hannibal's body again; his eyes seemed drawn to it. "You can take what comfort you can in the fact he didn't die in that noose. But don't say I told you, please. I ain't supposed to have told nobody."

"I won't say nothing." Sam took a final look at Hannibal's corpse, turned and walked away, back toward the woods.

"Good-bye," the guard called after him. "Take care of yourself, young fellow." Just a friendly country man, taking his small part in something far too big for him to understand.

"Good-bye," Sam replied. Then, in his mind: *And good-bye to you, Hannibal Deacon. Good-bye, and thank you . . . and I hope you know how much I admired you, and how much I loved you, and that I'll never forget you. Never. Nor who it was who did you the shame of hanging you even though you were already dead. I'll never forget it, nor for-give them for it.* His next thought was one that he would have expected to rise in his brother Joe's mind, but not, until now, in his own. *And as many of them as I can make pay for how they've treated you, Hannibal, I'll make them pay.*

The guard watched Sam until he was out of sight, then shifted his posture and his heavy rifle, glanced at Hannibal Deacon's corpse, drew in a deep breath, and carried on.

Chapter 27

The colonel's name was Danville Leadbetter. Born in Maine, educated at West Point, he was an engineer by career and thus well-suited to his assignment of rebuilding the bridges sabotaged by the Unionists. The Confederacy brought him into East Tennessee and he went to work, overseeing replacement of the ruined bridges and helping spearhead the capture and punishment of those who had destroyed them. He brought a special intensity to the latter phase of his work, possibly, some speculated, because he knew his Yankee heritage could foster mistrust among southern-born Confederates. Leadbetter had married a southern woman but was an outsider by blood, and such a man in such a time and position as his had every reason to feel compelled to prove the strength of his Confederate allegiance.

The hanging of Hannibal Deacon marked the beginning of and set the tone for the Confederate answer to the bridge burners. Partly because of fear that regular jury trials in so Unionist a region as East Tennessee would not result in death sentences for bridge burners, the Confederate Department of War urged "drumhead court-martial" trials for all accused of that crime. If convicted, they were to be hanged at once, preferably from the remains of the bridges they had burned, as Hannibal Deacon's corpse had been.

Colonel Leadbetter set up his headquarters in Greeneville, the heart of some of the most Unionist territory in the region. He quickly issued two communiqués. One was a terse telegram to the Confederate Secretary of War, J. P. Benjamin: "Two insurgents have today been tried for bridge burning, found guilty and hanged."

The men to whom he referred were two of the Lick Creek bridge burners, Jacob Henshaw and Henry Fry. After trial in Greeneville, they were marched up Depot Street to a large oak near the railroad station, and there hanged before the populace, defiant and unrepentant to the end. They might have been hanged from the remnants of the Lick Creek bridge, but too little of that structure was left to make a decent gallows, and besides, it was far easier to gather a crowd in Greeneville than miles out in the midst of rolling farmland. Colonel Leadbetter made a point of affixing the nooses around the necks of the condemned pair with his own hands. Under no circumstances would he allow the people of Greeneville to develop any notion that he was to be trifled with. The hanging went off with some aplomb, and made quite a gruesome show.

The plan was to leave the corpses hanging from the tree for several days, though the effects of decay would cause them to be removed somewhat sooner. For the time they did hang, however, Confederate soldiers passing through the town had some fun with the corpses, striking them, disfiguring them, and firing the occasional shot into them. Such displays were not discouraged by Confederate authorities in that they helped to drive home Leadbetter's message to the public more firmly.

The second of Leadbetter's communiqués was a public proclamation designed to make that message all the clearer:

TO THE CITIZENS OF EAST TENNESSEE:

So long as the question of Union or disunion was debatable so long you did well to debate it and vote on it. You had a clear right to vote for the Union but when Secession was established by the voice of the people you did ill to distract the country by angry words and insurrectionary tumult. In doing this you commit the highest crime known to the laws.

Out of the Southern Confederacy no people possess such elements of prosperity and happiness as those of East Tennessee . . . At this moment you might be at war with the United States or any foreign nation and yet not suffer a tenth part of the evils which pursue you in this domestic strife. No man's life or property is safe, no woman or child can sleep in quiet. You are deluded by selfish demagogues who take care for their own personal safety. You are citizens of Tennessee and your State one of the Confederate States. So long as you are up in arms against these States can you look for anything but the invasion of your homes and the wasting of your substance. This condition of things must be ended. The Government commands the peace and sends troops to enforce the order. I proclaim that every man who comes in promptly and delivers up his arms will be pardoned on taking the oath of allegiance. All men taken in arms against the Government will be transported to the military prison at Tuscaloosa and be confined there during the war. Bridge-burners and destroyers of railroad tracks are excepted from among those pardonable. They will be tried by drumhead court-martial and be hung on the spot.

D. LEADBETTER,
Colonel, Commanding

Early in December, in Knoxville, other bridge burners went to their deaths, the Federal invasion they had tried to bring in having never come, diverted by the changing tides of war.

The fiery Parson Brownlow, who had come out of mountain hiding and surrendered to Confederate authorities upon promise he would not be harmed, was among those in Knoxville's Castle Fox who watched one C. A. Haun withdrawn from his cell and taken out for hanging. Two others, a Greene County father and son named Harmon, soon followed. The rebel executioners forced the elder Harmon to watch his son die first, and then forced him onto the gallows to hang by his side. Haun and the two Harmons, like Henshaw and Fry, had been part of the Lick Creek bridge-burning party.

Brownlow was also there when young Elizabeth Self, daughter of another accused Lick Creek bridge burner named Harrison Self, visited her father in what she thought would be her final visit. As she left, she approached Brownlow. "Sir," she said, "I know you are a great man of words. Though it may do no good, I want to send a telegram to President Davis and seek a pardon for my father."

Brownlow obtained a paper and pen from a cooperative guard, and wrote the following:

Hon. Jefferson Davis:
My father, Harrison Self, is sentenced to hang at four o'clock this evening, on a charge of bridge-burning. As he remains my earthly all and all my hopes of happiness center on him, I implore you to pardon him.

Elizabeth Self

The weeping young woman took Brownlow's terse composition directly to the Federal telegraph facility at the nearby courthouse and wired it to the Confederate president with many prayers, but little hope that it would make a difference.

But larger forces were already at work in her and her father's favor. Self was a respected citizen with a history of good behavior, a simple and kindly man who had never been strongly partisan in politics. He had already been the subject of many supplications for mercy directed to the Confederate government by many private and public figures, including several staunch and respected rebels. Even the very court panel that had voted his conviction had pleaded for his death sentence to be commuted, influenced in part by testimony that indicated Self had gone to the bridge burning to make sure his sons, who had trailed along, were safe, rather than to actually participate.

Elizabeth Self's poignant telegram, added to the weight

of earlier pleas, tipped the scale in the mind of Jefferson Davis, who sent back a wire of his own. Harrison Self received his pardon, his sentence was commuted to imprisonment, and the gallows that had been erected in public view in Knoxville were deprived of one scheduled victim.

But the Confederates left the gallows standing, a silent, visible warning to all that resistance would not be tolerated, and that the next man scheduled to die in the noose might not end up as fortunate as Harrison Self.

The close of 1861 and the beginning of 1862 brought many changes to the armies of blue and gray.

The high Confederacy relieved General Felix Zollicoffer of his command of the District of East Tennessee on December 8, replacing him with General G. B. Crittenden, whose father was a United States senator and whose brother, General Thomas L. Crittenden, served prominently in the Union Army. Zollicoffer, who had moved with his troops into southeastern Kentucky, was given command of the district's First Brigade.

On the Union side, meanwhile, General William T. Sherman, who had aborted the planned invasion of East Tennessee at the last moment, was replaced by General Don Carlos Buell, but this change did nothing to increase the likelihood of a Federal invasion of East Tennessee. Like Sherman, Buell believed the Union Army was poorly situated at the moment for such an invasion, and all the fervent pleas of Senator Andrew Johnson and General Samuel P. Carter did not sway him. It was not long before Johnson gave up on Buell and headed to Washington to seek to persuade Lincoln himself to order the invasion, in that he knew the president held a soft spot in his heart for loyal East Tennessee, an area with which he held some family ties. Lincoln responded to Johnson's pleas with a promise of an immediate advance upon Knoxville.

Yet even then it did not occur. Buell simply hung fire, until Lincoln himself sent a telegram seething with impatience: "Have arms gone forward to East Tennessee. Please tell me the progress and condition of the movement in that direction. Answer!"

Buell replied to the president that his forces simply were not ready to make such a move. Lincoln wrote back, sounding oddly plaintive and defeated, saying that his desire to enter East Tennessee was not intended to be "an order in any sense, but merely, as intimated before, to show you the grounds of my anxiety."

He informed Buell that his "distress" was that "our friends in East Tennessee are being hanged and driven to despair, and even now I fear, are thinking of taking rebel arms for the sake of personal protection. In this we lost the most valuable stake we have in the South." But even now Buell did not move.

Meanwhile there was some similar ignoring of high orders being exhibited on the Confederate side by General Felix Zollicoffer.

The Confederates, fearing the possibility of Federal advancement into Tennessee, turned their attention to a strategic little Kentucky spot called Mill Springs, south of the Cumberland River and slightly southwest of the town of Somerset. Should the Federals possess Mill Springs, they would have easy access to important sections of Tennessee.

Touring troop emplacements in the Mill Springs area after spending about a month settling into his Knoxville headquarters, Crittenden ordered Zollicoffer to encamp south of the Cumberland and keep his eye on any suspicious enemy movements. But Zollicoffer disobeyed, encamping north of the river and setting up infantry, artillery, and cavalry. Thus he placed the river at his rear and difficult-to-defend terrain at his front, terrain that lacked good forage besides.

When Crittenden received word of Zollicoffer's actions, he sent a messenger repeating the command: encamp *south* of the river. Yet when he returned in January, Crittenden found Zollicoffer stationed just as before, blaming the weather and the lateness of Crittenden's messenger for his lack of compliance with the order.

As heavy rains set in and soldiers labored to build

flatboats to carry wagons and supplies back across the now-swollen Cumberland, intelligence arrived that two large Federal forces were approaching Mill Springs.

Crittenden saw only one way to respond under the circumstances. Knowing the weather was surely slowing the two Federal armies, he ordered an attack upon the nearer army of the two, which was led by General George Thomas.

The brunt of this attack fell to Zollicoffer and his Tennessee troops. Slogging their way toward Thomas through the wet night, they met their first resistance at dawn and found their weapons, mostly old flintlock rifles, rendered useless by the rain. Falling back, the Tennesseans were replaced by soldiers from the 15th Mississippi, and action began along Fishing Creek, carrying on through forests and fields. It was January 19, a day that would not be forgotten.

Zollicoffer, plagued with nearsightedness made worse by the dust and smoke of battle, made a fatal personal error in the heaviest portion of the fighting. Seeing what he thought were Confederate troops firing upon fellow Confederates, he rode in to order a halt to the perceived friendly fire. Too late he found he had misjudged; the soldiers he was among were Union, not rebel, and a shot fired by Corporal James Swan of Company H of the 10th Indiana Regiment ended Zollicoffer's life on the spot, making him the first Tennessee general of the Civil War to fall in battle.

The Confederates fought on without their leader, but the battle tide had already turned against them. Eventually they fell back, then retreated in defeat all the way to Knoxville, bearing their wounded as they entered a city stunned by the unanticipated rout.

East Tennessee University and the local Deaf and Dumb Asylum were converted into instant military hospitals, and the Confederacy faced a grim truth: With the defeat along Fishing Creek, Tennessee lay open before the Federals.

Further, Zollicoffer's death jolted and saddened almost everyone, regardless of political conviction. Of all the Confederate military leaders in East Tennessee, Zollicoffer had been by far the most popular. Even caustic Parson Brownlow, the Unionists' Unionist, declared that Zollicoffer had been a man of great personal honor and honesty, bravery beyond dispute, and possessing no marr upon his life record beyond his joining of the Confederate cause.

But any grief Unionists felt for Zollicoffer was, naturally, greatly overbalanced by renewed hope for the long-awaited Federal invasion of East Tennessee. Surely, with Mill Springs in Union hands and the door open to the Federals, that invasion would finally come. Surely.

Yet still it didn't. Buell concentrated his generals and their forces on the state's center section; East Tennessee would have to wait.

Disappointing as this was to the eastern Unionists, Buell's strategy did help bring along a string of Union coups. Fort Henry on the Tennessee River fell victim to an attack of both army and navy Federal forces. Rebel forces in Kentucky, squeezed and threatened, fell back from their positions in response. Fort Donelson was also surrendered to the Union, while over in North Carolina, Roanoke Island fell, too.

Near the end of the month an event of great significance happened in the heart of the state: Nashville was given up by the rebels who had held it and Union forces swept in. The capital city of Tennessee was in Union hands, the first capital of a seceded state to fall to the enemy.

Tennessee's Secessionist governor, Isham Harris, fled with the rebel soldiers, and Greeneville's Andrew Johnson received an unusual and unprecedented political mantle from Lincoln: the position of Military Governor of the State of Tennessee. There had never been a position quite like it in prior American history. Johnson entered Nashville and began practicing his governorship with an iron fist that quickly made him a despised man in the Confederate-supporting Middle and West Tennessee regions.

Elsewhere, battles raged.

In early March, Confederates at Pea Ridge, Arkansas, fought for two days and then yielded yet another battle to the Union. At New Madrid, Missouri, the Confederacy rolled back again, and later in the month, Major General Thomas "Stonewall" Jackson, the popular Confederate leader, suffered a defeat at Kernstown in the Shenandoah Valley Campaign.

Then came April, an advance of McClellan's Union forces on the Deleware-Maryland peninsula, and an attack on Yorktown. In Tennessee the month brought a fearsome, hellish battle at an obscure little place called Shiloh, after which General Pierre Beauregard and his rebel forces retreated into Mississippi.

The ironies were hard to miss: Tennessee's Middle and West divisions, Confederate in sympathy, were now in Union hands, while East Tennessee, where Unionism held the hearts and minds of a majority, remained dominated by the Confederacy.

Much had changed in rather sweeping fashion, but many more battles remained to be fought. The war was not done by any measure, and for those in rugged, ideologically divided western North Carolina and East Tennessee, the worst was still to come. The war from now on was to be a civil war in the most real sense: painful, violent, bloody, often fought within circles of former friends and even families. It was to be a guerrilla war, a hateful war, a war often governed by the terrain in which it was fought. A mountain war, fought man-to-man by the harsh rules of the feud, and as often as not, fought in shadows.

Part V

G A T H E R I N G   S T O R M

Chapter 28

Late April 1862; Knoxville, Tennessee

Jim Matoy sat as still as if he were carved from wood, only his eyes shifting back and forth, up and down, to view the unique tableau of which he was a part. He was seated beside his friend and fellow soldier, Nikatimsi. Beneath him was a pew, before him a pulpit, above him the ceiling of the sanctuary of Knoxville's First Presbyterian Church, and all around were his fellow soldiers in the very first entirely Indian unit of the North Carolina Cherokee Company, CSA, which would soon be known as Thomas's Highland Legion. It was so named in honor of dimunitive Will Thomas, or Wil-Usdi, the white trader, Cherokee advocate, and political figure who had organized the band and now was its captain.

To the perimeter of the Indian group, which was seated in the midst of the sanctuary, was a huge gathering of Knoxvillians who had come to ogle this unusual force and hear the religious service they were just beginning to conduct. So great had the number of gawkers been that the entire service was shifted from the Baptist church to the much-larger Presbyterian sanctuary, just so more onlookers could be accommodated.

Since coming to Knoxville with his fellow Cherokee soldiers some weeks ago, Matoy had become accustomed to being stared at. He didn't much mind it; his group was indeed an unusual sight. Though they were dressed in standard Confederate gray, their hair cut short or tied up tightly behind their heads, this gathering of soldiers was quite different from the norm. Much of its membership spoke no English, and quite a few had only the vaguest idea of what the great war of the moment was all about. They had signed on, like Matoy, mostly because Will Thomas asked them to, and what he asked for, he generally received. He had proven himself a stalwart friend of the North Carolina Cherokee for many years now, and few questioned him.

Matoy's allegiance, however, was not only to Thomas, but also to his old, murdered friend Skaantee. Matoy well remembered that long trek up to gain the counsel of his old friend, and of his own reluctance at that time to become a soldier. That reluctance was gone because of what had happened to Skaantee. Matoy remembered a later day he had climbed Skaantee's Ridge, heart in his mouth, fear in his belly. "There were shots up there," a man had told him, looking up at the ridge. "And a scream, very faint, like a woman."

Matoy had climbed the ridge and found them: Skaantee and his daughter, and the white man, named Sloat, whom Skaantee's daughter had married. All of them dead. He had held Skaantee's head in his lap and wept like a child.

Thinking of it now, he closed his eyes and felt his heart surge with hatred for whoever had murdered his friend. No one could prove who it was, but all believed it was a white man from the town of Marshall, named Joseph Colter, who had reason to hate Sloat. Though evidence indicated that Colter—if it was really he who had committed the slayings—was wounded on Skaantee's Ridge, no body had ever been found. Maybe he had died in some remote spot no one had run across since. Maybe he was still alive. Alive while Skaantee was dead. The latter thought was the one that gnawed ceaselessly at Jim Matoy and gave him a dark ambition: *If ever I find this Joseph Colter, I'll kill him. I'll murder him just like he murdered Skaantee.*

He opened his eyes as the sound of John Astoogatogeh's voice rang out from the front of the church, speaking in the

Cherokee tongue. This entire service would be conducted in that language, to the simultaneous fascination and bewilderment of the white observers all around. Matoy smiled slightly. It was rather fun, being able to understand what was said while the outsiders didn't. Astoogatogeh could advocate the immediate murder of every white Knoxville citizen, and the encircling oglers would merely keep on gawking and nodding. Not that Astoogatogeh would ever do such a thing. A Christian convert, he was a devout and thoroughly well-behaved man, chaplain of the company. Along with Peter Graybeard, he was one of two second lieutenants in the company, and probably the single most popular man in the group. Matoy admired him as much as any of the others, and valued his wisdom, which surely had come to him through his bloodline. He was the grandson of Junaluska, one of the great Cherokee chiefs.

Matoy had once discussed his bitterness over Skaantee's murder with Astoogatogeh, and received counsel to "let it go, as much as you can." There was no point in seething in fury over a murderer who might never be convincingly identified. "You don't know who killed old Skaantee, and neither does anyone else," Astoogatogeh said. "Perhaps it was this Colter you mentioned, or perhaps not. In any case, don't let this murder destroy you as well by making you full of hate. The hate a man keeps inside himself harms only himself. God knows the guilty, and none of them escape punishment in the end."

Matoy had tried to adopt that attitude. So far, it hadn't taken. Skaantee's death and his own desire to punish the perpetrator were always at the back of his mind. They filled him and spilled out in a spirit of aggression that made him embrace the military service he had initially feared. When Will Thomas received official permission to form his company, Jim Matoy had been one of the first volunteers. His friend Nikatimsi had signed up only a day later.

The service went on at some length. Matoy listened sometimes, brooded sometimes. It was odd, being here in the middle of a great city of white men, wearing the gray uniform of a Confederate, hearing words of peace spoken in a time of war. Yet so far there had been no real war for

Matoy. He and his fellow soldiers had spent their time encamped just north of Knoxville on a hillside dubbed Camp Aganstata, after the Cherokee name of one of the officers who helped recruit and create the Cherokee Company: the half-Indian Major Gideon Morgan. So far it all had been quite boring, but a welcome rumor was circulating that soon the company would be ordered to a new location to actually begin *doing* something. Matoy was eager. With the Confederacy in trouble across Tennessee and clinging tooth and nail to its precious eastern mountain region, surely there was more to be done than merely passing time in a camp . . . drilling, marching, drilling some more, playing lacrosse, and brooding over the murder of an old man who hadn't deserved to die.

The service ended. The Cherokee soldiers rose and filed out of the church, heading into the darkness and back to Camp Junaluska. As he left the church, Matoy scanned the onlooking white faces. What if one of them was Joseph Colter? Not likely, he figured, but he pondered that same question every time he saw white men. He couldn't help it, and it was about to drive him mad.

Shelton Laurel Valley, North Carolina

Greeley Brown loved to talk and Sam Colter to listen, but these days Greeley restrained himself from much chatter while riding the mountain trails. It was simply too dangerous now, and every time they traveled, they did so in the manner of fugitives, or of scouts reconnoitering in hostile terrain.

The western North Carolina mountains had turned into a very dangerous place, and probably would grow more so as time went by. Sam had come to see that homefront war was something like a slow-simmering illness: at the beginning a vague kind of thing, a bit worrisome but sometimes not even noticeable, imprecise in how it displayed itself. But as time passed, the illness would set in, become stronger. The symptoms would grow pronounced, the suffering greater.

These days the mountains crawled with Confederate Home Guards, who scoured the hills for Unionists, particu-

larly those who became bushwhackers or irregular parti-
sans. They also looked for deserters, whose population
thereabouts was already sizable and surely would grow
steadily as the war dragged on. Many a mountain rebel who
had signed on early, eager for the "glory" of warfare against
intruding Yankee aggressors, had already seen the glory
fade, and with it their war spirit. Many waited until the end
of their enlistment terms, choosing to return home and fight
no more. Others didn't bother to wait out their enlistments,
and vanished from their lines to melt into the familiar
mountains, to see to the needs of their families and put war
behind them, if they could.

The situation of the mountain folks in general was
growing more dire. With men away because of the war,
there were fewer people to tend the fields. Livestock was
being taken for military use, and salt was already in short
supply. Come fall and winter, the salt shortage would
become a major problem, for without salt there was no good
way to preserve meat.

On top of it all, a new blow had just been dealt in the form
of the Confederate conscription law, which swept into service
able-bodied men between eighteen and thirty-five. The mountain people were stung particularly hard. How could any more
men be spared from the farms and fields? How could a mountain family hope to live if only women and children were left
at home? Who would hunt? Who would bring in the crops?
And who would protect the civilian population from bushwhackers, Home Guards, rampaging soldiers? The conscription law was nettling, burdensome, and already beginning to
create yet another variety of mountaineer refugee: the conscription dodger.

Both Sam and Greeley fell within the age bracket of the
conscription law, but neither had any intention of being
drafted. Yet they didn't consider themselves conscription
dodgers; to do so would imply a recognition of Confederate
authority neither was willing to give. They perceived themselves merely as free-ranging Unionists, hiding out in hostile
territory, unaffiliated with any official military organization,
but ready at any point to begin the service both had decided

was their wartime calling: guiding stampeders out of Confederate territory to the Union lines.

After Sam returned from his grim visit to the Colter bridge and the corpse of Hannibal Deacon, he and Greeley had rejoined, but returned only briefly to the Unionist encampment in the Carter County mountains. From there they drifted over into this North Carolina wilderness and lost themselves in it, roaming, planning, hiding, and, for Sam's sake, hunting for Joe Colter, or at least the truth about what had become of him.

This free-roaming life had turned them into windburned, sunbaked woodsmen. The lines around Greeley's eyes were deeper, the ridges of his brow more furrowed, his beard lighter from the bleaching of sun and dappled with the beginnings of gray. Sam was leaner than ever, and nothing remained of the town-dwelling, boyish store clerk he had been in Greeneville. Weathered and taut, his eyes bore a cold glint they had not possessed before. He was no longer Sam Colter the townsman, but Sam Colter the mountain Unionist, Sam Colter the bane of Home Guards and rebel bushwhackers.

Since the bloody encounter in old Jarrell Lynch's cabin, Sam Colter and Greeley had killed three more men between them. Sam could claim two of those, both of them self-defensive slayings of drunken mountain rebels out for blood. Greeley had killed the third man, a Home Guard who tried to disarm him and had not displayed the sense to heed Greeley's commands to let him be. For two men who sought no fights, Sam and Greeley had run across plenty of them. Neither man relished the killings he had done, but both were glad they hadn't neglected to do what required doing.

They kept on the move most of the time, living in a variety of caves, cabins, and rough shelters that Greeley knew about and, in some cases, had built long ago for lodging during hunts. They encountered other men fairly frequently, and of late had begun to put out word that should anyone desire to escape the mountains and make for the Union lines, Greeley Brown and Sam Colter stood ready to guide them. There would be cost—their job would be risky and deserved compensation—but it would be reasonable.

They had gathered quite a list of names of potential stampeders, but so far he and Greeley had not found anyone ready for immediate departure. They expected the new conscription law to change that soon.

They rode now in the remote region of Shelton Laurel, looking for Joe Colter. Sam had followed a potential lead or two before in his search for Joe, but they had come to nothing. A new rumor had lately reached him. He dared hope that this one might have merit.

It was late afternoon, the sun edging down. They had traveled far today, and barely missed detection by a group of six Home Guards. Now, as they reached a turn in the trail, they saw a narrow mountain road ahead and stopped for a few moments to listen and look. One did not ride out onto an open road without caution these days.

Greeley Brown slumped in the saddle and sighed loudly. "I'm give out, Sam. Plumb give out."

"We can't stop now."

"What'd you say the old gal's name was?"

"Cart. Jenny Cart. Her husband's name is Jimmy Cart. Or was. He's gone and nobody knows for sure whether he's living or dead."

"And this man that's been seen about her place, you think he's Joe?"

"It surely sounds like him, from the description."

"What if her husband's come back to her, and it's him and not Joe?" Greeley asked.

"Well, if it ain't Joe, it ain't Joe. But you know I have to go see, don't you?"

"I do. I just hope we don't get shot."

"Why are you so worried? There's no reason to assume we're going to get shot at even if it ain't Joe."

"I ain't so much worried that it won't be Joe as I am worried that it will be. The Joe Colter I know is quick to snap the trigger."

Sam mulled that over. Greeley was right. They would have to be cautious in how they made their approach, for Joe, if it was him, would know he was a wanted man, and he indeed might shoot them right off rather than wait around for a good, identifying look at them.

But still Sam was compelled to investigate. They moved off the trail and onto the road, feeling tension like tingles of electricity down their shoulders.

There were no dogs about the place, which was not only unusual, but quite a blessing under the circumstances. A man could hide from a human being, but it was cursed hard to hide from a dog.

"I'll bet they've eat up whatever dogs they had," Greeley whispered as they watched the house, which was nothing but a small two-room cabin that looked like it might be approaching a century or so in age. The woods grew right up onto it on the rear and the south side; the front was cleared out several yards until it reached the trees where Greeley and Sam now hid. To the north was a rolling hill cleared of all growth and cultivated at the top and down one slope. "That's the poorest-looking dwelling I've seen in a long time, not counting my own various hovels."

There was dim light inside, but the shutters were closed. Looking closely, they could make out occasional movements of shadows on the other side of the windows, but whether those casting them were male or female was impossible to tell.

"We ain't going to be able to see if it's him, setting out here," Greeley said. "Them shutters rule that out."

"Well, I don't much want to go to the door," Sam replied. "That's the way folks get shot these days."

"So what do you suggest? It seems to me that—whoa!" Greeley ducked lower in the brush, as did Sam, for the front door had suddenly swung open and a man stepped out onto the porch. It was dark and the faint light behind him in the doorway cast him in dim silhouette, so it was impossible to see his face, but the form, the stance . . . Sam thought they looked very familiar, though he couldn't be sure.

"Good Lord—he's coming this way!" This from Greeley, in a sharp but very soft whisper.

Indeed the man was approaching, and there was nothing they could do without revealing their presence. The fellow was limping very badly but moving at a good clip nonetheless. To rise and bolt now would catch his attention—and he was carrying a shotgun.

Sam looked toward Greeley, though he couldn't see him well in this dark copse. What should they do? Heart racing, he sank even lower, lying flat on his belly in the brush as Greeley did the same beside him. The man was close now, almost upon them . . . and now he came closer yet, right into the brush.

Sam was about to rise and hope for the best when the man stopped. He looked around, laid the shotgun aside, and fumbled at the fly of his trousers. Sam and Greeley lay unbreathing, listening to liquid splattering the leaves of the single bush that hid them from the man, smelling the caustic stench of urine.

When the man was done, he rehitched his fly and reached into a pocket, from which he produced a pipe, which he began to load. The shotgun still leaned against a nearby tree. If necessary, they could jump this fellow before he could reach it—maybe.

Sam's mind raced. *A pipe . . . that means a match, and light. It'll show his face. . . .*

He heard the snap of a match being broken off a block, then the scratch of it . . . flame flared, rose, touched the pipe and flared brighter as he puffed, revealing a face that was bearded, thin, but indeed very familiar.

"Joe." Sam said it softly, trying to minimize the inevitable startling effect. It didn't work, for the man spasmed as if shot, dropped the match and the pipe and went straight for the shotgun.

"Wait, Joe, don't! It's me. It's Sam."

Joe Colter had the shotgun up and leveled by the time Sam could finish speaking, but he did not cock it. He stood for a moment like a tense statue, then lowered the gun a few inches. "Sam? Is it you?"

"It's me. I'm going to stand up now, Joe. I've got Greeley Brown with me. Don't shoot us."

Sam and Greeley rose together. "Hello, Joe," Greeley said. "I ain't seen you in years. But tell me this: Do you always pee at folks who come to visit you?"

"Greeley Brown—by gawl, by dang, that *is* you! I know

your voice, you old mountain rat! Sam? Sam? Come on out, brother! Lord have mercy! How in the world . . . what are you . . ." Joe's words stammered away to nothing. He laid down the shotgun as Sam emerged, a dark figure in a dark forest, and wrapped his arms around the brother who had only months before told him he would be a brother to him no more. Much had changed since then. Sam all but crushed his brother in his arms, patting his shoulders soundly with both hands.

"I'm glad I've found you, Joe. I feared you were dead. Thank the Lord! Hallelujah!"

"I came close to dead, brother. Mighty close. Come inside and we'll talk about it all. You, too, Greeley."

"You won't pee at me again, will you? I've got a mortal fear of being peed at."

"No, no, no. Now come on inside where it's safe, 'cause it ain't safe out here, not no more. There's a multitude of eyes in these dark hills, and most of them you don't want seeing you."

They headed across the yard toward the cabin, Joe in the lead, limping fast in his excitement.

"I've heard talk of you lately, Sam," Joe said. He was seated on a three-legged stool beside a pine table with a candle burning in the center. That and a second candle in a stand nearer the door provided the only light in the room. In the corner a hardened-looking, hatchet-faced mountain woman who, like so many of her kind, might have been twenty and might have been forty for all you could tell from looking, stared at them and gnawed on a shriveled raw potato, eyes shifting back and forth between the two newcomers as she chewed with what few nubby teeth she had left. The men ate bread and drank water—the only sustenance available at the moment in this place, unless they too wanted to eat raw potatoes.

"Heard talk? From who?"

"From all kind of folks. They say there's been two men roaming the mountains, advertising to Union men they'll guide them to the Federal lines. They say these two have been hell on rebel bushwhackers and Home Guards. They say one's named Brown, and the other Colter. I knew it had to be you and Greeley." Joe grinned crookedly. "It made me proud of you, brother. I was wrong about you. You ain't a coward by a long shot, not doing what you and Greeley are doing."

"Things have changed a lot since that last time we was together, Joe. The truth was, maybe I was at least a partway coward then. I was scared of Sloat. I admit it."

Joe looked older than before—it seemed to Sam that everyone he knew had aged years in a period of months— and at mention of Sloat he looked older yet. "Sloat's dead, you know," he said. "I killed him."

"I heard. I figured it was you. The law figures the same." He glanced at Greeley, who leaned back and out of the way, removing himself from the line of conversation because he knew what was coming next. "As I hear it, there was more than Sloat killed. A couple of Cherokee Indians, too."

"That's right."

"Why'd you kill the Cherokees, Joe?"

"You going to scold me over it? Preach at me?"

"I just got to know."

"I killed the old one because he came out of his cabin with Sloat's flintlock. I'd caught Sloat outside, without his weapon for once. He let out a yell when he seen me . . . I should have shot him dead right there, but I hesitated. I don't know why. I believe it was because he was unarmed. That's when the old redskin came out of the cabin with Sloat's rifle. I swung my revolver about and shot the old man, but he'd done flung Sloat his rifle. Sloat fired at me and struck me in the leg. That ball angled out and lodged in my thigh right under the skin. A black hard little knot, right under the top of my flesh. When I knifed into it sometime later, it popped out again like a pea from a hull. But anyhow, after Sloat shot me, I shot him, dead as Ben Franklin."

"What about the woman?"

"I had to shoot her, Sam. She come out of that cabin a-keening and a-crying, as a squaw will do, and ran right at me with a knife. I shot her to keep her from slicing me open.

I'd have never shot a woman otherwise, not even an Indian woman."

"I didn't hear about a knife being found in her hand."

Joe's eyes narrowed slightly and for a moment he looked hard and judgmental, just like he had the day he ruled Sam a coward. "You think I'm lying to you about that?"

"I don't know what I think."

"They didn't find a knife in her hand because I took it. That's what I used to cut the ball out from under my skin. After that, bleeding pretty fierce, I headed off the back side of that ridge. I went as far as I could, getting weak, and finally I fainted and rolled off a shallow bluff and nigh killed myself hitting bottom. Knocked myself cold. But I came around by and by and dragged myself out of there. I believe now that falling off that bluff may have saved me, for it broke my trail and kept anybody from finding me."

"People did look for you, Joe, and never found a trace. That's how the newspapers have it. Joe, do you know that nobody knows right now whether you're living or dead?"

"I'd suspected it. Kind of reasoned out that it would be that way."

"It's a good thing they don't know. They'd be looking for you harder if they knew you were living."

"I don't figure nobody's going to look real hard in any case. There's a lot more for folks to be concerned about these days than finding somebody who shot a couple of cur Cherokees and a piece of trash like Dab Sloat."

"What you did is what put me on the run," Sam said.

"Why?"

"Because the law was looking for me, because of you. It was right there in the newspaper. They wanted to ask me questions about you. They'd have asked if you had ever made threats against Sloat and so on."

"You could have lied."

"I ain't a good liar. Don't believe in lying, anyway."

Joe rolled his eyes. "Same old Sam. All high, righteous, and moral."

Sam glanced meaningfully at the woman in the corner and spoke in a whisper. "I see you ain't so high, righteous, and moral yourself these days. Uncle Wilton would be real ashamed of you, sharing living quarters with a woman who ain't your wife."

Joe whispered back. "Don't go judging me, Sam. Jen has been fine to me, keeping me hid and fed, but living quarters is all we share. Nothing else." He whispered even more softly. "Besides, Sam, take a look at her! You think I'd want to mess with a woman who looked like that?"

"No, I guess not."

"Durn right." Joe coughed into his fist and cleared his throat. "So, once you got on the run, what all did you do? How'd you wind up with Greeley?"

"I commenced to looking for you, on my own. I wanted to know if you were alive. But I couldn't find no sign of you. I went to see Greeley over in Carter County just in time to see the rebs burn his house and barn to the ground." He described how he and Greeley had found the hidden Unionist camp, learned about Hannibal Deacon's arrest for bridge burning, and the bloody trouble he and Greeley had run across at the cabin of Jarrell Lynch. "In the end I was by myself when I found they'd hanged Hannibal. I saw his corpse there at the bridge he'd burned. But Hannibal had gotten the last laugh on them, in one way. He'd up and died on them before they could kill him. Natural death. He got away with his bridge burning, that's how I see it."

"But you said he was hanged."

"He was. They'd strung his corpse up like a ham in a smokehouse, for folks to look at. An 'example,' that's what they said. An 'example.' "

"This Deacon must have been a good man, as high as you and Wilton thought of him."

"He was the best kind of man. And the way I lost him, it taught me something that I wasn't looking to learn, but I've learned it anyhow. God above, how I've learned it! It's taught me how to hate. I mean, to hate till it burns in your gut. I hate the rebs, Joe. I hate them for a hundred reasons, but mostly for how they treated Mr. Deacon's corpse, and the fact they would have killed him if he'd give them the chance."

Joe looked deeply at his brother. A dark smile spread across his face. "I'm glad you've learned to hate, Sam. I'm real glad. Because I hate 'em, too. And I intend to put as many in their graves as I can before I go to mine."

Jen Cart, who had been seated in the corner so quietly that Sam had momentarily forgotten about her, cackled with laughter at Joe's dark words. Greeley Brown took another bite of bread and kept his thoughts hidden behind a studying but unrevelatory face.

"How'd you come to this house?" Sam asked.

"I was hurt bad after the shooting on the ridge. I crawled to the first house I could find. The place was empty. I passed out and was ready to die, but somebody come along. Stopping by for a night's shelter. DeWitt. That's all the name he ever told me. He found me. I don't know why, but he cared for me like I was his brother. Stayed with me for days. When I was well enough, he brought me to Shelton Laurel and put me up with Jen. She's cared for me ever since, putting poultices on my wound until it was healed over, keeping me fed and hid from the rebs and anybody else that might come looking." Joe leaned over and whispered so that Jen couldn't hear. "I believe that maybe DeWitt and Jen might have had a bit of a love affair going on at one time or another, if you know what I'm talking about. She denies it, but I got a feeling. I've wondered if that's part of the reason her husband left her."

"Where's her husband now?" Sam asked.

"Gone. Don't know where. He was a reb, Jen says, and she wouldn't go along with it, and so he left. That's what she says . . . there may be more to it than just that."

"Are you healing up good, Joe?"

"Yep. But slow. As soon as I'm able, I aim to take to these hills and start into some mighty righteous work."

"What's that?"

Joe was filling his pipe again. "Killing rebs, that's what."

"Oh."

"So you and Greeley aim on guiding stampeders, do you?"

"We do," Sam said. "But I don't like hearing that word about us has got around so much that you've heard it. I don't like being that well-known."

"For that matter, I don't much like the fact that you heard rumors enough about me to track me down," Joe replied around the reed stem of his pipe. "I'm glad you found me . . . but I ain't glad you was able to, if that makes sense."

"It does. And it makes me think we'd all best be leaving here soon as possible."

"Right. And I will leave, soon. My leg's doing a lot better. And my trigger-pulling finger's got nothing wrong with it at all." Joe lit his cob pipe and looked at Sam through the smoke, smiling around the stem. "My own brother, right here before me! I'd have never expected it. I'm proud of you, Sam. You're changing, boy! No more the smooth-faced little town clerk. You're a man of the hills, like you were born to be. And a scourge of them what kiss the rump of Jefferson See-cesh Davis! I'm proud of us both. Rebel killers! I believe Wilton would have been proud of us, too."

Those words, intended to stir pride, stirred in Sam a guilty pang instead. He knew that Wilton Colter, though he had been a man who believed in fighting for what he saw was right, would not have been proud of the hate, of the venom that dripped from almost everything Joe said. Wilton's favor would have gone more to Greeley Brown, who had lost his home and former life to the rebels, who fought with bravery and even killed when necessary, but who did not glory in hate or the spilling of rebel blood for its own sake. It came to Sam that there was a thin line between righteous anger and evil hatred, between civil justice and personal vengeance. Greeley seemed generally able to walk that line without crossing it, unlike Joe. And perhaps unlike himself, too, Sam reflected.

Maybe I'm more like Joe than I ever thought I was.

These somber thoughts left Sam feeling deflated, doubtful, and tired. "Is there a place we can sleep here?" he asked.

"There is if you don't mind it being the floor."

They didn't mind it. Many a night had been spent in far more uncomfortable conditions. Their horses, retrieved from the place they had hidden them before approaching the house, were stabled in a shed out back. With a roof above, blocking a pattering rainfall that had begun shortly after they came in, and walls and shutters to keep out the wind, they were safe from the probing eyes of any rebels who might roam this night.

They slept well in the house of Jen Cart, and for the duration of that sleep were able to lay down the burden of war and worry.

Chapter 29

In a rural area near Richmond, Kentucky

Amy Deacon was nervous and trying not to show it. She sat alone at a little table in the corner of a ramshackle old clapboard building that passed itself off as an inn but seemed little better than a barn. Poorly lighted, the floor covered with dirt, trash, burnt-out pipe tobacco, and spittle, the place had a rough bar across one end, across which an obese, greasy man served homemade liquor in dirty glasses to patrons who didn't seem to mind at all putting their lips to caked rim-crusts left by the lips of other drinkers before. Amy herself had ordered a cup of milk with no intention of drinking it, just to make sure the innkeeper didn't resent her taking up space in his enterprise. It had been a misguided move. The innkeeper, rolling his eyes and sighing like a man much put upon, had left with a glass and returned with it full of raw, hot milk, fresh from the teats of a cow out back. She stared at it now, watching it separate and having no urge at all to put the stuff to her lips.

She opened her small purse and looked at a pocket watch inside. Ten minutes after eight o'clock. Either the man she was here to meet was late or she'd come to the wrong place. Digging out the neatly scribed note that had drawn her here to begin with, she checked the location and knew that this was the place. Ten minutes more, she decided. If he didn't show up by then, she was leaving. She hadn't been all that comfortable with the idea of this rendezvous in the first place.

Nine minutes later the door creaked open and a man walked in, sweeping off his tall hat and nodding greeting to the half-dozen drinkers who turned from the bar to see the new arrival. They grunted and nodded back in a way that told Amy this fellow was as much a stranger to them as to her. When he saw her, he smiled and nodded. He had neatly combed black hair, parted in the middle and slickened back, a trimmed mustache and thick whiskers down the sides of his face. His suit was black and very well tailored. He would have looked elegant in any setting; against this foul backdrop he looked almost absurdly so.

He approached her table, hat in hand. "Good evening, Miss Deacon." His voice was like smoothly flowing water. The men at the bar eyed him and Amy with curiosity.

"Are you Mr. Wilson, who wrote to me in Crab Orchard?"

"I am indeed, Miss Deacon." He gestured at the stool across the table from her. "May I?"

"Certainly. You have me at a disadvantage, Mr. Wilson. You obviously know me, but I'm unsure I know you, and I certainly have no idea what you want of me."

He glanced at the bar patrons. Noisy before, they had grown much quieter when he entered, and fired surreptitious, curious looks at him. "We could talk better elsewhere," he said. "I have a carriage outside. Would you find me trustworthy enough to take an evening ride with me?"

Amy did harbor some caution, but her curiosity was much stronger. "I'll go with you. Be aware, however, that I have begun carrying a small pistol with me at all times, and will use it if you show yourself to be anything other than you claim to be."

"I don't doubt it for a moment," he said, smiling. "Would you like to finish your milk before we go?"

"I don't believe so," she replied.

He pushed back the stool and stood, came around and, in a perfect gentleman's style, helped her with her chair.

He reached into a pocket and left a generous amount of money on the table, bringing a smile to the wide face of the fat innkeeper. Then he walked with Amy to the door, opened it, and admitted her and then himself into the warm night.

The carriage was of high quality and featured lamp head-lights, but he left them unlit. Amy sat beside him, enjoying the ride despite her own self-reminders that she shouldn't put too much trust in a man of whom she knew nothing more than his last name.

She learned at once that in fact she hadn't even known that.

"My name, I should tell you, isn't Wilson," he said. "It was unnecessary for me to be so cautious, perhaps, but in my line of work one learns that an excess of caution is far better than a lack of it."

"Then who are you, sir, and why did you deceive me?"

"I wasn't trying to deceive you, only anyone else who might chance to see the letter I wrote you. You're familiar with my name, if not with me. You know my cousin Horatio, I believe."

"Horatio . . . Horatio Eaton? That would mean that you are—"

"Jonathon Eaton, at your service," he said, nodding and touching his hat. "And also in the service of the United States government, in ways and means not generally aired before the public."

Amy gazed at him, surprised and fascinated. "Horatio told me once that he had a cousin named Jonathon Eaton, and gave all sorts of strange and subtle hints about him . . . about you. He said something about your being 'situated to provide opportunities for important service.' He never explained what that meant."

"Good for him. The less known and said about me, the better."

"Then why, Mr. Eaton, are you sharing these things with me?"

"Horatio has told me very much about you, and of course there's the newspapers and the gossip mills. Amy Deacon, the betraying Judas of a daughter of the late, great Secessionist himself, is a figure both celebrated and reviled, depending upon the viewpoint of the observer."

Amy found something insulting in the frankness of this bit of talk. "You speak a bit freely, Mr. Eaton. And you also speak in riddles. Explain why you've arranged this meeting, or stop this carriage and let me be on my way."

"I wouldn't want to lose you just yet. Nor do you want to miss what I have to offer, if you're a young lady of the temperament and mettle that Horatio declares you are."

"More riddles. Speak clearly or let me go! But first tell me how I can know you are who you say you are?"

He smiled. "I knew you would get around to that. You are far too intelligent not to." He pulled the horse to a halt, reached into a pocket and pulled out a small, rectangular something that he handed to her. It was hard and metallic. Producing matches, he struck one an held it so the light revealed what he had given her. It was a photograph of him standing in a stiff parlor pose beside Horatio Eaton. He held the match long enough for her to examine the photograph closely, then shook it out. She handed the picture back and he put it in his pocket. In its place he produced a folded piece of paper, which he unfolded and handed to her. Another match, then another, and by then she had finished reading the paper's handwritten contents. It was in effect a letter of introduction written in the familiar scribing of Horatio Eaton, testifying that Amy should trust the letter's bearer to be exactly who and what he claimed to be.

She handed the letter back and he put out the match.

"I am satisfied," she said. "I'll trust you. Now tell me what you want with me."

"I want your service on behalf of the United States government," he said. "I am aware that since you have come to Kentucky you have been sending out subtle word that you wish to be of use in some manner for the cause. Very unusual to get that sort of request from a woman, but you've gone about it quite well, working in the proper channels and showing the kind of discretion that is vital when covert activity is involved. And from Horatio I know your personal qualities and your honesty of conviction. I know that you must despise the Confederate government, considering the wicked way they treated your uncle."

"I'll never forgive what was done to Hannibal," Amy said.

"I was sure you would feel that strongly. Good. It's the spirit that's needed in the special service I have in mind. But restraint and common sense are needed as well. And the ability to carry on deception—which your experience with Horatio's journal shows you possess."

"Thank you. Tell me: What kind of service do you have in mind for me?"

"You must understand from the outset that what I will tell you is very secret, very sensitive. I'm charged to carry out a very covert plan, and choose my own civilian agents to help me. If you refuse to participate—and I hope you don't refuse—it will be essential for you to tell no one, no one at all. Do I have your pledge of silence, whatever your decision is?"

"You do."

He picked up the reins, gave them a shake and clicked his tongue. The carriage lurched off, and he began to talk, his smooth voice flowing without a break for the next half an hour as Amy listened, enthralled, fascinated, alternately thrilled and frightened—but mostly thrilled.

A few miles south of Jonesborough, Tennessee

The splinter was a long one, and dug at least an inch into the flesh. The neophyte carpenter who was its victim let out a screech and loud curse and dropped the plane with which he had been vigorously smoothing a wide plank that was to be part of a tabletop.

"Language, Ben Kirby! Language!" declared an elderly, white-bearded man who had just come through the door. "We do not curse in this household! You know my rule: When you feel the urge to curse God's name, give God's blessing instead!"

"I'm sorry, Mr. J.W.," Ben Scarlett replied. "But take a look here what happened." He held out his hand, where a big drop of blood was gathering at the point of puncture. The splinter remained jammed well under the skin.

J. W. Mainard approached and looked closely, squinting. "Oh, my! I'd say that does hurt—though I hardly see even so mean a splinter as cause for trampling on the name of our creator."

"I said I was sorry." Ben meant it. J. W. Mainard's scoldings, which came from time to time, did not irk him but authentically shamed him. He owed much to this viceless old saint and did not like to offend him. Since he had come to live at this place, Ben had worked harder than ever in his life to control his behavior. He had substantially put aside his shiftlessness, his laziness, his attitude of hopelessness regarding himself. Most astonishingly, he had even done without liquor for quite a long stretch now, something he had never believed would be possible.

Nobody had forced this altered behavior upon him. He had reformed himself out of his own desire, as a sort of payback for all the Mainard family had given him: an open door, affection, a sense of family and home. And pride. That was the greatest gift of all: pride in who he was, and what he was. No longer a vagrant and a drunk, but a true citizen. A worker. A *man*.

"Let me get that out for you, Ben," J. W. Mainard said, reaching for Ben's bleeding hand.

Ben stuck the hand out. "Be careful when you— eeooww!" Old Mainard had yanked the splinter out without much care about how he went about it. "By God, old man, you like to have—" He stopped, chilled by Mainard's reproving gaze, and swallowed down a mouthful of unreleased cursings. "I mean, God's blessings on you, Mr. Mainard, and on this here splinter He in kind providence allowed me to jam into my hand for God only knows why." He paused, examining Mainard's face to see if he had said enough words of holiness to please the old saint. For good measure he added, "Glory be to His name."

J. W. Mainard, struggling to suppress a smile, examined the bloodied splinter. "Maybe this splinter going into your hand had a bit to do with a certain Ben Kirby being, of his own God-given free will, an overly careless carpenter.

Maybe he ought to blame himself a bit more and the Lord a bit less." He laughed quickly, tossed away the splinter, and slapped Ben on the shoulder. "We'll turn you to the path of righteousness yet, Ben Kirby. I expect to see you a full-fledged Christian one of these days. By the way, this all reminds me of the joke about what the old Calvinist said after he sat down on a tack: 'Thank God that's over with!' " Mainard threw back his head and laughed heartily, making his beard shake.

Ben could only grin, having no knowledge of Calvinists or doctrines of predestination. The Mainards, a devout bunch of folks, were very knowledgeable about religion and often spoke in terms he didn't understand. One thing was clear even to him, though: They had been trying to stir to Christian conversion the man they knew as Ben Kirby almost since the day he had come to them. So far conversion was one idea that had scared him far too badly to consider. Maybe someday. Not just yet.

No one had tried harder to reshape him than the Mainard who brought him here, the preacher Lucas Mainard, whom he had found beaten by the roadside after fleeing Knoxville. The pair became unlikely friends—a pro-Union preacher and an allegiance-shifting drunk—but the friendship was as real as it was odd, and Ben credited Lucas Mainard with instilling in him a flickering but real spark of desire to become a better man. Mainard, beaten by Secessionists for refusing to announce God's sanction of the rebel effort, had been forced out of his church and returned briefly to his family home here at Jonesborough. He had brought Ben with him, introducing him as a friend and "rescuer" to his father, J. W., and mother, Elizabeth. Without any real plan for it to happen, Ben had been drawn into the Mainard family as something of an unofficial, latter-day adopted son. This, even though he was in his thirties. But if there ever had been a thirtyish child, it was Ben Scarlett. He needed someone to take him in, dote over him, give him support and encouragement. Someone able to make him face what he was doing to himself in all these years of drinking. Someone kind enough to even care that he was doing it.

Lucas Mainard eventually left his home place again,

heading into Kentucky on the sneak to offer his service to the Union Army. Ben, who in this typical chameleon fashion had declared himself a devoted Unionist under the influence of the Mainards, stayed on, working about the place, relearning some youthful carpentry skills from J. W., and becoming the closest thing to a happy man he had been at any time of his life. Mainard had given Ben a profession as well, a job in a niter mine. This required of him several miles of daily travel, but provided a sideline benefit far more important to Ben than the money: exemption from the Confederate draft.

"Ben," J.W. said, growing solemn all at once, "I have a worry for you."

"What's that, Mr. J.W.?" From the beginning it had been "Mr. J.W.," a way of addressing the man that struck a natural balance between the respect for his age and the informality of their friendship.

"There was a reb conscription officer nosing around today, asking about you."

"When?"

"While you were at the niter cave."

"Oh. Was it a big man, with a great big onion-bulb nose and yaller hair?"

"Yes, that was the one. Trotter, I believe his name is. I know some of the family. Some in Fall Branch, some in Knoxville. A fine bunch, apart from being rebs."

It was Mr. J.W.'s habit, Ben had noticed, to find something good to say about most everyone. "Maybe they're a good family, but that feller has a dislike for me, Mr. J.W., and I don't know why. I've seen him three times that I recall, and every time he's snarled at me like a dog."

"He was asking me questions. Such as your name. I says, 'He's Ben Kirby,' and this Trotter, he just grins and says, 'Kirby. Is that right?' I don't know what he was trying to get at."

Ben knew. He had never revealed his true surname to the Mainards. There seemed no reason to, though the moral atmosphere about the Mainard house sometimes made him feel guilty for being deceptive about his identity. It made a walking lie of him. But as time went by and he put aside his liquor and old ways, it came to him that since he was something of a new man, maybe having a new name was appropriate. Now he even was beginning to think of himself as Ben Kirby as much as Ben Scarlett.

Maybe it wasn't going to be as easy as he had thought to put all of that old life behind, though. It sounded as if this Trotter fellow had an idea that Ben Kirby might not be who he claimed.

For a moment Ben was slightly tempted to reveal the truth to his benefactor, but he held back. "I don't know what that man's up to," he mumbled. "Got no idea."

"Well, I doubt you have cause to worry. I suspect he may see you as rebel conscription fodder. But you do have your exemption papers."

"Yes." Ben instinctively patted his pocket, the place he stored the paper guaranteeing his exemption from the Confederate draft. He was an employee of J. W. Mainard's niter mining operation under authority of District 7 of the Confederate Niter and Mining Bureau, created earlier in the year to promote and supervise the mining of saltpeter used in the creation of badly needed gunpowder. It was not particularly odd that Mainard, a Unionist, operated a mine generating war-making product for the Confederacy. For one thing, he was quiet about his Unionism and cooperative with the ruling authorities. For another, his niter cave, located about two miles north of his house, was too rich a site for the Confederacy not to utilize, meaning those authorities had every reason to cooperate with him. And niter mines and Unionists tended to go together, to the chagrin of many rebels. So vital was the niter to the war effort that employees of niter mines were exempt from conscription. Naturally, Unionists seeking to avoid being drafted into the rebel army vied hard for jobs at niter mines, eager for the precious exemption papers that came with them. It was the exemption benefit of his work that Ben most treasured. He could hardly believe his fortune in stumbling upon a situation that provided him pride, employment, friendship, shelter, and conscription exemption to boot.

"You keep an eye out for Trotter, Ben," Mainard said.

"He has a threatening, sneaky way about him that concerns me."

"I'll be careful, Mr. J.W."

Days passed, and Ben worried about the inquisitive soldier. Maybe he was just an overzealous fellow under orders to examine all conscription exemptees. But Ben suspected there was more to it than that, something personal. He scoured his brain, trying to recall if he might have known anyone named Trotter at some time past, but he could not remember any such person. Yet that meant little. In his last few years in Knoxville, Ben had spent much of his time in a drunken and very unobservant state. He had encountered hundreds, thousands, of people. A denizen of the streets, he was seen aplenty even by people he had not met in turn. How could he be sure the agent was not one of them?

But eventually he mostly forgot the matter. Busy every day, working almost all the time either at the niter cave or in J. W. Mainard's carpenter shop, Ben didn't have much time for brooding. Thus he was unprepared for it the day he mounted the old but strong horse Mainard had sold him, rode out toward the niter mine, and came face-to-face with the yellow-haired officer and three gray-clad privates, well-armed, on a dark and shady portion of the road. He stopped and faced the man.

"Hello, Ben Scarlett."

He knows me. "My name's Kirby. Ben Kirby."

"No. You might fool that old man you work for, but you don't fool me, Ben Scarlett. I've seen you many a time. My name's Trotter. Michael Trotter. You recollect that name?"

"Don't believe I do, sir."

"I'm a man that once had a pocketbook full of money stole by a drunk in Knoxville. The year of 1860, third of January. A drunk that was named Ben Scarlett."

Ben did remember now. Suddenly Trotter's face was familiar. He even remembered the brand of whiskey he had bought with Trotter's money, and how he had hidden a bottle of it from Charlie Douglass because he was too selfish to share it. He swallowed hard and found his throat had gone dry. "My name's Ben Kirby," he repeated, voice scratching.

"They tell me you got an exemption paper."

"Yes sir."

"Let's see it."

Ben reached a trembling hand into his pocket and pulled out his precious document. Unfolding it, he held it up.

"Hell, give me that! I can't read it from here with your hand trembling so! And why are you trembling, Ben? You got something to worry about? Secrets? Lies? Huh, what is it? Give me that paper!"

Ben found himself unable to move. One of the soldiers heeled his horse over close to Ben, snatched the paper from his hand and took it back to Trotter, who looked it over and grunted disdainfully.

"This here paper exempts Ben Kirby from Confederate conscription. Don't say a thing about Ben Scarlett."

"I ain't Ben Scarlett. I'm Ben Kirby."

Trotter sighed and rolled the paper up tightly, making a tube. He peered through it at Ben, like a spyglass, and laughed. Then he said, "I believe I'd like to smoke right now." He pulled a cigar from a pocket, popped it into his mouth, then dug out matches. Striking one, he lit the rolled-up exemption document, then with it lit his cigar. Puffing, he let the exemption paper burn almost to his fingers, then tossed it to the ground.

"You can't do that," Ben said weakly, though the act was already done and it was obvious Trotter could do just what he pleased in any case. "You got no right."

" 'Right,' you say? Let's talk about what's 'right,' Ben Scarlett. What's right is that every able-bodied man enjoying the benefits of living in the Confederate States of America is duty-bound to wear the proud rebel gray. Duty-bound to fight against the Yankee aggression. No man has the right to change his name and hide behind an exemption he don't deserve. Especially a drunk and a thief."

"I ain't a drunk. I ain't a thief. And I do deserve exemption," Ben argued timidly. "I'm working in a niter mine. I'm helping provide powder for the Confederacy. Soldiers can't fight without powder."

"Well, if you're a niter miner, you ought to have an exemption paper on you. Let's see it." Trotter flashed a grin at his fellows.

Ben was bewildered. "You just burned it up."

Trotter put on a face of astonishment. "What? You got no exemption paper?" He looked at the privates again, winking. "I believe we've found ourselves a dodger here!"

"Looks like it," one of them replied.

"Mr. Ben Scarlett, how old are you?"

"Forty-six," Ben lied.

"He says he's thirty years old. Well within conscription age. You heard it, didn't you, soldiers?"

"I heard it," one of the soldiers said. "He said it clear as day. Thirty years old."

"You're coming with us, Mr. Scarlett. You can consider yourself duly conscripted by the army of the Confederate States of America."

Ben shook like a man dying of ague. He felt tired; sweat beaded his forehead. "I can't . . . I don't want . . ." There was nothing to say. He was caught and didn't see how he could escape.

"You'll come peacefully, I reckon?"

"Can't I . . . will you let me go back, Captain, and fetch my things?"

"You got pants, shirt, a horse. That's all you need, Ben. The generous Confederacy will provide you everything else."

Ben slumped over, feeling hot fire in his stomach.

"Straighten up there, man! Don't act the sickly child on us. You've enjoyed the benefits of your little deception, and now the time's come to do your duty. Be a man about it. Come on, Ben Scarlett. Let's take a ride."

"I need to tell Mr. Mainard."

"We'll see that he's informed."

"I want to tell him myself."

"Ben, you're wasting our time."

Ben straightened. Trotter and the soldiers grinned at him. He was a mouse surrounded by cats. Fear put a metallic taste on his tongue . . . but then anger came, surging. "I'll not go!" he yelled. He spurred his horse and ran it straight through the midst of them, then cut off the road and onto the wagon track that ran across a field and over to the cave where the niter was mined.

"After him!" Trotter yelled. "Shoot him down!"

Shots cracked. Ben tucked down low in the saddle, wincing, anticipating being pierced by bullets, but the shots sailed high. More shots burst, loud, flat, popping noises behind him. He spurred his frightened mount to greater speed and glanced behind. They were after him, but farther back than he had thought they would be. Apparently he had thoroughly surprised them, and his quick motion might have spooked their horses enough to slow their chase.

In any case, he pressed what little advantage he had and rode hard along the wagon road, ducking and listening to their shots. Firing from the saddle, they were missing him widely. Teeth gritted, face twisted in a grimace of fright and determination, he flew along, coming now into view of the big cave entrance in the hillside. Men moved about there among iron kettles and hoppers. Smoke billowed up from their fires and leveled out low across the terrain, a white, level ledge against a rich blue sky. He heard yells from the miners: "That's Ben Kirby!" "Look! There's soldiers chasing Ben Kirby!" Then he was past, out of earshot, and racing up at an angle across the hill.

Another glance back. They were closing in. His horse was strong and fast, but old and lacking endurance for a long run. He urged it on as best he could and reached the top of the hill. Starting down the other side, he picked up speed. But they would be upon him soon. He could not hope to outrun them.

Moments later the soldiers pounded up over the hilltop and saw Ben's horse standing, riderless, on the field beyond. They rode down to it, then scanned the land in all directions, looking for him. They could not find him.

"He's hid out somewhere," a breathless, excited Trotter said. "Hell, we'll find him! He can't have gone far on foot!" He turned to one of the soldiers. "Go back around to that cave and fetch them miners! Put them to searching! We're going to find Ben Scarlett!"

* * *

The hunt went on for hours, but no Ben Scarlett turned up. They probed the hillside, dug into bushes, scoured the woods beyond the field for hundreds of yards. No Ben.

It was as if he had dissolved into smoke and drifted away. Trotter raved and cursed and yelled at the hills, telling Ben Scarlett that he might as well come out and give himself up. It did not good. By nightfall even Trotter knew they had been bested and withdrew, taking Ben's horse with him.

Ben did not emerge until midnight. He came crawling out of a narrow crevice well-hidden by thick brush. The crevice was barely big enough to accommodate a man, but it was deep, leading all the way back into the niter cave, and Ben had wriggled into it so far that they couldn't have detected him even if they'd shoved a torch into the crevice itself. As it was, they hadn't even found the crevice.

Slimy, damp, filthy with clay and soil, Ben stood on the hill and knew he could not go back to the Mainard house. Most likely they'd be watching the place, anticipating his return. Even if they didn't, he couldn't afford to implicate the Mainards in his escape by returning and telling them what had happened.

He was on his own again. Without money, weapons, exemption papers, or even a clean set of clothing. He couldn't remain in the county. Trotter would be after him until he caught him.

The world had been very good to Ben Scarlett the last few months. He should have known it couldn't last.

For the first time in a long time, he thought about how comforting it would be to have a good drink of very strong liquor.

Chapter 30

Like a slow but increasing rain that first loosens then washes away a field of topsoil, the pressures of wartime eroded the lifestyles of the people in the valleys and mountains of East Tennessee and the rugged wilderness highlands of western North Carolina.

Such former commonplaces as coffee and processed sugar became rare or expensive. Southerners tried to find coffee substitutes: toasted and ground rye or wheat, even dried sweet potato chips boiled in water. Nothing satisfied like the authentic item. Tea also became scarce, forcing deprived Confederacy residents to drink brews made from sassafras root or raspberry leaves. Candy and the like vanished from store shelves and went unreplaced. Dry goods dwindled, cloth became expensive, and women who had relied on store-bought fabrics turned back to the spinning wheels and looms that had been used in recent times mostly to clothe the poor or enslaved. Store-bought dyes were hard to find. Natural dyes were utilized in their place: black walnut hulls for brown, pokeberries for purplish-blue, elderberries for black.

Gold went out of circulation, hoarded by those fortunate enough to possess it. Silver vanished as well; even cutlery was put into hiding. The notes of state-chartered banks, worth a quarter on the dollar more than Confederate notes, soon were hoarded right along with the silver and gold. Confederate notes became suspect and unwanted, forcing the rebel government to give out warnings that refusal to accept Confederate money would be treated as a crime. Those to whom money was owed were therefore in a bad position. They disliked receiving payment in low-value Confederate dollars, yet could not refuse them. So they gritted their teeth, dealt in Confederate money, and hoped the economy of the South wouldn't collapse around their ears.

In the rural areas of the highland country, what was perhaps the most threatening shortage of all, that of salt, grew worse as 1862 went by. Those in the mountains worried for the coming winter.

The Confederates had begun hoarding salt in guarded warehouses and appointing agents to oversee its carefully regulated distribution, generally in quanities insufficient to meet the needs of meat curers. And known Unionists were often overlooked altogether in the distributions.

Cattle, lacking salt to lick, suffered right along with their owners. Salt-deprived people fell back on such desperate and inadequate measures as soaking old brine barrels and salted fish boxes to obtain what meager salt they could from the runoff. They sometimes obtained enough for daily use in this way, but never would they be able to obtain enough for meat curing in such a manner.

Makeshift measures might do for coffee and clothing dye, but salt couldn't be conjured or substituted. Many a mountain Unionist father mulled the coming cold season and thought with resentment about the precious salt of which he was being deprived—deprived by a government that had been forced upon him against his will, took freely of what little he had gained through years of hard labor, and, besides all that, sought to force him and his sons into military servitude against a foe that to him was no foe at all.

Angers that had seethed and simmered for months grew hotter, and hatreds more bitter. Salt became the subject of

conversations, of longing dreams, and the object of hoard-
ings, thefts, and secret quests.

In the mountains come winter, salt was life. And life was
something even usually peaceable men would go to desperate measures to preserve.

The Confederate military oversight of East Tennessee had
quite an unstable feel about it almost from the beginning,
mostly because the overseers kept changing.

Crittenden had replaced Zollicoffer as commander in
East Tennessee, but lasted only until March, when Major
General Edmund Kirby Smith succeeded him. Crittenden
had been mostly an absentee commander in any case, away
from the Knoxville headquarters since the Mill Springs fight
that had cost Zollicoffer's life.

Kirby Smith sought to oil the gears of the Confederate
conscription machine by issuing pledges of pardon and
cooperation with Unionists who came in, confessed their
error, and took the Confederate oath of loyalty. Almost at
the same time, though, a more dire proclamation went out
from W. M. Churchwell, colonel and provost marshal of the
District of East Tennessee, concerning the families of Union
men who had fled East Tennessee to join the Federal army.
The proclamation assured the "disaffected people of East
Tennessee" that those "who have fled to the enemy's lines,
and who are actually in their army," would receive
"amnesty and protection, if they come to lay down their
arms and act as loyal citizens, within the thirty days given
them by Major General E. Kirby Smith to do so. If at the
end of that time, those failing to return to their homes and
accept the amnesty thus offered, and provide for and protect
their wives and children in East Tennessee, will have them
sent to their care in Kentucky, or beyond the Confederate
States' line at their own expense." The proclamation con-
cluded with the terse and somewhat threatening note that
the "women and children must be taken care of by husbands
and fathers, either in East Tennessee or in the Lincoln government." The message was clear to Unionists who had
stampeded and left families behind: See to your own, or

they will be left to do without. As if to underscore the point, Kirby Smith ousted the families of prominent Unionist Horace Maynard and famed propagandist Parson Brownlow, sending them beyond Confederate lines.

June brought an event that cheered the highland Unionists and dealt a major blow to the Confederacy. Union General George W. Morgan and a group of subordinate officers guided a multipronged army through rugged, seldom-traveled country toward the all-important mountain pass of Cumberland Gap, the key gateway from Kentucky into East Tennessee and southwestern Virginia. Morgan, who had recently taken command of the Seventh Division of the Army of the Ohio, coordinated the Cumberland Gap campaign with Gen. Samuel P. Carter, a native of Carter County, Tennessee, whose force consisted mainly of former East Tennessee refugees formed into the ragtag, ill-equipped Third and Fourth Tennessee Regiments. Two other Tennessean brigadier generals took part as well, James G. Spears and Absalom Baird, along with an Irish mercenary named Colonel John Fitzroy de Courcy.

Attacking the gap in a flanking movement that required moving armies through a maze of mountainous wilderness, Morgan took his prize without losing a man. The Tennessean soldiers, eager to press on against Kirby Smith in their homeland, pursued for a few miles, but turned back after seeing the retreating rebels had too lengthy a lead.

The capture of Cumberland Gap brought a time of reunion to many East Tennessee Unionist families who had been separated from sons, husbands, and fathers who stampeded north months before to join the Federals. Entire clans swarmed out of the Tennessee hills and valleys and sought out their loved ones at the Gap. The highland loyalists were heady: With Cumberland Gap in United States control, surely East Tennessee would soon be retaken as well.

George Morgan contacted Washington, seeking support for an invasion, but in the distraction of more pressing Federal actions elsewhere his request was not answered.

While Unionists cheered the occupation of Cumberland Gap, the Confederacy was not sitting idle. Seeing Federal

General Don Carlos Buell moving across Alabama, his sights on Chattanooga, the Tennessee River, and East Tennessee, the Confederate leaders struck on a plan to cut off Buell's lines of supply and thus isolate him. The plan centered on the officially neutral state of Kentucky and involved a dashing rebel raider named John Hunt Morgan.

At about the same time Cumberland Gap was falling to George Morgan of the Union, John Hunt Morgan of the Confederacy came to Knoxville, set up quarters, and began recruiting volunteers for raids into Kentucky. Dapper and handsome, Morgan enjoyed much success and pushed on ahead with his plans despite a lack of good weaponry and uniforms for many of his men. Training under the watchful eye of an English soldier-of-fortune and Crimean War veteran who had cast in with the rebels, George St. Leger Grenfell, Morgan's recruits drilled twice a day in Knoxville, following French patterns and in many cases bearing clubs because of the lack of rifles.

When Morgan's Kentucky raiding began in July, many still bore no better weapons than clubs. Morgan was unconcerned, anticipating the capture of many Federal weapons.

Throughout the summer John Hunt Morgan proved himself a terror to Federals and a figure of dashing heroism to rebels. Raiding almost to Cincinnati, he struck terror into the hearts of northerners, received a reputation as a capable guerrilla fighter, and pulled off his daring raids with an elegant panache that would make him legend. With many of his raiders clad in jeans and civilian clothes, and armed with outdated and even primitive weaponry, he nevertheless took more than twelve hundred prisoners, captured thousands of Union rifles, burned bridges and other structures to the tune of more than $10 million in damages to the Union infrastructure, and suffered only a few losses himself before heading home to raid for the remainder of the summer in Union-occupied Middle Tennessee.

In the rebel-held eastern highlands, Union men looked north longingly, picturing the American flag waving over Cumberland Gap, luring them toward Federal lines that had never seemed more accessible. But to reach those lines meant travel through hard mountain country and broad valleys crawling with Home Guards, regular Confederate troops, and rebel guerrillas. For such journeys men needed guides who knew the terrain and the skill of moving undetected through rugged country—guides such as Greeley Brown and Sam Colter, who by now had left Joe Colter behind at the Cart cabin in Shelton Laurel, North Carolina, and returned to a hidden Unionist camp in Carter County, Tennessee.

The time of the Union "pilots," as they would come to be known, had arrived. Men in groups of ten to a hundred or more sought out those able and willing to undertake the hazardous duties, and set out on dark nights with hopes as high as their fears. There was, at least, comfort in company. Few were willing to attempt to "stampede" across such hostile and dangerous country alone.

On a rainy twilight in August one of the rare ones rash enough to attempt a lone stampede sat on a darkening mountainside, lightly gripping a left hand that had been badly cut two days before and now was showing unmistakable, repellent, alarming signs of mortification.

Ben Scarlett, sick to his stomach, his head spinning with fever, and his pus-oozing hand throbbing miserably with every beat of his pulse, sat on a log and wondered just where he was, just how long it would take him to die, and if anyone would ever find his corpse.

Alone on the mountainside, tears in his eyes, he watched night come on, a great dread settling in with the darkness. In the daylight even a sick man dared to hope, but suffering by night was ten times worse. Ben doubted he could make it through this night. He was sure that in the blackest part of it, death would find him. The only comfort he could find was that, as sick as he felt, the thought of dying wasn't as hard to abide as before.

So he prayed, talking to a God he had generally ignored, asking for what mercy could come to a hardened old sinner such as himself. He prayed for salvation should he die, but prayed harder yet for a rescuer, promising God that should one be sent, he would be a better man for the rest of his life than he had been up until now.

When his amen was said, he looked up and watched the last light fade. His fever grew hotter as the night cooled. "Who'd a-thought it would be a bottle of water that done in Ben Scarlett?" he said aloud. "I always figured the whiskey would kill me."

A water bottle indeed was responsible for his infected injury. After his escape from the conscripting officer near the niter mine, Ben roamed without direction for weeks, sleeping in barns, sheds, living the life he had lived in Knoxville for years, but with two differences: His setting now was rural, and he was no longer drinking.

It amazed him that he had managed to avoid liquor after the jolt of being forced out of the good life he had enjoyed at the Mainard house. Alcohol would be a great comfort at such a time. But he had managed to say no to it so far, though this resulted as much from liquor being hard to find just now as from personal willpower.

"I believe I'd have enjoyed a few drinks if I'd known it was going to end for me like this," he said to the sky. "I'd have been better off passed out in a still house than dying on this mountain from no more than a cut hand."

His injury had resulted from a fall while crossing a creek with a glass bottle of water gripped in his left hand. The glass had shattered, cutting the hand badly. Slime from the stones had infiltrated the cuts as he tried to rise, and infection had set in very promptly. Now he was too sick to go on, and too deep in the mountains somewhere between the Clinch River and the Cumberlands to find a farmstead and help.

"I should have stampeded in a group, not alone," he muttered as he sank down onto the leafy forest floor. "Should have." They were the last sensible words he said. Fever overtook his mind and he babbled and writhed alone on the dark mountain, his mind full of fearsome images conjured by the sickness that comes of infection.

He did not know it when hands touched him and weary eyes examined him by the light of dawn. He was unaware of it when he was lifted and carried into a nearby cavern and there relieved of his infected hand by the same keen knife

Greeley Brown had used to kill two bushwhackers in Carter County the prior fall. This was the first time Greeley had ever amputated any portion of a man, but he proceeded with the assurance that only in this way did this poor fellow, whoever he was, have any hope of living. The crude surgery was done by the light of a candle and what shafts of sunlight penetrated the heaps of stones laid in the entrance of the cave.

Sam Colter sat beside Greeley throughout the operation, hands resting on Ben's throat to choke off any screams. They had moved him into this cave and laid the stones up in the entrance, to further muffle any shouts Ben might give out. Outside, a group of weary, scared Unionist stampeders, unhappy that their guides had paused to dally with an obviously doomed man encountered solely by chance, sat about the cave and ate raw green corn while rubbing feet that were worn to blisters by days of hard hiking, climbing, and wading through rivers of rushing water and broad fields of tangled briars.

No screams arose from the cave. Ben Scarlett was too ill to be much aware of the knife that sliced away his hand. When the amputation was done, skin folded over the stump, and the wrist tied off and bandaged with strips torn from the single extra shirt Greeley carried, Sam knocked out the stones blocking the cave entrance and came out into the light, Greeley following.

"It's done," Greeley said. "If he ain't too poisoned in the blood, he might live."

"And what are we going to do?" one of the stampeders asked bitterly. "Sit around here on this mountain, waiting for that man to get well before the rebels find us? We're paying you good money to pilot us, Greeley Brown. I believe in mercy as much as the next man, but your duty her is to us . . . and there's no point in mercy for a man bound to die anyway."

"He won't die," Sam Colter cut in. "With that putrefied hand gone, he'll get better right fast."

The stampeder opened his mouth to voice some further complaint, but Greeley cut him off. "Listen to me, all of you: You'll be guided on, just like I pledged, and just as fast. The only difference will be that Sam won't go on with us. I'm leaving him here to keep watch over this poor pilgrim, whoever he may be. Caesar Augustus! Would you want to be left to die on a mountainside if you was in his shoes?"

"I wish I *was* in his shoes," one of the stampeders muttered. "I've done walked the soles out of mine."

"I'll have you to the Cumberland Gap before too much longer, men, and there the Federals will see you provisioned out, fed, clothed, everything. And that poor fellow back in the cave will not slow you at all. Are you satisfied?"

"I want half the money back I paid to young Mr. Colter," one of the stampeders said. "He only helps half the way, then he only gets paid for half the way."

Greeley looked at Sam. "I'll split the difference out of my share, Sam. I'll not see you hurt for being Good Samaritan to that man." Greeley turned to the others. "Fine, upstanding, merciful men you are! Fussing because there's some of us believe in helping them who are hurt. Caesar Augustus! I've knowed some of you for years, and this surprises me."

The stampeders did not seem bothered by his chiding. They were too weary to care. They had set out from near Elizabethton by night, traveling hard trails and avoiding the roads, hiding out by day and moving by night, until they had reached the high ridge of Bay's Mountain, which they passed by circling its northeasternmost prong near the Long Island of the Holston River. Passing through the valley beyond they went on to the long and ominous Clinch Mountain, which they had passed over with great difficulty. Winding through the rugged Clinch River valley, then wading the Clinch itself with their clothing bundled on sticks held above their heads, they had finally reached Powell's Mountain, and here they had encountered this pitiful, sick stranger. One of them had literally tripped over his body in the dark.

Greeley's proposition to lead the stampeders the rest of the way to Cumberland Gap seemed to satisfy them, and they passed the day with sleep, nibbling at their supply of corn—stolen from fields in the Clinch River valley and on the southeastern slope of the mountain—and smearing their blistered feet with grease from a bottle of it brought along by one of the more forward-thinking stampeders.

They set off again at dusk, heading down the slope, leaving Sam Colter alone with the amputee, whose fever had declined and who began to moan and show signs of the beginnings of recovery. Sam passed a sleepless night as the man tossed and writhed in his cave, letting out occasional unconscious yells when he happened to roll on his arm stump. When sunrise came, Sam found the man awake.

"Howdy," he said. "My name's Colter. Sam Colter. I need to tell you that, in case you ain't noticed, your bad hand has been cut off."

Ben Scarlett raised his arm and took a look. "So it has," he said. Then he closed his eyes and slept. True sleep, the sleep of a recovering man, not the stupor of illness.

Sam slept, too, drifting off as he wondered how long it would be before Greeley returned. *If* he returned. The valley across which the final stretch of the escape would have to be made was populous and filled with rebels. Only the Gap itself was in Union hands. There was no guarantee that Greeley could get his stampeders across, nor that if he did, he would be able to make it back the opposite way again once they were delivered.

By the time he awakened in the afternoon, Ben Scarlett had regained just enough wits to avoid revealing his real name to the young stranger who had taken up with him. He introduced himself as a Dandridge native named Ben Clinch, borrowing his surname from the Clinch River because nothing else came to mind quickly enough. There was trouble associated with his true name of Scarlett and his recent pseudonym of Kirby. So again he was changing his persona. *I reckon I change my name more often than I change my underwear,* he thought.

Sam Colter, a likable if exceptionally skinny young man, was full of questions but managed to ask them without being nosy. Ben was careful how he answered until Sam told him that he was a Union man himself, at which point Ben declared that he was a Union man, too, on his way through to Kentucky to "join Abe's army." This was not true; he had sought only to escape Tennessee and the rebel conscription, not to join the Federal force, but it sounded more noble to tell it that way.

"My guess is that missing hand will keep you out of the soldier business, Mr. Clinch," Sam told him.

Ben lifted the stump, looked at it without being able to quite believe that this was his arm, and realized Sam Colter was right. That broken bottle had done him a favor in a way. Unless the Confederates were more desperate for soldiers than he thought, the stump at the end of his left arm was as good as an exemption. And this exemption no one could argue with, or roll up and use to light a cigar.

"I'll be!" Ben said. "I hadn't thunk of that. I expect you're right, sir."

"So what will you do now, Mr. Clinch?"

"I don't know. I'll figure that out when I reach Kentucky."

"You still aim to go there?"

"I don't know what else to do. Tennessee ain't much of a place to be these days."

"You're right about that. That's why I'm a Union pilot. That's what brought me to this mountain. There was a bunch of us here, me and another guide and a gang of stampeders. One of them stampeders tripped over you in the dark, and me and Greeley Brown took you into that cave yonder and sliced off your hand. You'd be dead now, I reckon, if you hadn't parted with it. I know you don't remember none of this. You were way too sick to know what was going on."

"Well, better a live one-handed Ben than a dead two-handed one," Ben replied. He knitted his brows in thought. "Mr. Colter, you being a Union pilot, would you guide me on to Cumberland Gap?"

"I'd be proud to, Mr. Clinch, but Greeley would never allow me to take the risk for just one man, especially one—no offense—who ain't going to be fit to fight in the Federal army. There's hundreds of Union men back in the mountains, Tennessee and Carolina Union men both, waiting to go and able to make soldiers. Greeley likes to pilot big groups. He says if you're going to take the risk, you might as well run as many through as you can."

"That makes sense." Ben's disappointment came through despite an effort to sound bright and nonchalant.

Sam thought it over a few moments, then said, "Tell you what, Mr. Clinch: You could come back to Carter County with Greeley and me, once Greeley gets back, and go with us on the next run."

Ben closed his eyes, thinking, then shook his head. "Reckon not. I've made it most of the way alone. I'll make the rest of the way, too. Why should the rebs care anyway? With a hand gone I'm no more use to the Federals than to the Confederates."

Ben, who was lying on his back under a blanket Greeley had left him, opened his eyes and looked over at Sam. "I thank you again for saving my life. It was providence that sent you. It must have been."

Sam grinned. "You never know, I reckon."

"I know," Ben said. "I know it for a fact. When you've lived the life I have, you know providence when you see it. I believe in it strong. You could put it on my gravestone: 'He was no count to nobody, but he did believe in providence.' And I do believe. If it wasn't for providence, I'd be dead long ago. Why I ain't, I can't imagine. It has to be providence."

Sam Colter and Ben talked very much that night, moving off the topics of war, providence, stampeding, and the loss of hands and into the more personal areas of their hearts. Sam found in Ben a man who listened well and did not pass judgment. He was easy to talk to, and the things he said back, though often funnily worded, often proved to have a deeper kind of sense to them once they had time to sink in.

Sam talked at last about Amy Deacon, though he never called her name. So Ben sat listening to Sam speak of his unrequited love, never imagining that the woman of whom he spoke was the same one whom Ben held in such esteem, the same one whose father had tried to make a murderer of him, and because of whom he had fled Knoxville in '61. Ben hadn't returned there since, even though he had read in the papers long ago that Doc Deacon had died in a fire on Secession Hill. Though Knoxville was still his town, his home—if a homeless man had a home—he hadn't been able to imagine going back there. Not yet. Ben didn't fully understand why. In any case, he didn't think much about Knoxville anymore, or about Doc Deacon.

But he thought often about Amy. He thought of her now, as this young stranger talked about the young woman he loved but who had told him there could be nothing between them while war was under way. Ben thought as well of another woman he had known years before, the one whom Amy Deacon reminded him of in so many ways. Angel. His lost Angel. The beloved one who had told him he must choose between her or the bottle. He had made his choice, his awful choice, the choice that had left him lonely for so many years. As Sam talked about his own loneliness and desire for the one he loved, Ben looked into his own soul and thought that surely the loneliness he saw there was far deeper and blacker than anything one so young as Sam Colter could feel.

Sam finished his talk and fell silent for a moment, then asked, "Have you ever been married, Mr. Clinch?"

"No. I came close . . . but no."

"She didn't die or nothing, I hope."

"No. No. She didn't die." Ben paused. "Nothing happened to her. It happened to me. There was a time in my life when I drank to excess, Mr. Colter."

"Oh. And she wouldn't marry you. Is that it?"

"Yes. She was wise. I'd not have made a good husband. She deserved better than me." Ben looked over at Sam. "Somebody good and decent, like you seem to be."

"I'm just a Carolina boy who was looking toward being a merchant, then got himself knocked off his tracks by the war."

"When the war's over, you will go find this gal you love, won't you?"

"I will. If I'm still living. And if the war ever does really end."

"You'll marry her?"

Sam picked up a stone and fiddled with it, then dropped it. "If she'll have me," he said softly. "If only she'll have me."

"I'd say she will, Mr. Colter. You seem a fine young man, the kind any girl would be lucky to have. Not at all like me. I'm sorry and worthless, and any woman who'd have the likes of me, why, she wouldn't be worth having herself."

Sam chuckled. "Don't be so critical of yourself, Mr. Clinch."

"I'm just testifying to the truth about Ben Scar—about Ben Clinch. I'm a man who seems bound to make the wrong choice every chance I get. You line a string of choices up before me and bet on me picking the worst dang one, you'll get your money every time." He looked at Sam squarely. "Don't you be that way, Mr. Colter. You make the right choices. Go find yourself that young woman and tell her again you want to marry her, you tell her you'll do anything it takes to please her and win her over, that you'll stick by her every day of her life and yourn. Don't you let yours get away, like mine did. Don't you do it."

Ben's tone had grown increasingly forceful as he spoke, and Sam was a little taken aback. Quite evidently he had just heard a man speak from the deepest well of his soul. "I'll . . . I'll keep your words in mind, Mr. Clinch. I won't let her get away. Not if there's a thing I can do about it."

"Well, good. I'm glad to hear you say that. You don't want to ruin your life like old Ben has."

"You don't look ruined to me, sir."

"Well, I've done a little better lately. But I doubt it will last. Like I say, you line up them choices like little baby shoats on mama sow's teats, and I'll pick the worst of the litter nine times out of ten. Now, if you'll pardon me, I'm feeling tired and my stump here is hurting like perdition, so I believe I'll try to get me some sleep."

He lay down, closed his eyes, and licked his lips, trying to imagine the taste of whiskey.

Greeley Brown was pleased to see how thoroughly his surgical subject had recovered when he showed up again on

Powell's Mountain. Sam introduced Ben "Clinch" to Greeley, who became the recipient of abundant thanks and even a heartfelt kiss on the hand. Ben was a man glad to be alive and grateful to those whose crude surgery had allowed his life to go on. He had recovered his strength and health with amazing speed, as so often happens to those who have been freed of gangrenous extremities.

Greeley shared with his companions food and beverages given to him by grateful Union officers at the Gap, who had welcomed the new recruits he brought to them. Greeley related how the first sight of the American flag waving over the fort had brought a jag of joyous weeping to his weary Unionist band, and he admitted that he hadn't been exempt from tears himself. "I look forward to the day them stars and stripes wave over the whole Southland again," he said. "It was a beautiful thing, seeing that flag there in the gap. But I received no encouraging word about invasion."

"Who'd you talk to?"

"General Sam Carter. The same one who's brother to the Preacher Carter who set up the bridge-burning plan. He said that there ain't going to be an invasion anytime soon, as much as he'd like to see one."

"So you and me, we'll likely be making more of these stampeder runs," Sam said.

"Likely so. Maybe a good many."

"I'm going on through the Gap myself," Ben said. "After that, I don't know what will become of me."

"Why don't you go back to Dandridge?" Sam asked. "The rebs will leave you alone, I'm sure, considering you can't fire a Union rifle very well with one hand."

Ben couldn't answer Sam truthfully, the truth being, of course, that he had not come from Dandridge in the first place and therefore had nothing there to return to. But he did momentarily consider the possibility of returning to the Mainard home in Washington County. Trotter would surely leave him be now that his hand was gone. Or would he? Considering that he had fled from conscription and evaded military arrest, Trotter would probably see him punished. And how would he earn his keep with the

Mainards now that he was maimed? A man couldn't shovel niter-bearing dirt very well with one hand, nor do any decent carpentry.

"I believe it's Kentucky for me," he said vaguely. "Then I may head north, to walk again on free Union soil." This he said for effect; there was nothing in the North that particularly drew him. He was running from, not to.

But his companions took him at his word. "Then best wishes, and God go with you, sir," Greeley Brown said, lifting the bottle of water from which he was drinking.

Ben and Sam lifted their own bottles. "Hear, hear," Sam said, and they drank together.

Then Sam looked at Greeley and said, "I want to go with Mr. Clinch."

"What? Go north, you mean?"

"Just as far as the Gap. I want to guide him. I want to see that American flag flying for myself."

"You know my policy on guiding a lone man, Sam."

"I know. But I want you to make an exception this time. We're so close to the Gap, and I've never explored all the way to it. I could learn the terrain and make sure Mr. Clinch was safe at the same time."

Greeley argued against it, but Sam pressed the matter and, to his own surprise, prevailed, though Greeley declared it to be against his better judgment. So when Ben set out, with Greeley heading back toward Carter County, agreeing to meet Sam at a designated place near his old burned-down house, Sam was with him.

They reached Cumberland Gap without incident and Sam enjoyed the sight of the flag as much as he had hoped. He lingered for a day until he was able to see Ben safely placed with a band of other refugees, then headed home.

He was nearly across Powell's Valley when he heard the sound of approaching horsemen just around a curve in the road he was crossing. Panic struck him; some inner warning instinct told him that rebel soldiers were about to come around that bend. He ran for the woods on the far side of the road just as they came into view.

They *were* rebels, a full squad of them, mounted and armed.

"Halt! You there—halt!"

He didn't halt. He ran as hard as he could, scared beyond description. Branches slapped and scratched, vines grabbed at his feet, trees loomed before him as if they had leaped from hiding, making him dodge. He heard shots, lead missiles tearing through underbrush and smacking wooden trunks. Shouts, curses, trampling feet behind him. He ran harder, but so did they.

He came into a clearing all at once, the woods behind, a house ahead, a startled-looking man in the yard splitting wood with an axe. A woman at the doorway screamed and dropped a basket of fresh-washed laundry.

"You got to hide me, sir, they're after me—"

The man raised the axe, a wild, fearful look in his eye. "You stop there! Who are you? Why are you running?"

"They'll catch me, mister! Please hide me, please—"

He heard them in the woods behind, almost ready to emerge. No time to hide now. He began running again, veering right to pass the man with the axe, but the fellow stepped before him and rammed the butt of the handle into his forehead. Grunting, vision firing with a burst of sparks, Sam fell to his knees. Blood ran into his eyes.

"Running from the Confederacy, are you?" the man with the axe said. "Indeed you are—there they come now! I'll not give aid to no damned Lincolnite nor any conscription dodger . . ."

The man kept on talking, but Sam didn't listen. He could see little because of the blood, but he felt and heard them surround him, felt them grasp his arms and yank him up with guttural sounds of triumph.

"What will happen to me now?" he asked a figure that loomed before him through the red haze in his eyes.

"We've caught you now, boy!"

"He tried to make me hide him, officer," the man with the axe said. "I wouldn't help him. I've got two sons wearing the gray, and I'll give no aid to Lincolnites."

"What will happen to me now?" Sam asked again.

No one would tell him.

* * *

Greeley waited as long as he could, but at last he had to conclude the worst. He longed to go back into the valley and make inquiries, but this was impossible. Far too dangerous.

He could only pray that Sam was still alive, vying to maintain that hope against a strong and stubborn intuition that said he was surely dead. Greeley tried not to listen, yet still the malevolent voice whispered.

With a weighted heart and sorrowful soul, Greeley turned his back on the broad valley—a hungry-looking, wicked valley it seemed to him, like a wound across an otherwise healthy land—and headed back toward home, alone and very sad.

Chapter 31

John Hunt Morgan's distracting effectiveness as a guerrilla raider was only one part of a mounting southern aggression in 1862, his summer raids only the first probe of a planned Confederate sweep into Kentucky. Surly-looking General Braxton Bragg, now leading the Confederate effort in the west, hoped to rouse support among the Kentucky populace as Kirby Smith marched his army through Cumberland Gap itself in defiance of the Union force holding it.

The massive Kentucky invasion started in late summer. It was soon bolstered by news that General Robert E. Lee had won a strong victory in a second battle at Bull Run and was expected to attack Washington itself.

Moving around, rather than through, Cumberland Gap because of the strength of the Federal fortifications there, Kirby Smith took Richmond, Kentucky, which stood near the place where Amy Deacon had rendezvoused with Jonathon Eaton. Frankfort fell soon after. Other Confederate armies swept in and took Lexington. Across the river, a nervous Cincinnati dug in for an anticipated attack. The South was pressing the North in its own territory, showing an aggressiveness that was daunting, all the while trying to stir a grassroots, pro-Confederate uprising within the Kentucky populace.

Yet the latter hope simply didn't play out. Recruiting efforts enjoyed only minimal success, and Kentuckian Unionism was unexpectedly rampant. Bragg grew discouraged, and in September informed the Confederate War Department that "unless a change occurs soon, we must abandon the garden spot of Kentucky."

Countering Bragg's misfortunes, the tide still rolled in the rebels' favor elsewhere. The Confederate offensive isolated Federal General George Morgan at Cumberland Gap and forced him into a northward retreat, drawing tears and fury from his Tennessee troops, who had waited so long for a chance to retake their homeland.

Despite some problems, opportunity loomed before the Confederacy like the yawning mouth of the great Cumberland Gap itself. Aggressive and motivated, the rebel armies seemed on the verge of great achievements. Hope was at its height—a height it would never reach again.

In the end, some would blame Bragg.

He was a capable general, a stern disciplinarian of his troops—yet also a self-doubter, hesitater, second-guesser. With the chance to unite with Kirby Smith and seal the success of the invasion, he instead vascillated, and while he did so, Buell reached Louisville and was reinforced.

A fight at Perryville gave Bragg a victory of sorts, but he withdrew under false impressions of the enemy's numbers and sacrificed his advantage. As Bragg fell back, Kirby Smith withdrew from Lexington, carrying loot, ammunition, captured weapons, refugees trailing behind so that the entire procession was some forty miles long, with Buell in close pursuit.

By mid-October it was clear that the South had lost its upper hand in Kentucky. The weary rebel armies left a force of about three thousand to hold Cumberland Gap and straggled back into East Tennessee, a thousand miles of marching completed in two months. Many soldiers were sick and injured. The weather was cold, snow heightening the miseries of the marching troops. Knoxville's doctors were pushed to their limits, tending the exhausted, wounded, and ill.

Yet the military undertaking hadn't been a complete failure. The Federals had lost Cumberland Gap, the threat of a Union advance into East Tennessee was for the moment averted, and the South had gained some valuable war booty. Jefferson Davis, a Bragg admirer, praised his general despite the great failure at Perryville.

On the Federal side, Buell was removed and General William S. Rosecrans put in his place. General Ambrose Burnside, who was to play quite an instrumental role in East Tennessee's wartime future, replaced McClellan.

These were days of great campaigns, great successes, great failures, great changes. But in the East Tennessee and western North Carolina highlands, one thing had not changed: The people, most of all the Unionists, continued to suffer, and the winter was now almost here. In the worst of the deprived mountain regions, many wondered which would kill them first—an enemy's army, or starvation.

Ben "Clinch" had never left the vicinity of Cumberland Gap. While there, he had chanced to meet a grizzled old mountain hermit who lived high on the Kentucky side of the mountains, up in the Cumberlands, a few miles' hike on mountain trails from the Gap itself. The mountain man was named Coburn Handy. He had homemade whiskey with him when he and Ben met, and offered Ben a swallow. From somewhere outside, or maybe somewhere within, an old demon had arisen, and Ben accepted the offer. "There's more where that come from," Handy told him. "This here's good whiskey, my own product and pride. You come with me, Mr. Clinch, and I'll share it with you."

So Ben followed Coburn Handy back through the mountains to his home, and remained. The whiskey was as good as promised, and he drank it in abundance. When he was sober, he hated himself for his failure. So he made sure he wasn't sober all that often.

Handy was a strong supporter of the Confederacy, so

Ben became one, too. He flowed through changing alle-
giances with the ease of a fish piercing smooth waters. Let
the war go on and take whatever direction it would. He
would ride with the currents. As long as he had Handy's
roof to sleep under, Handy's wild game and homegrown
vegetables to live on, and most of all Handy's homemake
whiskey to drink, nothing else mattered. He could stay here
forever. He didn't even care that he was missing a hand. It
required only one hand to hoist a whiskey jug.

Sometimes he and Handy drank with another hermit of
the area, a younger, stocky, bearded man named Hendrix
Cart, whose eyes had been ruined by bad whiskey and were
failing him by the day. Like Handy, Cart was a rebel sympa-
thizer. He was a married man, he told Ben; his wife, Jen,
still lived in his old homeplace in the Shelton Laurel Valley
in North Carolina. She came from a family that was strongly
Unionist, and that had created some problems for him when
war talk began. The tensions had grown worse, and he suspected his wife of being unfaithful. Disgusted, Hendrix had
left her and come here.

Cart talked a lot about his wife, Ben noticed. When he
was sober, he declared he was glad to be apart from her,
wanted to never see her or her Lincolnite kin again. But
when drunk, he would weep and pine about going back to
her. Times were growing hard in the North Carolina mountains, he had heard. Union folk like his wife were suffering
in particular, and he hated to think of it. "I'll go back to her.
I'll take her away from there and find a safe place for her."
Then he would sober up and declare again that he detested
her and didn't care if she starved.

Ben wasn't sure which Hendrix Cart was the real one:
the Cart who despised his woman, or the Cart who loved
her. He was inclined to cast his bet on the latter.

Once again there were changes in the Confederate high
command in East Tennessee. Kirby Smith, who blamed
Bragg for the failure in Kentucky, requested of Jefferson
Davis that he be relieved of command under Bragg. Davis
denied that request but did grant Kirby Smith a leave of

absence. Ultimately that leave would become a transfer to the Trans-Mississippi Department based in Louisiana, and a promotion in rank.

General J. P. McCown took over command of the Knoxville Confederate base and quickly became friends with Will Thomas of the Cherokee band, who had marched into Knoxville earlier in the year with Jim Matoy among their number. Thomas now called his command either the Highland Rangers or the Battalion of Indians and Mountaineers. He had been made a major in July and saw his rank rise to colonel in September, when his troops were formally organized as a regiment with several new companies transferred in under his command so that now the group consisted of a mix of whites and Indians. In October, Thomas became a lieutenant colonel, with seven companies under him. His dream had long been to command a true legion, and he was nearly there.

But so far Thomas's soldiers had seen little action. Matoy's company, for example, had spent most of its time guarding the railroad bridge at Strawberry Plains, suffering from boredom and an epidemic of measles that proved fatal to several. Matoy himself fell sick briefly, but recovered.

His friend Nikatimsi was not so fortunate. He died of the disease, raving in fever and making Matoy regret he and Nikatimsi had become soldiers at all.

The Highland Rangers' inactivity was not to last. Word reached McCown at Knoxville that Federal troop movements had been spotted in the Cumberland Gap region; it was vital that all mountain passes be guarded.

So Matoy's company was at last called into real action. The Cherokees marched toward Cumberland Gap, aligned with the Confederates already there, and were sent to guard another mountain pass on down the range.

The Indian soldiers advanced toward their position, led by Lieutenant John Astoogatogeh, who wore a uniform of standard Confederate issue, with one exception: a full Cherokee turban that made him stand out among all the others there. Matoy had never heard of the place they were going. It was a small, remote notch in the hills, known in the area as Baptist Gap.

* * *

The volley seemed to come from nowhere, and without warning. Jim Matoy hardly realized what had happened until he saw John Astoogatogeh pitch over, bloodied, move and groan for a moment, and then expire. Death was like a deflating, a relaxing of muscles and an exhalation of breath, then the beloved Astoogatogeh's form grew as still as the very stones of the mountain upon which he had fallen.

Ambushed! Matoy thought. *We've been ambushed!*

He waited for some instinct to tell him what to do. The instruction he had received in training seemed worthless just now, almost forgotten, and what he remembered was inapplicable to the wild wave of confusion sweeping through the Cherokee ranks. More shots came and Matoy simply froze where he was, rifle half raised, breath held by reflex, as if he had been plunged beneath water.

For nearly a minute everything and everyone seemed in utter disarray. Many Cherokee soldiers leaped for cover; others fired at the puffs of smoke that marked the place where the Yankee sharpshooters were hidden, and others merely stood, as Matoy was.

Then an odd thing happened.

An awareness that John Astoogatogeh was dead swept the entire group like some simultaneous mental revelation. No man among the company had been more admired than the devout chaplain and lieutenant; hardly a man among them would have hesitated to trade his life for Astoogatogeh's. But no such choice had been offered. Astoogatogeh was dead, slain in the first Yankee volley, and the infuriating injustice of it overwhelmed every Confederate soldier there and, for Jim Matoy, became the catalyst that pulled him out of his paralysis and into action.

By all common sense they should have run. The ambush had been well-laid. But fury was strong, and as one, almost every man in the rebel band gave the whoop of war and rushed straight into the Federal gunfire.

Several of the Cherokees fired their rifles, then threw them aside and drew long knives from belt sheaths. Racing in on the Federal riflemen before they had time to reload, they commenced a bloody slaughter. At this moment they were no longer regular soldiers fighting for a cause they only half understood. They were warriors, fighting out of the same primal urge that had enabled their ancestors to gain and hold what became their homelands long, forgotten years before.

The Federals were unprepared for what had come upon them. Most were enlistees out of Indiana; none had come into this war anticipating a fight with what looked like savage devils out of some early pioneer's nightmare. Federals rose and ran, but many fell under the rebel gunfire or the slashing of the long knives. It was fierce, bloody, and while it lasted, bloodthirstily rousing for the enraged Confederates.

In the midst of the carnage was Jim Matoy, one of those who had cast off his rifle to join the knife-wielders. Moving as if by some external manipulation, watching his own actions rather than feeling that he was guiding them, he overran a young Federal soldier, grabbed him with a forearm around the neck and brought his blade up and then down. The young blue-clad soldier shrieked and shuddered, then collapsed to the ground beneath Matoy, bleeding and dying.

Matoy rolled him over and without a thought about what he was doing, carved a furrow beneath the soldier's hairline and around the back of his head, above and around the ears. Twining his fingers in the sandy hair, he gave a whoop and a pull, and took the scalp only a moment after the terrified soldier mercifully died.

Matoy rose, exulting in the hot pleasure of battle. This was a sensation he had never known before and would not have thought could be possible for him on that day he climbed Skaantee's Ridge, his heart full of dread and fear at the prospect of going to war. He had feared this? He couldn't imagine why. At this moment he felt he was born for warfare.

Around Matoy other Cherokee were taking scalps from both the dead and the wounded. The Federals were fleeing in

stark horror. They had come to fight soldiers, not beings so
fearsome that at this moment they seemed fully supernatural.

Filled with the heat of war, Matoy chased another soldier, this one a man in his mid-thirties who still carried his
rifle. The man raced up a small ridge. Matoy followed.

He was moving away from the center of the battle but,
preoccupied with the man he was chasing, did not notice.
Matoy was gaining on him with every pace. The soldier was
wheezing and puffing and struggling to run despite being
completely winded. The man slowed, turned. Matoy raised
his knife, let out a war whoop, then started into the muzzle of
a rifle that suddenly belched fire and smoke. Something hit
him in the side of the skull, hard and stinging, and he fell.

Time passed, untrackable. Matoy rose, half blinded from
blood, and sensed that the fight was continuing behind
him. He was afraid now, and could not see the man who had
shot him.

The battle spirit in him died suddenly. In its place came
primal fear, and the instinct that stirred any wounded living
thing: *I must hide. I must hide!*

He staggered farther up the ridge and then across it,
putting the rise between himself and the battle. He began to
grow weak, and the amount of blood running down his face
and soaking his shirt was appalling. *I'm going to die here!*
He ran harder, like the soldier had run, as if by flight he
could outrace death.

More blood filled his eyes and he was completely
blinded. He ran on still, smacking branches, hearing his own
gasps and tasting his own blood. Then he seemed to swim
into an ocean of white and felt the ground vanish from
beneath his feet. Suddenly he was falling, striking something stony and rough. He slid down, felt a hard pinch
around his middle. Jim Matoy was instantly unaware of
battle, blood, and fear. Unaware of even his own existence.
The whiteness turned to black, and he saw no more.

He awakened in darkness. Or perhaps he was still blinded . . .
no, because when he blinked he could see variations in the
depth and richness of the blackness engulfing him. It was a

gorgeous, full blackness, oddly inviting. He would have enjoyed watching it, except his midsection hurt distractingly, as if he were a bird being squeezed to death in the fist of some cruel boy. He tried to move and his head throbbed. Oddly, he seemed to be nearly upside down. Was this death? No, he didn't think so. He felt too much pain to be dead.

He remained still for a time, until his vision slowly returned and the blackness took interpretable form. It gaped beneath him . . . a hole. A deep, swallowing hole right into the earth itself. Turning his eyes in their sockets until they hurt, he saw that he had fallen into a depression in the ground, with a hole in the bottom that went to cavernous depths he could not guess. The mountain had a mouth and was trying to swallow him into its black belly. There was dim light coming in from above and behind him; the blackness he had initially seen was merely the blackness of the hole.

He tried to move his hands and found that his right arm was pinned but his left relatively free. Feeling about, he detected that he was caught in the gnarled grasp of some root. He was intensely grateful for that root, and thanked the great Creator that He had, in His foresight, placed that root there for Jim Matoy. Without it he would have fallen into that rocky, earthen mouth, and he knew that what the earth swallowed, it seldom vomited forth again.

He felt about some more, found a portion of the root that fit his hand and felt strong enough to bear his weight if he could shift it. He strained, closing his eyes so he wouldn't have to watch the hole swallow him should he fall. Then he pushed hard on the root, shifted his body and got his right arm free. It was numb. He hefted it out from under himself like a dead thing; it dangled down toward the hole. He rested, exhausted from his exertion. The numb arm began to tingle painfully. He waited until he was finally able to wriggle his fingers and the tingling gradually diminished. It took an agonizingly long time.

He must try again. He gripped the root in two places now, with both hands, and pushed up. He felt his form rise, and though he was a lean and strong young man, his body felt like it carried the weight of three men. Arms trembling, he moved his legs, found a foothold on the root, gave a straining heave and upward push, and came upright, perched on the root and now able to see a dimming twilight sky above.

He rested again, then climbed completely out of the depression and onto the solid earth around it. Collapsing, he rolled away from the hole and came to a stop against the base of a tree in a pile of old leaves. Closing his eyes, he slept, and wondered how long he had been here. There was no sound of human activity within his earshot. He seemed to be alone.

The next thing his senses revealed was sound . . . voices, speaking English with the inflections of white men.

"Where'd you find him, Ben?"

"Up under a tree. A pretty good distance from where the fight was."

"Hell, why'd you bring him here? I don't want no redskins around me. I hate them."

"I couldn't just leave him there."

"How'd you manage to carry him?"

"It wasn't easy. Made my wrist stump hurt, just from the effort."

"We ought to kill him and be done with it."

"No! I'll have no part of killing nobody, not even an Indian."

"Then what'll we do with him?"

"Show a little human mercy, I reckon. Tend to him. See if we can make him better. I s'pose we can turn him over to the Confederates at the Gap after that."

Matoy loved the one who spoke of mercy and healing, and hated the other, though he could not move or speak to express his feelings. He sensed that they were bending over him.

"Look there, Coburn—he's got a furrow in the side of his head like a plow's pushed through it. And he's all mashed up and bruised. I fear he won't live."

"Then let's kill him now."

"No!"

"This is my house, Ben. Not yours."

"You kill him, and I'll tell. You'll hang for murdering a soldier."

"An *Indian* soldier, that's all! Indians don't count for real soldiers. They're just . . . Indians."

"He's a soldier, Coburn. Got him a uniform and everything. See?"

Jim Matoy heard it all as if through wads of cotton stuffed in his ears. He tried to open his eyes but was too weary to do so. He seemed to be on his back, and what was beneath him felt softer than a pile of leaves. The kind one had talked about carrying him. He surmised that he had been found, carried to shelter, placed on a bed. He managed to flutter one eye open long enough to see that he was indeed inside a structure of some sort, seemingly a cabin or shed, and there were two white men looking at him intently from the side. The eye drifted shut again.

"Look there!" said the voice of the one who had advocated his killing. "He moved his eye. You see it?"

"Yes. That's a good sign. He'll be waking up here in a while."

Jim Matoy drifted toward sleep as the harsh one replied to the kind one, and he couldn't understand what was said. His head hurt very badly, and he wondered with a casualness he couldn't account for whether the harsh one would talk the other into letting him kill him after all. He hoped not.

He fell back into a stupor and dreamed he was hunting ginseng with Skaantee. It was a good dream, one he would have been content to remain in for a very long time.

But like all dreams, it faded and Jim Matoy woke up. Fully this time. His head still hurt. He tried to sit up, moaned. A man came to him. Matoy saw a bearded, bedraggled face with a gentle smile and watery, weak-looking eyes. The same kind of eyes he had seen in the Cherokee men back in Carolina who fell victim to too much liquor. He scanned the fellow up and down and noticed with some interest that he had only one hand.

"My name's Ben Clinch, and you can just call me plain old Ben," the man said. Matoy knew from the voice that this was the kind one. "What's yourn?"

"Jim Matoy." Matoy was pleased to find he still had a voice, weak though it was. "Private Jim Matoy, from North

Carolina . . . serving in Lieutenant Colonel Will Thomas's Highland Rangers, Confederate States of America."

"Pleased to meet you, Mr. Matoy. I ain't never knowed an Indian before. You are an Indian, ain't you?"

"Yes."

"I thought you Indian boys spoke some kind of foreign tongue. I didn't know you spoke American."

"Some speak American . . . speak English . . . some don't." He forced crusty eyes into better focus. "When is the other man going to kill me?"

"Why, he ain't going to kill you. That's just Coburn Handy a-talking, just rattling on. I done talked him out of it."

"Where are the other soldiers?"

"Gone. You boys sure put a fright into them Yankees. We could hear the shooting from here."

"My head hurts."

"That's because a bullet grazed through it. Cut a right smart furrow. But it's scabbed up fine and I believe it'll heal. Hendrix Cart—he's a third fellow lives around here— poured some whiskey on it while you was sleeping, so you wouldn't feel it so much. Whiskey is good for wounds, you know."

"I thank you. My sides, they hurt, too. Was I shot there?"

"No. But somehow you've sort of crushed up your middle. Busted a few ribs, I think."

Matoy remembered. "I fell into a hole, caught myself on a root."

"That's what done it, then. Hey, I'll bet you're hungry. Want some corn?"

Matoy ate a few bites and drank some whiskey, and felt somewhat stronger afterward, and also warmly fond of this bleary-eyed Ben Clinch fellow, especially after the whiskey took hold. He had known only a few white men in his day, Will Thomas best of all, and it seemed odd to be under the care of a white-skinned stranger. He looked around for the others and asked where they were.

"Outside drinking, I believe," Ben said. "Coburn don't seem to much like having an Indian in his place. No offense to you intended, Mr. Matoy. Me, I know what it is to not be wanted. I was a drunk in Knoxville for years and years, and Lord knows nobody wanted me around, neither."

"I've been in Knoxville," Matoy said. "Before coming here I was near Knoxville. Strawberry Plains."

"I been there a time or two. Ain't much to see at Strawberry Plains, is there? Little town, the river, the railroad bridge."

"What happened to your hand?"

"It got cut on some glass, and mortified, and a couple of fellers cut it off for me so I wouldn't die."

"I am very weak. I don't think I've ever been this weak before."

"You probably ain't ever been this hurt before."

"Why are you taking care of me?"

"Why not? With this here war a-going, I reckon folks need to take care of each other."

"Thank you."

"No thanks needed."

"I want to sleep again. You won't let the other man kill me while I sleep, will you?"

"Lord, no. Don't you worry. He's a good man, just a bit rough. Hendrix Cart's from North Carolina, just like you. He's got him a wife back there, and has been saying the last day or two he's going to be back and see her while he can. He's losing his eyesight, you see. Going blind. That'd be a terrible thing, going blind. I think I'd rather have just about anything quit working on me except my sight. I've lost a hand, but I swear I'd rather lose that than ary one of my eyeballs . . ."

Ben kept on talking, but Matoy heard only a little of it. The whiskey made him very sleepy, and he drifted off with Ben's voice still chattering dimly in his ear.

Chapter 32

In spite of the reassurances Ben had given about the harm-lessness of his fellow mountain dwellers, he kept a close eye on Jim Matoy for the first couple of days he was at Coburn Handy's cabin. Though Coburn had been the one who spoke about killing Matoy, Ben was actually more worried about Hendrix Cart. Cart had known some Chero-kees back in his home mountains and obviously had under-gone some kind of trouble with them. The Cherokee were in Cart's eyes the most despised branch of a despised race.

Cart grumbled and frowned at Matoy quite a lot when-ever he was at the Handy cabin, saying he couldn't under-stand why a "damned redskin heathen" should be given quarter in the home of a white man. But Ben realized even-tually that Cart wasn't any threat to the Cherokee. Cart was one to talk, not to do. Furthermore, Cart had something far more close to his own heart to worry about than the pres-ence of a wounded Indian. His failing vision was worsening almost by the day, his eyes beginning to hurt. The prospect of true blindness loomed for the man, preoccupying him.

Matoy, young and strong by nature, healed quickly and steadily. He soon detected Cart's eye problems and made some suggestions to him about how he might deal with it—a bit of Cherokee poultice medicine he had learned from Skaantee during their old-ginseng-gathering days. Cart, who was interested in such folk medicines anyway, attempted Matoy's remedy, grudgingly and in secret at first, and found it helped alleviate the pain, even if his vision didn't improve. Something that did improve was his perception of Jim Matoy. Ben watched with some astonishment as Cart began to talk about the uninvited guest less as a "redskin heathen" and more as a "danged decent kind of fellow, for a Cherokee."

Matoy and Cart, men from two different worlds, soon engaged in conversations about North Carolina, argued about the Cherokee removal—Cart defending and Matoy condemning—and about ginseng, herbal medicine, and woodcraft in general.

Before long Matoy left Handy's cabin and moved over to Cart's. Though Ben knew Cart would never admit it, an odd, grumpy friendship had been formed. Ben was glad to see it. Sometimes he could get oddly sentimental, thinking about how two such different men had come into fraternity, and would wipe away a tear or two.

Winter brought a circumstance that threatened to bring Ben tears of the sorrowful kind. Handy announced that the big supply of sugar he had stockpiled for years near his hidden still house—even Ben didn't know where the still house was—was gone, and his supply of whiskey dwindling. Since the beginning of the war, Handy had developed an underground business of selling whiskey illegally to soldiers who would sneak over from Cumberland Gap; what whiskey remained, he said, would need to be sold rather than consumed, because he needed the money. Ben was heartbroken, and as shocked as a financier just told he was facing financial ruin. He became moping and sorrowful, lingering around the Handy cabin like a mourner at a funeral chapel.

Cold and snow came. Coburn Handy developed a cough that worsened, and his lungs began to hurt. Ben grew worried and urged him to seek medical help among the military men at the Gap, but Handy was stubborn, declaring he would get better. He didn't. One chilly morning, Ben woke up to find the old fellow dead in his blankets. He and Cart, grieving like sons who had lost a father, buried him beside his cabin. Ben's sorrow was not only over Handy himself, but over a growing intuition that his situation here in this mountain retreat was about to change.

Only one good thing could Ben find in the death of Coburn Handy: He and Cart could go ahead and drink up the last of the whiskey instead of selling it to the soldiers at Cumberland Gap, as Handy had intended.

Ben moved in with Cart and Matoy because Cart's cabin was warmer than Handy's. There he lingered and brooded, waiting for a life situation he loved to be taken away from him, as almost all the other good things he found in life had been taken away.

At the rare moments he was courageous enough to look inside himself, he found an emptiness and aching that frightened him, but which he had no idea how to fill, unless with liquor.

So he drank, watching the supply of whiskey dwindle, and grieved in private over his losses and his slow, steady destruction of himself.

Jim Matoy could no longer understand his own mind. There was no reason he could think of why he should enjoy a limbo of a life in the mountain retreat of a gaggle of white-skinned drunks, yet he was enjoying it.

He was well now, fully capable of returning to his command and to military service. But the idea held no appeal.

Matoy was haunted. The memory of battle and the brutal nature it had unveiled in him was troubling. But here with these odd companions, he had rested, been at peace, and reverted back to being the Jim Matoy who had once climbed Skaantee's Ridge in vain hope of being told there was no reason he should become a warrior in a white man's conflict. He didn't want to go back to warfare. He wanted to live the life he had lived up until the great conflict—hidden away among the high mountains, doing what he wanted, living at peace in a small but cordial world. This was what Jim Matoy loved, and what war and violence had changed.

Matoy was glad he had not been born in the early days of his people, when all men were expected to be warriors and crave battle. He would never have fit into that world. It troubled him to realize that, but truth was truth.

When he looked back on what he had become during the fight, Matoy saw ugliness. Killing men, taking their hair . . . should anyone take pleasure in that, under any circumstance? Yet he had taken pleasure in it, a wild, fearsome, raw kind of pleasure that now seemed very wrong.

He was a young man lost in a moral confusion. He felt guilty when he considered how he had found pleasure in warfare, but felt just as guilty, in another way, because he no longer wanted that pleasure. Was it not his duty to be a warrior? Had he not taken a pledge to see this task through? Had Skaantee not told him it would be dutiful for him to fight in this war, and had he not sworn a hundred secret oaths on Skaantee's spilled blood that he would see that duty through, and if possible, also avenge Skaantee's murder by finding and taking the life of the murderer?

There was the most haunting, troubling reality of all: He no longer was even sure he wanted to avenge Skaantee. He wished he had never heard the name of Joe Colter and never sworn to kill him for what he had done.

I must leave here and go back to my command, Matoy told himself many times. *It is my duty. That's what Skaantee would tell me. And I will go back. Soon. Not yet, but soon.*

He stayed where he was, hunting the meager small game that could be found in the surrounding winter woods, watching Ben Clinch drink himself toward the grave and Hendrix Cart slowly go blind.

One cloudy morning when melting snow was turning the forest floor to mush, Hendrix Cart opened his eyes and found that the world had been lost to him sometime in the night, leaving for him only patches of light, blobs of vague color. He wept with eyes that would no longer see, and by the evening of that sad day informed his companions that he wanted to go back to North Carolina and find the wife he had left behind and whose face he would never actually perceive again. This time, unlike maudlin and drunken times before, when he had played with the idea of returning, Cart was sincere. He was ready to go home, and to get there he would require help.

Jim Matoy, troubled as he was by his inner conflict over duty, suddenly found a decision spilling ready-made and welcome into his mind. "I'll guide you," he said to Cart, hardly thinking about it. "I'll take you back." And after he had done that, Matoy told himself, he would go back to his own home and the life he had known. He would desert. He was tired of fighting mental moral battles. Let Will Thomas and his rebel band fight their fights if they wanted. He would be part of them no more. He had tasted the sweet bitterness of battle one time, and that was enough.

This liberating decision filled Matoy with a wild sense of joy and freedom, but at once another image arose: Skaantee's face, looking sadly at him, telling him in silence that his decision was not honorable. Matoy felt a twinge, but shrugged it away. Skaantee was dead. It was the place of the dead to hold silence, not to speak to those who still lived.

For his part, Ben thought it a fine thing that Matoy was volunteering to play guide to Hendrix Cart. It was also a sad thing. His friends were leaving and he would be alone. Unless he went with them . . . but why would he do that? Cart was from the Shelton Laurel, deep in the North Carolina mountains, and there was trouble there. In those mountains the war was less one of soldiers and armies than a personal, terrifying battle of individual against individual, small band against small band. It was not the kind of place for a man like him.

Matoy and Cart set out for Carolina two days later, traveling on foot and carrying with them almost all the meager rations that had been about the place. Ben had cut Matoy's hair close and traded his Confederate uniform for some of Coburn Handy's extra clothing, and the plan was for Cart to pass him off as a free mulatto, should it become necessary, though he didn't look much like a mulatto to Ben. Matoy had the kind of looks that betrayed his Cherokee heritage no matter how you decorated him up. The best hope was that they would never be challenged by anyone. They would keep to the remote ways, the untraveled wilderness, as much as possible. Sort of odd, Ben thought. Most folks who sneaked through the mountains did so to reach Kentucky, not to leave it. Matoy and Cart were to be mirror-image stampeders, going opposite the usual flow.

Ben wondered why Matoy was going with Cart rather than returning to his military unit, but down deep he didn't really care. All that mattered was that Matoy and Cart were leaving, and he would have to find some other place and means of living.

When they were gone and Ben was alone, he sat down and listened to the wind. It howled terribly, colder than a devil's soul. Ben huddled inside the cabin and wiped tears, missing the woman he had lost years before, missing his three companions, missing the Mainard family back in Jonesborough, missing Knoxville, missing his lost hand, even missing old Daniel Baumgardner and the warm shed behind his store. Right now, with only a little effort, he might even miss his days of living on Secession Hill with Dr. George Deacon, back before it all turned so ugly and terrible.

Most of all he missed someone he had never really known, but would have liked to: the Ben Scarlett that might have been, if he had followed other and better paths.

The wind howled louder. Ben rose and went for the last jug of the late Coburn Handy's homemade whiskey.

He stayed at the Handy cabin until the whiskey was gone and his meager store of food ran out, then traveled to Cumberland Gap and begged sustenance from the rebel soldiers there. They were as generous as their situation allowed, and he wound up staying around the Gap for many days, taking residence in a privy behind a burned-down house, near a grove of brush wherein he discovered a broken-down old wagon. It was a remarkable if valueless find. Wagons in any state of repair were rare hereabouts, most of them having been confiscated for military use. For that matter, groves of brush were becoming rare, too, the occupying army's firewood demands having substantially denuded what had always been a heavily wooded landscape in peaceful days.

Ben got on fairly well in his privy dwelling. He would build a fire just in front of the privy door, prop the door open and sleep sitting up, shoulder leaned against the wall. The soldiers who became aware of this thought it hilarious, and Ben became sort of an instant, secret mascot for them. Despite their own meager rations, the soldiers began slipping food to "Outhouse Ben," as they called him. Some even obtained liquor from time to time, and occasionally shared it with him. Ben, who had learned what it was to have pride in himself while living at the Mainard house and mining niter, watched the last of that pride dwindle. "Outhouse Ben." What a low name for a man to have, a low role for him to play! To be fed like a dog, gotten drunk and made to do absurd things for the entertainment of bored soldiers, to be laughed at for living in the only structure he could find . . . there was nothing of pride in such a life. He pondered somberly over it often, but did not seek to leave it.

He was lost in broodings one January day as he shuffled slowly along the road that led from the Gap up into the Yellow Creek Valley. He looked up to see a carriage broken down beside the road, a wheel snapped cleanly in two. Beside it stood a woman in a heavy cloak, looking helpless. He stopped and looked at her, and her face turned toward him. For a moment he was staring into a visage from his past: Angel Beamish, who would have become Angel Scarlett if not for his drinking. But this wasn't Angel. The woman stared at him, seeming puzzled or troubled.

It was snowing, but Ben took off his hat as he approached, watching recognition light her face. He used the hat to hide the stump where his hand had been, embarrassed by his imperfection in the presence of this young woman.

"Hello, Miss Deacon," he said, smiling a yellow-toothed smile. "You likely don't remember me. I'm Ben Scarlett, who used to be a drunk in Knoxville, and it's mighty good to see you again."

Amy Deacon was astonished. She had sensed something familiar about this man the moment she saw him, but had he not identified himself, she would have never known him. Back in Knoxville, Scarlett had looked grizzled and older than his years, but now he was haggard beyond anything she had seen before. Thoughts and feelings crowded through her mind: *This man knows who I am . . . this is the fellow who lived with Father on Secession Hill after he sent me away . . . this is the man who wrote that letter to Horatio Eaton that said my father killed Charlie Douglass. . . .*

She nudged up her will and took control of her thoughts. *Be calm, Amy. This could be a difficult situation, and you must be calm.* "Hello, Mr. Scarlett," she said, smiling. "I'm so pleased to see that you are well. Are you here as a soldier?"

It seemed a foolish question; he was more raggedly dressed than the most ill-clad Confederate she had seen, and looked anything but military. But the question had a purpose: She had to know where Scarlett stood in relation to the rebel military occupying the Gap ahead.

"No, ma'am, I ain't a soldier. I ain't fit . . . see here." He moved the hat and showed her the vacant place where a hand should be, looking away with a shamed expression, quickly covering the stump again. "I'm just here as a no-'count. Living in a . . . little place back up the road, and begging off the rebs."

"I see." His answer hadn't given her all the facts she wanted to know. She cast a glance at her baggage in the rear of the carriage, in particular a heavy carpetbag mostly covered by a blanket. A more direct question was in order. "Have you finally decided what side to take in the conflict, Mr. Scarlett?"

"Ma'am, I've been rebel when need be, Union when need be, and at the moment I reckon I'm rebel again, since it's rebels what feeds me. But the truth is I ain't nothing. I'm just me. Just like when you knew me before." He felt embarrassed, telling these things to her. "But I want you to know, Miss Deacon, that I've been better than I am now. For the longest time I was off the liquor, and working for money in a niter mine. Making my own way. I was proud then. I had reason to be."

Amy looked past him; coming up the road were soldiers in gray, a squad of them riding slowly and just about to spot the crippled carriage.

Amy grasped Ben's arm and pulled him around behind the carriage so it blocked both of them from the soldiers' view. "Mr. Scarlett, there is no time for me to explain myself, but you must listen, and you must help me. There are soldiers coming up the road. When they reach me, I will present myself as Mrs. Rosadean Mayberry, and show them some official-looking papers that present me by that name. I want you to do something for me." Reaching around, she pulled out the carpetbag that had been beneath the quilt. "Take this and go into those woods there, and hide with it until I am through dealing with the soldiers. If they take me off with them, keep the bag with you and hide it wherever it is you live. I'll find you later, somehow. And Mr. Scarlett: You must not look inside that bag. And you must not talk about me to anyone, and most of all you must not call me by my real name. Do you understand?"

"I understand." In fact he was quite confused—but he would do what she asked.

"Here." She thrust the bag into his hand. "Go for those woods, and keep this carriage between yourself and the soldiers. Don't let them see you."

"Miss Amy . . . I mean, Miss Rosadean, why are you—"

"No time! Go!"

He trotted off, glancing back and watching to make sure he kept hidden. He entered the woods just in time. The soldiers rode in close, greeted Amy politely with tips of their hats, and gathered around the carriage. An officer talked to Amy, who gestured and pointed at the broken wheel and acted upset, and at one point produced two or three papers that she allowed the officer to study. He nodded, handed them back, and set his men to working on the carriage. Ben watched it all. An hour went by and the soldiers seemed to

be having no luck fixing the broken wheel. Two soldiers
spoke to the officer; he examined the wheel himself, then
talked some more to Amy. Moments later the soldiers were
unloading her bags from the rear of the carriage and placing
her on a horse. Another unhitched the horse, pulling Amy's
carriage. The entire group then turned back toward the Gap,
taking Amy and her horse with them and leaving the broken
carriage where it was.

Ben rose and made his way through the woods back
toward the little outhouse where he lived, carrying the mysterious carpetbag. He wondered what was in it and when
Amy would come for it. Then he was ashamed, realizing
she would see the conditions under which he was living.
Outhouse Ben. It made him feel like nothing, like less than
nothing.

He went into the grove of trees near the burned-out shell
of the house near his privy and found the wagon that Cart
had hidden here long ago. He put the bag up on the back of
it, reasoning that if the soldiers hadn't found this wagon by
now, they probably wouldn't find the carpetbag here, either.

I wonder what's in it? He ached to look, but she had told
him not to. *Got to be strong. Got to resist the temptation.* He
turned away from the wagon and took two steps. Then he
stopped. *I ain't got much of a record of resisting temptation
anyhow. May as well not resist this one, either.*

He went back and fetched the bag. Squatting in the
thicket, he opened the top of it and saw a few items of
clothing. Moving those aside, he saw a surface of plain
cloth just below the clothing. He felt it; something was
beneath it. He tugged at the cloth and found it was in fact a
cloth sack, and what he had thought was beneath it was
inside the sack. He pulled it out, opened the drawstring, and
turned the bag over.

Feminine undergarments fell out, but also money. Neatly
stacked and bound with paper strips, falling out of the frilled
personal wear in which it had been hidden. Confederate
bills, mostly hundred dollar denominations. Thousands of
dollars in all.

He stared at the money for a long time, then played with
it a little. He lifted it to his nose and sniffed it, even put his

tongue to one bill to see what wealth tasted like. Finally he put it into the bag . . . but not all of it. A couple of stacks of bills he retained for himself, stuffing them into the pockets of his ragged clothing. He just couldn't resist it.

"I don't know how you done it, Miss Amy, but you've sure made yourself rich," he whispered to no one. "There must be a hundred thousand dollars or more here."

He brushed the leaves and so on off the bills, put them back into the sack and then into the carpetbag, and arranged the clothing on top of it as close as it had been before. *I wonder if she'll miss them bills I took?* He thought about putting them back . . . but again temptation was stronger than his liquor-weakened will. He hated to steal from Amy Deacon, of all people, but there was just so much money there, so much more than he could ever hope to get in any other way. He knew Confederate money wasn't worth all that much, but in quantities that huge, even devalued dollars counted for a lot.

He went back to his privy, built up his fire, and sat inside, flipping through the bills he had taken but keeping watch all the while to make sure Amy didn't appear and catch him at it.

She didn't show up that day, nor that night, but when Ben awakened the next morning she was there, standing beside the dying remnants of his fire and staring at him inside the privy. He blinked, turned red, then felt bitterly ashamed that she had seen him like this. He supposed some soldier must have told her where she could find him. Told her, and probably laughed about the old drunk who lived in an outhouse. He wondered if she had laughed, too.

"Good morning, Mr. Scarlett," she said.

"Morning," he mumbled without looking up. *Where's them bills? What did I do with them?* He remembered: He had hidden them under a loose board on the other side of the little outhouse.

"I suppose I owe you an explanation of why I behaved so strangely yesterday."

He finger-combed his hair and looked for his hat. It was on the floor. He picked it up, brushed it off, and put it on.

"You don't owe me nothing, Miss Amy. I mean, Miss . . . Rosa . . . Rosadean. That's right, ain't it? Rosadean."

"Mr. Scarlett, let me ask you a question that I will trust you will answer truthfully: Would you betray me if I told you something very secret?"

"No ma'am. I'd never betray you." He came out of the privy. It was humiliating, just having her look at him.

"I'm here under false pretenses, Mr. Scarlett. I can't explain them all fully to you, but suffice it to say it is important that the Confederates not know who I am. Rosadean Mayberry—the thoroughly made-up woman I am pretending to be—is a staunch rebel woman from Morristown, Tennessee, a young woman who has been living in Kentucky since her marriage before the war, but who has lost her husband and is now going back into Morristown to care for her aging parents—both of them good Confederates, too—who have both fallen ill. I have papers giving me passage through any Confederate lines I encounter between here and Morristown. Forged papers, I should say. Forged by agents of the United States government, for who I am acting as an espionage agent." She paused. "Do you understand what I mean, Mr. Scarlett?"

"Yes, ma'am. Means you're a spy."

"That's right. And in telling you that, I've put my life, in effect, into your hands. But you were faithful in what I asked you to do yesterday, and I feel you have the right to know why I asked your help . . . especially in that you might have faced some serious consequences yourself if the truth about me had been uncovered and you were caught as well. To be quite honest, you were a godsend. I had felt like the . . . certain items I'm carrying wouldn't be discovered, but the closer I came to the Gap, the less sure I felt, and when the carriage broke down I felt that somehow that made it more likely they'd search it all very thoroughly and I would be caught. I was right . . . they did search everything I had. If I hadn't been able to pass that certain bag off to you, then . . . I don't much want to think about it."

"I'm pleased I was able to help you, ma'am," he mumbled. "Proud you trusted me."

She smiled. "For some reason, Mr. Scarlett, I believe you

are a trustworthy man. Maybe it's because of the letter you wrote to Horatio Eaton, warning him about my father. I learned all about it, later on."

Ben had nearly forgotten. He nodded.

Her demeanor changed subtly, and her voice. "Tell me something about that, Mr. Scarlett. Did my father . . . did my father kill Charlie Douglass?"

He despised the answer honesty compelled him to give. "Yes, ma'am, I believe so. He wanted me to do it, and I wouldn't. He had took me in at Secession Hill, give me food and liquor and let me sleep in your old room. It was all to ply me and get me to doing what he wanted, and what he wanted was for Charlie Douglass to get shot."

"You didn't do it?"

"The fact is, Charlie was shot in a whole different way before the decision even come up to be made. A rebel fellow shot him there on the street. But if he hadn't, I still wouldn't have done it, no ma'am. I left Doc Deacon right after that, and a few days later Charlie was shot again, this time shot dead. I didn't see it happen, but I know it was the Doc. I had no reason to question it was him."

She did not argue. She had no reason to question it, either.

"I knew the Doc was after your friend Horatio Eaton, too, and that's why I sent him that letter. But how'd you know?"

"Horatio Eaton came to Greeneville. Fleeing from my father, who had threatened him in his yard with a shotgun. I saw the letter then." She looked wistful. "My father's dead, you know. And Secession Hill is burned to the ground."

"I read about it in a newspaper. I'm sorry for you, miss. I know losing a father's hard, no matter what the circumstance."

"Thank you." She sighed. "I suppose maybe I'm trying to make up for some of his sins, working for the Union. My! I'm speaking far too freely with you, Mr. Scarlett. I'm in violation of everything I've been taught. But I just can't help but trust you."

"I 'preciate that." He thought of the two stacks of bills he had taken and felt guilty.

"Where is my carpetbag?" she asked.

"It's hid. I'll take you to it."

He led her to the grove and the edge of the thicket inside. "I'll go fetch it," he said. "You'll just mess up your clothes in there." He went in, vanished from her sight a minute or so, then came out again, the bag in hand.

"Here," he said.

"Thank you." She hefted it in her hand, as if testing its weight. "Mr. Scarlett, did you look inside?"

"No! No, ma'am. No. You told me not to, and I didn't." The guilt burned like fire now.

"I knew I could trust you." She smiled. He smiled back, with difficulty, and very feebly.

"Did they get your carriage fixed?"

"Yes, though not too well. I don't know if it will make it the rest of the way."

"Too bad I can't go with you," he said. "I was a carpenter some while I was working the niter mine. Pretty good at it. I reckon I could fix a wagon if it busted. Even with one hand."

"Is that right? Yes, it's too bad you can't go."

"Uh-huh. Well, it's been a pleasure to see you, Miss Amy . . . Miss Rosadean. I hope you make it through safe and sound with that bag of . . . bag of whatever it is you're carrying."

"Yes. Thank you, Mr. Scarlett. You've been a boon to me yet again. Can I count on you to keep everything I told you secret?"

"You know you can."

"Thank you." She hesitated, then approached him, leaned up and kissed his whiskery cheek. Kissed him despite his smell, his appearance, his raggedness—despite everything, and it was almost enough to bring tears to his eyes.

"Thank you, miss. Thank you. God bless you." He paused. "And God bless the United States."

"Amen, Mr. Scarlett. Amen to that. And good-bye."

She returned to the base camp of the Confederate guards and managed to sneak the bag in among her other luggage without it being seen. She was thankful now that her luggage had been searched, because it would not be searched again. She was not the first courier of counterfeit Confederate money to pass through Cumberland Gap, sent down with bills printed at Frankfort, Kentucky, and passed into circulation among the Confederate states in an effort to devastate an already trembling economy. Some couriers had been caught; she did not want to become one of them. This was service she wished to do well, the work she had taken on under the recruitment of suave Jonathon Eaton.

This was dangerous work, but for the first time since the war began, she was satisfied. Amy Deacon had never been one to sit to the side. She was a participant, an activist, a young woman with a vision of what the world should be and the desire to try to make that vision real. She kept her eyes forward, seldom looking at what was past.

But as she rode along now, however, she did look back. Meeting Ben Scarlett had made her think of past days, before war, before division and the destruction of families and the deaths of good men like Hannibal Deacon. There was much in her past that Amy was glad to be free of, but there were portions, isolated points of sunlight and happiness, that were bittersweet in her recollections. Oddly, one of those bright occasions was the time Ben Scarlett had helped her hang flyers for that star-crossed secession rally, the time he had told her how she put him in mind of a fine lady he had loved and lost. That had meant much to her; it was a sweet and endearing thing she would not forget.

She thought about Ben Scarlett and wondered how he had lost his hand. She had declined to ask about it, for it was obvious that the mutilation embarrassed him.

She rode on for many miles and was deep in isolated forest hills when the wagon wheel broke again. She realized at once, with a glint of cold fear, that she would be passing the night here.

Perhaps more than a night. She would have to find some means of having the wagon fixed again, if it was fixable. She examined it, unable to make the determination herself. It was unnerving to feel so isolated and vulnerable, but she vowed to herself to tough it out. It was her duty.

She hid the carpetbag with the money in the woods

nearby, in case anyone should come along tonight and steal what was in the carriage. Her luggage could go; she was willing to sacrifice any of that. But the counterfeit money had to make it through to its designated drop-off point near Knoxville, whereupon she would—if all went well—be conveyed by prearrangement to Union-held Nashville, from there to circle back into Kentucky and begin the process anew and in some other fashion.

She threw another wrap across her shoulders and wondered just how cold it would get before morning came, and if, after all, she really had the grit it took for this kind of work.

Chapter 33

Ben dreamed up several plausible reasons to explain why he set out on the track of Amy Deacon's carriage not an hour after she left Cumberland Gap. He told himself he felt guilty for stealing the currency and wanted to return it—which was true, though not as great a motivator as he pretended—and that she shouldn't be traveling alone in such dangerous country, but required for safety a man with her, even if only a no-account, one-handed vagabond. These were his calculated reasons, but in fact there were reasons far more fundamental, if not as consciously explicated.

It was simply a matter of options. If he remained at Cumberland Gap, Ben Scarlett had nothing to look forward to except living in a privy and receiving scraps of food from soldiers who were themselves underfed, and who held him in scorn even as they fed him like a dog. He couldn't take any more of that. Seeing Amy again, and receiving her kiss, had stirred up what little flame of pride remained in him, and made him ashamed of what he had fallen to.

It was manifestly foolish, this walking out in the open, dressed in tatters, moving through heavily occupied territory where he might be stopped at any point merely because he looked suspicious. But what the devil! What was there to lose except the shame of being "Outhouse Ben"? No more of that. He was leaving that behind, and good riddance.

She had said she was going toward Knoxville. Very well, he would go toward Knoxville, too. If he were lucky, he'd find her. If not . . . well, he'd worry about that later, if need be. For now it simply felt good to be doing *something*. And he figured he had little to fear. One glance at this one-handed bag of tatters would tell anyone there was nothing here worth bothering with in any way. Maybe softhearted folks along the way would even take him for a maimed former soldier and give him help.

He hoped that if he could move fast enough and Amy slowly enough, he might actually catch up with her on the road and she'd invite him to go with her. He imagined what that would be like, sitting up there in that carriage with so fine and pretty a woman, feeling proud to be in her company just like that day he had walked Gay Street at her side, carrying those broadsides.

It didn't cross his mind to analyze very deeply how he felt about Amy Deacon. He hadn't yet bothered to consider that he was suddenly obsessed with a young woman who until recently he hadn't seen since the night of Doc Deacon's Secession rally, a woman maybe a decade and a half his junior, who had no reason to think of him as anything more than something to be treated kindly out of pity.

He strode on, whistling, swinging his arms—hand forward, stump back, hand back, stump forward—energized by purpose. Happier than he had been in weeks, he made remarkably good time along the road.

He was soon exhausted, and stopped at the first real community he came to and took shelter in a shed almost as nice as the Baumgardner shed back in Knoxville. Furthermore, it was built up against a barn that contained a root cellar in one corner, and in that cellar he found vegetables, to which he helped himself, stuffing his pockets full and leaving by way of a back fence with his clothing bulging with the stolen food.

He headed toward the Clinch River, cheerful about the food but more sober about what he was doing. The novelty was wearing off, reality settling in. How reasonable was it for him to expect Amy Deacon to be pleased to see him? She was a Union agent, for heaven's sake, carrying a wealth of Confederate currency for some reason, a woman who had to be unencumbered, ready to move and react without the burden of an old drunk hanging around. He didn't like those thoughts but couldn't help thinking them. He also couldn't help marching right along in spite of them, determined to see Amy Deacon again whether it made sense or not.

He was three miles along his day's journey when he realized that just maybe, at the moment she planted that kiss on his cheek, he might have fallen a little in love. Maybe he had been in love with Amy Deacon all along, from that evening he helped her hang broadsides in Knoxville. Maybe her resemblance to a woman he had once planned to marry had his instincts confused. At this point he couldn't say.

He passed soldiers, mostly small groups of two or three, but one time encountering a big squad of them that marched across in front of him at a crossroad. No one paid him any heed beyond glancing at his stumped arm. No one asked any questions.

He kept on walking, muscles growing sore, unaccustomed to this much exercise.

He encountered the carriage on a cold, shaded stretch of road, still sitting where it had broken down. There was no luggage in it. No one around. Ben grew concerned. This surely looked like Amy's carriage. The same wheel was broken as before, and as he studied it he could see the signs of repair done at the Gap. Her carriage indeed. But where was Amy?

He peered around, saw no sign of her. "Miss Amy!" he hollered, cupping his one hand beside his mouth. "Amy Deacon! Where are you? Are you all right?"

A movement in the woods behind him made him turn. Amy Deacon emerged, covered with brambles and carrying her money-filled carpetbag. Her face was red with fury and in that state bore a resemblance to her father's countenance—a little unsettling to Ben.

"How *dare* you shout my real name, Ben Scarlett!" she scolded. "Didn't I tell you that under no circumstances were you to use it?"

Ben gaped, mouth hanging open for several moments. "I forgot, Miss Amy . . . Miss Rosadean. I seen the carriage broke down, and feared something had happened to you, and I plumb forgot."

Her expression softened. "Well, don't forget again. And tell me why in the name of heaven you've followed me."

"I . . . well, I followed you, you see . . . I wanted to . . ." He hung his head, reached into his pocket and pulled out the two stacks of currency. Holding them out, head still down, he peered upward to see how she reacted.

Her first response was to stare at the money for a moment, then at him—there was that Doc Deacon look again—then to rush up, snatch the bills, and quickly stuff them inside the carpetbag. "And I thought I could trust you!" she said. "Is that all you took?"

"Yes, Miss Amy . . . Rosadean. I'm sorry. So sorry I decided I had to bring it back and give it to you."

"It's a good thing you did." Though they were surrounded by woods and well away from any house, she began talking in a near whisper. "You know what that is? It's counterfeit Confederate currency, that's what!"

"Counterfeit . . . you mean, not real?"

"No, of course it's not real. It's printed by the United States government and transferred into the Confederacy and put into circulation."

"Why would the Union want rebels having more money?"

"It's because it's false money, don't you see? It hurts the Confederate economy for it to circulate."

"Oh. I see." He didn't. Economics beyond simple exchange or barter was far beyond his ken.

Amy went on: "It's my job to deliver this money to a recipient at Knoxville. If every dollar hadn't been accounted for, I would have been held responsible. Do you realize how deep the trouble you almost got me into? Are you sure every bill is back?"

"Yes, Miss Amy . . . Miss Rosadean. Every bill. I promise. I didn't know I was getting you in trouble. I didn't!"

"Oh, so you thought the money was simply mine, and you would steal it from me. Is that it?"

"I brought it back!"

"Yes, you did, but . . ." She paused, sighed. "Yes, you did. And I thank you for that—though I'm furious that you took it in the first place."

"You got every right to be mad. Every right."

There was a long, uncomfortable silence. Desperate to end it, he dug into his pocket and produced a raw potato. Slapping on his most pleasant look, he asked, "Want a victual?"

She looked at the potato, at the bedraggled, grinning man holding it, and burst into laughter. Partly it was a venting of tension, partly a recognition of something funny and a bit touching in Ben's look and manner. "I do," she said, taking the potato, which she polished clean like an apple with her cloak. "I haven't eaten since yesterday." She took a big bite and chewed it. "Not bad. I've never eaten a raw potato before."

Ben produced a potato for himself and bit into it without bothering to clean it first. "I've eat many a tater like this. And raw beans, raw turnips, corn. A man in my situation eats what he can, whatever form he finds it in. Why, once when I was drunk, I ate a dead roach. Thought it was a bit of hard candy. He crunched like a . . . oh, sorry. Not the kind of thing to think on while you're crunching a tater." He took another bite. "How'd the carriage break down?"

"It just broke down, simple as that. The wheel gave way just like the first time."

"I ain't a mechanic, but I've worked on a wheel or two in my time, and I don't believe that one can be fixed again."

"Neither do I. So what do you suggest we do, Mr. Scarlett?"

He didn't miss that she had said *we*. "Walk, I guess. Or steal a horse or two. Where's your horse, anyhow?"

"Gone. And horses are hard to come by, they tell me. The rebel army has almost all of them."

"Then I reckon we'll walk. I'll carry that bag for you, if you want. I promise I'll not run off with it."

She handed it to him.

"You got more bags than this, ain't you?"

"They're gone. In the night I grew a little scared out here alone, and went into the woods. Somebody came along on the road—I heard them, didn't see them—and this morning all my baggage was gone. The horse, too. Everything except for the money, which I had taken into the woods with me. It's a good thing I did. And I have my pass papers still, thank God. I always keep them on me."

"Smart, you doing that."

"If I'd been smart I'd have taken all my baggage into the woods, and my horse, and not lost anything."

"Well, like I always say, what's did is done, and what's done is did. Ain't nothing gained by worrying over it. And if you'd took that horse in the woods, it might have made noise and drawed them thieves right to you. Want another tater?"

"Yes. And that carrot in your shirt pocket there. Good heavens, Mr. Scarlett! I just realized you don't have on a coat! Aren't you freezing?"

"I got on three pairs of pants and four shirts." He peeked down his collar. "No, five. I'm warm, don't you worry."

She laughed again—a sound as sweet to him as the first time he had heard it. He gave her the vegetables. Hefting the bag in his hand, he set out striding, with Amy keeping pace right beside him.

"What will happen to us if rebels find us carrying this money?"

"We'll be robbed at the very least. Taken prisoner, most likely. Maybe worse."

"Oh."

"You still want to go on with me?"

"Yes. I'd go anywhere with you, Miss Amy . . . Miss Rosadean. I don't care what happens, long as I'm hoofing along with you."

She smiled oddly, lips together, and quickly looked away. He wondered if he'd said something he shouldn't have.

They paid a black boy to ferry them by canoe across the river at an unfrequented spot, then skirted around Maynardville and slept in the woods in a recess where warmer air lingered and the cold wind couldn't reach them. Amy curled up on the leaves, her head on her carpetbag. Ben sat up against a tree, "keeping watch." In fact he snored the night away. His days as Outhouse Ben had accustomed him to sleeping upright, and he was quite comfortable under the tree, though he was stiff by morning.

They went on, heading south toward Knoxville. By now Ben was sure he was in love and willing to fully admit it to himself. By the time they traveled through the vicinity of Gravestown, he was equally ready to confess that he was a fool. He had no business falling in love with anyone. He had nothing to offer any woman, especially one so fine as Amy.

They ate the last of Ben's purloined food and soon were hungry again. "There'll be food for us at Knoxville," Amy said. "And I'll try to arrange some payment for you for the help you're giving me. I can't make promises, but I think I can do it."

Once again he was to be paid for helping out Amy Deacon. Just like in Knoxville, hanging those broadsides. He smiled. Amy Deacon always seemed to bring good things to him.

They came to a spring and drank, kneeling side by side and dipping water in their hands. It was difficult for Ben to gather much water in his one hand, and Amy, seeing this, cupped her own hands together and lifted them to his lips. He hesitated, then drank. She dipped her hands again, offered him another drink. He shook his head. His face had gone solemn and thoughtful.

The ripples in the water stilled. For a few moments they lingered there in the quiet. Ben leaned over and looked deeply at his own reflection, then at Amy's.

"What are you thinking about?" she asked.

"Just thinking about me. Just thinking about . . . nothing."

She smiled. "Well, thinking about yourself, that's thinking about something, isn't it?"

He didn't smile. "No," he said. "It ain't. Not for Ben Scarlett."

He stood and splashed through the stream to the other side. Amy stood, troubled by his manner and words, and followed.

When they reached the northern fringes of Knoxville, Amy pointed to a decrepit old two-story building. There was no sign above the door or in the yard, but Ben knew this place —an old hotel, operated by an even older man and his bent-over wife.

"There's the place I'll be leaving the currency," she said. "There'll be a man there, waiting for me."

"So you've done your job. Congratulations to you."

"Yes." She smiled. "And you've helped me so very much. I've felt much more safe, traveling with someone."

"It wasn't much. I had nothing better to do."

"You wait for me, Ben. When I'm finished inside, I'll come back. I've been thinking. I'm going to see if I can make arrangements to take you on to Nashville with me . . . if you want to go. The Union has Nashville, you know. There'd be safety there for you."

"Nashville . . ."

"Would you like to go there with me?"

"I'll . . . think on it. While you're inside."

"Good. Good. Now wait for me. See that grove of trees? Wait there. I'll be back soon."

"Good luck to you in yonder, Miss Amy."

"Thank you, Ben."

He entered the grove and sat down beneath a tree, wishing he had something to drink. He felt very sad just now, and liquor would help. It always helped, for a little while.

He had a partial view of the old hotel from where he sat,

but the shutters were closed and he could not see past the windows. Closed shutters seemed to fit the situation. The kind of business Amy Deacon was involved in couldn't be done where people could see.

Nashville . . . a city he had never seen. What would it be like? How long would it take to get there? Traveling with Amy, it wouldn't matter how long. Long was good, if he was in her company.

For a time he pictured it, seeing the journey in a light of hazy glory, seeing himself proud and fine-looking, envied by those who saw him at Amy's side. . . .

Then rose the image he had seen reflected in the spring-water earlier. The reality that was Ben Scarlett. He smiled sadly and shook his head. "Ah, well."

Digging into the pocket of one of the several shirts he wore, he produced a stubby pencil, and from another pocket an old bill of sale for barrel staves, made out in the name of the man who had owned and cast off the ragged shirt before Ben picked it up. Turning the bill facedown, he spread it over his knee, licked the dull pencil tip and began to write, pinning the paper against his knee with the stump of his wrist.

Absorbed in his work, he did not notice the old man who slipped out the front door of the hotel, looked furtively from side to side, and began heading down the road at a surprisingly fast pace toward a place about a half mile ahead, where lines of rising smoke gave evidence of a rebel encampment.

When the note was done, Ben read it to himself, mouthing the words silently. A frown creased his forehead; he chewed on the end of the pencil.

"No, Ben. You'd best not say that," he muttered aloud. "She don't need to hear that from you. You just keep that there little thought to yourself, old fool." He pinned the paper on his knee again and carefully tore off the bottom of it, thereby removing the last words on the page. He flipped that scrap away and read the letter one more time.

Finished, he nodded. No fine bit of writing, certainly, nothing to impress a talented wordsmith like Amy Deacon, but it said what needed saying, and left unsaid what needed to be unsaid, and so it would do.

He left the note beneath a stone in as visible a spot as he could find. Glancing at the hotel, he lifted his one hand in a brief wave, sighed, and began trudging through the woods, heading into town by a route that would not take him past guard posts or rebel camps.

It probably made little sense to stay around Knoxville, he figured. For all he knew, the name of Ben Scarlett had been tied to the death of Charlie Douglass and the law was looking for him. Yet he went on nonetheless, drawn by the need to be near that which was familiar, and not finding himself much able to care whether there was danger for him where he was going. He was leaving the best he had known in years behind him in that hotel, and it hardly seemed to matter now what became of him.

In his mind he prayed for Amy Deacon, and for liquor.

Ben was well on his way to town and out of sight of the hotel when the little band of soldiers rose to its porch, dismounted, and walked swiftly in. Ben was not there to hear the muffled hammering on a closed door, the gruffly shouted demand for entry under authority of the Confederate States of America, nor to see Amy Deacon and a dapper, defiant-looking slender fellow being hustled out the front door some moments later, Amy's carpetbag of counterfeit currency in the hand of a triumphantly grinning soldier.

Another soldier tied the dapper fellow's hands behind his back, roughly. They did not tie Amy, but put her on one of the horses, giving her many stern warnings and telling her that any attempt to escape was futile and could result in injury. Bawdy commentary and laughter rose from some of the soldiers, aimed at the terrified female prisoner, but an officer quickly quieted that.

They headed up the road toward Knoxville, the dapper fellow walking, looking surprisingly nonchalant, and Amy Deacon trying to look brave, giving one wide-eyed glance across her shoulder toward a nearby grove of trees.

* * *

A roaming young boy meandered into that grove half an hour later and saw a paper weighted to the ground by a stone. Curious, he picked it up. Squinting, he read it, picking out the words despite their atrocious spelling and poor penmanship:

Dear ~~Miss Amy~~ woops Miss Rosa Deen,

Sorry but I had to go on and not wate for you. Thank you for being so nise to ask me to com with you to Knashville, but I reckin I had better stay abowt Knoxville, sinse it is my home and it is time I com back to it. I want to tell you I am prowd to have traveled with you and that you have give me much joy jist by your kind and frendly ways with me. You ar the nisest woman I no. I thenk hyer of you than you can no, but I am no more than a drunk and will never be no more than that so you do not need to be abowt me for long. But wear ever it is you go I want you to no there is one fellow who will alwase smile to thenk of you and will alwase wish he was mor than he is so that you mite thenk hyer of him than you can now. I thenk you are Fine. Please do not forgit me but when you can say a prair for old Ben and no he has not forgot you neether.

Good by my good frend and God bless you for you desarve it.

Your frend,
BEN S.
Good by.

None of it made much sense to the boy. He shrugged, wadded the paper and threw it into the brush. He noticed a smaller torn scrap of the same paper lying among the leaves. Picking it up, he smoothed it and read words penned by the same hand that had scribed the letter. Apparently it had been torn from the very bottom of the page, below the closing:

Be keerful Miss Rosa Deen for I love you.

The boy shook his head. The scrap meant no more to him than had the letter itself. A love letter, as best he could tell, just a lot of gush and sentiment, nothing interesting to a boy. Rolling the torn-off paper scrap into a little ball, he popped it into his mouth just to have something to chew on, and meandered out of the grove, going on his way.

Chapter 34

Sometime in the harsh North Carolina winter of 1862–63, demons came to the mountains.

They whispered in the ears of tormented people and those who brought the torment, stirring hatred, cruelty, vengeance. Suffering was their pleasure, hunger their meat. The demons of war feasted well that season, glutting themselves on the hunger of the deprived folks, a hunger so deep it put despairing mountain wives to writing plaintively to their men on distant military lines:

My Dear Edward—

I have always been proud of you, and since your connection with the Confederate army I have been prouder than ever before. I would not have you do anything wrong for the world, but before God, Edward, unless you come home, we must die. Last night I was aroused by little Eddie's crying. I called, "What's the matter, Eddie?" and he said, "Oh, Mama, I'm so hungry." And Lucy, Edward, your darling Lucy, she never complains, but she is growing thinner and Edward, unless you come home we must die.

Many soldiers who received such letters did come home, risking the ultimate penalty paid by deserters. They were weary men who had long ago forgotten the notions of "glory" that had sent them to the lines. They were no longer sure for what reason they fought, or why they were expected to leave their families to suffering and death while they were away. And so, many such men spat off their military servitude like bad and bitter food, and returned to the mountains to do what they could for those they loved.

But once home again they found themselves not really home at all. In the mountains were others who sought to catch and punish such men as they. Rebel Home Guards ranged and hunted, often behaving little better than the bushwhackers who committed depravity in the name of both sides or neither. Those who desired merely a peaceful life away from war had much to fear from the Home Guards and the conscription enforcers, and were compelled to hide. In caverns, crude hovels, and even hollow trees throughout the North Carolina highland wilderness lived men who dared not return to their own houses, houses perhaps within sight of the miserable places they took shelter, because they knew that hostile men were waiting and watching for them to show themselves.

The demons whispered in the ears of these exiles, and in the ears of those who pursued them, and hatred grew like a well-fed parasite. There was violence, more and more of it, worse and worse. The old people who claimed to have "the sight" declared they heard death howling in the nighttime wind. Even those who could not hear death's howls could see its results. Corpses were found with growing frequency, lying open-mouthed and fatally shot in woodland hollows or kneeling in an eternal pose of prayer across logs and tree stumps, bullets fired into the backs of their heads at close range. Many slain ones were never found at all, their fates forever unknown to the wives and children they left behind.

Those left behind cried often, because they missed those who had been taken from them, and because they were hungry. There was little meat to be had, and little salt with which to preserve it, anyway.

Yet there were warehouses full of salt in the towns, controlled by Confederate overlords. At those dispensaries, desperate mountain families were told that of course they could have the salt they needed—all they need do to obtain it was have the deserted, Unionist, or conscription-dodging father of the household turn himself in for his due punishment. Then salt would be theirs. If they were uncooperative, however, there would be no salt, and quite possibly no survival through the hard winter.

Even the fortunate ones who had salt and meat, however, could not be assured of survival. Women and children lived in mortal fear of those who rode in without warning and threatened the lives of the old grandparents, or the weak new babies of the household, unless the wives would do their "duty" and reveal to them the whereabouts of their hiding husbands. Sometimes the worst of such men would torture those they questioned, beating women with hickory canes until they bled, tying old men and old women to trees by their wrists, leaving them hanging in the cold. They leashed new mothers to trees and lay their squalling newborns naked in the snow, just out of reach, saying that of course they were reasonable, of course they were humane, and of course the wailing mothers could have their babies back . . . just as quickly as they told where their husbands were hidden.

The demons cajoled, whispered, laughed in the deep hollows and on the high peaks. It seemed to many that they sometimes took the form of men, and that hell had come to the hills.

It was into that hell that Jim Matoy and Hendrix Cart came in the first cold days of 1863.

They appeared without warning, five men with five raised rifles and grins that weren't really grins, ugly and threatening in the twilight.

"That's far enough, both of you'ns," said one of them, a stocky fellow with an auburn beard and wide nose. "Get them hands up, and stay still until we can get a good look at you'ns."

Jim Matoy and Hendrix Cart raised their hands slowly. Matoy's hands trembled. He was glad for the biting cold, because it gave an excuse for the trembling, but he knew that faced with men like these, he would have been trembling, cold or not.

"Thunder!" One of the others exclaimed. "That there's Hendrix Cart right there, or I'm a darky!"

"Why, so it is!" said the stocky man. "Hendrix, I thought you'd gone from these hills forevermore."

"Frank? Frank Stricklin, is that you?" Cart said.

"It is, Hendrix. What? Can't you see me?"

"I can't, Frank. I'm almost blind. It's been coming on slow. All I see is light and shadow. That's all."

"You don't mean it! Blind? Law, I'm sorry to hear that."

"Can we take our hands down?"

"Depends. Who's this red coon with you, and why you with him?"

"That there ain't no red coon, just a free mulatter who's helping me get home."

"Mulatter? No! Looks like an Injun to me, Hendrix."

"He does, or that's what I been told. I can't see him my own self, of course. But everybody says to me, 'That there mulatter sure does look like an Injun.' Sort of interesting, don't you know, everybody saying that, and him not being an Injun at all."

"Go ahead and put down your hands, Hendrix. But I want your friend here, whatever breed he is, to keep his up. I don't trust niggers of any color, red or black."

"Frank, he ain't going to hurt nobody. If you won't trust him, you can trust me."

"Can I, Hendrix? They tell me you're Secesh."

Cart paused, having detected a new and subtle cold undertone in Frank Stricklin's voice. Jim Matoy, hands still up and muscles already beginning to hurt from holding them that way, detected it, too, and thought: *Oh, no.* He knew right off that trouble was coming. They had run across Union men here, and if Cart was too blind to see the ice in Frank Stricklin's gaze, Matoy was not.

"Well," Cart said, picking through his words like he was tiptoeing shoeless through shards of glass, "I reckon I've leaned toward the Secesh, yes, but I try to get on good with everybody, no matter where they stand." He chuckled impotently, his useless eyes rolling in their sockets.

"There ain't no fence-straddling nor getting on good anymore, Hendrix. Things have got bad since you left these mountains. Real bad. Why'd you leave, anyhow?"

"My Jen and me had a falling out. I had come to think she warn't faithful. Hey, Frank, why you talking in so mean a tone? I ain't here to harm nobody."

"War's war, Hendrix. War's war, and war's mean."

War's mean. Matoy found those words foreboding. Something was afoot here, and it would not end pleasantly.

"Well, won't you at least let my mulatter friend put his hands down?"

As much as Matoy longed to put his hands down, he wished Cart would quit asking about it.

"Hendrix, I can't let him put 'em down. You see, that ain't no mulatter, no matter what you say. That there's an Injun, and there's been a whole bad piece of trouble for Union folk from the Injuns. They've took up for the Secesh, them stinking heathens have, and they've been cruel, bloody-handed cruel."

"Frank, I can tell you ain't happy with the situation. I can sure tell it. But I want to tell you, my mulatter, whether he's really a mulatter or not, he ain't one of them Secesh redskins you're talking about. He ain't been causing nobody trouble hereabouts. Why, he's been with me, up in the Cumberland Mountains in Kentucky."

"Why you come back here, Hendrix?"

"I want to be with Jen again. Living ain't going to be the same for me from now on, me being blind. It's my fault, drinking bad whiskey and such. But I want to be back with my woman again."

Jim Matoy's arms were made of stone. Holding them up was torture, but he was sure that if he let them fall, he would die on the spot.

"Your woman ain't your woman no longer, Hendrix."

"What'd you . . . what's that, now?"

"You deaf as well as blind? I said Jen's not your woman no more. She's took up with a Union man. Did you know that? He's living right there in her house with her. His name's Colter. Joe Colter, from over at Marshall. She's hiding him from the rebs, and from the law, too. They say he's a murderer."

Jim Matoy felt something kick inside his stomach and blood surge hot in his temples. He wondered, quite seriously, whether his ears had just fooled him. No, they hadn't. Frank Stricklin had just called the name of Joe Colter! Colter, the very slayer of Skaantee, a man that not long ago he was swearing to kill in vengeance —he was living in the house of Jen Cart!

Cart said, "Frank, don't you be goading about that. Not about my woman."

"Ain't no goading to it. It's true. This here man's living with your Jen, right there under the same roof. Sleeping on the same bed, too, I'll lay a wager. Ain't no telling what else he's doing with her. That woman of yours, she'd lay with anything on two legs. She'd probably lay with that Injun you got there with you, or with a darky buck."

"Frank, you shut that kind of talk up! You hear me?"

"Facts is facts. Your Jen ain't no better than a common harlot, Hendrix. But you know what? I hold her in higher regard than I could ever hold you, just because she's Union. She's faithful to the flag even if she ain't faithful to her man."

Matoy knew Cart well enough by now to detect when he was losing his self-control. An odd quiver would come into his voice, and a subtle scratching undertone. So it was as Cart spoke his next words. "You're mighty brave, ain't you, Frank! Talking that way to a blind man! You put a knife in my hand and a blindfold on your eyes and we'll fight it man-to-man, even terms!"

"Hear that, men? He threatened me. You hear it? Threatened to knife me! Why'd you threaten me, Hendrix?"

Matoy spoke. "Mr. Cart, they're looking for a reason to shoot you. Don't let them make you mad."

The men with the guns laughed. "Hear that? He says we're wanting to shoot you, Hendrix. Why should I shoot you? You think I still carry a grudge over what your brother done to me? That was a long time ago. You think I ain't forgot?"

"He wasn't my brother! He was a half brother, and I didn't like having to claim even that. And none of that was my doing!"

Jim Matoy wondered what the pair were talking about. Whatever it was, it indicated longstanding bad blood between Cart's family and Stricklin's, and, he suspected, was far more truly at the root of the present tension than anything that had been talked about openly so far.

Matoy was destined never to know what Cart's half brother, of whom Cart had never spoken to Matoy, had done to anger Stricklin. After Cart's last defensive comment, Stricklin swore, lay down his rifle, pulled out a revolver in its place, and shot Cart through the heart. Cart fell with a grunt, blood spreading fast across his chest, arms flailing, but only for a moment. Death came quickly.

Matoy didn't stand to gape. He turned and ran into the thickest part of the woods, dodging behind a tree and then a laurel thicket. To his surprise, no one shot at him for a moment or two, perhaps astonished by the speed of his flight. He ran hard, hitting a hill and going up it at full speed. Glancing over his shoulder, he saw one of the men raising his rifle. Matoy ducked and cut left just as the shot was fired, and was not hit. He kept running, and heard them coming after him.

It went on like this for a very long time. Matoy lost track of direction and distance, the impetus being to run, always run, no matter to where as long as he was getting away from those who chased him. Another glance back revealed he had left all but two of them behind. Redoubling his effort, he sucked air in through a mouth stretched wide against his teeth, breath hissing. He looked back again. Only one chasing him now.

He had escaped! If he had outrun all the others, he could outrun this one as well. He reached another hill, ran up it and came out at the top just in time to see the land vanish beneath him. He kicked in the air, turning to the side, and fell fifteen feet to the woods floor below the bluff he had just found in the most undesirable way.

Years' worth of leaves gathered there were sufficient to save him from injury, but not enough to keep him from being badly stunned, the wind knocked from him. He lay with head spinning and hurting, lungs suffering for want of air, and heard the last pursuer coming around and down the bluff behind him, where it was more hill than precipice. He tried to get up but couldn't move.

The man loomed above him. He was big and the run had been hard on him, so for a while he did nothing but stand heaving, sweating, hunching over, staring red-faced at Matoy while his hard breath drove droplets of spittle out of the corners of his mouth.

"Gotcha . . . redskin, " he said when he was able.

Matoy regained his own breath at last and sucked it in with a hard moan.

"Gotcha . . . sure did have to . . . run hard to do it."

Matoy's lungs ached, strained by the sudden intrusion of air. Yet he still had no strength to stand, and his vision was blurry.

"Well . . . here we go," the man said, pulling a pistol from his belt. It was an old flintlock pistol of Revolutionary War vintage. He clicked back the lock and aimed it at Matoy's face. His finger squeezed down, but at the last moment he diverted his aim and sent the ball blasting into the ground a foot to the right of Matoy's head. The sting of the powder bursting into Matoy's skin made him think at first that he was shot, but passing moments and clearing gun smoke brought comprehension: He had been spared.

"A Cherokee spared my grandpap in just such a way many a year ago," the man said, putting away the pistol. "Now I've returned mercy for mercy. The others will have heard the shot and figure I killed you. You lie there and get your wind back, and if you find you can move, you can get out of here come dark. Don't you never show yourself around here again, though. The balance has been set right, and I'd not show such mercy again. Your kind ain't welcome in these mountains no more. Get on out of here and back to your own places, or lie right here and die, if you want to. It's all the same to me. You understand me, you red coon?"

The man turned and strode away without waiting for an answer. Matoy watched him climb the escarpment with much effort and grunting. He reached the top, looked down one time at the fallen Cherokee below, then vanished from sight.

That night, salt raiders struck in the little town of Marshall.

They swept into town without warning, a band of fifty or so, many of them driven by months of mistreatment and deprivation, and the looming threat of starvation for their families. They carried no fire, gave out no whoops or yells, and in fact worked to make as little stir as possible.

Of the salt raiders, some were common hill farmers, others mountain irregulars, but most were deserters from the 64th North Carolina Regiment. All had suffered, and watched their loved ones suffer, too. They broke into the warehouse and began stealing the salt supplies, as well as blankets and bolts of cloth stored in the building.

Among them was Joe Colter, who had within the past week left the house of Jen Cart. He had seen frequent suspicious movement in the woods near the house, felt eyes upon him, sensed danger hidden around him. For the sake of Jen Cart's safety, he had left the protection of her home and taken to the hills, taking on the netherworld of life of an outlier or "scouter." He, as much as any single man among the raiders, had concocted the idea of the salt raid.

The raiders worked feverishly. Joe Colter helped move the stolen goods at the beginning, but because of the slowing effect of his old injuries, he was relieved of that work. He stood outside the warehouse, standing guard.

A lone man in a gray military uniform rode in some minutes later and approached the warehouse. He accosted Colter, demanding to know what was going on here, demanding that this obvious theft stop at once. Joe spat angry words back at him. Another of the salt raiders stepped forward and put an end to all conversation with a blast from his rifle. The challenger in gray fell from his horse. He rose quickly, gripping a wounded arm, and ran back into the night, the raiders laughing at him, cursing at him. They went back to their work, unloading the contents of the warehouse, then dissolved into the night, scattering in different directions.

Not all of them, however, dispersed. Some of the more bitter among them, driven to their deed not only by need but also out of hatred for those who oppressed them, came quickly together in the hills near Marshall. The spirit of vengeance was high. The war demons circled and whispered encouragement to them, and they listened.

This group was made up mostly of deserters from the 64th Regiment, along with Joe Colter and a few others with no affiliation with the 64th, but with a driving hatred for it and any other rebel military force. They headed for the house of Colonel Lawrence M. Allen, commander of the 64th. He was not home; the 64th was at the moment stationed at Bristol, Tennessee, guarding—of all things—salt that had come from the works at Saltville, Virginia. But Allen's wife and three children were home, along with some servants.

The raiders burst into the house without warning and began to plunder. They found two of Colonel Allen's children deathly ill with scarlet fever, but showed no pity. They took blankets, shoes, clothing, money—even the garments of the ailing children, folded beside their beds. So sick they could hardly understand what was going on, the children watched the grizzled intruders through slitted, fever-weakened eyes. The raiders gave them no word of sympathy. They had children of their own who also suffered. Suffered because of rebel conscripters and rebel officers, such as Lawrence Allen, who punished men for deserting, even when desertion was the only way those men could keep their families alive.

They left the Allen house at last, and raided the homes of some other Confederates and Confederate sympathizers nearby. Then they were gone, appeased for the moment, the work of vengeance done and fury sated, waiting now for the responsive fury that would surely come in turn.

Jim Matoy had never been more perplexed in his life. Alone now, very sore from his run and his fall—but seemingly uninjured, thankfully—joyful to be alive, yet shaken by the near touch of death that had come during the day, hating the man who had chased him and made him fall, yet loving him because he had shown him mercy . . . how could he know how to feel and think at such a time? Matoy was living just now on the sharp edge where conflicts and contradictions come together, and trying to make sense of matters inherently unsensible.

One aspect of it rang clear through the muddle: the name of Joe Colter. Joe Colter, Skaantee's murderer, living in the house of Hendrix Cart's estranged wife!

Mere weeks ago, when his fire for avenging Skaantee was still burning hot, he would have welcomed this news. Now he did not. He would rather not know, rather not have to deal with the sudden sense of responsibility that knowing thrust upon him. Until now the idea of finding and punishing Joseph Colter had been airy and unreal. But now he knew that Joe Colter could be found at the cabin of Jen Cart, a cabin he could manage to locate if he made a true effort. The formerly theoretical had become solid and close at hand. There was opportunity to put action to words, and the opportunity was not welcome.

He sat in a laurel thicket, aching and sad, grieving for Hendrix Cart but mostly for his own unhappy and confused self. He wondered what counsel Skaantee would give him right now if he were here. He was glad that Skaantee's counsel was cut off to him, because he knew what he would say. Skaantee would counsel war. Skaantee would counsel vengeance. He would say what Jim Matoy did not want to hear.

But Matoy needed counsel from someone, anyone who could penetrate for him the mysteries of duty and personal obligation, and the even deeper mystery of war, in which right and wrong seemed to turn upside down and mix until both became nearly impossible to discern. He remained huddled in his hiding place, wishing he had someone to tell him what to do. He sat thinking and afraid, hungry and tired, until he decided to let himself fall asleep. But as he surrendered his mind to rest, a thought arose that made him open his eyes wide again: *Perhaps I do have the counselor I need. Perhaps I always have. Perhaps the person who should decide the duties of Jim Matoy has never been Skaantee, or my father, or Nikatimsi, or Wil-Usdi, but Jim Matoy himself.*

It was a thought that gave him simultaneous feelings of liberation and deep personal responsibility. Yet it made more sense to him than anything that had crossed his mind for a long time. He mulled it over again and again until his eyes closed once more and his mind drifted to silence.

Chapter 35

She stood on the porch, rifle in hand, and peered into the twilight forest.

Someone out there. She could sense it, almost smell it. Whoever it was, he—or they, maybe—was silent enough. The average person might never suspect, but Jen Cart was a native-born mountain woman, raised rough and gritty and close to the wooded land, and she could not be fooled.

"Come out here and show yourself, whoever you are!" she shouted at the forest. Not one to hide behind shutters was Jen Cart, nor to seek cover. She brandished her rifle, daring anyone to do harm to a lone woman on her own cabin porch. "I'll do no harm to any except them who hide theirselves!"

"Don't shoot me," a male voice said from the same spot in the woods that had once yielded up Sam Colter and Greeley Brown. This voice, however, was neither of theirs, and it had an inflection that put Jen Cart on edge. If she were forced to declare, she'd swear that voice sounded like an Indian's.

"Come out and show yourself! I'll do you no harm if you do none to me! Who are you?"

The figure emerged—an Indian, sure as the world, though his hair was hacked short and rough. He wore tattered clothing that didn't quite fit him. He was unarmed. "My name is Jim Matoy," he said.

"An Injun!" She raised the rifle and aimed it squarely at him. "What are you doing here, boy?"

"Are you Jen Cart?"

"You speak your speaking right good, for a redskin. Why you asking who I am?"

"Because if you are Jen Cart, I have news to tell you about your husband. I'm a friend . . . was a friend, of Hendrix Cart."

She lowered the rifle, staring at him frostily but thoughtfully, her face hidden by the twilight shadows cast by the porch roof above her. A few moments passed. "Was his friend. So you've come to tell me he's dead."

"Yes, he is dead."

Another pause. A dog barked off in the distance, out in the woods. A rifle cracked about two ridges away. Someone hunting, maybe. Maybe something else. Jen Cart's rifle came up again, leveled. "Did you kill him, Injun?"

"No. He was murdered by a man named Frank Stricklin, who stopped us in the woods. He had other men with him, but I don't know who they were."

She lowered the rifle completely this time and closed her eyes. "Stricklin," she said. "Stricklin. It would be him who would do that. Oh, Hendrix. Poor Hendrix."

"I'm sorry. Your husband was a good friend to me."

Jen Cart's manner became different, her voice softer, her rounded shoulders a little more so. "Just who are you?"

"I'm a Cherokee from the Oconaluftee. I was a . . . *am* a soldier with Thomas's Highland Legion. I was hurt at a fight many miles northwest of here, near the Cumberland Gap, and separated from my command. Your husband and some of his friends took me into their home and helped me to get well. When Mr. Cart said he wanted to come home again, to you, I told him I would guide him."

"Hendrix wouldn't have needed no guide."

"He was blind, or almost blind. He said it was from his drinking."

"Blind," she repeated, lowering her head and staring at the dark ground while absorbing yet another sad and surprising fact. "Blind. And now he's dead." She lifted her head again. "Where's his corpse?"

"I don't know. When they shot him down, I ran. They chased me, but I . . . got away. I went back later to where it happened, and his body was no longer there."

"It'll never be found," she said. "Stricklin will see to that. Damn him! Damn his murdering soul!" Conversation stopped for a time while Jen Cart cried and Jim Matoy stood silent, watching, feeling out of place and uncomfortable.

She brought her emotions under control very quickly. Some mountain women wailed and moaned their grief. Jen Cart was not one of these. When she spoke, her voice was steady again, by force of a strong will. "How'd you know where to find my cabin?"

"I hid in the woods. A boy came by, I stopped him. He was afraid of me, and when I asked him, he told me."

"I ain't afraid of you," she said. "I ain't afraid of no Injun, nor of the whole reb army, nor of the devil himself. And I ain't afraid of Frank Stricklin, but he has cause now to be afraid of me." She came off the porch and walked up closer to Matoy, examining him head to toe with curiosity. It was nearly dark now.

"You hungry, Indian?"

"I am."

"I got little, just some bread and old sorghum. Come inside and I'll feed you."

Matoy didn't move.

"Didn't you hear me, boy? Come inside and I'll feed you."

"Are you alone here?"

She wondered if he had bad intentions for her—robbery, or worse. She had heard many sobering stories about Indian wickedness. "Not as long as I got my rifle I ain't. Don't you be thinking of trying to harm me. I'll kill you if you try. But if you behave yourself, I'll feed you."

"I don't mean . . . I wasn't trying . . . it's that I've been told there was someone else here. A man. Joseph Colter."

And so it was true, what she had been hearing from Joe,

that too many people were becoming aware of his residency in her cabin. *Not safe no more,* he had said. *I have to leave, for my sake and yours.* "There ain't no Joe Colter here no more."

"But there was?"

Jen Cart wondered if she should answer . . . but what did it matter? She sensed trustworthiness in this Cherokee stranger, even if he was a rebel soldier. At the moment rebel or Union didn't matter so much to her. It had been a Unionist, a man who held to the same side of this war as did she, who murdered her husband. "Joe was here. Now he's gone . . . out there." She gave a general wave at the engulfing, looming mountains around them. "It wasn't safe for him to stay here no more. It had become knowed by too many. So he left here."

Matoy's eyes closed a moment; it seemed to her that a look much like relief came over his face.

"You going to eat or not, boy?"

"I'm going to eat," he said. "Thank you."

He followed her inside.

She told him he could remain the night, if he wished, sleeping on the floor near the hearth. He didn't want to stay, not in a house that had sheltered the murderer of Skaantee, but the night was cold and he was hurting and tired. He accepted.

He remained all the next day, unwilling to travel by daylight. He ate much less of her food than he would have liked, because she had little, would have even less as the winter progressed, and he didn't want to deprive her. So he ignored the rumblings of his stomach and shook his head at most of what she offered him.

As she grew accustomed to his presence, she let her grief show. Oddly, he couldn't tell whether she grieved more for the death of her husband or the leaving of Joseph Colter. Though she told him that she had merely been Colter's protector, he was perceptive and knew there was more to it than that, at least on her part.

As the day waned, Matoy prepared to leave. He was weaponless, without provisions beyond a few old, hard biscuits Jen Cart gave him, sore from his old wounding and his ordeal at the hands of Stricklin and his men, and he had no money. But Greeneville lay over the mountain, a hard but not impossible journey for an unprovisioned man.

"Thank you for your kindness to me," he said to Jen Cart as he readied himself to go. "I'm sorry I had to bring you such sad news."

" 'Twarn't your fault, I don't reckon." She looked past him and into the mountains. "I wish Hendrix hadn't of been murdered. And I wish Joe hadn't of left." She wiped a stray tear. "I hate Frank Stricklin. I hate him. I hope someday I can kill him."

He had to speak. "Mrs. Cart, there is something you should know. There was a time not long ago that I wanted . . . that I knew a man who wanted to kill your friend Joseph Colter, just like you want to kill Frank Stricklin."

"Kill Joe? Who wanted to?"

"Just a man. He didn't know Joe Colter, had never met him, but he knew what Colter had done. Joe Colter killed some people, one of them an old Cherokee man named Skaantee, who was like a grandfather to the man I knew. Skaantee was a good man. He didn't deserve to die. So this man decided he should kill Joe Colter for what he had done." He looked at her squarely. "But it won't happen. The man decided he won't kill him, even though he has reason."

"Why?"

A few moments passed before the answer came. "Because Skaantee is dead and vengeance would not bring him back. Because this man, he knows now he wasn't born to be a killer or a warrior." He thought for a moment more. "Because if this man has learned to hate Joe Colter, he's learned to hate vengeance and war even more."

She stared at Matoy, wordless.

He went on. "I understand why this man chose what he chose. I know now what it is to hate war, too. I do hate it, this war above all wars. It should have never been my war, not my people's war. We should never have become part of it. But we have. I had thought I might desert like so many have, go hide in the mountains until it is over. By now I've been listed as missing in battle and presumed dead. No one would look for me . . . but I won't desert. I said I would be a soldier. So I'll be a soldier. Even though it's not my war."

"It's a wicked war," Jen Cart said.

"Yes. It is." Matoy pulled his coat up around his neck, the cold wind rising. "Thank you again for your kindness. I'll go now." He strode away, then turned. "Mrs. Cart, when you see Joe Colter again, you tell him what I told you. You tell him that Skaantee was a good man. You tell him he should not have killed him. But you tell him, too, there will be no blood vengeance. You tell Joe Colter that the vengeance he will know will be knowing he has killed a man who didn't deserve to die."

"I'll tell him."

"Good-bye, Mrs. Cart."

"Good-bye, boy."

He strode off into the forest, heading in the direction of Greeneville and the Confederate conscription station there. Along the way he would come up with a reasonable-sounding explanation as to why he was turning up so far removed from the place where he had gone missing in battle. He'd say he had lost his memory and good sense for a while, as sometimes happened to men hurt in battle. He would give no hints to how close he had come to desertion. He would report that he was ready now to find and return to his command.

And they would not ask many questions. The Confederacy needed soldiers far too badly to ask too many questions of a healthy young soldier ready to return to war, even if it was a war he despised.

Word of the salt raid at Marshall spread, told mouth to ear, written in letters and newspapers, and chattered in code across telegraph wires. Soon it reached the ears of Colonel Lawrence Allen and his fellow officer James Keith. They sought permission from their commander, General Henry Heth, the latest in the seemingly endless string of commanders of the Confederate troops in East Tennessee, to retaliate against the raiders who had not only committed the major crime of salt theft, but deliberately insulted and injured the family of Colonel Allen as well. Heth agreed.

The raid generated other responses. Rumors grew that it, like the East Tennessee bridge burnings of autumn '61, was a portent of a general Unionist uprising. Confederate militia units, ten units of cavalry, and even Thomas's Highlanders began scouring the hills from Tennessee to Georgia, looking for Unionists and seeking to put down the expected revolt before it began.

But there was no Unionist revolt. Few of the rebel search squads scoured up much in the way of Union radicals, though there was one small battle in Madison County that brought a few casualties among rebel deserters and the roundup of some prisoners.

Meanwhile, Keith and Allen were moving in two columns of troops. One, under Keith, came into the valley across the high, windswept Bald Mountains, twenty-five of his men falling victim to frostbite. The other column, under Allen, entered the valley by the usual, lower pass at the other end.

In the distance, hunting horns touched the lips of civilian sentinels and announced to all who heard their blasts a message the mountain people had long dreaded: The gray soldiers have come.

In the woods, men whom war had driven into hiding watched the movements of the soldiers into the valley and wondered what would come before they left it again, and whether they themselves would be living to see them go.

As Allen and Keith began their push through the valley, they encountered gunfire, fired out of hiding, and returned it as best they could. The snipers had the advantage of being hidden, but the Confederates were better equipped, greater in number, and commanded by a man fired with a sense of personal vengeance. The rebels killed eight valley men at one farm, six at another, then joined Keith's column, which had completed its difficult march over the mountains.

A courier brought word to Colonel Allen that one of his ailing children who had been terrorized by the Unionist raiders had died and the other was expected to die as well, soon. As snipers fired at him, Allen rode to his home and for the first time received a firsthand description of how the salt raiders had insulted his family. Implications were strong that the terror the raiders had struck into the sick children contributed to their deaths. Allen filled with an even more bitter hatred. His second child died while he was there, and he buried both of his young ones the next morning and returned to his soldiers.

They began a search of the valley. About a dozen suspects were found; some were jailed in Asheville, others sent into Tennessee and up to the conscription center in Greeneville. Three other men turned themselves in at Marshall and were jailed.

The 64th swept the valley of Shelton Laurel for salt raiders, deserters, and Unionist irregulars. One man that a small detachment drove out of a hidden little mountain hut put up a fight, shouting defiance while blasting away at the lot of them. They opened fire, riddling him, driving him back to fall on the leafy forest floor, where he lay writhing, living for several minutes by the sheer force of will before death finally came, his last word a spit of defiance at the soldiers who had killed him.

Those soldiers remarked with sullen admiration about how he had clung to life. He must have been a stubborn and hard-fighting kind of man to die that way. The assessment was correct. Joe Colter had indeed been stubborn and hard-fighting all his days, but for him the fighting was now done forever.

They left him lying where he had fallen. As far as they were concerned, the mountains could have him.

The death of Joe Colter was only the beginning of violence in the valley of Shelton Laurel, much of it sensationally brutal.

The men of the valley were hard to find, the soldiers of the 64th learned. They all seemed oddly absent, away from home and farm. But their families weren't absent, and families usually knew where their men were, though they didn't want to tell. But often they would tell, if persuaded in just the right way.

The Confederates whipped some of them, lashing one ancient woman with switches until the skin of her back was shredded. They strung a woman of eighty-five up by the neck and let her hang with toes barely on the ground, then let her down just at the point of death, revived her, questioned her, then strung her up again, and again, and again. They used the old trick of snowy day, leashed mother, and naked baby in the snow at one house, and at another, occupied by one of the families of Sheltons who had given their name to this valley, they whipped and repeatedly hanged another woman, demanding to know where her husband was.

Their methods worked, at least somewhat, and soon they had sixteen prisoners, men and boys.

The 64th lingered, with their prisoners, for another couple of days, then began an abrupt march toward Tennessee. The prisoners—now only thirteen of them remained, the others having escaped—asked where they were being taken. To Knoxville, they were told.

But at a certain grassy field encircled by hills from which unseen eyes were surely watching, they stopped. Colonel Allen was conspicuously not present, having ridden on ahead, but Keith was there. He dismounted, went to some of his soldiers and gave a quiet order, and five of the prisoners were pulled away from the others and shoved to their knees.

What was about to happen was as obvious to the prisoners as it was unbelievable. Keith ordered a few of his men to line up before the prisoners and ready their rifles for firing. Faces paled among the rebels. Some of the men shook their heads; they would not commit murder, not even in the name of the Confederate States of America.

Very well, Keith said, those who faltered could kneel beside the prisoners and be dealt with in just the same manner.

No soldiers joined the prisoners. Trembling, they lined up and raised their rifles.

Old Joe Woods, a mountain patriarch and one of the five

kneeling men, said, "For God's sake, men, you're not going to shoot us?"

No one answered him. Keith drew his sword.

"At least give us time to pray!" Woods begged.

"You promised us a trial!" another prisoner shouted.

Keith swung down the sword and the rifles fired. Four of the five died at once, another writhed, screaming and bleeding, until someone put a ball through his brain. For a few moments there was silence in the mountains, broken only by the receding echo of the last shot.

Another five prisoners were dragged out and made to kneel. One was David Shelton, a boy of twelve, whose father had been among the first five to die. He begged to be spared, but no one responded. "At least don't shoot me in the head!" he asked. "My mother will want to stroke my hair after I'm dead."

So they didn't shoot him in the head, but the shots only broke his arms. Rising among the four freshly dead beside him, he stumbled toward those who had wounded him, bleeding and weeping. "You've killed my father, you've killed my brothers, you've shot me in my arms, but I forgive you—I can get well if you'll let me alone. Let me go home! Let me go to my mother and my sisters!"

Two soldiers dragged him back among the dead and shot him again. This time they did shoot him through the head. They wanted him to die quickly. It was far too terrible to have to hear him beg.

The last three who died did not bother to plead for mercy. They looked into the faces of the men about to shoot them and held onto the only thing men in their situation could keep: their dignity. Another volley rang out and it was done.

They buried them all in a common, shallow grave in hard ground. Before they buried them, the grave diggers had to strike at some of the shot ones with a heavy hoe because they would not stop twitching and moving. When the grave was covered, one of the rebel soldiers, driven nearly mad by the wickedness in which he had participated, danced atop the grave and sang a minstrel tune, declaring he would "dance the damned scoundrels down to and through hell."

The rebels marched on, leaving the dead behind. The

unseen watchers, the shadow warriors all around, had witnessed it all, and word of the massacre at Shelton Laurel
spread across the valley. The families and friends of those
slain came into the killing field the next morning and found
that wild hogs had gotten to the grave and devoured portions of the corpses. Some of the fallen could be identified
only by their clothing.

Of all the ugly brutality of the war in western North
Carolina, the Shelton Laurel massacre was the worst so far.
But it would not be the last. The death demons still haunted
the high ridges, and many feasts were yet to come.

The mountain war had only just begun.

Chapter 36

The shed door opened slowly, with a creak. Ben Scarlett opened his eyes and squinted into the light. A figure stood limned before him. He put his hand to his brow and squinted even more.

"Mr. Baumgardner?"

"Ben Scarlett, is that you?"

"Yes, sir. I'm afraid it is."

Baumgardner stood silent, moving his protruding lower jaw from side to side.

"I'll leave, sir. I know you don't allow folks to sleep here."

Baumgardner asked, "Where you been? I ain't seen you in a long time, Ben."

"I been a lot of places, sir. It's been a long road for me."

"You're hand's gone."

"I know, sir. It got cut and mortified, and I had to lose it or lose my life." Ben stood slowly, joints stiff. "And the truth is, Mr. Baumgardner, it ain't much of a life that I live, but it is mine, and I'd like to keep it if I can."

"Yes. I can understand that."

"Ain't you going to grab me and drag me out like you used to do?"

"No, Ben. I'm not." Baumgardner looked at him, eyes thoughtful and weighted with what looked to Ben like some deep sadness or pain. He paused, brows knitting, thought churning almost visibly in his mind. "In fact, Ben, I want you to come inside. There's a kettle of stew simmering on the stove in the store, and I was just getting ready to eat a bowl or two. Would you join me?"

Ben was amazed. "I'm obliged, Mr. Baumgardner. I'll join you, yes sir."

Baumgardner nodded. "Good, Ben. Good. I get tired of eating alone. And being alone."

"Are you alone now, sir? Where's your sons?"

"My sons, they're . . ." He choked off and swiped his hand down his mouth and beard a time or two, and when he spoke, his voice was different. "I lost them, Ben. Both of them. One put on blue and the other gray, and now they're both dead."

"I'm sorry to hear it, Mr. Baumgardner."

"Thank you, Ben."

"We all seem to be losing things in this cussed war," Ben said. "I lost this hand. I've had friends, and good situations, and pride and even work—that's right, sir, I had me some good work for a time, and even kept sober—but I've lost all that. There was even a woman I grew right fond of, and I lost her, too." He paused. "Well, no, I reckon I didn't. The truth is I never had her to lose. I ain't the kind of man women are likely to fall in love with, Mr. Baumgardner, in case you didn't know that."

Baumgardner eyed Ben, shook his head, and suddenly chuckled. Ben wasn't sure why Baumgardner chuckled, but laughter was better than grief, and he grinned back at the merchant.

Baumgardner said, "Ben Scarlett, you are a sight, you know that? You've always been a strange bird. Why in the world I'm inviting you in for stew is beyond me."

"I believe I know, Mr. Baumgardner."

"Tell me, then."

"Because in this sorry war about the only thing left to a man sometimes, after he's lost everything, is being able to be good and kind to somebody else. Even when it don't make a bit of sense. Even if the one he's kind to is no more than a one-handed drunk who ain't never been no good to nobody."

Baumgardner said nothing for a time. Then he said, "Ben, you are a strange bird. Mighty strange. Now come on. Let's go inside before that stew cooks away to mush."

"Yes, sir, Mr. Baumgardner."

Ben closed the shed door and they walked around through the alley toward the front of the store. Baumgardner had to hurry to keep up with Ben Scarlett. It was a cold day, and Ben was weak with hunger, eager to get to the stew.

AFTERWORD

THE SHADOW WARRIORS, like its two companion novels in THE MOUNTAIN WAR TRILOGY, is a novel strongly rooted in fact. Though its foreground characters are fictional, the settings, scenarios, and circumstances in which they live and move are accurate to the time and place of the story. Additionally, several characters and events of the novel either are fully historical or are heavily based on historical realities.

For example, there was in fact an outspoken, hard-drinking Unionist named Charles Douglass who lived in Knoxville during the early days of the Civil War. Like Charlie Douglass of THE SHADOW WARRIORS, he was prone to heckle Secessionists and did sometimes beat a bass drum in Knoxville's streets as a show of Unionist pride. Douglass was wounded on a Knoxville street in a manner substantially like the wounding depicted in the novel, and was later murdered by a party or parties unknown. Nevertheless, the Charlie Douglass of THE SHADOW WARRIORS is not intended to exactly parallel his historical counterpart, and is best interpreted here as a fictional character.

Likewise, the shooting incidents that are depicted as having occurred in Marshall, North Carolina, on the day that state's voters went to the polls on the Secession issue, almost exactly parallel some violent incidents that did occur in that narrow mountain town that day. Some minor fiction-alization has occurred, however, and in particular I wish to note that the Madison County sheriff as depicted in this novel is presented in fictionalized fashion and is not intended to portray the actual county sheriff who died in Marshall that day.

The Unionist bridge-burning campaign of late 1861 occurred as presented, except for the portion concerning the burning of the Colter bridge, that bridge being fictional. All the other bridge burnings presented, however, and the men who carried them out, come directly from history. So does the stern response of the Confederate government, which tried, convicted, and hanged several bridge burners as depicted in the novel.

The character of Greeley Brown is inspired in large part by a remarkable but little-known historical figure named Daniel Ellis, of mountainous Carter County, Tennessee. Ellis, born in 1827, was a farmer and wagonmaker who epitomized the staunchest Unionist elements of his native mountains. When the Civil War broke out, he participated in the bridge-burning campaign and the subsequent ill-fated Unionist uprising, then commenced a successful but intensely dangerous career as a Union pilot, guiding more than four thousand refugees out of Confederate territory and to Union lines before the war ended. He went on after the war to publish his adventures in a thoroughly fascinating book (despite its purple-prose style) with a jawbreaker of a title: *Thrilling Adventures of Daniel Ellis, the Great Union Guide of East Tennessee for a Period of Nearly Four Years During the Great Southern Rebellion, Written by Himself.* Ellis's book was so thoroughly pro-Union and so bitterly anti-Confederate that he made himself plenty of enemies with it, resulting in the necessity of his going armed for almost the rest of his life. The fact that he published his book in 1867, when war wounds were still fresh, no doubt guaranteed it would generate the most rancor possible.

The brutal massacre of Unionists in Shelton Laurel, North Carolina, occurred substantially as described in this novel, though different accounts of the tragedy vary somewhat in details. The bitterness left by that terrible event has not fully vanished from the western North Carolina mountains, many portions of which remain almost as rugged and isolated as they did during the period depicted in this novel. Many descendants of the victims of the Shelton Laurel massacre still populate the mountains.

A final, personal note: If the novels of THE MOUNTAIN WAR TRILOGY present Unionist characters more sympathetically than Confederate ones, that is no accident, but neither is it an attempt on this author's part to stir up contrary feelings about a terrible war that is, thank God, long behind us. Though I lived in what was one of the most staunchly Union counties in East Tennessee and readily admit to a certain affection for the Unionists who lived, struggled, and sometimes died on my home soil, the primary reason THE MOUNTAIN WAR TRILOGY must inevitably seem biased toward the Unionist side is simply that it is primarily *about* Unionists. It is only natural for an author to present his main characters in a positive light, if only to gain for those characters the sympathy of the reader. I am aware, however, that the Civil War and the reasons behind it were complex, that the interests of different involved regions varied, that modern Americans tend to "take sides" based on which side of the conflict their ancestors came down on, and that there are two sides or more to every story.

The saga begun in THE SHADOW WARRIORS will continue in the second volume of THE MOUNTAIN WAR TRILOGY. That novel, entitled THE PHANTOM LEGION, will be available in midyear, 1997, and the third novel, SEASON OF RECKONING, will reach the shelves shortly before Christmas.

If you've enjoyed THE SHADOW WARRIORS, you won't want to miss the rest of the trilogy. The adventure only grows from here.

CAMERON JUDD
Greene County, Tennessee

ABOUT THE AUTHOR

CAMERON JUDD is a former newspaper reporter and editor and the author of more than twenty published books. Noted for its historical accuracy and marked by a love of the land and the people who lived on it, his writing is authentic and entertaining. Cameron hails from near Greenville, Tennessee, where he is at work on the remaining two books in *The Mountain War Trilogy*.